Popcorn LOVE

KL Hughes

Acknowledgements

First and foremost, I would like to thank my love. Thank you, my darling wife, for all your encouragement and support, your confidence and faith in me, and your endless supply of laughter and kisses. Your bright spirit always keeps me going.

I would also like to thank my editor and project manager, Michelle Aguilar, for sticking with me every step of the way, helping me to grow as a writer, and helping this book to bloom into what it was always meant to be.

Finally, I would like to thank my publisher, Astrid Ohletz, and the incredible team at Ylva Publishing for giving this book, and me, a chance. Please accept my deepest gratitude.

Dedication

For Swen

Chapter One

"Stop whining," Vivian huffed before stuffing a forkful of Cobb salad in her mouth.

Elena rolled her eyes as she took a sip of her sparkling water and crossed and uncrossed her legs under the café table. "*You* stop whining," she hissed at the other woman. "A refusal does not equate to whining, Vivian. You continuing to push the issue, however, *does*."

Vivian finished chewing her food in silence before dabbing at the corners of her mouth with her napkin. Both she and Elena were no strangers to proper manners. They had been raised to never forget them after all.

"Oh come on, Elena. It's time for you to live a little. It's time for you to move on. It's *time* for you to get your sexy ass out there and share it with the world!"

Elena quirked a brow at her best friend. "The world?"

Running a hand through her long, ash blonde hair, Vivian leaned back in her chair. "Okay, so maybe not the *world*. That would put a whole new meaning on the phrase 'sleeping around', wouldn't it?"

"I am not *sleeping* with anyone," Elena said. "I have no desire to dabble in the dating world, let alone jump into bed with a string of nameless, faceless one-night stands that could only offer momentary satisfaction, and at the risk of heavy consequences." Elena knew well that some of those consequences could change one's entire life.

"*Exactly!* That's the problem!"

"No, dear. The problem is *you* continuing to hound me about this ridiculous idea of yours to set me up on a string of dates that I have absolutely no interest in."

"How do you know you have no interest in them? You haven't met any of them yet. *I* haven't even met any of them yet." Vivian pointed a finger at her friend as if she had just made the most brilliant argument for her case. Elena simply stared at her, unblinking and unfazed.

"Look, Elena, it doesn't have to be some big ordeal," Vivian said. "It's not like I am going to put you on a strict schedule of dates or try to marry you off to the first good-looking man or woman—"

"Woman?"

"Well, there *was* that time in Cancún." Vivian's soft laugh grew louder as she watched Elena's cheeks color. "That was the one and only spring break I convinced you to take with me during college." She let out a blissful sigh. "Best spring break of my life."

Elena's blush spread as she ducked her head and lowered her voice. "Dios mío," she muttered. "I should *never* have let you talk me into that trip. It was a complete circus, a circus, may I remind you, of which you swore to never speak again!" She snatched at her glass of water and took a long sip, the cold liquid an instant relief. "Oh, and in my defense, I was *highly* inebriated that night. I'm sure you recall the nine tequila shots I took. *Nine.*"

"Oh I recall." Vivian turned a wicked grin on her best friend. "I recall you took all nine of those shots off of nine different parts of that chick's body."

The pink tint painting Elena's cheeks deepened into a rich cherry red. She cleared her throat roughly as she glanced around the café before hissing, "*Still,* it was only one time."

"Not true. Have you forgotten about that girl in sophomore year? What was her name, the one who somehow talked you into pledging ADPi?"

Elena's voice lowered to a near whisper. "Audrey."

"Audrey, yes! That's the one! She was a real nut job."

With a silent wish that this conversation would fall into the fiery pits of hell, never to be spoken of again, Elena cleared her throat. "She was *eccentric.*"

"She stalked you for a *month* after you quit the sorority! You had to get a restraining order!" Vivian laughed. "Oh my God, remember when she sent you that teddy bear?"

Elena's blush crept down her neck to turn the visible parts of her chest splotchy and red. "Please don't."

"When you pressed its ear, it played that recording of her..." Vivian's speech was broken around her laughter. "...her singing 'Wind Beneath My Wings' and audibly crying!"

Elena sighed and pressed her forehead into her palm. "That was a rather unfortunate experience."

"It was *hilarious!*"

"Why am I friends with you?" She practically guzzled down the remainder of her water, eager to be done with this ridiculous affair.

"Because I am incredible. Anyway, my *point* was—"

"Oh, you had a point?"

Vivian smiled at her, nudging Elena's leg under the table with her foot. "My *point* was that I could set you up on dates with both men *and* women, if that is something you are interested in. It's obvious that you are at least a little gay. I swear I will only set you up with the best of the best, and who knows? I could introduce you to your Mr. or Ms. Right! If nothing else, I could at least set you up for a good lay."

"Okay, this conversation is over now." Elena clucked her tongue as she rose quickly from her seat and grabbed her purse.

"Oh, come on!"

Stepping around the table, she bent to peck Vivian's cheek. Their waiter returned with the check at that moment and Elena smirked as she pointed to Vivian and said, "Lunch is on her," then headed for the door.

"Think about it!" The door jingled with Elena's exit, and Vivian was left there to cover the bill.

The sound of Elena's heels clicking against the marble floor of her parents' foyer reverberated off the walls as she made her way quickly through the place. She was eager to see—

"*Momma!*"

A pint-sized ball of energy crashed into her side from seemingly out of nowhere, and Elena stumbled but caught herself before she could fall. With a laugh, she turned and swooped up the small boy attached to her leg. "Munchkin!" She twirled her son around and planted a dozen little kisses across his face.

"*Mooooooom!*" He whined as she set him back on his feet, then giggled, even as he made a show of wiping at the bright red smudges marking his puffy cheeks. "You got lickstick on me!"

"And it looks fabulous on you." Elena reached out and ruffled his dark brown hair, the same deep shade as her own, just as she noticed her mother Nora standing in the doorway of the kitchen, watching them.

The elder woman's long sable hair, bits of gray peeking in, hung in a single braid over her shoulder, and her chestnut eyes, so like Elena's, were warm and kind as she smiled at her daughter and grandson. Small wrinkles around her eyes showed years of both joy and stress, but Elena thought she looked ever young. She hoped to age as gracefully.

"It looks like Momma gave you a makeover, Lucas," Nora said. "Come and let me see."

Grinning, Lucas ran back over to his grandmother. She crouched down so that she could be eye-level with the boy as he asked, "Does it really look fablous, Gram?"

"Oh absolutely!"

"You see?" Elena said. "I told you. Now, can you say 'thank you' to your Gram."

"Gracias Gram."

Nora kissed his cheek. "De nada."

Stepping over and scooping her son up, Elena squeezed him against her in a loving hug. "Good boy." The sensation of one of his small hands tangling in the hair at the base of her head made her sigh. He always played with her hair when she held him. Over the years, it had come to soothe them both.

She leaned forward and pressed a kiss to her mother's cheek. "Hola, mamá. How was he today?"

"Oh, he was fine." Nora smiled. "You know he is always a perfect angel." She crooked her finger at her daughter to beckon her to follow, as she turned to head back into the kitchen. "I was just making some tea. Would you like a cup?"

"Yes, please." Elena dropped onto a stool at the kitchen bar and settled Lucas on her lap. He continued to play with her hair as she and her mother carried on.

"How was your day, dear?" Nora asked. "Everything going well at the office?"

"The spring fashion shoot is developing smoothly." Elena gently bounced her son on her knee and patted his pudgy little thigh. "Honestly, things could not be better at the office." She sighed. "Things with Vivian, however..."

"Oh?" The tea kettle whistled from the stove, and Nora poured the heated water into two waiting cups. "The dating thing again?"

"Yes. She will not give—"

"Momma, I drawed a dinosaur today," Lucas dropped his head on his mother's shoulder and played with the necklace dangling from her neck.

Elena patted his leg as she corrected him. "*Drew*, Lucas. Not 'drawed'. You *drew* a dinosaur today, and I am sure it was the best dinosaur drawing ever. I can't wait to see it, munchkin, but what did Momma tell you about interrupting people when they are talking?"

"Uh, not to." Lucas chewed on his lip, his reply a guilty murmur.

But Elena's smile stayed warm. "That's right. You are such a smart boy."

He grinned and hid his face in the crook of his mother's neck, letting her short dark locks fall over his features as Elena turned back to her mother. "She will not give up on this ridiculous idea that I am in dire need of a love life."

"Oh, I don't know that she is necessarily focused on providing you with a *love* life, per se."

"*Mother!*" Elena hissed, scandalized at her mother's teasing smirk.

Laughing softly at her daughter's reaction, Nora said, "Lucas, dear?"

When his little face peeked out from under his mother's hair, Nora smiled at him. "Ear muffs, please."

Lucas huffed out a disapproving sigh as he brought up his hands and cupped them tightly around his ears to block out any sound.

"Perhaps Vivian is right, Elena. You need to get out more, and not just to the office. It would do you some good to meet new people, and truth be told, dear, your sex life is lacking. Let off some steam. Have some fun."

"You, of all people, are telling me to have fun," Elena drawled, "to go out and have s-e-x with someone I don't *know* just to 'let off some steam'?"

"Well, *do* be responsible about it, but yes," Nora said. "I know your father and I kept you on a rather tight leash when you were younger, and things were admittedly strained when Lucas was born, but you are an adult, Elena. We have treated you as such for quite some time now, and you are a responsible woman. I trust that you will take care of yourself, but it may be good for you to simply let loose for once and stop holding onto things you cannot change. Stop being afraid to connect with people."

Elena sighed as she took the cup of tea her mother offered her and blew at the hot liquid. "Thank you."

"At least think about it," Nora said as she blew at her own tea. "It's time to move on from the past. You know what your father always says."

"Sólo se vive una vez." Elena nodded.

"It's true," Nora said. "You only live once, and you are in your twenties. You don't get those years back, my darling. So have a little fun."

Elena tugged on Lucas's arm to let him know he could drop his hands from his ears. She then rested her head on top of his and closed her eyes. Maybe her mother and Vivian were right. Maybe it was time.

"I will think about it." Though her eyes were closed, she knew her mother was smiling.

Later that evening, after putting Lucas to bed, Elena collapsed onto her plush leather couch and reached for the remote. With a sigh, she flicked through the channels on her flat-screen television. She cycled through all of them twice before giving up and clicking the damned thing off again.

She laid her head on the arm of the couch and closed her eyes, the events of the day spiraling through her mind. Her mother and

Vivian were right: She was only twenty-seven and already extremely successful and wealthy, but if she was deeply honest with herself, she was also lonely. She was so lonely she could feel it in her bones.

A single tear slipped from the inner corner of her eye and over the bridge of her nose, and before Elena even realized what she was doing, her cell phone was pressed to the side of her head and a soft ringing echoed in her ear.

"El—"

"Okay." Elena began before Vivian could get a word out. "I will do it. I will let you set me up."

Vivian's squeal of excitement made Elena roll her eyes as she swiped at her cheeks, thankful that her friend couldn't see her. "See?" Vivian said. "I knew there was some good sense still floating around in that head of yours. Why the change of heart?"

"Is insanity a fair answer?" Elena could only imagine how pitiful she looked in that moment.

"No, but I will let it pass for now. I can't wait to get started. I already have at least two people in mind."

She interjected before Vivian could get swept up in her excitement. "I have a condition."

"Of course you do. What is it?"

"A babysitter."

"You want me to set you up with a babysitter?" Vivian asked, confused. "Seriously? I was thinking someone more your status, Elena."

"I don't care about status, Viv." She sighed. "You know that, but no, I was referring to my condition. You have to find me a suitable babysitter for Lucas. My mother already keeps him during the days while I work, and I don't want to put any extra burden on her. Oh, and also, no more than two dates a week, maximum. I refuse to give up too much of my time with Lucas."

"Yeah, yeah, you're the world's best mom." Vivian's voice fell into a bored drone. "I'll buy you a trophy later."

Elena chuckled. "Those are the terms. Do we have a deal?"

"Oh, we definitely have a deal. I find you a babysitter, and then we work on finding you a spouse."

"Let's not go overboard."

"I'm just saying. You never know. Anyway, I'm guessing you will want to meet the sitter ahead of time?"

"Of course. Just let me know when you have someone for the position, and I will set up a meeting."

"Deal."

"Oh, and Viv?"

"Yeah?"

Elena sighed, blowing a wild strand of hair from her face. "Thank you."

She could practically hear Vivian's smile through the phone, even though she spoke in a whisper. "You got it, babe."

Her hand shot into the air as Elena rushed to the curb for a cab. She was already ten minutes late for her lunch date with her potential babysitter. Thanks to Vivian's last-minute phone call a few hours before Elena's lunch break, information on the applicant was limited. In fact, Elena knew absolutely nothing about the young woman she was about to meet except that she was a senior at New York University. Vivian hadn't even given her a name or appearance to go by, so Elena could only hope that the café she chose wouldn't be too terribly packed; she didn't want to spend half of her lunch searching for the girl. Then again, it was entirely possible that there would be no one waiting for her at all. She would be nearly twenty minutes late by the time she got there, after all.

When the cab pulled up to the curb by the café, Elena handed the driver a few bills and dashed inside. She let out a breath of relief when she saw that the café was mostly empty, only a few people dining. So she let her eyes shift from occupied table to occupied table. When a young woman with a long yellow-blonde ponytail and startlingly bright green eyes smiled awkwardly and waved her over, Elena let out another sigh and crossed the café to meet her.

The young woman rose from her seat, and Elena took in the old jean jacket, white tank top, and skin-tight jeans with narrowed eyes. Her style was bland, but the girl was definitely in good shape; that much was obvious, and Elena hoped it meant she would be able to keep up with Lucas. The boy was a bundle of energy during the day, but he could be even worse in the evenings, transforming into an unholy nightmare the moment she tried to put him to sleep, if he wasn't yet ready to go.

"Hey, uh, Elena Vega, right?" She held out a hand, and Elena watched the girl's emerald eyes rake the length of her body quickly before darting back up to lock onto hers. Women were strange in that way, always scanning one another, sizing each other up, and comparing. It didn't bother Elena, though, or she never would have survived the fashion industry.

She plastered on a smile and nodded as she took the outstretched hand and shook it firmly. "I am," she said. "How did you guess?"

"Your friend said you were some big business something-or-other." The girl plopped heavily back down into her seat. "You're the only person who's come in here in the last fifteen minutes wearing anything even remotely expensive and looking all shit-my-meeting-ran-late."

Elena arched one slender brow at the young woman's blunt speech, but she could hardly help the chuckle that escaped her as she lowered herself into the opposite seat. "Yes, I apologize," she said. "It has been a terribly busy day."

"It's cool."

"I'm sorry," Elena said, blushing slightly. "I just realized that I don't even know your name."

"Oh, it's Allison. Allison Sawyer."

Chapter Two

"ALLISON." ELENA REPEATED THE NAME softly on her tongue. "It's lovely to meet you."

"Wow." Allison laughed. "No one's ever said it was 'lovely' to meet me. Good, yeah. Nice, definitely. But *lovely*? That's a new one. Let me guess. You went to some fancy prep school immediately followed by Harvard or Yale or something, right?"

The surprised look on Elena's face made Allison smile. She slipped a pair of thick black-rimmed glasses out of her backpack and onto her face as she pulled the menu toward her. *This is going to be a trip*, she thought as she glanced back up at the woman, who was still just staring at her.

"Yes, actually," Elena said as she shifted uncomfortably in her chair. "I earned my MBA from Harvard Business College."

"Knew it," Allison said smugly. This woman certainly wasn't the first upper-class person she had worked for. She had had several catering jobs at random high-class events throughout her first couple of years in college, and she had babysat a lot of friggin' kids, for rich and poor families alike. So, she was used to the five-minute delay that the wealthy folks sometimes required in order to acclimate themselves to what Allison referred to as *normal-people speak*, but they all eventually caught on. Or they sneered and decided not to hire her.

Whatever.

"So, what's good to eat here, Elena?" She paused. "Is that okay?"

Elena looked up at her, confusion in her eyes. "I'm sorry? Is *what* okay?"

"That I called you Elena. I can call you Mrs. Vega if you prefer that instead, or whatever."

"Actually, it's *Ms.* Vega." Glancing away, Elena rubbed a hand down the side of her neck before clearing her throat and turning back to Allison. "I am not married, but the formality is unnecessary. You are welcome to call me Elena."

"Awesome!" Allison smiled before letting her gaze fall back to her menu. "So, what's good to eat here?"

The small smile that tugged at the corners of Elena's mouth did not go unnoticed. It was soft, more natural than the tight smile she had worn before, and Allison hoped it meant the woman was relaxing a bit.

"Well, I suppose I almost always order a Cobb salad."

"Okay." Allison shrugged. "Let's go with that then." She put her hand up and waved the nearest waiter over.

When the young man reached their table, he pulled a pad and pen from his apron and politely asked, "What can I get for you ladies?"

"Uh, yeah." Allison chewed on her lip and pointed at Elena. "She's ready to order, and I'll have whatever she has plus another water with like three lemons."

An audible chuckle escaped the waiter as he turned to Elena, who was staring at Allison as if she was some sort of natural phenomenon.

"Okay," Elena said, "then I will have a sparkling water and the Cobb salad, and I suppose Ms. Sawyer will have the same."

"I'll have it right out, ladies."

"Thank you," Elena replied at the same time that Allison said, "Thanks, man."

As soon as he walked away, Allison scrunched up her nose. "Can we not do the whole 'Ms. Sawyer' thing?" she asked. "Ever again, preferably."

"Is it a problem for you?" Elena asked, intrigued.

"It's just that a few of my professors call me Ms. Sawyer, and it grates on my nerves. I know it's supposed to be respectful or whatever, but it just makes me feel old, and I'm way too young to feel old." Allison winked at her. "You know what I mean?"

Clearing her throat, Elena rested her hands in her lap and crossed and uncrossed her legs. "Yes, I can certainly understand that."

"I figured you would get it. You can't possibly be older than twenty-five, and I bet you get that *Ms. Vega* crap all the time, right?"

A soft blush decorated Elena's cheeks even as she smirked and corrected Allison. "I'm actually twenty-seven, but you have just earned a few points in your favor for making me feel at least two years younger."

"Go me!" Allison took a sip of the extra-lemony water the waiter had delivered.

Elena laughed in a soft sigh. "But yes, I am often only referred to as *Ms. Vega* while at work."

"Right." Allison nodded as she pulled off her glasses and stuck them back in their case before slipping them into her bag, having forgotten for a moment that she was still wearing them. She only needed them to read, drive, and sometimes to watch television and hardly ever wore them otherwise. In fact, she tried to avoid handling them when she could, because she was a tad clumsy. She had broken a pair before and had had to save up to afford the ones she now owned. She was in no hurry to break those as well.

"You look younger with your glasses on," Elena said, tilting her head. "Striking either way, of course, but younger."

Struck momentarily speechless, Allison scratched at the back of her head and let out a choked gurgle of a laugh. "Uh, thanks," she said, "for the 'striking' part or whatever."

Elena smiled, and Allison could see the amusement dancing in the woman's eyes. "You are welcome."

"So, you're like some super successful businesswoman, right?" Allison asked, quick to change the subject. "You must be pretty awesome at what you do to be so successful when you're so young."

"I would like to say that yes, I am quite successful at what I do. However, Allison, I believe we are here so that I may interview *you*, not the other way around."

"Right. Totally. Fire away. Oh, and you can call me Alli if you want; that's what my best friend and a few others call me. Or, you know, Allison is fine if that's what you prefer. Just throwing that out there."

"Allison it is, then."

Allison let out a small laugh and nodded. "All right, then." She wasn't terribly surprised by the choice given how much Elena seemed to favor formalities, but it might take some getting used to.

The waiter returned then with their Cobb salads, and the two women began to eat as Elena started in with a list of questions.

"Why don't you start by telling me a bit about yourself," Elena suggested as she nibbled at her salad. "Vivian mentioned that you were a senior at NYU. I'm guessing that puts you at around twenty-one or twenty-two, unless you are an accelerated student."

"Nope, no acceleration here. I'm twenty-two, and yeah, I'm a senior at NYU. I'm a social-work major with a lit. minor."

Elena arched an intrigued brow. "Social work and literature," she said. "That is an interesting combination. Why the interest in either?"

"Well, the first is a little complicated," Allison admitted. She didn't like to go into detail on this particular subject. "Let's just say that a lot of stuff gets overlooked in the system or doesn't get looked into hard enough, and I want to help correct that, or at least, I want to make strides in correcting that."

Allison's stomach lurched when Elena visibly stiffened at the words. She should have just said she wanted to help people or something, but she tended to ramble and give herself away. She hoped Elena wouldn't read too much into it, but the way the woman's smile slipped back into its earlier strained form made Allison suspect otherwise.

"And the other is simple," Allison said, clearing her throat. "I just really like to read."

"I see," Elena said. "I enjoy reading as well. I have quite the collection at home, so, perhaps, if I hire you, you may find a book or two to entertain you while Lucas naps or once he has gone to bed for the evening."

"Lucas?" Allison grinned. "Your son's name is Lucas? Is he the only one you've got? How old is he?"

Elena smiled brightly, clearly unable to help herself. "Yes, his name is Lucas. He is three, and yes, he is the only child I have."

"Three." Allison cooed. "That's a great age. I bet he's adorable."

"Beyond, but he is also quite the handful."

"Most toddlers are. I'm sure I can handle him."

The way Elena narrowed her eyes gave Allison the impression that the woman was a bit skeptical about that statement.

"How has he been with other babysitters?" Allison asked.

"I have never hired a babysitter before." Elena shifted in her seat. "My parents keep him when I cannot."

"Ah." That explained a lot. Elena was obviously very protective of her son, and parents tended to be a little skeptical when starting out with babysitters anyway. "Well, hopefully I'll be a good fit."

"So, you like children?" Elena asked. "What I mean is, do you actually *enjoy* caring for children or are you simply in it for the money? Is this your first potential babysitting job?"

"The last family I babysat for moved across the country. So, Lucas would be my one and only if you hired me, and yes, I like kids. I love kids, actually."

"Oh? Do you have any siblings?"

Allison laughed so hard that she snorted, and Elena simply stared at her with a perplexed expression. "Sorry. It's not really funny, but yeah. I've had siblings before. If you count them all up, in fact, then I had twenty-nine siblings by the time I was sixteen."

The surprise in Elena's widened eyes quickly gave way to an understanding nod. "You're a foster child." She whispered the words so softly that they were almost inaudible.

Scratching at the back of her neck, Allison shrugged to hide her discomfort. "Yup. I'm an orphan. Spent most of my life in the system. Anyway, I don't really like to talk about it, so if we could move on to the next subject, that would be great."

"Yes, of course." Elena glanced away and licked her lips before turning back to Allison. "I apologize. I didn't mean to pry."

"You didn't. You asked a perfectly acceptable question and I answered it. That's that."

"Very well." Taking a quick peek at her watch, Elena sighed. "I'm terribly sorry, but I should be on my way. I am already late in returning to work."

"Oh, right." Allison nodded and forced a smile. "Yeah, I get it. I have my next class in an hour anyway." She stood as Elena did and stretched out a hand. "Well, uh, it was nice to meet you, Elena."

"You as well, Allison." With a firm shake of Allison's hand, Elena collected her things and laid several bills on the table. "I will take care of lunch."

"You don't have to do that, but thanks. I appreciate it."

Elena nodded in answer and turned to leave, but she whirled around again when Allison called her name. She began walking over until they were a little closer than was typically considered appropriate.

"Look, I know you don't know me," Allison said. "And I know that you probably just want the best you can get for your son. I get that, and I'm not asking you to pity me or to throw me a bone just because of my past or because I need the money. I'm asking you to give me a chance because, unlike a lot of people who get these jobs, I *do* actually care, and I'm a good person. I work hard, really hard. I'm an honor student. I'm trying to *make* something of myself. And I may not know a lot about family, but I *will* take care of your kid. I'll make sure he's safe and happy anytime you need me to. I'm punctual and I'm clean and I'm a good choice for this job."

Allison reached into her pocket then and pulled out a small slip of paper with a string of numbers scrawled across it. "This is my number," she said as she handed it to her. "I hope you'll give me a chance, Elena." She gave the brunette one last smile before slipping by her, out the door, and into the rush of the city.

The soft sound of Lucas's breathing sang like a comforting and familiar lullaby in Elena's ears as she drove home from her parents' house with her sleeping son in the backseat. Lucas always fell asleep in the car, whether the drive was five or fifty minutes. Something about the hum of the road always knocked him out.

Elena watched the road beneath the orange sky as the sun set and her thoughts wandered. She thought of the hectic day she had at work, but mostly she thought of the woman she met on her lunch break, Allison Sawyer. Something about Allison stuck with her after she returned to work and even now. Elena was accustomed to taking command of the majority of the social situations she found herself in, and considering she had intended to interview this young woman as a potential employee, she had assumed this situation would be no different. Boy, had she been wrong. Allison Sawyer had slipped right in and taken the reins like she was entitled to them, like she had bred and raised that horse herself, and strangely enough, Elena had simply let her—no arguments, no fuss. Elena couldn't stop thinking about it but as she contemplated the young woman, she made a split-second decision.

She drummed her fingers on the steering wheel impatiently for the remaining few minutes it took to reach her house. As soon as she parked the car, she dug through her purse until she found the small slip of paper she had been given earlier that day and punched the numbers into her cell.

"Who's this?" the voice on the line asked without any form of greeting, and Elena couldn't help the small smile that formed on her lips. *So blunt,* she thought.

"Hello Allison. This is Elena Vega." Before she could say anything else, Allison jumped right in. Elena was surprised that she had been expecting anything else from the woman.

"Elena, oh my God, are you hiring me?"

"Well, I was hoping that we could do a trial run. I want to make sure that Lucas is comfortable with you before I make a final decision. If you are interested, when might you be available to come meet Lucas and perhaps spend a bit of time with him?"

"Yeah, I'm definitely interested." Elena swore she could hear her grinning over the phone line. "And well, it is now officially the weekend. I just got out of my last class, so I'm available right now. I mean, if that's okay with you and everything."

Mouth agape, Elena tried to think of an excuse to pick a different time and day. She hated impromptu anything. It always made her feel flustered and nervous, but, then, impromptu seemed to be the definition of Allison Sawyer. So if Elena was going to hire her, she had better get used to it. She glanced at the small digital clock above her stereo. Five forty-five blinked back at her. She swallowed before stuttering, "Oh, well, okay. Um, yes, I suppose that right now would be fine."

After she had rattled off her address and listened to a pen scratch down each word, Allison's voice came back over the line. "Sweet. I just need like fifteen or twenty minutes, then I'll be there."

"Very well." Elena's palms were beginning to sweat as she thought of everything she had to do prior to Allison's arrival. She wanted to tidy up, despite the fact that her house was almost always immaculate, considering she cleaned up after Lucas on an hourly or even half-hourly basis. Clutter drove her mad. She supposed she should also provide dinner, considering Allison said she had only just left class, so she likely had yet to eat. What could she cook in fifteen minutes?

"Elena?"

Elena snapped back to attention, her cheeks flushing for no one to see. "Yes, I'm here. I will see you soon, Allison."

As soon as she hung up, Elena jumped out of her car and quickly collected Lucas from the backseat. He rubbed at his eyes sleepily as she carried him into the house, but, by the time they reached the living room, he was wide awake again. Elena chuckled as the boy smiled slyly at her and said, "Momma, you wanna make dinosaur nuggets."

"Oh I do, do I?" she asked, still laughing as she carried him into the kitchen, held him at the sink to help him wash his hands, and then put him in his seat.

"Uh-huh." His nod was overly dramatic.

Elena opened the freezer and looked inside. "I suppose I'm in luck then, because we happen to have an entire box of dinosaur nuggets." She pulled out the box of grilled chicken nuggets cut into dinosaur shapes and waggled it at her son.

Giggling, Lucas threw up his arms. "How long?"

"Not long, baby." She stopped to drop a kiss to his forehead and muttered to herself. "Now, what to make for Allison?"

When the doorbell rang, Lucas had already devoured his dinosaur nuggets and sweet peas and had run off to play. Elena still found it strange how much her son actually enjoyed peas. He was one of few kids she knew to actually love them, but she was far from complaining. She finished straining the pasta before going to answer the door. The pitter-patter of Lucas's feet running toward her from the other room meant he was too curious to stay away, but he was also quite shy. He hid behind her leg as she pulled open the door.

Allison looked exactly as she had earlier that day—long blonde ponytail, jean jacket, and everything.

"Ms.—sorry." No formalities, she remembered. "*Allison*, hello. I'm glad you could make it."

"Hi," Allison chirped with a little wave. Her eyes raked down Elena's body as they apparently were going to do every time she saw the woman, then shifted to the little hand clinging to Elena's pants and wide caramel-colored eyes peeking out from around Elena's leg.

Smiling and shaking her leg, Elena softly said, "Stop hiding, dear. Come out and say hello."

His little head poked out just a bit farther with a shy greeting. "Hello."

"Hi Lucas." Allison waved at him, and the boy narrowed his eyes at her. She glanced back up at Elena. "He looks like you."

"Yes," Elena said and then suddenly realized that they were still standing in the doorway. Stepping back, she motioned for Allison to enter. "Come in."

They barely managed more than a few steps inside before Lucas tugged on Elena's pant leg. He crooked his finger at her, motioning for her to bend down. When she did, he cupped a hand around his mouth and pressed it to his mother's ear.

"Momma, who's that?"

"That is Allison." Allison offered him another small wave, but he just continued to look at her with narrowed eyes. "She is a babysitter."

"What's a babysinner?" He shrank behind Elena a little more.

Both Elena and Allison laughed. "Babysit-ter," Elena repeated.

"Yeah, kid," Allison said. "I sit on babies."

Lucas's eyes widened comically and so did Elena's.

"I'm not a baby. I'm a big boy!"

Winking, Allison said, "Well then, I guess you and me can just be friends then."

Elena watched closely as Lucas seemed to consider Allison's words, and when he took a step out from behind her leg, she couldn't help but smile.

As if testing the water, Lucas quietly asked, "You like dinosaurs?"

"Are you kidding me?" Allison gasped dramatically. "I *love* dinosaurs!"

That was all it took. A wide smile spread over Lucas's face and in seconds, he ran right past them and into the next room, shouting to Allison over his shoulder. "Come on!"

Allison looked up at Elena and smiled. "Can I go and play with him?"

Pure childlike excitement filled the younger woman's bright eyes in that moment, and Elena could see why babysitting was a good fit for Allison Sawyer. "Go ahead. Oh, and I am making pasta. I thought you might be hungry."

"Awesome! Yeah, I'm starved. Thank you. That's really nice of you."

"My pleasure," Elena said. She watched as Allison darted off after Lucas and out of sight. Only minutes later, giggles from both of them echoed into the kitchen from the living room, and Elena grinned as she brought her pasta sauce to a simmer.

"Perhaps this will work out after all," Elena murmured, now only hoping that Vivian could keep her word and set her up with at least a *few* decent dates.

Chapter Three

When Elena finished preparing dinner, she set two places at the dining-room table and then headed toward the living room. She reached the open archway that led into the large living room and stopped and leaned against the frame. A tender smile graced her lips.

Allison and Lucas sat on the floor together as they played with Lucas's dinosaur figurines, and Elena had to cup a hand over her mouth to keep from laughing aloud when she realized that her son was slowly but surely scooting closer and closer to Allison. Within a few moments, he was sitting hip-to-hip with her, and completely surprised Elena by crawling up into Allison's lap and resting his back against her chest. That moment alone was enough to convince Elena that Allison was right for the job.

She was only further convinced as Allison simply seemed to roll with the changes, letting Lucas make his own decisions and set his own pace. She patted his leg as she reached around him and quietly asked, "What about this one?"

"That's my tricertops."

"Triceratops," Allison corrected.

Lucas pulled the dinosaur from her hand. "That's what I said," he muttered. He then held up another figurine and added, "And the rex eats him."

"Oh yeah?"

"Yeah, 'cause the rex is a carnival." Lucas gave her a confident nod. "That means he eats meats."

Allison giggled and so did Elena, unable to hold it in any longer. Allison's head snapped up and she smiled when she saw Elena leaning against the door frame and watching them.

"Hey Elena, did you know that Rex is a carnival?" Allison asked her, winking.

"I did, actually." Elena nodded. "He only eats meat."

"You're sposta say thank you." Lucas's hand poked at Allison's chin.

Allison grabbed his hand and held it. "What for?"

"Because I teached you something."

"Taught," Elena and Allison corrected simultaneously.

Huffing out a breath, Lucas tried to roll his big honey-brown eyes but only ended up crossing them. Allison gently moved him off her lap and placed him in the middle of all the dinosaurs. He seemed content to play alone, so she popped up off the floor and walked over to Elena.

"He has trouble with tenses," Elena explained.

"Well, he *is* only three," Allison said. "He'll get the hang of it. I had a brother once whose speech didn't really develop until he was like four, and then I had a sister who was talking up a storm by the time she was two. It's different with every kid. There's no hard and fast rule to it, you know?"

Nodding, Elena continued to watch her son play. "He's normally very shy around strangers," she said. "He seems to have taken quite the liking to you, though. I'm surprised."

"Ouch. Are you saying that I'm not likeable?" Allison gaped comically and pressed a hand to her chest.

A smirk formed on Elena's lips as she shook her head. Allison seemed like a genuinely kind person with a good head on her shoulders, and she was refreshingly at ease with herself. It actually made it easier for Elena to be more comfortable with her.

Allison leaned against the opposite side of the door frame as she, too, watched Lucas play. "He's pretty awesome." She nudged Elena's arm with her elbow. "Like his Mom."

That pulled a loud laugh from Elena. "Flattery will get you nowhere, Ms. Sawyer."

"It's Allison, and I think you're wrong about that," she argued. "I think flattery will at least get me some food."

"You would have gotten it anyway. The dining room is just around the corner and to your right. I've already set the table for us. You go ahead. I am going to move Lucas to his playroom so I can see him from the table."

"Okay, thanks." Allison darted off toward the dining room while Elena collected her son.

"So, what do you think, munchkin?" Elena quietly asked as she picked Lucas up. "Do we like Allison?"

His fingers tangled in the hair at the back of her neck as he offered up a wide grin.

"Is that a yes?"

The answer came in the form of an enthusiastic nod as they passed the dining room, where Allison had just finished filling a bowl with salad and was now piling some pasta onto a plate, and then into the playroom next door. "She's pretty," he whispered, his cheeks flushing a gentle pink.

Elena patted his bottom and put him down on his feet. "I know," she said, tapping her finger on the tip of his nose. "Momma's going to eat now. You be good."

"Okay."

When Elena took her place at the dining room table, adjacent to her guest, Allison pointed toward the playroom. "The kid likes dinosaurs, huh?"

"More than almost anything," Elena said. "He got a dinosaur T-shirt for his second birthday, and ever since then, it has been dinosaur everything—clothing, room décor, toys, and anything else we can find. I have yet to understand the obsession."

"I always liked dinosaurs too." Allison leaned back in her chair and stretched her arms out. "They're cool because they actually existed."

"I suppose so, yes."

"So, you think I'm pretty, huh?" Allison asked, then, taking Elena by surprise.

Elena shook her head, laughing quietly. "Do you ever stop?"

"Rarely." Allison nodded to accept the wine glass Elena offered. "Unless it bothers you? Because if it bothers you, I can totally stop."

"It doesn't bother me." Elena took a sip of wine. "I am simply unaccustomed to it. That's all."

"Unaccustomed to what? Unaccustomed to people who don't talk like they just climbed out of a textbook, or people who actually speak their opinions to your face instead of behind your back? Lifestyles of the rich and famous and all that, right?"

One slender brow rose at the daring remark. "My, my. Am I sensing a hint of bitterness?"

"Not at all." Allison shoved a forkful of pasta into her mouth and moaned softly as she chewed the food and swallowed it down. "Holy crap! That's good."

"Thank you."

"Thank *you*. Anyway, no, not bitter. Just my opinion, I guess. You disagree?"

Elena stared at her a long moment before sucking in a breath and confessing, "Unfortunately, no."

"It's no big deal, really." Allison shrugged. "I mean, minus the general textbook talk, the middle and lower classes are really no better. There are bitches in every group, you know?"

Elena's eyes cut quickly to the side to see if Lucas had heard that word, but he was completely immersed in his own little world, making loud screeching and roaring sounds as he played with his dinosaurs. Allison followed Elena's eyes, and her cheeks instantly flushed.

"Oh sorry. I didn't mean to say that so loudly. I swear I won't ever cuss around the kid."

"Thank you. I would prefer that you don't in his presence, but I don't believe he heard just now. Anyway, I find I rather agree with you. However, I *am* curious to know..."

"If I see *you* like that?"

Elena nodded as she took a dainty bite of pasta and avoided Allison's eyes. It wasn't until she heard the quiet words "Not even close" that she finally looked up.

"At least, not yet," Allison added. "You can always tell which people think they're better than you. It's in their eyes and in the way they sneer, you know? I've had a lot of rich people turn me away just because of how I dress or how I talk or whatever. But I don't get that from you, even if you *do* secretly think you're better than me. You definitely don't show it."

"I don't," Elena said quickly.

"You don't show it?"

"I don't think I am better than you."

Their eyes locked across the table. Allison winked and pointed her fork at Elena before twirling it in her fingers and poking it down into her pasta again. "Okay then."

Her smile was echoed on Elena's face. "Okay."

When they were finished eating, Allison immediately stood up and reached for Elena's plate. All stacked together, the dishes were easy to carry to the kitchen, and Allison deposited them next to the sink.

Elena started to thank her but then noticed Allison pulling off the jean jacket that she seemed to wear like a second shirt and turning the faucet on.

"Oh Allison, you don't have to do that."

"I know. You didn't have to cook me dinner either, but you did. I want to, so just let me, okay?"

Elena's shoulders relaxed as she laced her fingers together in front of her waist and stepped over to the counter. "Very well. I appreciate it. Thank you."

"You're welcome. Thank you for dinner."

Just then, Lucas sprinted into the kitchen, shouting that he wanted to help Allison. When he tried to skid to a stop, his socks slid on the tiled floor, and he crashed into the lower cabinets beside Allison's leg. The dishes sitting on the counter near the edge trembled as Lucas's little body banged against the cabinets, and before Allison could stop it, the salad bowl on the top of the stack slid off and went tumbling down.

A yelp of fear escaped Elena as Allison threw herself to the floor and covered Lucas's body with her own. The salad bowl clunked on top of her head with a hard thud, rolled down her shoulder and then onto the floor where it cracked on one side from impact.

Elena was on the floor next to them in seconds, just as Allison was turning Lucas in her arms and looking him over. "You okay, little man?" she asked. He nodded like it was no big deal and then bent to pick up the fallen bowl.

"This bowl is not okay." His eyes widened as his voice jumped up an octave. "Look Momma, a crack!"

"I see," Elena said. "I'm just glad that you are all right. Let's not touch it anymore, though, okay?" She took the bowl from him and placed it back on the counter, far from the edge. "Lucas, why don't you go to your room and change into your pajamas? You think you can do that by yourself like a big boy?"

"But I wanna help wash." He knotted his hands in the bottom of his shirt as he danced in place from foot to foot.

"You can help Allison the next time she comes to see you, okay?"

That seemed to be enough for him. "Okay!" he cheered before taking off for his room.

Once he was out of sight and Elena turned back around, she found herself face to face with an amused Allison. "So, there's gonna be a next time, huh? That mean I got the job?"

"Are you kidding me?"

Allison's smile dropped from her lips. "Oh, uh, well, I—" she began to stutter.

"Allison, you just threw yourself in front of a flying salad bowl to protect my son. Of course you have the job."

A sigh of relief slipped through Allison's lips before dissolving into laughter. "Sounds so much more badass when you put it like that."

Elena stepped to the sink, nudging Allison's shoulder with her own, and reached for the dish soap. "Come on, hero. Let's finish these dishes."

Lucas's small hand slapped against Allison's in a firm high five when she accompanied Elena to bid him goodnight. "So, I'll see you soon, okay?"

Grinning at her, he nodded and climbed into his bed. "And we can play more dinosaurs?"

"Totally."

"Totally," he repeated, and Allison chuckled as she ruffled his hair. She was already pretty taken with him. "Night kid."

She left the room and waited for Elena in the hallway. Elena's voice drifted from the room as she told Lucas she would be right back to tuck him in. When she emerged from the room, they walked quietly down the hall, through the foyer, and to the front door.

"So, I guess you'll call me when you need me?" Allison asked as she opened the door and leaned into the frame.

"I will," Elena said. "I'm glad we were able to do this, Allison. I think Lucas will enjoy having you around when I am out."

She smiled. "I think I'll enjoy it, too." She gave a small wave before stepping through the open door. "Okay, well, goodnight Elena."

"Good night." Elena gently closed the door behind her.

A resounding squeal spilled through the phone. "This is fantastic! We can get started right away."

"Please stop making it sound like a project, Viv." Elena groaned as she lay in bed with the phone pressed between her cheek and her pillow. "I'm not a test subject."

"Sure you are. And we are testing how fast we can find you a man."

"Or woman." Elena bit her tongue as soon as she realized what she said.

"Oh really? What happened to all that 'it was only one time' stuff?"

Burying her face into the pillow, Elena let out another exaggerated groan. "You are incorrigible."

"I'm not incorrigible. You just hate it when I'm right, and I was right. You are at least twenty-five percent gay."

The pillow muffled Elena's snort of laughter. "Gayness is not measured in percentages. It's not a heritage."

"Well, it is now." Vivian was cracking herself up. "I am one-sixteenth Irish, and you are one-quarter gay."

Elena rolled her eyes and glanced at her bedside clock. "I'm hanging up now."

"Okay, but see if you can get the babysitter for tomorrow. You are lucky you called me on a Friday, because I can definitely have a date set up for you by tomorrow night."

"Viv, no—"

"No excuses. You agreed, so you're going. That's final."

"Fine, *Mother.* He or she better be incredibly attractive."

With that, Elena hung up, buried her face into her pillow again, and sighed as she pulled the blankets over her head and shut out the world.

Heels clicked loudly against the floor as Elena hurried to the door and pulled it open to see Allison standing there with her blonde hair cascading around her shoulders in loose curls and a backpack hanging off her back. Elena smiled as Allison's eyes trailed down her body.

Perfectly coiffed hair fell in shining waves ending just above exposed collarbones, and Elena's tight black dress hugged her body and accentuated her curves. Toned calves were on full display, drifting down to slender feet adorned in black heels.

Allison let out a quiet whistle. "*Daaaamn.*"

Cheeks flushing a faint pink, Elena nodded in appreciation.

"I'm gonna take a wild guess and say that you're going to some big company party tonight, because you are definitely dressed to impress." Stepping inside, Allison set her backpack on the floor beneath the table by the door.

"I'm afraid not. My friend, Vivian, the woman you spoke to about the babysitting job, has been incredibly determined to set me up with someone."

"Whoa, hold up. Are you telling me that you hired a babysitter so you could go on dates?"

Elena rolled her eyes as she walked through the house with Allison trailing behind her. "Unfortunately, yes."

"Oh wow. That's rich. I hope she's at least screening the dudes."

Elena's lip curled as she thought on that. "Do you think I should be worried?"

Allison followed Elena into a bedroom at the end of a long hallway and collapsed on a large bed. "*I* would be," she sighed as she stretched and pressed her body more fully into the mattress. She cracked up when Elena playfully smacked her knee.

"Oh *do* make yourself at home in my *bedroom*, Ms. Sawyer."

Grinning, Allison rolled around on the bed a bit. "Allison," she sing-songed in response, "and it's *your* fault. You walked. I followed. If you didn't want me in here, you should've said."

The daring, confident nature of this young woman was ever surprising, and Elena could only shake her head and laugh. "I suppose it is fine."

"Good."

Elena walked over to a large vanity and pulled a pair of earrings from a small jewelry box that rested atop it.

"Where's my little guy? Or did you call me here to babysit your house?"

Pressing the earrings into her lobes, Elena took the opportunity to double check her makeup in the mirror. "He's in his room watching a movie," she said. "He likes to lie in bed while he watches."

Allison's brows rose in appreciation. "Smart kid."

Elena blotted her lips, and Allison popped her own, as if to fill the silence. "So," she said after a moment, "you're not even a *little* bit worried?"

"About?"

"Well, I'm assuming these are blind dates, right?"

"Yes."

"Okay, so they're called blind dates for a reason. You don't know the guys ahead of time. So, I'm just saying...."

"You are just saying what?" Elena huffed, arching a brow at Allison's reflection in the vanity mirror.

"I'm saying I hope Vivian at least knows the guys, because you don't want to like end up, you know."

"No, I'm afraid I *don't* know. Perhaps you should elaborate."

"I'm just saying, you don't want to end up playing out weird 'mommy' fantasies with some deranged Momma's boy or you know, like, trapped in some dude's basement being told to put the lotion on your skin or else you get the hose again."

Elena's lip curled in disgust even as her brows furrowed. She turned toward Allison looking utterly confused. "What the hell are you talking about?"

Allison gaped. "Oh no, *seriously*?"

"Seriously *what*?"

"You haven't seen *The Silence of the Lambs*? That is a *must*-see!"

"I'm afraid not, and if what you just said is from that film, then I am afraid I would rather not." A shiver ran down her spine. "I'm going to have that unfortunate image stuck in my head for the rest of the night."

"Well, you're welcome." Allison stuck her tongue out. "It'll remind you to be cautious."

The doorbell rang, echoing to them from down the hall, and Elena cursed as she glanced at the clock. "He's early."

"Overeager," Allison said, playfully shaking her head in disapproval.

"Oh hush."

Allison followed Elena back down the hall and to the door. When Elena opened the door to reveal a tall, dark-headed man in a light gray suit, she smiled, seeing how Allison narrowed her eyes, sizing him up. He had to be in his mid-thirties, probably pretty wealthy, considering his attire and the Rolex on his wrist.

Instead of introducing himself, the man offered up a cheesy smile and said, "You look lovely."

Elena smiled tightly and noticed Allison rolling her eyes at the compliment. An urge rose in Elena to do the same, but she knew her manners. Thus, she nodded her head in appreciation and returned the compliment. Asking him to wait in the foyer, she walked down the hall to Lucas's room with Allison following.

Lucas barely acknowledged her goodbye kiss, too wrapped up in his movie, and Elena was able to slip in and out without a fuss. She turned to Allison once they were out of the room.

"You have my cell number?"

Allison nodded.

"Okay, and I left emergency numbers on a pad for you in the kitchen. There is plenty to choose from for dinner or you can order something; I left some money on the counter. Also, I prefer Lucas be in bed by no later than eight, though he can be difficult to put down at times."

"I got it covered. Go on. You don't want to keep your fancy date waiting."

"I shouldn't be home too late."

Allison followed her to the door once more. Just before Elena stepped out, Allison leaned in with a whisper. "Watch out for the lotion."

Elena's cheeks flushed with pink as she tried not to laugh. She subtly kicked Allison's shin before following her date out the door.

Chapter Four

"So, Elena, Vivian tells me you have a son. Larry, is it?"

"*Lucas*, and yes, he is three."

"Oh, and the father?"

Brows shooting toward her hairline, Elena leveled the man with her piercing gaze. "My, Brice, you cut directly to the personal questions, don't you?"

Brice grinned far too widely to be natural. "Forgive me. Was that out of bounds?"

"Considering we have only just met, I would certainly say so." She pulled her napkin into her lap and took a careful sip of her water.

"Well, perhaps we will know one another much better by the end of the night," Brice replied softly and with a subtle wink that Elena assumed the man thought was either charming or seductive.

Brice had selected a high-end restaurant that Elena frequented with her parents, and she found it much too predictable, given his obvious wealth. Why so many men assumed all women wanted an expensive meal, an expensive wine, and a ride in an expensive car was completely beyond her. Would it kill them to try for a little originality?

Elena, as was her nature, kept a mental list of strikes against her date, and, thanks to the man's overly personal question and suggestive behavior, he gained his first before they ever even placed their orders. He earned his second strike only seconds later when the waiter arrived to take their orders.

Before she could even open her mouth to speak, Brice flashed a smug grin and addressed the waiter. "Yes, thank you," he said. "We will take a bottle of your finest Cabernet Sauvignon to pair with two house sirloins, both medium rare, and the lady will enjoy a side salad while I will take a—"

That was about as much as Elena could stomach. How dare he speak for her? Fifteen minutes into this date, and Brice was already stripping her of choice.

She far from approved.

"Actually," Elena interjected, "*I* will have a glass of chardonnay to pair with the roasted salmon in lemon butter. I would like that with a side of seasoned vegetables, and please, ask the chef to apply any salt lightly. Thank you."

The waiter smiled at her and nodded before smirking at Brice, who was staring at Elena with his lips slightly parted and his brows furrowed. "Sir?" the waiter asked.

"Oh right, yes," Brice said quickly, snapping back to attention. He placed his order and offered Elena a tight smile. "I was unaware you didn't eat red meat. I apologize."

"Oh I do eat red meat, Brice." Her revelation came with an equally forced smile. "I simply am not in the mood tonight. You would have known as much if you had simply bothered to ask."

Brice cleared his throat and glanced around the restaurant. He took a sip of water and smacked his lips. It was clear to Elena that the man had only just figured out that she was nowhere near the type of woman he was looking for. He undoubtedly wanted a piece of arm candy that would worship his every decision.

Elena was hardly a trophy. She was the entire goddamned competition—a complex yet worthwhile challenge, not a mindless reward.

Sighing, she crossed and uncrossed her legs underneath the table, avoiding eye contact with Brice. *Great,* she thought. She was going to have to sit through an entire undoubtedly awkward dinner with this man now, and it was likely that little conversation would take place. Then again, perhaps that would be a blessing.

She could only hope the waiter returned soon with their meals and then soon after again with the check.

"Hold on, kid." Allison grunted. "Let me just get my feet right."

Lucas giggled as Allison finally got her feet positioned gently against his belly. She then took his hands and squeezed them. "Hold on tight, okay? Tight tight!"

"Okay!" He squealed and squeezed her hands as tightly as he could when Allison then easily lifted his body into the air. She held his arms out with her hands and kept his body up with her feet so that he looked like he was flying just a few feet above her. She couldn't help her laughter when Lucas screamed at the top of his lungs, "I'm an airplane!"

"You are!" She separated her feet so that Lucas fell quickly from his position in the air and she caught him in a fast embrace, tickling him as he squealed and wriggled around, rolling off her chest to the floor.

Lucas laughed so hard that little sound escaped, but then his eyes went wide and he clapped a hand over his mouth.

"Whoa," Allison said, her smile fading. "You okay, buddy? Are you gonna be sick?"

Perhaps it was a little too soon after dinner to be flying the kid around on her feet. She didn't want to end up covered in stomach-pureed sweet peas.

Cheeks flushing a bright red, Lucas popped up on his feet and whispered, "I peed."

Allison had to bite her tongue to keep from laughing, because it was obvious that the little guy was fairly embarrassed about his accident, but his pink cheeks and quiet admission were incredibly cute. She tucked a finger under his chin and pushed it up so he would look at her. "Hey, that's okay, Lucas. Everybody has accidents."

"Even you?" he whispered.

"Even me." She was certain she hadn't peed her pants since she was in diapers, but he didn't need to know that. "It was my fault anyway, okay? I shouldn't have tickled you so much."

Lucas nodded, but he still didn't raise his voice above a whisper as he held his hands over the wet spot on the front of his pants and said, "Okay."

"Okay, let's go get cleaned up then. It's bath time before bed anyway, right?"

"Uh-huh." Lucas nodded and then shyly took one of Allison's hands. He walked with her down the hallway and toward the large bathroom across from his bedroom.

Once Allison got the water to a decent temperature and the tub filled about halfway, she shut the water off and turned to Lucas. He had already stripped down to nothing and stood shyly in front of her with his hands over his privates and his lip tucked between his teeth. His round belly poked out over his hands and Allison saw that he was an outie. She'd had a foster brother with an outie belly button too. As weird as other people sometimes found it, Allison thought it was very cute.

She poked it with her index finger as she asked, "Okay bud, you ready?" He nodded and held up his arms so that she could pick him up. She lifted him over the high edge of the tub and settled him slowly down into the warm water.

He was a shorty, even for his age, Allison noted as the water rose to his chest and she looked him over. His hair was a dark brown, just like his mother's, and his eyes were brown too, though they were lighter than Elena's. Elena's eyes were a deep espresso, while Lucas's were a brighter, more golden brown, like a sun-soaked field of wheat. He had puffy cheeks slightly fairer in color than the rich olive tone of his mother's skin, and they had the same slender nose and full, pouty lips. His chin, however, was entirely his own, and that made Allison wonder if he had gotten it from his father or perhaps a grandparent.

Lucas quickly regained his confidence as they played with his floating rubber boats, and by the time Allison carefully tilted his head back to rinse away his shampoo, he was jabbering up a storm about all of his favorite things.

"No way," Allison said, splashing a little water at the boy. "Green is *my* favorite color too!"

"Dinosaurs are green!" Lucas shouted.

"Yeah!" Allison gave him a wet high five before pulling the plug out of the drain. Lucas stood up and shivered as Allison grabbed a small towel to pick him up with. Once she got him out of the tub, she dried him off and helped him into his pajamas, which of course were covered in dinosaurs. Sitting on the closed lid of the toilet seat, she watched as the boy stood in front of a small mirror his mother had obviously installed just for him and carefully combed his damp hair. Afterward, he brushed his teeth with expert precision, rinsing his mouth with a Dixie cup and then smiling so wide at Allison that she could see his gums.

"Whoa!" she gasped. "Great job! They're super white and clean."

Turning, Lucas ran out of the room and into his bedroom. He cannonballed into his bed, pulled his blanket up onto his head like a hood, and laughed hysterically when Allison came in after him.

Seriously, she thought as she sat down to read him a story. *Could this kid get any freakin' cuter?*

Leaving the restaurant with Brice was even more uncomfortable than *being at* the restaurant with Brice. Elena walked silently beside him until they reached his sports car where he opened the door for her to slip inside.

"Thank you," she said before gracefully sliding into the low-set seat.

When Brice dropped into the driver's seat and the engine roared to life, Elena's thoughts were dominated by a single mantra. *Please let traffic be minimal. Please let traffic be minimal.* Of course, Elena knew that the hope was not even a long shot. It was a complete impossibility.

A Saturday night in New York City? Not a chance.

As the car crept through the busy city streets, Brice cleared his throat and asked, "So, have you been on many blind dates?"

Elena stared out her window as she quietly responded, "I have not."

"I would have guessed that," he chuckled. "You seem a little on edge, perhaps a little uncomfortable. It takes a while to get used to. I would guess from your reaction at the restaurant that you don't date much at all. Not quite used to being pampered? That's a shame for a woman as beautiful as you."

"Pampered?" Elena could hardly mask the disbelief in her voice.

"Mm," Brice hummed and turned to flash a smile that reminded her of the shark in *Finding Nemo,* a movie she'd watched countless times with Lucas. That smile was predatory and smug. She wasn't facing him, but she saw the bright white reflection of it in the glass pane of her window.

Elena wasn't even going to touch this conversation with a ten-foot pole. If this man actually thought that making blatant assumptions and speaking *for* her rather than *to* her or with her were the equivalents of pampering, then what was the point of even bothering with a response?

"Turn here," Elena snapped bluntly, pointing to the right turn quickly approaching. She scratched at the side of her nose and avoided looking at the man in the driver's seat as she added, "It's faster."

That must have been enough of a hint for Brice, because he said nothing else for the remainder of the ride back to Elena's house.

Lucas's long, dark lashes fluttered as he tried to keep his eyes open, but his breathing had grown deep and heavy, and Allison knew that the kid was a goner. He hadn't been nearly as hard to put down as Allison had been expecting, though he put up a good struggle. She stopped reading and laid her hand on his belly over the covers, rubbing in small circles. Within seconds, he was out. She leaned over and kissed his forehead before quietly slipping out of the room.

"What to do?" she muttered as she checked the time on her cell phone and saw that it was barely after eight. She probably had quite a bit of time left before Elena would be home. She could kill some time on homework. Grabbing her backpack from the foyer, she carried it into the kitchen and pulled out a bag of microwavable popcorn and a few small bags of Reese's Pieces candy. She popped the popcorn in the microwave and poured it into a large bowl she found in one of Elena's cabinets before pouring all the bags of candy into the popcorn and mixing it all up.

Carrying her backpack and the large bowl of popcorn into the living room, she pulled out one of her textbooks, a notebook, and a pen and began jotting down notes while she stuffed her face. She fully expected to be at it for another few hours, but it was only about thirty minutes later that Allison heard the front door open. The soft clicking of heels on a hard floor then echoed through the house.

The soft click of the front door closing behind her sent a wave of relief through Elena's body. She let out a heavy sigh as she leaned against the heavy wood, thanking God that that horrid date was finally over. The large ornate clock on the wall in the foyer told her it was nearly fifteen 'til nine. Lucas would be long asleep by now. Still, she wanted to check on him.

Walking as quietly as possible, which wasn't easy with heels, Elena made her way to his room and peeked in. A smile settled across her lips as she saw his little face in the light spilling in through the open door. His thumb was stuck firmly in his mouth as he slept. She watched him for several long moments before closing his door again and seeking out the babysitter.

The living room coffee table was littered with textbooks and notes, the homework laid out in front of the couch where Allison sat with a bowl of popcorn in her lap. She looked up as Elena came into the room, glanced quickly down at her cell, and then back up at Elena. "Ouch," she said as she tried to fight a laugh. "Not even nine yet. I'm guessing the date didn't go so well?"

Elena rolled her eyes and let out an annoyed huff as she slipped off her high heels. "That is the understatement of the year."

Chuckling, Allison set aside her popcorn and rose from the couch. "Sit down," she told her. "I'll be right back."

The couch cushion sank with a gentle sigh as Elena settled in, wrinkling her nose in disgust upon looking into the bowl Allison left behind.

When Allison returned, she carried a hot cup of coffee. She set it down on a coaster on the table in front of Elena and asked, "Sugar or cream? I guessed that you're a black-coffee kind of girl, but I can grab some if you prefer. Or I can drink the coffee if you'd rather have wine or something."

Elena just smiled as she shook her head. "No, thank you. You guessed correctly, but you certainly didn't have to do that, Allison."

"Yeah, I know." She shrugged as she stepped around the small table in front of the couch and reached for her popcorn.

Grabbing the coffee with her left hand, Elena used her right to gesture toward Allison's snack as she settled back into the couch. "That looks terribly fattening."

Allison completely surprised Elena when she lifted up the front of her tank top to expose a rigid set of perfectly toned abs. "I think I'm good."

Heat surged through Elena's cheeks, turning them red. She cleared her throat roughly and shot her gaze back up to mirthful, green eyes. "I suppose you are." She quickly brought her coffee cup to her lips, distracting herself by blowing on the hot liquid and avoiding eye contact with her incredibly shameless babysitter.

Clearing her throat roughly, Elena asked, "How was Lucas?"

"Best kid ever." Allison settled back into her spot on the couch. "He *did* have an accident, though."

"Really?" Elena was surprised. "That is a rare occurrence."

"Yeah, well it was my bad. I was tickling him, and he was pretty embarrassed. But I just told him that everybody has accidents and then gave him a bath. He cheered right up."

"How did he do with the bath?" Elena was pleasantly surprised that Allison had even bothered with a bath. She had assumed that she would simply keep Lucas entertained and then put him to bed. This only made Elena further approve of her. "He can be rather shy."

"Nah, he did great," Allison beamed. "Babbled on the whole time and then combed his hair like a perfect gentleman, brushed his teeth, and climbed right into bed."

Elena smiled, and Allison just stared at her until Elena cleared her throat. The sound seemed to break Allison's trance, and she blinked and glanced quickly away, her fair skin flushing.

"Oh shit," Allison blurted out. "I'm sorry. I didn't even ask if you wanted to hang or whatever. I can totally go now. I'm sure you're tired or something. Sorry."

Elena considered her options. She wasn't necessarily tired. She never went to bed this early, though after that date, she was more than ready to bury her head in her pillow and sleep until the new day, when she could put it all behind her. Yes, that seemed like the perfect plan;

or perhaps a nice bubble bath and then bed. Oh yes, that sounded even better.

However, when she opened her mouth to tell Allison that she would show her to the door, she found herself saying something entirely different. "No, it's quite all right, Allison. I would not mind actual *bearable* company, considering my date was anything but."

She barely masked her surprise upon hearing the words spill from her own lips. However, they were already out of her mouth, and Allison's bright smile was enough to keep her from taking them back. She could spend a bit of time with the babysitter. Why not?

"That blows." Allison got comfortable on the couch beside Elena, putting her popcorn down on the table and tucking her sock-clad feet up under her so that she could turn on the couch to face her new boss. "Was it the lotion? He was a total creeper, right?"

Elena laughed out loud as she ran a hand through her short, dark locks and took a sip of her coffee. A satisfied hum vibrated between her lips at the bitter, familiar taste on her tongue and the heat of the liquid as it slipped down her throat. Exactly what she needed.

"He was a dissatisfactory date, to be sure," she said, "though he managed to avoid any mentions of lotion, thankfully."

"Only because you didn't go home with the guy."

"Of course I didn't go home with him, Allison." Elena turned an expression of disbelief onto her. "I only just met the man. What sort of woman do you think I am?"

"The kind that guys *really* like." Allison waggled her eyebrows. "No, you're right. You're a classy bitch, and classy bitches don't do that."

"Oh?" Elena asked, amused by the label. "And what, may I ask, *do* classy bitches do?"

"Well, wouldn't you know? I mean, you *are* a classy bitch after all."

Elena snorted into her coffee, which only made Allison laugh harder, saying, "Classy bitches always drink their alcohol out of fancy glasses."

Agreeing, Elena gave an appreciative nod and hummed her approval.

"And classy bitches wear high heels, no matter the occasion."

Tilting her head, Elena tried to think of a way to refute that one, but there was no point. It was true that she wore high heels basically everywhere she went except when she went for the occasional run. "Agreed."

"Classy bitches always do that eyebrow arch thing too," Allison said, only for Elena to *immediately* arch a brow at her.

"See?" Allison pointed. Elena scoffed and forced her reaction back down.

"Oh, and classy bitches *never* sleep with a dude on the first date."

"Absolutely." Elena tipped her head in satisfaction.

It had been quite some time since Elena had laughed this easily and naturally with another adult. Vivian was hilarious and she often made Elena laugh, and of course her parents had their moments, but Allison was an entirely different animal. It amazed Elena how easily Allison pulled it out of her, the laughter and the playfulness.

"So, what was wrong with the guy?" Allison asked.

Elena sighed and swiped a hand through her hair again. It fell in gentle waves around her face. "What *wasn't* wrong with him?"

"That bad, huh?"

"Well, for starters," she said, "he was overly confident, and unjustly so."

The curl of Allison's lip made her disgust obvious. "That annoys the hell out of me. My roommate dated a guy last year who always tried to order for her, even at places like McDonald's."

"*Yes*," Elena groaned, turning more toward Allison. "That is exactly what he did, and I positively loathed it. I can select my own meal, thank you very much!"

"Right? Like, eat what you want, dude, but let me order for myself. Oh, and why do guys always order a salad for girls? What *is* that?"

"Yes!" Taking a quick sip of her coffee, Elena cleared her throat and then mimicked Brice's snotty voice as she said, "Oh, and the *lady* will have a side salad."

Allison snorted. "Did you eat it anyway?"

"Oh no," Elena replied, letting a wicked smile grace her lips. "I didn't even let him finish the order. I dismissed his and placed my own."

"Seriously?" Allison clapped her approval. "That's great. I bet he felt like such an idiot."

"Oh, oh!" Elena added, suddenly finding herself rather enjoying this, absorbed entirely in the exchange. "He *then* proceeded to imply during the car ride home that I refused his order because I am unaccustomed to being *pampered*!"

Allison brought her middle finger up to her mouth and mock-gagged herself on it.

"Exactly. I didn't even bother replying."

"I wouldn't have either. The guy sounds like a douche. What was his name?"

"Brice."

"*Brice?*" Allison grimaced. "Even his *name* sounds douche-y."

Elena smiled. "Now you're just trying to make me feel better."

"As long as it's working." Allison winked.

Elena ducked her head a bit as she took another sip of coffee. "It is," she said quietly, like it was an admission. "Thank you."

"Don't worry," Allison said, awkwardly patting Elena's arm as they lingered by the front door. "I'm sure the next date will be better."

"One can only hope." Elena chuckled. She handed Allison several bills that she had pulled from her purse before walking the babysitter to the door, and Allison stared wide-eyed down at the money.

"Whoa, no." She pushed the money back toward Elena. "That's way too much."

Elena reached out to curl Allison's fingers around the cash. "You earned it." She squeezed Allison's hand before releasing it. "Please take it."

Sighing, Allison nodded. "Well, thank you. Really."

"Thank *you*." The warm night air rushed in as she opened the door.

When she was halfway out, Allison turned and shifted from foot to foot as she adjusted her backpack. "So, I'll see you soon, right?"

Elena nodded. "I will call when I need you again."

"Okay then." Feet shuffling, she offered Elena her signature little wave, muttering, "Goodnight."

Elena leaned her head against the door. "Goodnight Allison," she said softly, standing in the doorway until Allison was long out of sight.

Chapter Five

Hazy eyes fluttered slowly open and began to focus. Elena chuckled low in her throat, the sound muffled and raw from sleep, as she came face to face with her son. He lay in her bed, curled up in a ball beside her with his face so close to her that they were nearly touching. His eyes blew wide the moment his gaze locked with hers, and Lucas burst into a wild fit of giggles, clutching his belly. "Hi Momma!"

"Good morning munchkin." She reached out and palmed his cheek.

"Time to get up!" Lucas leaned into his mother's touch. "Time to go to Gram's!"

Confused, Elena glanced at the clock on her bedside table. It was barely after seven, which was late for a work day. She started to jolt out of bed before remembering.

"It's Sunday, baby," she said. "Momma doesn't work on Sunday, remember?"

Lucas's eyes widened. "Just me and you?"

The sight of his smile made her heart swell. She hoped her son would always show such enthusiasm about spending entire days with her. Lucas adored his grandparents and the time he spent with them each weekday, but he was a Momma's boy through and through. Elena was his "most favoritest person" in the world and that was why the weekends, Sundays in particular, were his favorite days.

"Just you and me," Elena whispered, tapping her index finger on the tip of Lucas's nose.

He clapped his hands happily. "Where we going, Momma?"

Elena rolled onto her back and stretched her limbs, groaning as she did so, then laughing when Lucas began to imitate her. He scooted down on the mattress and threw his arms over his head, then groaned and grunted as he twisted about, opening his mouth wide in a fake yawn and scrunching his eyes closed.

His mocking sounds quickly turned into shrieks, though, when Elena suddenly turned and pounced on him, her fingers finding home just under his arms. She tickled his sides while he squealed and tried to wriggle away from her. She let up after only a moment so as to avoid any accidents on her bed and planted a loud, smacking kiss on his forehead before slipping out of bed and pulling her robe on over her night gown.

"Where would *you* like to go today?" She motioned for him to vacate the bed so she could make it up and he crawled across the top of the bed, latching onto Elena's hands, so that she could help him slide down. "I wanna see the dinosaur bones!"

"Of course you do," Elena said.

"Can we?"

"Of course we can." She reached down to stroke the back of his head before moving around to the other side of the bed to adjust the sheets and blankets. "We will go after breakfast, okay?"

"Okay!" Pumping his fist into the air, he took off in a wobbly sprint down the hallway and toward the kitchen.

Elena ran a hand through her hair as she followed her son through the house.

The sudden, surprising blare of her phone nearly caused Elena to bump her head against the door frame as she strapped Lucas into his car seat. Once she got everything buckled, she pulled her phone from her purse and rolled her eyes as she saw Vivian's face light up the screen.

"Hello darling!" Vivian's voice echoed through the line as soon as Elena accepted the call. "How was your incredibly sexy date last night?"

"Incredibly disappointing," Elena said. "In fact, he was *so* disappointing that I have determined to despise you for a minimum of one week."

"Wow, a whole week?" Vivian gasped. "What did he do? Proposition you for sex before dinner?"

Elena slipped into the driver's seat and buckled her belt. "Make it two weeks," she huffed.

"Okay, okay. I'm sorry. I thought he was sexy." Vivian chuckled. "What went wrong?"

"He was decently attractive," Elena admitted. "Until he opened his mouth."

"Are you sure you weren't looking for reasons not to like him?"

"Please. Give me a bit of credit, Viv. The man attempted to order for me and then suggested that my disinterest in him doing so was due to the vast lack of pampering in my life."

Vivian snorted into the phone. "Wow. That is just sad."

"Where did you even find him?" Elena asked.

"Where else?" Vivian asked. "Work. He is a friend of my assistant. She suggested him."

"Fire her," Elena joked.

"Momma! We're not moving!"

Elena glanced in the rearview mirror to see her son squirming in his seat. "I know, munchkin," she said. "Just one more minute."

"Vivian." She turned her attention back to her phone conversation. "I will have to call you back. I've just gotten Lucas in the car, and we are headed to the museum."

"Which one?" Vivian asked. "I have no plans for today. I could meet you there."

"The American Museum of Natural History." Elena started the car.

"I take it Lucas wants to see the dinosaurs again?"

"Of course," Elena said. "Call me when you arrive, and Lucas and I will meet you."

Elena glanced in her rearview mirror to find Lucas looking right back at her. His eyes were narrowed, and Elena couldn't help but let out a loud bark of laughter.

"Okay, okay, we're going," she told him, and his expression morphed into a smile.

Allison spread the small blanket out atop the grass, plopped down on top of it and pulled out her current reading material from her backpack—*Invisible Monsters* by Chuck Palahniuk. She had always enjoyed his minimalistic writing style, and Allison had nothing but love for any author who didn't shy away from the ugly details and horrors of life.

Sticking her backpack under her head to use it as a pillow, she lay back and sucked in a deep breath, letting the smell of the Central Park breeze tickle in her nose. It was nice to get out of the dorms from time to time.

It was a gorgeous Sunday morning, and Allison wiggled around until she was comfortable, thinking about the night before. Elena Vega was like a puzzle—complex and intriguing. She was far from the typical rich girl who cherished money and material things above all else, and Allison wondered what more she might learn of the woman as she began to put all of the pieces together—*if* she was able to spend more time with her.

Tucking her bookmark into the back cover of her book, Allison began to read. She only managed a few pages, however, before she was suddenly and unexpectedly tackled. She yelped as a small body barreled into her, and Allison struggled for a moment to get away before recognizing her tiny attacker.

"Lucas?" she managed to choke out despite the boy having knocked the wind out of her. He giggled and nodded as a shadow cast over them both. Allison raised a hand to shield her eyes as she looked up to see the glowing form of Elena Vega.

Allison felt a gentle stirring in her stomach as she looked up at Elena and watched a bright smile spread across the woman's face.

"I'm terribly sorry, Ms—Allison," Elena said. "He saw you and took off before I could stop him."

Allison pushed herself into a sitting position with Lucas in her lap and patted his back. "No, it's totally cool."

"Hey little man. I missed you," she said, tickling Lucas's belly. She then looked up at Elena and softly added, "Hi."

"Good morning, dear. Quite the coincidence running into you today."

"Wanna see dinosaurs?" Lucas squeaked as if he had just had the most brilliant idea of his young life.

"Uh...." Allison didn't have a clue what Lucas was talking about.

"I am taking him to the museum," Elena said. "He loves the fossil exhibits."

"Oh right. Gotcha. I like that place too."

"Come see!" Lucas pleaded as he bounced on her thigh and squeezed her hand.

"Oh, Lucas," Elena said. "I'm sure Allison is rather busy with her own Sunday plans."

"Nah, I'm good actually." Allison bounced her knee with Lucas atop it. "I'd love to see the dinosaurs with you guys. I mean, unless you don't want me to come, which is totally cool. I wouldn't take offense or anything. I can understand wanting to spend time with your kid, just the two of you."

Lucas had apparently chosen to hear only the beginning of her answer, because he yelled his excitement, jumped to his feet, and tugged on Allison's arm before she ever finished speaking.

"No, it's fine," Elena said. "Vivian is meeting us there anyway."

"Oh, well okay." The blanket and book were quickly shoved back into Allison's backpack. "Let's go then."

"Are you sure you don't mind, Allison?" Elena placed a hand on Allison's arm to hold her back. "I noticed you were reading. I would hate to interrupt your day simply because my son is overeager. You are more than welcome to decline his demanding invitation."

Nudging Elena's shoulder, she shook her head. "It's fine, really. I'd take you guys over books any day, and hey, that is seriously saying something. I love books."

A faint hint of pink painted Elena's cheeks as she nodded. "Very well."

Lucas hopped up and down beside them. "You have to hold hands!" he shouted.

Without really thinking about it, Allison slipped her hand into Elena's, only to see Lucas's face immediately scrunch in confusion. Elena cleared her throat, the pink tint of her cheeks now a deep crimson. She laughed as Lucas loudly explained, "No, Alson, you have to hold hands WITH ME!"

"Oh, uh, right." Allison released Elena's hand and swiped her own through her hair. "Um, yeah, because that makes *so* much more sense. Duh, Allison."

Lucas squished himself between the two women. One of his tiny hands slipped into one of Elena's and the other into one of Allison's, and they walked together like that all the way to the museum.

Elena met Vivian at the main entrance of the museum while Allison and Lucas remained with the fossil exhibits.

"Where's Lucas?"

"Well, hello to you, too." Elena pecked her on the cheek. "He's with Allison." They linked arms and made their way inside.

Blonde brows knitted together. "Who the hell is Allison?"

"That would be the young woman that *you* found to be my babysitter for Lucas."

"Oh!" Vivian clucked her tongue and nodded. "Right. I remember now. Wait, you're paying your babysitter to go to the museum with you? Babe, that's just sad."

A manicured hand swatted her arm. "No, of course not. She was reading in the park, and Lucas saw her and invited her along. I think he may idolize her a bit. He went on and on about her during breakfast and in the car."

"So you like her?"

"What?" Elena asked. "What do you mean?"

"I mean exactly what I asked. Do you like her? As a babysitter? What else would I have meant?"

"Oh!" Elena nodded. "Oh, yes. Yes, she is a wonderful babysitter. You know how shy Lucas can be, but he took right to her."

"See? I *am* good at picking people."

"For babysitting, perhaps. You should apply that skill to your choices in dates. I would rather not end up with another Brice."

"Hey!" Vivian nudged Elena's side with her elbow. "Give me a chance. You have only gone on one date, and the guy had excellent potential. How was I supposed to know he was a jerk?"

"Douche."

Vivian cackled. "Come again?"

"Allison called him a douche." Elena shot her a wry grin.

"College kids."

"You *do* realize that we are only five years older than her, yes?" Elena bumped her side. "You forget that it hasn't been long since you and I were those college kids."

A wistful sigh escaped Vivian's lips. "Yeah, those were the days. Though, even in college, you never would have used the word 'douche'."

Elena squeezed her friend's arm and pointed across the room where a woman with long blonde hair and her back to them stood in front of a massive dinosaur skeleton. Lucas was tucked against her side as she held him and pointed up at the bones.

Scanning over Allison's body, Vivian raised a brow at the ribbed tee, skin-tight jeans, and scuffed black boots. "Christ," she muttered. "*That's* the babysitter I chose?"

"You didn't meet her?" Elena asked, surprised.

"No, I put an ad on Craigslist and she called me. I only spoke to her on the phone but she sounded sweet."

"She is."

"Yeah, and she apparently does Pilates all day long every day," Vivian said, her tone envious. "Look at her legs."

Elena nodded as they both stared at the babysitter. "She is quite in shape. You should see her stomach."

Without another word, Elena took off toward Allison and Lucas, leaving Vivian to stare. "Wait, what?" she said. "When did you see her sto—Elena!"

"Momma, look!" Lucas pointed up at the massive dinosaur skeleton, his eyes wide even though he had seen each and every dinosaur in this museum multiple times.

With Lucas still bouncing on her hip, Allison whirled around and saw Elena standing there with another woman beside her. Elena cooed at Lucas: "I see, baby. Which dinosaur is that?"

"That's Rex," Lucas told her before stuffing his fingers in his mouth and sucking on them while he continued to stare up at the skeleton.

Both Elena and Allison chuckled before Elena motioned toward the other woman. "Allison, this is my friend, Vivian Warren, the one you spoke to about the babysitting position."

Allison's gaze shot to the blonde at Elena's side. "Oh right, yeah." Smiling, she stuck out her free hand to shake Vivian's, while her other arm remained firmly tucked under Lucas's bottom. "Nice to finally meet you in person, Vivian."

Vivian slipped her hand into Allison's and shook it gently. "You as well, Allison. I see you and Lucas have become fast friends."

"Oh yeah." Allison nodded. "We're besties."

Vivian reached out to pat Lucas's arm. "Hey buddy."

His head never turned but his small hand pointed up again as he said, "Aunt Viv, look!"

"I know!" Vivian feigned excitement. She then turned her attention back to Allison. "So, how is college life treating you? You're at NYU, correct?"

"Yeah, it's pretty cool," Allison said. "Got a bed and food and a bunch of people obligated to carry on conversations in class with me, so it's all good."

The three women laughed together before Vivian asked, "What is your major?"

"Social work." Lucas tugged her to the side when he dove toward his mother, who caught him and transferred him from Allison's hip to her own. He pointed to the places he wanted to go, and Elena carried him accordingly, leaving Allison and Vivian to follow.

"Fascinating," Vivian said. "Now, let's get to the good stuff, shall we?"

"Sorry?" Allison asked. "What good stuff?"

"Elena's date."

"Oh that. She wasn't too hard on you, was she?"

"*Should* she have been?" Blue eyes narrowed. "Or was she merely exaggerating?"

"I can *hear* you, dear," Elena sing-songed from a few feet in front of the two of them.

"Congratulations, babe. Your ears are functioning."

It was obvious the two women had been friends for a long time.

Allison shoved her hands into the rigid pockets of her tight jeans. "Uh, she only talked about it a little bit before I left, but yeah, the guy sounded like bad news."

"*Thank you*, Allison."

Vivian rolled her eyes at Elena's words and ignored the glare shot her way when she said, "You know, Allison, if she's not paying you to be here today, then you don't have to have her back. You can tell me the truth."

"No, it really did sound like a bad date," Allison said. "You can do way better."

"You hear that, Elena? She doesn't even know me, and yet she already has faith in my skills."

"Perhaps that is *because* she doesn't yet know you, Vivian."

"Ah, my best friend." Vivian winked at Allison. "Her sweetness *abounds*."

"Alson!"

Allison was still laughing as she stepped up to Elena's side. "What's up bud?" she asked Lucas as she elbowed Elena's side with a conspiratorial nudge.

"Look!"

"Whoa!" Allison gasped, making a good show of looking up at the skeleton. "Which one is that?"

"Aptosaurs."

Elena leaned closer to Allison and whispered, "*Apatosaurus*."

"Ah, okay. He's a big one, isn't he, Lucas?"

Lucas nodded as he continued to suck on his fingers and stare up at the skeleton.

"All right," Elena said, patting Lucas's thigh. "Let's move on. We have a lot of bones to see, and I imagine someone will be hungry soon." She headed toward the next exhibit, Lucas's hand already pointing up, while Allison and Vivian trailed along behind her.

Vivian tapped her nails against the kitchen counter as she waited for her coffee to brew. Her phone was pressed between her ear and her shoulder, and it was taking Elena nearly as long to answer as it was taking Vivian's coffee pot to fill.

"Hello Vivian." Elena's voice greeted her after the fourth ring. "I was just finishing up dinner."

"So am I," Vivian said. "I'm having coffee."

Elena snorted. "I know you've already eaten. You rarely make it to five o'clock without whining about your growling stomach."

"True. I had sushi. So, today was fun."

"It was."

"Allison seems great." Vivian was curious as to how Elena would respond. She had noticed how at ease Elena had seemed to be with Allison at the museum, and it had surprised her. Elena had always been rather closed off with strangers, especially where Lucas was concerned. She had perfect manners and could acclimate quickly to different social situations, but she preferred her own circle of people. That much had always been clear to Vivian.

"She is," Elena said.

"You seemed really comfortable with her."

"I suppose so, yes," Elena said. "Why do you mention it?"

"No reason." Vivian did her best to sound casual. "You just don't usually warm up to people that fast, and Allison is obviously your complete opposite. I was just surprised."

There was a long pause before Elena spoke again. "She seems to have that effect."

Vivian nearly snorted. Allison certainly seemed to have *some* sort of effect, because she and Elena had made their way through that museum like old friends, or perhaps even something more. She had noticed the way Allison almost unconsciously always stepped to the side to allow Elena to pass through each doorway first, and she even placed her hand on Elena's lower back a few times when they squeezed through a particularly crowded area. Vivian had gaped the first time it happened and Elena didn't move away from the touch.

"She does," Vivian said. She reached for her coffee pot as the machine finally wheezed out its last few drops and she poured herself a large amount into a waiting mug. "I'm glad she is working out for you."

"Me too. Thank you again for finding her even though I suppose she technically found *you* through Craigslist."

"Well, it was *my* ad, so I'm taking credit." Vivian let out a soft laugh. "All right. I won't keep you on the phone. I just wanted to kill time while my coffee brewed."

"Glad to be of service," Elena said, and Vivian made loud kiss noises against the speaker of her phone.

"Bye, babe."

The call ended with Vivian sipping at her coffee and contemplating the other two women. There was obviously some chemistry there, though it was equally obvious that both Elena and Allison were entirely oblivious to it. Knowing Elena, it could take ages for the woman to realize it herself. Vivian decided that she would have to intervene to help the process along. She nearly clapped her hands with excitement, but instead held tightly to her coffee cup and took another hot sip.

"Where to begin," Vivian muttered under breath, a smile quirking at the corners of her mouth.

Chapter Six

Elena sat at the head of the table in the design room and tapped her nails rhythmically against the hard surface. Wendy had been rambling on for nearly ten full minutes about flower arrangements and centerpieces for the gala to follow the spring show, and such things had always been Elena's least favorite aspects of planning meetings. It was, however, her job to give final say on nearly all projects; thus, she had to endure.

She sighed, laying her hand down flat against the table and drawing the room's attention away from Wendy, who had let her terrible tendency of going off on tangents take over, and back to her. "Let's not turn this into an ordeal, Wendy," she said. "I said simple and elegant, and neither should be difficult to accomplish. I want the hanging pieces for the outer edges of the banquet hall—nothing bushy or heavily scented."

Wendy rapidly scribbled down notes as Elena spoke. She nodded along and muttered, "Oh, of course," and "Absolutely," after every other word.

"Centerpieces equal size to the dinner plates and lower than eye level," Elena continued. "Tell Gregory I want clear vases, not gold, no matter *how* popular they are right now, and I want a splash of color in the arrangements—a *splash* not a spate."

"Only a splash?"

Elena closed her eyes for a moment and took a deep breath through her nose before turning to Elliot and arching a brow at the man. "Yes, a splash, Elliot," she said. "I presume you have an objection?" He always did.

The man had been a pain in Elena's ass since her first day on the job, and Elena didn't have to guess why. He ranted about it enough in break rooms and between cubicles that everyone knew—he believed he deserved her job more than she did. Elena had overheard all his complaints before—family privilege, wealth, sex appeal. He had even gone as far as to suggest sexism, as if women had professional advantage over men. It was ridiculous, and for him to claim any sort of privilege won Elena the position, given that he was a white male and she was a Latina woman, made her laugh. She had earned her job.

"Well," Elliot said, adjusting his square gold-rimmed glasses on his nose, "bright colors are appropriate for spring, wouldn't you say? Given the line-up for the show, I would say even *more*-so." He glanced around the table pointedly and then smirked as he turned back to Elena. "I'm sure I speak for everyone when I say I'm concerned that just a 'splash' of color might not be enough to match the season."

She had to fight the urge to roll her eyes. She knew Elliot didn't care about the damned floral arrangements. He simply liked to voice dissent any time Elena made a decision. He seemed to gain an immeasurable amount of glee from challenging her, and Elena found it not only annoying but also pathetic.

Rather than throw her phone at his head like she wanted, Elena simply stared him down in a tense silence. When he began to visibly squirm, she let out a long sigh and said, "We are about fashion, Elliot, not flowers."

"Yes, but—"

"The arrangements should complement the season, not match it," she said. "Or are you suggesting that we fill a room of designers in designer clothing with centerpieces that draw attention *away* from them?"

"Well..."

Elena turned to the rest of the table and cleared her throat. "Would Elliot be correct in speaking for you all then?" she asked. "Do you share his *concern*?"

Every other employee at the table quickly jumped to reassure that they didn't have any issues with a splash of color. Peter, who was probably her sweetest employee but also her most timid, even looked like he was on the verge of crying. The more people made to reassure her, the more uncomfortable Elliot became, and Elena reveled in him getting a taste of his own medicine.

She turned back to him and smirked. "Reassured, dear?" she asked, her amusement evident in her voice.

With pursed lips, Elliot avoided her eyes, and Elena smiled. "Excellent," she said. "Now, if there are no other *concerns*, let's move on to the next order of business."

Her phone vibrated as Nia stood at the other end of the table and began addressing an issue with construction in one of their upcoming shoot locations. Elena glanced at the screen to see a text from Vivian. She slid her finger over the screen to unlock it and quickly read the message.

Date tonight! Call your babysitter!

Elena sighed but made a mental note to call Allison before turning her attention back to Nia.

Allison sprinted out of her dorm building, her hair disheveled and her clothes wrinkled. She spit a wad of toothpaste onto the grass as she took off across campus. She was already fifteen minutes late for her Narratology exam.

She cursed when her phone rang. Tugging the shrill device from her pocket as she ran, she glanced down and saw *Elena Vega* flashing across the screen and smiled unconsciously as she tapped to answer it. But as soon as she put the phone to her ear, Allison looked back up to see that she was headed straight for a pole.

"Shit!" She dodged the pole at the last second but still managed to trip over her own feet.

A faint reply of "*Pardon me?*" echoed from Allison's phone, but she was too busy yelping as she tumbled forward with a string of curses: "Fuck shit damn ow!"

Her textbook shot from her hands as she landed roughly on her side, and Allison groaned as she rubbed at her elbows and rolled onto her stomach so that she could push herself up to her feet again. Just as she started to move though, she heard the muffled sound of a voice saying, *"Hello? Allison?"*

"Shit!" Allison grumbled again. She scrambled to get her phone and quickly put it up to her ear. "Uh, Elena?"

"Allison?" There was utter confusion in the other woman's voice.

"Yup, sorry 'bout that." With a grunt, she used her hands to push herself up onto her knees and then into a squat so that she could stand up again and collected her things.

"Are you all right, dear? It sounded like you were having quite the struggle."

Allison blushed. "Oh, yeah, well I may have, possibly, sort of, fallen down or whatever."

"You *may have* fallen down, Allison, or you did fall down?"

A smile stretched Allison's lips even as her cheeks maintained their reddish tint. "Shut up," she grumbled and was rewarded with a burst of laughter over the phone line. "Yeah, I fell. I was running and wasn't paying attention. So, yeah, laugh it up, I guess."

It took a while for Elena's laughter to die down. "I apologize." she said. "Are you sure you're all right?"

"I'm good, yeah. Thanks. Just late for an exam."

"Oh. I will let you go then. Perhaps you could give me a call once your classes are finished for the day?"

"It's cool." Allison sighed and glanced at the time on her phone as she plopped down on a campus bench. She was already far too late to make it for the exam. She shook her head, disappointed in herself. "I'm never gonna make it now anyway."

"Are you sure?"

"Yeah, I'm sure." Allison leaned her head back and soaked in the morning sun. Her eyes stung with tears that she blinked quickly away.

"I'm sorry," Elena said.

"Don't be." Allison swallowed down the lump in her throat. "I stayed up really late with my roommate last night, and I slept through my alarm. It's my fault. I just hate screwing up like this. It makes me feel like an idiot, you know?"

Elena was silent a long time before saying, "Could you talk to your professor about it? Perhaps you could make it up?"

Allison bounced her knee rapidly as she pressed a hand to her eyes. "Yeah, maybe," she said. She was fairly friendly with her professor, so maybe Elena's suggestion could work. She could email him and say that she was sick or something. Her stomach rolled at the thought, as if it was trying to make the lie true. He might let her make up the exam since she otherwise had near-perfect attendance and a perfect grade in that class. It was worth a shot, but that didn't stop Allison's chest from aching with guilt.

"I hope it works out for you." Her voice was sincere and even tinged with a bit of sadness and that, for some reason, made Allison feel the slightest bit better.

"Thanks." Allison ran a hand through her ratty hair and hissed as her fingers snagged in several tangles. This was really *not* her morning. "So, what's up?"

"Right, yes." Elena cleared her throat. "I was calling to inquire if you might be free this evening. I apologize for the last-minute call, Allison. Vivian only just sprung this on me. I was hoping an early call might make the difference."

Allison propped her phone up against her ear with her shoulder. "It's fine. You don't have to keep apologizing, Elena. I'm pretty much free all the time, so, yeah, I can come over tonight."

Elena sighed. "Excellent. I greatly appreciate it."

"No problem. What time should I be there?"

"Would six be acceptable?"

"Yup, six is good. I'll see ya then."

"Okay, wonderful. See you then."

With a groan, Allison hung up the call and forced herself off the bench to head back to her dorm room. At least her day had just gotten a lot better.

Elena was just slipping into her dress when Lucas shuffled into her bedroom. Cheeks red, he stared at the floor as he quietly said, "Momma."

Her lips tugged with a frown when she saw his head ducked down and his body slowly swaying from side to side. He always stood like that when he was guilty of something.

"Lucas," Elena said. "What is it?"

He didn't say a word as he moved his hands out of the way and Elena was able to see the large wet spot on the front of his pants. She frowned as she walked over to her son and kneeled in front of him. "Did you have an accident, munchkin?"

His wide expressive eyes shot up as he quickly shook his head back and forth in adamant denial.

"Lucas." Elena ran a hand through his hair and then tapped her index finger gently against his nose. "It's okay if you had an accident. You can tell me."

"I didn't!" His voice turned into a high-pitched squeal. "Swear!"

"Well then why are your pants wet?"

Ducking his head down again, he whispered, "I spilled my juice."

Elena slipped her index finger under his chin and pulled his head up so that she could look him in the eyes. "That's okay, baby."

"Really?" he asked, shuffling a little closer to her.

She pursed her lips as she pretended to think about it. "I will tell you what. If you give me a super special kiss and hug, then it is definitely okay."

A massive grin stretched Lucas's lips and he giggled as he threw his arms around Elena's neck and pressed a big, smacking kiss half on her cheek and half on her nose. Elena squeezed him and planted a dozen little kisses all over his face, causing him to squeal and squirm, but he never actually tried to escape.

"Okay, munchkin, let's get you some new pants before Allison gets here."

"Alson!" Lucas sprinted down the hallway toward his room. Elena made to follow him, but she only managed a few steps down the hall when the doorbell sounded.

"I will be right there, Lucas."

She passed Lucas's room and made her way toward the front of the house instead.

Allison was standing at the door, gaping at Elena with a dark blonde eyebrow rising in question. "Um..."

"What?" Elena frowned. "Is something wrong?"

"Running late? Or are you just happy to see me?"

Elena just stared at her, blinking. "What are you talking about?"

Blushing, Allison pointed at Elena and muttered, "Your dress is uh...it's open."

Glancing down, Elena was greeted by the sight of her dress hanging loosely on one side, making her bra clearly visible. Her own face flushed as she cleared her throat. "Right, yes...well. Children can be distracting, I suppose."

Allison slipped by Elena and into the house, kicking the door closed behind her. "Well, let's not just stand here and show off your bod to the whole neighborhood, yeah?"

The red of Elena's cheeks only darkened as Allison quickly reached out and latched onto her shoulders. With a quick spin, Elena's back was facing her. "I can get it for you." Settling the dress back into proper position, she slipped her hand to the base of Elena's spine where the zipper began.

Allison didn't even realize the way she held her breath as she slowly zipped up the dress, but she *did* feel the tug low in her abdomen when her fingertips brushed over warm flesh. She shrugged the sensation off as her body's basic reaction to a beautiful woman. It wasn't the first time and it wouldn't be the last, so she quickly finished zipping the dress before awkwardly patting Elena on the back and clearing her throat as she squeaked, "All done."

Elena turned to smile at Allison. "Thank you."

An awkward silence grew between them as they stared at each other. Green eyes traced the length of the Elena's body, and both women jumped when a loud yell of "MOMMA! PANTS!" echoed into the foyer from down the hall. Allison raised a brow in question.

"He had a spill," Elena said and then motioned for Allison to follow her down the hall.

Once they got Lucas fixed up and settled him down with his toys, it wasn't long before the doorbell rang again. Once again, Allison found herself following Elena to the front door while Lucas played with his dinosaurs in the living room.

When Elena opened the door, the man on the other side offered a wide smile. He was short, Allison noted with amusement—like *really* short, much shorter than Elena. He wore an obviously expensive suit and shoes that Allison figured some poor reptile had to have died for, but it did little to distract from the man's appearance. It wasn't that he wasn't decent-looking, because in all fairness, the guy was pretty attractive if you could look past his height and the strange situation at the top of his head. It was just...well, who *could* look past the situation at the top of his head?

His hair sat oddly, almost unnaturally, on top of his head. The color didn't quite match his eyebrows or short sideburns, and the front of his hair swooped dramatically to the left side. Allison could not stop staring at it. She tried to look away, but it was useless. She didn't know how Elena was going to get through an entire evening with the guy without gawking at him.

Completely ignoring Allison's intense stare, the man held out a bundle of red roses and introduced himself in a rush of minty breath. "Elena, hi. I'm Garrett. Wow! You are even more beautiful than Vivian said. These are for you."

Allison grunted and Garrett finally looked at her. He frowned momentarily before plastering on a smile as he glanced at her clothes and asked, "Oh, are you the help?"

"Ha!" Allison barked. "Dude. Wow." She shook her head as she turned and walked back into the house.

"Allison is my son's babysitter." The words were spoken in a clipped tone as Elena thrust her hand out and took Garrett's flowers and asked him to wait outside while she slipped them in water and grabbed her clutch.

Allison followed Elena into the kitchen. "Oh, Miss Vega, would you like me to take those flowers for you? I can clip and arrange them in a lovely vase for you, Miss Vega."

They shared a disgusted look, Allison rolling her eyes and Elena curling her lip. "We haven't even left the house yet and already I have a headache," she said.

"Wanna fake sick?" Allison offered. "I can go run the guy off for you."

Elena chuckled as she pulled a vase from a cabinet. "Oh, the temptation."

As she filled the vase with water, Allison pointed at the waiting roses and asked, "Overkill, don't you think?"

"Oh? Here I was thinking the roses were the saving grace of that greeting. Flowers *are* a lovely gesture, after all."

"*Roses*?" Allison scoffed. "No, that's a lame, clichéd gesture that men put way too much stock in. You don't get a woman like *you* roses. Seriously."

"No?"

"No way. You're way too, I don't know…just a lot better than roses. Roses are generic. Orchids maybe, because they're unique and way prettier than roses. Wildflowers even, but definitely not roses."

When Elena's brows rose in surprise, Allison immediately went over her own words in her head. Should she not have said that? Was it too unprofessional? Allison wasn't even sure if she and Elena were friends, or if Elena was simply *friendly* with her because Allison babysat her kid. The small, almost shy smile that Elena gave her a moment later, though, made Allison's stomach flip pleasantly and she couldn't bring herself to regret the words at all.

Elena slipped the roses into a vase and carried the arrangement to the living room. The roses got a new home on an end table, and Lucas got a brand new imprint of his mother's lips on his cheek. Allison laughed when the boy grumbled and wiped at the mark, only for Elena to press a fresh one in the smudged spot.

After a quick wave in Allison's direction, Elena was heading out the door. Allison watched her leave, shaking her head for a good minute before going to play with Lucas. She had a feeling this date, too, would end with a lot of complaining.

As Elena expected, Garrett whisked her away to yet another fine-dining experience. She sat across from Garrett and desperately tried to keep her gaze away from his hair. It was quite distracting, though, considering the fact that every time the man laughed a little too heartily or shook his head, it would move rather unnaturally; and this was a man who liked to laugh at his own jokes whether they were funny or not.

This was how Elena realized that Garrett was wearing a rather unflattering toupee. It honestly made her feel a bit sorry for the man, because he wasn't that old, likely only a decade older than her at most, yet obviously was already bald or balding beneath his mop of a toupee. Elena would have wagered the man looked much better without the thing. The toupee wasn't the only issue Elena took with the man, however.

When the waitress arrived to take their order, Garrett thankfully made no attempts to order for Elena. However, he turned to the waitress and asked, "How is the Cajun shrimp and sirloin? Is it heavily spiced, because I'm afraid I suffer from a bad case of irritable bowel syndrome and overly spicy foods tear right through me?"

Elena nearly choked on a gasp that she covered with a soft cough. She was completely appalled. She could certainly sympathize with the man's struggles, but to speak so bluntly of such things at the dinner table was practically a form of table-manners blasphemy as far as Elena was concerned.

"I do like a bit of heat, mind you," Garrett continued, "just not in the restroom!"

He laughed loudly at his own joke as he glanced back and forth between the waitress and Elena, both of whom were completely mortified. The waitress stuttered out a quick reply, while Elena merely ducked her head and fought to choke down the bile that had risen in her throat from the unfortunate imagery Garrett's confession had produced in her mind.

I will kill *Vivian,* she vowed. *I will kill her!*

Music blasted from the television in the living room as Allison danced around kitchen, cooking dinner. Thrilled to discover that Elena had satellite music channels, she put on the eighties pop channel and danced and sang for Lucas while he sat in his chair. He clapped his hands, sang along with his own made-up lyrics, and bounced and swayed around.

Allison loved eighties pop music. She had fallen in love with it when she was really young, living with a foster mom that had an obsession with Prince. It was one of her favorite memories, riding in the car with one of the few foster mothers she had actually really loved, and just dancing to Prince and Michael Jackson. The eighties had quickly become her favorite musical decade; it was so *free*. To Allison, eighties music practically screamed fun.

Pouring the pasta sauce she had made onto a small plate of spaghetti noodles, she whirled around to face Lucas and brought the long wooden spoon up to her mouth, pretending the spoon was a microphone as she danced around him and sang "Raspberry Beret".

Giggling, Lucas sang along with murmured random words and sounds as he danced in his chair and clapped his hands on the offbeats. Allison laughed with him as she cut his spaghetti into tiny bites. When she set the plate in front of him, she leaned forward and kissed his forehead.

"You're such a cool kid," she told him. "You know that?"

Lucas grinned as he scooped up his spaghetti with a spoon. "Mhm." Within seconds his face was decorated with bright red sauce.

"So, Elena, tell me a bit about yourself," Garrett said around a mouthful of shrimp. Elena cringed when he grabbed another large shrimp with his fingers and popped it into his mouth before he was even finished chewing. He pulled the tail from his mouth with a loud slurping sound and dropped it onto the side of his plate as he stared at her and waited for her to speak.

Elena, whose appetite had waned the instant the man mentioned his unfortunate bowel issues, had ordered only a small bowl of soup. She sipped daintily at it while attempting to avoid looking at Garrett.

She could feel his eyes on her now, though, and she knew she couldn't ignore him.

Her smile strained around clenched teeth. "What would you like to know?"

"Well, for starters," Garrett said with a smirk, "you can tell me how a beautiful woman like yourself hasn't gotten a good man yet."

Elena offered him another tight, strained smile when he chuckled loudly. Clearing her throat roughly, she told him, "Relationships have hardly been high on my list of priorities."

"That's a shame. But lucky me that you've decided to make it a priority now, right? You deserve a good man, Elena. You're worth it."

"I would never measure my own or any woman's worth by her relationship status," she responded coolly as she subtly signaled to the passing waitress that she was ready for the check. "I would certainly never measure a woman's worth by her ability to garner a man's attention or affections either. I am worth *much* more than that, Garrett, as are all women."

A choking sound gurgled in Garrett's throat as he tried to speak before he swallowed. He coughed and spluttered, and Elena merely stared at him uncomfortably while he cleared his throat several times. "Of course, of course," he choked out. "I didn't mean to imply that you weren't."

Elena did nothing more than hum in response. The waitress thankfully arrived with the check, but Garrett snatched it away before she could grab it. "I can take care of this."

"As can I," Elena said, arching a brow. She was irritated, and every word from the man's mouth grated on her nerves. She relented, though, and let the man cover the check simply because she was eager to get home. The sooner this date was over, the better.

Chapter Seven

"But I'm not tired." Lucas huffed as he squirmed around in his bed and used his charming caramel eyes to his advantage.

"All right, that's enough with the eyes, Puss in Boots." Allison tickled his belly. "I'm not fallin' for it. It's already ten minutes past your bedtime, so come on. Settle down. It's time for not-sleepy boys to get sleepy."

Sheets twisted around Lucas's body as he rolled and kicked. "But *you* don't have to go to sleep!"

"Yeah, well, that's because I'm a grown-up. When you're a grown-up, you can go to bed whenever you want."

"Why can't I stay up with you?" His bottom lip poked out far enough for Allison to see his bottom teeth. "I'll be really quiet. Swear."

Sighing, she pushed his lip back in with her index finger. "I'll tell you what," she said, climbing onto his small bed and settling in beside him. He instantly curled into her side, laying his head on her chest when she moved to put her arm around him. "How about I just hang out in here with you for a bit, just until you get sleepy, okay?"

Already the kid had been rubbing at his eyes and yawning more than once in the last hour.

He nodded against her chest. "Okay," he mumbled, already falling asleep. She dug a hand down into the pocket of her jeans and pulled her cell phone out. Holding it up above them, she whispered, "Want to take some pictures?"

She felt him nod against her chest again.

"Okay, buddy, look up at the camera."

He rubbed his eyes and turned his head. Allison reached down and tickled his side to get him to smile. As soon as he burst into laughter, she snapped the picture, hoping that the light streaming in from the hallway would be enough to make their faces visible.

She chuckled. "Okay, one more. Big smile."

Pushing up off of her chest a little bit, Lucas smiled one of the biggest, cheesiest smiles that Allison had ever seen. She snapped the picture and laughed when Lucas instantly snuggled back into her side. "Gettin' sleepy now?" she whispered.

"Mhm." His breathing deepened and his little hand twitched as it clung to Allison's shirt.

The snap of the shutter sounded through the room as Allison took a final picture. When she turned her phone around to look at it, her heart melted at the image. Lucas's puffy cheek was squished against her chest, his hair a little unruly on top of his head, and his fingers were curled tightly in her shirt right at the neckline. Even with her giant, dorky smile, Allison thought it was a great picture.

She set the picture as the background wallpaper on her phone and then turned to press a kiss to the top of Lucas's head before slipping out from under him as carefully and quietly as possible. When she pulled his hand from her shirt, Lucas let out a tiny groan but then simply smacked his lips and rolled over. She tucked him in once more before slipping out of the room.

Elena contemplated pulling a pen or two from her purse, jamming them into her ears, and bursting her own eardrums just so that she wouldn't have to listen to her date continuously talking throughout the entire drive back to her house. The man had no filter, and he was also apparently oblivious to the innumerable amount of hints she had provided to indicate that she would prefer silence. One could only huff, scoff, disagree, or simply remain quiet so many times to get a point across.

"There she was, right there in my office, being bent over the desk by my secretary. I mean, can you believe the nerve? Well, you can just imagine how quickly I sent her packing, right?"

She merely rolled her eyes as she rubbed at her temples and stared out the window.

"So, that's how I ended up back on the dating scene. I told myself, I said, 'Garrett, don't you spend a minute dwelling on her,' and I didn't. I jumped right back into dating, because I knew, you know? I knew that things could only get better for me once I was out of that toxic relationship. I knew there was a good woman out there who would appreciate all that I bring to the table. And then look, here you are."

He laughed again, and she let out a heavy sigh as she tilted her head forward and pressed her forehead to the window. When was this going to end?

"And I know we had that little upset at dinner. But, of course, that was a mere misunderstanding. When we met, though, Elena, when I saw you at your door, I felt something, you know? I think there was a connection, a little spark."

Rolling her eyes yet again, she softly banged her forehead against the window.

I wish *there was a spark. I* wish *there were flames. I* wish *I could set myself on fire.*

She nearly cheered when she saw Garrett turning onto her road. As soon as he pulled into the driveway, Elena reached for the door handle and was out of the car in seconds, not giving the man the opportunity to open her door for her.

Any hopes that he would just leave were dashed when Garrett met her as she came around the car to the small walkway that led to the front door. She shuddered as he placed his hand on the small of her back and led her toward the door.

"I think this could be a good thing, Elena." She had to look away because the slight breeze outside was catching just under his toupee, pulling it up on one side. He smiled at her as he carried on. "So, that spark. Didn't you feel it?"

"No," she sighed as she slipped her key into the lock.

"I'm sorry?" Garrett responded. "I didn't quite catch that."

She exhaled a heavy breath, realizing that she was going to have to give up the subtleties, and whirled back around to face him. "No,

Garrett," she said. "I said no, I did not, have not, nor *will I* feel a connection."

She turned back and opened the door, thinking that would be the end of it, but then he spoke up again. "Well sometimes it takes more than one date to really feel and build that connection," he told her. "Perhaps you and I could—"

"*No*."

Allison stood staring at the microwave, listening to her popcorn cooking, when she heard Elena's voice echo softly into the kitchen. Frowning, she checked the clock on the wall. It had only been about twenty minutes since she put Lucas down to sleep, so that meant that Elena had most likely had another dud date. She started to make her way toward the foyer, toward Elena's voice.

"Well sometimes it takes more than one date to really feel and build that connection," she heard Elena's date say. "Perhaps you and I could—"

"No." That was Elena. It sounded like Garrett wasn't too keen on letting Elena go. It made all the alarms in her head go off and she raced to the foyer.

"You never know until you try. Maybe a second date would—"

"I am sorry to be so blunt," Elena said, cutting him off again, "but it is apparently the only way I can get you to hear me. I feel *no* connection, and if I am being perfectly honest, Garrett, this date was little more than sad. I truly do not wish to see you again for a second date."

"Are you sure?" Garrett asked just as Allison appeared behind Elena in the doorway.

Glaring at the man over Elena's shoulder, she calmly asked, "Is there a problem here?"

The sound of her voice caused Elena to jump, but when Allison placed a comforting hand on her back, she unconsciously leaned into it.

"No, Allison, there is no problem. I was just saying goodnight to Garrett."

Garrett narrowed his eyes at Allison but then turned his focus back to Elena. "Well, okay then," he sighed. "I can respect that you didn't feel the same way about our date. Still, I'm glad to have met you Elena, and I suppose I should thank you for your candor."

Elena nodded and offered him a strained smile. "Thank you for dinner. Goodnight."

"Goodnight." But before Elena and Allison could retreat into the house, Garrett whirled back around with a hand on his stomach. "Uh, sorry, just one more thing. I hate to be a bother, but do you think I could use your restroom? I think those Cajun spices are going to be a problem after all."

Lip curling in disgust, Elena opened her mouth to respond, but Allison beat her to it. "No way," she answered, moving out onto the porch. "You can hold it until you get home, or you can stop at a restaurant or something."

Allison wasn't an idiot. She knew when to draw a line, and she had been in enough dodgy situations to know how fucked up people could be. She wasn't about to let some stranger into Elena's house. It wasn't that she thought Garrett was much of a threat. The guy mostly just seemed awkward and a little desperate, but she wasn't about to take any chances.

"He has IBS," Elena whispered.

"He's got what?" Allison asked, not even bothering to lower her voice.

Sweat started to bead along Garrett's forehead, and his cheeks were red in the glow of the porch light. "I have IBS."

Allison frowned. "The hell is that?"

"Irritable bowel syndrome," Elena supplied as she hovered just behind Allison.

Crossing her arms over her chest, Allison shook her head. "Sorry but I don't really care if your bowels are irritated, dude. You're not coming in this house. We don't know you and we've got a baby inside."

Elena gently placed a hand on Allison's shoulder. "Relax, Allison."

It wasn't enough to shake Allison, and she only continued to stare Garrett down. "Go on, man. Get out of here."

Green eyes remained glued to Garrett even as he turned and practically waddled back to his car. Allison didn't move a muscle, watching until his car was out of sight. When she turned back around, her eyes met Elena's, and the two women stood on the porch for a long moment.

"Thank you," Elena said. "But you didn't have to do that. I can certainly protect myself."

"I know. But you're also nice enough to let that guy in, and I was kind of afraid you would."

Elena smiled softly at her. "You are right. I may have let him in to use the restroom."

"See, don't do shit like that. Do you realize how dangerous that is? People are screwed up. They'll give you some crap excuse to get inside, and then you…Elena, you could get hurt. Lucas could get hurt, okay?"

The slight tremble in Allison's voice made Elena frown. She reached out again and squeezed her shoulder. "Allison," she whispered. "Stop worrying. Do you honestly think he would have hurt me?"

"No," she admitted. "I really do think the guy was just about to shit his pants."

Elena laughed quietly. "I agree. You see, *I* am a good judge of character as well, dear." She then poked Allison's arm. "I let *you* in, didn't I?"

"Oh, well, yeah. You're totally an awesome judge of character."

Pleased to see her smiling again, Elena led them inside, sniffing the air as they entered. "Popcorn again?" She dropped her purse onto the small table in the foyer before making her way toward the kitchen.

"Oh snaps! My popcorn!" Allison shot around Elena and into the kitchen, yanking the puffy paper bag from the microwave and dumping its contents into a giant bowl. She then grabbed a couple bags of Reese's Pieces and dumped them in as well. She gently shook and bounced the bowl until the candies disappeared into the popcorn and smiled as she turned around and held it out toward Elena.

Elena wrinkled her nose and shook her head. "No thank you."

"One of these days," Allison said. "One of these days, you will try it and then the heavens will open up and angels will sing and you will be like, 'I should've listened to Allison sooner!'"

"Well, if that day ever arrives, you are more than welcome to your 'I told you so'. For now, though, I shall stick to my theory that it is as disgusting as I imagine it to be."

"Suit yourself." Allison dug a hand into her popcorn. Before she put any in her mouth, though, she looked back up at Elena and said, "If you want me to go, I can just put this in like a billion Ziploc bags and take it with me. No big deal. Unless you would rather change into your jammies, plop down on the couch, and rant to me about your undoubtedly lame date with crap-your-pants guy?"

Elena's lips parted with a wide grin.

"That option is totally on the table, too. Just sayin'. You look like you wanna bitch about him, and I'm a good listener."

Her smile never wavered as she sighed and said, "Very well, but I am most definitely going to need a glass of wine for this one."

"Ew, seriously? He did *not* say that at dinner!" Allison gasped when Elena informed her of Garrett's IBS confession.

"Oh yes, he certainly did," Elena told her, shaking her head. "I was utterly mortified, of course, as was the waitress; poor girl."

"*I'm* mortified and I wasn't even there." Allison shoved some more popcorn into her mouth as she relaxed into the arm of the couch opposite Elena.

"Honestly, *who does that*? At dinner, no less, and also while attempting to woo a woman!"

"Apparently Garrett does that," Allison said, shaking her head. "Poor dude. No one ever taught him proper date etiquette."

"And what do *you* consider to be proper date etiquette?"

"I consider *not* talking about the high probability of shitting your pants to be proper date etiquette. Also, one should either bring their real hair with them or no hair at all."

Wine burned in Elena's nose as she coughed and laughed at the same time. Allison burst into loud laughter and leaned across the couch to whack Elena on the back a few times. "Sorry, didn't mean to nearly kill you."

"I am so glad I wasn't the only one to notice that awful toupee."

"Notice! What do you mean *notice?* I didn't *notice* the toupee; it noticed me. The damned thing was flapping around in the breeze and waving at us, Elena! He apparently forgot to extract the animal before he pasted its hide to his head, because I'm pretty sure that thing was still alive."

Elena laughed so hard that tears streamed down her cheeks. She waved her hand for Allison to stop.

"What? Don't pee your pants from laughter, Elena, because then you'll have to admit that you and Garrett are a perfect match for each other."

Elena attempted a glare but it was a hopeless pose while still laughing. Allison merely smirked.

"Seriously, though," she said once Elena regained her composure. "That dude should come with a warning label attached to his forehead or something."

She pointed her index finger at her own forehead and mimicked writing the words she then recited in a robotic voice. "Warning: Avoid Strong Winds and Spicy Foods. Subject is likely to lose hair and shit pants."

Elena dissolved into laughter once more until the best kind of ache throbbed in her ribcage. She hadn't laughed this much in such a long time; in fact, she didn't think anyone had *ever* made her laugh like that.

The decision to have Allison stay had been surprisingly easy. Elena had always been such a solitary person, but she liked having Allison around. Maybe it was because they were so different. Maybe it was because Allison embodied everything Elena had never been—easy-going, fluid, carefree.

It intrigued Elena even as it confounded her. She was ever impressed by the younger woman's confidence. Elena herself was an extremely confident woman, but Allison's confidence was different. It was present in everything—the way she carried herself, the way she laughed with abandon, and the way she interacted with her.

Elena was drawn to it and she didn't have a clue why. She entertained the thought that it was because there was a part of her that had always wished she could be more like Allison—younger at heart, wilder.

Allison Sawyer was like a cheesy comedy movie—an instant way to cheer oneself up after a bad night.

A happy sigh left Elena's lips as she tucked her feet under her and rested her head against the back of the couch. "He was quite short as well, wasn't he?"

Allison nodded as she finished up her popcorn and sat the bowl on the table beside her. "Totally. I bet you were regretting your heels as soon as you opened the door."

"I think Vivian must not have actually met the man prior to setting me up with him."

"I think Vivian must have been drunk or something when she set you up with that guy. You sure you wanna trust her to set you up on a third?"

She shook her head. "I know. I must be losing my mind."

"Eh, maybe this guy will be the worst of 'em, yeah?"

"I certainly hope so."

About an hour later, after Allison finished cleaning her dishes and tidying up, Elena walked her to the door. Once Allison was out of sight, she retreated back into the house and walked down the hall toward Lucas's room. Once she made sure he was still sound asleep, she retired to her own room, dropped onto her bed and pulled a small bottle of lotion from her bedside table.

As she lathered the lotion over her feet and hands, her phone beeped on her dresser. *It must be Vivian asking about the date,* she thought. Elena hopped off the bed and went to grab the phone; she had quite a few words for her best friend.

But when she swiped her finger across her lock screen, a notification box popped up and informed her that she had one new text message from Allison Sawyer.

Elena's brow arched but she quickly pressed to open the text. A soft chuckle escaped her as she saw that it was a photo of Allison and Lucas. Her son's face was tucked into Allison's chest and it was obvious that he was laughing. Allison was smiling brightly as well.

Elena smiled and pressed to save the picture into her phone's photo gallery. She felt that smile still painted across her lips even as she crawled back into bed and even when her eyes fluttered closed and her breathing grew deep.

Chapter Eight

"ELENA, PLEASE, MUST YOU ALWAYS take so long to dress yourself?"

Elena's neatly flipped hair swished around her face as her head poked out of the open closet doorway. She narrowed her eyes at the woman sitting on the end of her bed. "Mother, it has barely been twenty minutes. Stop being so dramatic, and, for the record, I have done much more in that time than dress myself."

"Do tell, dear, because as far as I can see," Nora replied, pointing toward the visible parts of Elena's crimson bra and the naked flesh of her stomach, "you *haven't* actually dressed yourself yet."

A few strands of hair flew away from Elena's face in the gust of air she huffed out. "Perhaps that particular task would have been finished already had I not been repeatedly interrupted by your barks of impatience and endless questions about my utterly disappointing dates."

Elena ducked back into the closet as Nora chuckled deeply. The elder woman glanced toward her own reflection in the mirror above Elena's vanity and patted a hand at her hair where it was pinned up and rubbed down a few wild strands.

"Speaking of," she said, "when is Vivian due to arrive?" The three women were attending a Broadway show that afternoon.

"Soon."

"Oh, well thank you for being *so* specific, darling."

Appearing from within the closet a moment later, a smile planted itself across Elena's painted red lips. She slipped on her heels then posed dramatically in front of her mother, one hand on her hip and another lain delicately across her forehead. Bright red pumps made for a striking splash of color, paired with Elena's form-fitted black dress. Her hair was slightly curled around the edges and lay gently against her olive complexion.

She had done this often as a little girl. She would dress up in various outfits carefully selected from her own clothes and a few of her mother's, decorate her hair with a sparkling headband or clip, and paint her face with bits of lip gloss and eye shadow. All dolled up, Elena would put on a mini-fashion show for her mother, walking an imaginary runway while stopping every few steps to strike a pose. Nora, of course, applauded the show while praising her daughter's stunning beauty and stylish attire. She and Elena frequently liked to joke that those little shows had been the promising start of Elena's career.

Nora clapped now at her daughter's pose as well. "Flawless, my dear. Simply flawless. Takes me right back to when you were a child."

Elena laughed and walked over to kiss to her mother's cheek before using her thumb to wipe away the lipstick left behind. She then turned back to her vanity to grab a few pieces of jewelry to match her outfit.

"So, Daddy is taking Lucas to the children's museum?" she asked as she popped in her earrings.

"That was the plan, though you know your father," Nora said. "I'm sure he and Lucas will have had quite the adventure about the city by the time we return from the show."

Before Elena could respond, the sound of the front door closing echoed through the house, followed by the clicking of heels, and then Vivian appeared. She smiled brightly at the two women before turning her attention to Elena.

Vivian bugged out her eyes. "How did you do it, Mom? She's actually dressed and ready to go *on time?!*"

The small hairbrush Elena sent soaring in her direction pulled a shriek from her lips, and she laughed triumphantly when she successfully dodged it.

"You are lucky that you are even invited."

"Ah, what did I do now?"

"From what I've heard, dear," Nora cut in, "you have made Elena's dating life even more of a hell than it was prior to this little adventure the two of you agreed upon, and in only *two* dates. Well done, Vivian."

"Mother! Don't encourage her." She turned back to her best friend. "Honestly, last night was a simply horrific experience."

"I think you are too harsh of a judge." Vivian pursed her lips and attempted to look serious despite the mirth dancing in her azure eyes.

"He spoke about his bowels at the dinner table."

Vivian actually gagged while Nora shook her head.

"My dear, I would love to have seen your face."

"It wasn't pleasant, I can assure you." Elena's dark eyes turned back to Vivian, who was now laughing about the entire thing.

"That was only the beginning, Viv. It ended as uncomfortably as it began. I was beginning to think you set me up with a dud on purpose."

Vivian's laughter instantly died in her throat. Her eyes widened just slightly. "That's ridiculous, Elena."

"As was the date." She propped her hands on her hips.

"I can't learn a person's entire life story prior to setting him up with you, Elena. If that were the case, then *I* would be dating him. He looked good on paper. What more do you want me from me, woman?"

"You didn't even meet him first?"

Vivian's cheeks flushed a light pink as she turned and her eyes pleaded with Nora for help. The older woman shook her head. "You're on your own with this one, my dear."

"Gee thanks, *Mom*."

"Look, Elena, I will make it up to you. The next date will be better, *much* better. Oh! I will set you up with a woman this time! How about that?"

"A woman?" Nora arched a brow. "Elena, I'm surprised. Have you finally embraced your inner lesbian?"

Elena's entire face flushed as she dropped her forehead into her hand. "Please, can we not talk about this?"

"Oh honey, it's nothing to be ashamed of."

"I'm not ashamed, Mother." But she kept her head down, avoiding Nora's eyes and teasing smile.

"Well good. Because it's about time you were honest about it, Elena."

Vivian cackled as she watched Elena's cheeks grow redder under the thin curtain of dark hair that had fallen around her face. "That's what *I* said!"

The familiar glare shot in her direction only caused her to laugh harder.

"What? I *did*!"

"I hate both of you." She grabbed her small clutch from the vanity and strode by Vivian and out of the room. Vivian and Nora followed Elena down the hallway.

"It's perfectly natural, Elena." Gathering their purses, they made their way to Elena's car. "I was a lesbian once myself."

Elena halted in the middle of the walkway and whirled around. "Excuse me?"

Vivian clamped a hand over her mouth. Her entire body shook with the laughter she fought to contain as Nora shrugged and repeated herself. "I was a lesbian once."

"What do you mean '*once*'? How can you be a lesbian '*once*'?"

"Oh dear," Nora said, waving her hand dismissively, "it was the seventies and I was a teenager."

"*And?*" One red pump tapped impatiently, Elena's expression severe as her mouth pressed into a thin line.

"And everyone was still hung over from all of that 'free love' crap from the sixties."

"*And?*" She could not believe what she was hearing. How had she never known this?

"*And* I went through a bit of a lesbian phase with a girl at school."

"What about Daddy?"

"What about him? I hadn't met your father yet, dear. I was completely within my right to engage in certain *activities* with my friend." Nora then sighed almost wistfully. "Still the best sex I've ever had."

"*Mother!*"

"Oh my God." Vivian's voice squeaked between rolling giggles. "This is the best day of my life."

Allison finally woke up at around three in the afternoon, having slept her Saturday away. Rolling onto her back, she stretched out her limbs, her body tangling in the sheets. She hadn't gotten much sleep the night before, fully amped by her hilarious night with Elena, and, once she got back to her dorm, she had stayed up most of the night watching movies.

The muscles of her biceps strained and her toes curled down as she stretched her body as far as it would go. She groaned and yawned. Sufficiently stretched, Allison popped her knuckles, her elbows, her knees, and her neck, and crawled out of bed to finally start her day.

After a shower, she slipped into a pair of black leggings, a long gray V-neck T-shirt, and fuzzy socks. She poured herself a bowl of cereal and then crawled back into bed. She had absolutely zero plans for the weekend, and her roommate was out of state until Monday, visiting some distant cousin or something. The note she left on the massive dry-erase board that hung between their beds made Allison laugh as she read it again.

Alli,

Would've said goodbye but didn't want to interrupt your snore-fest.

Be back Monday. No sex in my bed unless you wanna buy me new sheets.

XX, Macy

Allison munched on her cereal as she clicked on the small television she and Macy shared, flipping channels before settling on something random she only paid partial attention to as she ate her cereal and reached for her phone on the bedside table. When she saw she had a text from Elena, she smiled, causing milk to dribble down her chin and onto her shirt.

"Shit." The blanket became her napkin as she opened the text message, grinning again as she saw the photo she had sent to Elena the night before. There were six simple words Elena had sent in response.

Thank you for the picture, Allison.

That was it, but for some reason, Allison could not stop smiling. She stared at it for several long moments before putting her phone back on the bedside table.

For the next few hours, Allison cycled through a number of random activities, none of which were very entertaining. She watched TV for a bit, washed the dishes, and played Bookworm on her phone. She even tried to read for a while, her favorite pastime, but simply could not get into it.

She hated days like this, when she desperately wanted to do something, *anything*, but everything she actually did just bored her. It drove her mad. She finally gave up after a while and figured she might as well do something productive, since there was apparently nothing that was actually going to please her. There were a few chapters she needed to review and take notes on for class, so she went to grab her textbook from her backpack, but her backpack was not where it usually was on the floor at the end of her bed.

After going through everything twice, Allison finally accepted that the damned thing just wasn't there.

"I must've left it at Elena's."

It was most likely still sitting on the floor next to Elena's couch. Allison grabbed her phone again.

Hey Elena. Sorry to bother you, but I think I might have left my backpack at your house last night. Could you check?

Hopefully, she would be able to just swing by and grab her bag. She sent the message and then plopped down on her bed to wait for an answer she hoped would be swift.

After the show, Elena drove her small group to her mother's house, and the moment the three women went inside, they were instantly bombarded by a tiny flying boy. Lucas crashed into Elena's legs with a loud squeal of "Momma!" before jumping over to Vivian's legs and then Nora's.

Hugging each of them, he began to babble in rapid-fire excitement about his day. Elena reached down and grabbed her son by the shoulders. "Lucas, Lucas, slow down," she said. "Did you have a good time with Pop?"

"Yeah! I slided down a fire pole!"

"You *slid*. That's great! Did you save anyone from a fire?"

"No silly."

"Silly?" Elena gasped and poked Lucas's belly, making him giggle. "*You're* the silly one, mister."

A light blue tint coated her sons' lips, teeth, tongue, and cheeks, and Elena frowned as she noticed it. It felt sticky on her thumb as she rubbed across his cheek. "What is all over you?"

"I may have given him a popsicle," another voice said, and Elena glanced up to see her father leaning in the doorway of the kitchen, smiling at her, "or two."

"Daddy." Elena scowled. "You know how he is when he's had too much sugar."

"I'm so fun!"

Everyone in the room burst into laughter, and Elena kissed Lucas's forehead. "That you are, munchkin." She licked her thumb and used it to scrub away the gunk on his cheeks while he squirmed and pushed at her hands.

"Mooooooooooom. That's gross."

"Oh hush." She licked her thumb again and scrubbed a bit more, but threw her hands up when he grumbled and pushed at her again. "Fine," she laughed and stuck her tongue out at him. "You can just be sticky."

"Gram will give me a bath."

"Oh, I will, will I?" Nora asked as she crossed the room and pressed a brief kiss to her husband's lips. He wrapped an arm around her shoulders and tucked her into his side.

"Yeah!" Grinning widely, Lucas looked at his mother. "Can I stay with Gram and Pop, Momma?"

"Overnight? I don't know, munchkin. You will have to ask Gram and Pop."

Lucas whirled around to face his grandparents. "Can I?!"

"Of course you can, Lucas," Nora said.

After a cup of coffee with Elena's parents and listening to Lucas ramble on about his day for a while, Vivian and Elena made to leave. Hugs and kisses were passed around, and Elena propped Lucas up on her hip to give him extra. "I'll pick you up in the morning, okay munchkin?"

"Okay Momma." Little fingers tangled in Elena's hair. "Miss me!"

"I always do, baby."

Vivian leaned in and smacked a kiss on Lucas's sticky cheek before Elena put him down again. "Be good for Gram and Pop," she said, and he nodded that he would.

As she pulled out of the driveway, Elena could see him standing at the window and waving as Elena and Vivian left, face pressed to the window until the house was out of sight.

"Elena, whose bag is this?"

Elena came around the corner and into the living room with two glasses of wine just as Vivian held up the item in question, a green and blue backpack. "Christ, it's heavy."

"Oh. It must be Allison's."

"I see," Vivian whispered to herself, taking the small glass of wine from her friend before settling onto the couch. "Well, you should probably text or call her. I'm sure she will need it for school. Maybe she could pick it up tonight."

"That's true." Elena set her wine on the coffee table and retrieved her phone from her purse. "I will text her. She is probably out with friends tonight anyway, but perhaps she could come and collect it tomorrow."

Dropping back onto the couch, Elena held her phone out to show Vivian a message. "She apparently beat us to it."

Hey Elena. Sorry to bother you, but I think I might have left my backpack at your house last night. Could you check?

Vivian watched as Elena tapped out a quick response.

Yes, it is here.

Not even ten seconds later, the phone beeped with a response. "Wow," Vivian said. "She must really want that backpack."

A quiet laugh slipped from Elena's lips as she read the message, while Vivian read it over her arm.

Sweet, any chance I could get it from you? I mean, are you busy? Are you home?

It was interesting how Elena seemed to slip into another world while responding to the babysitter. Vivian wondered if Elena even had a clue how she looked in that moment—her eyes fixed on her phone screen, a small smile gracing her lips, and her teeth gently biting at her full bottom lip. She looked like a teenager again, having just gotten a text message from her ultimate crush.

This is just sad, Vivian thought, willing herself not to laugh. *How blind can you be?*

The clicking sounds of the phone keys were the only sounds in the room as Elena typed out her message—*Yes, I'm home. Are you not out with friends?*—and pressed the *send* button. She then frowned and speedily wrote another message—*I'm sorry. That really isn't any of my business.*

Ha! came the reply from Allison. *It's all good. No, I don't go out a lot, and my roomie is out of town. So, could I come get my bag now then? I'm bored as hell and have nothing else to do. Might as well do some homework, right?*

Vivian cleared her throat as she read more messages over Elena's arm. "Maybe *you* could just take it to *her*."

Elena looked at her, arching a brow, but Vivian only shrugged. "What? She always comes to you, you know, babysitting and whatnot. It's not like you're doing anything, and that'll save the girl from having to take the subway. Life is good when you can avoid the subway on a Saturday."

"That is true." She chewed on her lip. "But you and I are spending time together."

"Elena, we see each other nearly every day. I think I will survive. Besides, I have quite a bit of paperwork to catch up on this weekend anyway."

"Are you sure?"

"Absolutely positively."

Elena poked Vivian's thigh. "Well, don't sound so enthusiastic about it. You're going to make me feel as if I'm bad company."

"Oh please. You know you're my favorite company."

Elena grinned at her as she turned back to her phone. It amused Vivian to see Elena's lip suck right back between her teeth as she typed another message. She just shook her head and laughed internally while she waited for Elena to finish.

Perhaps I could bring it to you, Elena typed, *if that suits you.*

The response was nearly instantaneous. *You'd do that?*

Of course. Elena grinned unconsciously yet again. *It would be no problem.*

Ten minutes later, Elena and Vivian were walking out of Elena's front door and toward their respective vehicles. Elena carried Allison's heavy backpack in one hand and her clutch and keys in the other. They stopped in the middle and hugged one another, planting a kiss on each other's cheeks.

"Have fun with the college girls," Vivian teased as she poked Elena's ribs. "Don't do anything *I* wouldn't do."

"So, basically *everything* is fair game?"

"Exactly."

They said their goodbyes, and Vivian grinned all the way to her car. She had a feeling they were on the brink of a breakthrough.

As she walked up to the large building that was Allison's dormitory hall, Elena texted to let her know she had arrived, because each building required key-card entry. She was thankful that it was spring, so it was a fairly warm night. She would not want to have to wait in the cold for Allison to come collect her, not to mention the fact that it had taken her some time to find parking and it hadn't been terribly close. A freezing walk back to her car would not have been fun.

It was only about three minutes before Allison came bolting out the front door of the building with a lopsided smile on her face. Elena's eyes traced down Allison's body—her messy ponytail, baggy gray V-neck, and her black leggings, which perfectly accented her toned thighs and calves. Laughter bloomed in her chest as she realized that Allison's feet were protected by only bright orange fuzzy socks and slip-on house shoes.

Allison whistled as she reached Elena, checking out the woman's black dress and red pumps. "You know, it's just a dorm," she teased, reaching out to take her backpack. "You didn't have to get all dressed up."

Elena looked down at herself, blushing slightly. "Oh, right. I went to see a show earlier with Vivian and my mother."

"Ah, makes sense then." Scratching at the back of her neck, Allison glanced toward the ground. "You look really nice."

"Thank you, dear. You look quite comfy."

Allison followed Elena's gaze down to her feet and laughed as she wriggled her toes around inside her socks. "Oh yeah, they're my faves. My feet get really cold."

"Mine too."

"Well, you need some fuzzy socks then."

Elena smiled. "Perhaps I do."

"So, uh, thanks a lot for doing this," Allison said as she held up her backpack. "I really appreciate you driving all the way over here to bring me this; that was really nice of you."

Elena just nodded, smile still firmly in place, as she tucked her clutch under arm and tangled her fingers together in front of her, resting her hands against her abdomen. "It was no trouble at all."

"Cool." A long silence fell between them as they stood together in the warm night air, nothing but the sounds of traffic echoing around them. The moment dragged until it was almost awkward, both of them just shuffling in place, until Allison looked up at the exact same time that Elena did, and their eyes locked together. Stomach flipping, she quickly cleared her throat.

"Um, well, do you wanna come up?"

Elena's eyes widened slightly. "Up to your dorm room?"

"Yeah. I mean, we could just hang or whatever for a while if you want. The roomie and I have a lot of movies. Unless you have other plans. That's cool, too. It's no bi—"

"No, no. I have no plans. I…all right, yes, I suppose it would be nice to have a companion for the evening."

Allison laughed. "All right then, *companion*."

When Elena only rolled her eyes, Allison slung her backpack over her shoulder and began walking backwards toward the front door of the building. "Come on," she said, motioning for Elena to follow her.

Elena didn't hesitate, her heels clicking against the concrete as she hurried to catch up.

Chapter Nine

"So, this is it," Allison said as she opened the door to her dorm and waited for Elena to pass. "Sorry about the year-long wait to check you in downstairs. They're really strict about that here."

Elena waved a dismissive hand and took slow steps into the dorm, as if she wasn't quite sure what she was doing there to begin with. Three feet into the room, she stopped to stare at everything. She wasn't positive, but she felt fairly safe in assuming that the left side of the small room was Allison's.

Stacks of books lined a small shelf beside the left twin-sized bed and also at the end of it. The walls were bare but for a small dream catcher that hung just over the pillow. The blankets on the bed were all green, including the sheets and pillowcase, and Elena could see what looked like the end of a guitar case poking out from under the bed.

The other side of the room was much darker—lots of crimson and black. Music and movie posters and magazine cut-outs covered the walls surrounding that twin-sized bed. The blankets were red and black as well, and there were various stacks of CDs, DVDs, and a few books sitting about.

A large dry-erase board was pinned to the wall between the two beds, hanging just above a small flat-screen television propped up on a short and rickety-looking old wooden dresser. Elena chuckled as she read the message scribbled across the dry-erase board.

"Hey," Allison said, "I know the room's small, but you don't have to laugh at it."

"No, I was laughing at the message," she said, a little concerned that Allison had actually misinterpreted her laughter and taken offense, despite the smile firmly planted on Allison's face. She pointed at the dry-erase board, and Allison glanced over at it.

"Oh, right." She laughed. "Yup, *that's* my roommate."

Smirking, Elena read the girl's name on the message. "Well, Macy seems to believe that there is a high probability of you committing inappropriate acts in her bed. Had this problem before, have you?"

Allison's cheeks flushed pink as she cleared her throat and stammered a little. "No, no, of course not. No, she's just kidding. I don't really...I mean, it's not something that I—"

"Allison. Relax. I was only teasing."

A slightly choked laugh left her lips as she scratched at the back of her neck again. "Right, I mean, duh. Of course you were."

Another awkward silence ensued. Allison smacked and popped her lips, while Elena continued to observe her surroundings. "So," Allison said. "It's probably safe to move more than three feet from the door."

Elena stood stiffly as she looked at Allison, unsure of what exactly she was expecting of her. There was obviously nowhere to sit except the bed, and Elena didn't want to assume that she was welcome to do so. She was entirely in Allison's element now, and it made her feel like someone had come along, peeled off her skin, and applied one that simply didn't fit; at least, not yet.

"Where would you like me to go?"

"Oh, right." Allison laughed. "I guess there's nowhere else to go, huh? I just meant that you could sit down if you want. Make yourself comfortable."

"On your bed?" Elena asked, just to be sure.

Allison felt a strange tickle in her stomach. She nodded. "Yeah."

It only took five steps to cross the room, and Elena sat gingerly on the very edge of Allison's bed, her posture rigid. She rested her clutch on her lap with her hands atop it. When she looked back over to Allison, the blonde was grinning at her.

"What?"

"Nothing. Just, how did you know which bed was mine?"

"The day we met, you told me that you loved books." The various teetering stacks of books surrounding Allison's bed drew her gaze.

"Oh yeah, I did." Allison walked over to a small black mini fridge at the foot of her roommate's bed. She extracted a silver can and held it up. "You want a beer?"

Before Elena could respond, Allison scoffed at her own words. "What am I even talking about? You are *so* not the type of woman who drinks beer. There's some soda in here too, and I think that we've got some juice and some water in the common fridge out in the suite kitchen."

"What will *you* be having?"

"I'm gonna drink this beer. There's like two six-packs in here, so I might as well."

"Very well then. I will have the same."

She was determined to try to fit into these particular surroundings. At the moment, she felt rather uncomfortable, but hoped that would pass if she made an effort to be more at ease, be more like the woman that actually lived here. She could be more than a privileged rich girl.

Allison's eyebrows shot up. "Really? You like beer?"

"Not at all." They both laughed. "However, I will make an exception."

Another can of beer was opened and passed her way, and Elena sipped delicately at it Her lips pinched tightly together at the first few sips, but she grew accustomed to the taste. Allison smiled the entire time she watched her. "You're just full of surprises," she said.

"So, where's Lucas? Is he having some sweet Saturday night toddler rave at your house right now? Anyone not in pull-ups gets kicked out of the party, and that's how you ended up here, right?"

"How ever did you guess?" Elena asked with mirth in her eyes. "He is spending the night with my parents."

"Ah, cool." Allison stepped around Elena's knees and dropped down onto the mattress beside her. House shoes dropping to the floor with two soft thuds, she pulled one socked foot up under her as she sipped at her beer. "You pretty close with your parents?"

"I am, yes."

"That's cool." Allison's gaze traveled down the exposed flesh of Elena's legs, down to her feet, still arched inside the bright red pumps. Bottom lip tucked between her teeth, she leaned over to put her beer on her bedside table before hopping off the mattress and dropping to her knees in front of her guest.

"I always wondered what that would be like," she murmured as she avoided Elena's eyes and reached out, delicately wrapping one hand around Elena's left ankle.

Eyes narrowing, Elena tilted her head slightly to the side as she watched, but said nothing.

"These can't be comfortable," Allison muttered as she grasped one ankle and pulled a shoe off, her fingertips just barely brushing over the smooth skin of Elena's foot. The limb jerked in her hand and Elena felt a small smile tugging at the corners of her mouth.

"I'm a bit ticklish." She saw a wide grin spread across Allison's face at the admission as she immediately reached for the other foot, but Elena was quick to throw out a hand to stop her. "Don't even think about it."

Allison cracked up but froze, her hands wrapped around Elena's shoe. "That's a pretty serious threat for someone who is only a 'bit' ticklish."

Elena rolled her eyes. "Perhaps I am a bit more than a bit."

"Like pee-your-pants ticklish or just squeal-and-squirm ticklish?" That mischievous little grin remained on her face.

"The latter," Elena said. "However, I warn you to consider your next move quite carefully, Ms. Sawyer."

"Oh, should I?"

Elena nodded seriously.

"And why is that?"

Cheeks growing warm, Elena glanced down to her lap. "When I was sixteen, I accidentally kicked my father in the face when he tickled my feet, and it knocked one of his front teeth out. He has a fake tooth now."

Allison tried not to laugh but it burst out of her. "Oh my God, that is hilarious!"

"It was quite horrifying when it happened, actually. There was a lot of blood."

"I bet." The remaining shoe was pulled free, and Allison put it next to the other. "I'll try to resist the urge then. I can't afford a new tooth."

"Wise decision, dear." Elena stretched her feet down, curling her toes and letting out a small sigh of contentment. It was nice to finally be freed from the confines of those shoes. "Thank you."

The bed bounced a bit as Allison plopped back down. "So, you wanna watch a movie or something?"

Elena, still poised on the very edge of the mattress, glanced to the small television and then back to Allison. "I suppose that would be fine."

"Cool. Let's get you out of that dress then."

Elena's eyes widened as her gaze locked onto Allison's. "I'm sorry?"

"Uh, wow, that sounded better in my head." Allison smacked a hand against her forehead. "I just meant that you probably won't be comfortable sitting through a whole movie in that dress. You can borrow some of my clothes. I mean, if you want?"

"Oh." The word came out in a rush of breath. "Oh, right, I see. Well, I suppose—"

"You know you don't always have to 'suppose' everything." Allison leaned over to nudge Elena with her elbow. "You could just say 'yes'."

"I suppose you're right."

Allison threw her hands up and Elena, realizing what she'd said, reached over and swatted her arm. "Excuse me." She rolled her eyes. "I meant to say 'yes'."

"That's more like it." Hopping off the bed, Allison pulled out another pair of leggings and a random old, ratty red T-shirt from a small dresser. She handed the items to Elena and took the woman's beer and clutch. "These should fit you. The bathroom is just through that door over there. You get changed and I'll pick us out a movie."

Elena rose from the bed, Allison's clothes clutched in her hands, and crossed to the bathroom. Before she could fully close the door behind her, she heard Allison let out a groan.

"Let's get you out of that dress then?" Allison said. "Way to sound like a friggin' perv, Al."

Elena smiled and clicked the door softly closed.

The mirror in the bathroom showed Elena her own wide-eyed reflection, Allison's clothes still bundled between her hands. She was immensely uncomfortable, not only because she was about to don someone else's clothes, but also because she felt so completely and utterly at a disadvantage. She had never been this type of person—this carefree, hang-out-in-your-lazy-clothes, movie-marathon, beer-in-a-can type of girl. She never even had any friends the likes of Allison Sawyer.

She didn't know *how* to be that type of girl, not that she felt like she needed to be. She had no intentions of trying to be something she wasn't. It was more that she didn't want this experience to be an awkward one for either of them.

The fact that Allison made her feel somewhat more at ease at least gave her comfort. When the silences set in or when there was a moment of miscommunication, things became strange, but never to the point that Elena wanted to cut and run. As long as Allison was talking, joking and teasing and being herself, it helped Elena to relax.

Setting Allison's clothes on the sink counter, Elena angled her arms back so that she could latch onto the zipper of her dress. When she managed to lower it enough to ease her body out, Elena's eyes fell to her chest. Her stomach clenched uncomfortably as she was reminded that she was most definitely *not* wearing a bra.

"Shit." She had been wearing a crimson-colored bra when she had first dressed for the show, but when she had decided to wear *this* particular dress, she had divested herself of the garment.

She glanced to the door then down to her naked chest, over to the red baggy T-shirt on the sink, then back to her naked chest. The rather dim lighting in the dorm room was a plus, she thought. Allison had the room lit by only a single lamp, which might or might not be extinguished during whatever movie they were about to watch. If the room was dark, then surely the fact that she would be braless would go unnoticed.

Wait—was it cold in the other room? Elena glanced down at her breasts again.

"Well, it is apparently cold in here," she murmured.

She couldn't remain in the bathroom for an hour, she reminded herself; so she grabbed the two items of clothing from the sink, slipped the red T-shirt over her head, and nearly purred at how comfortable the material was. It was a rather thick material as well, which helped conceal her obvious chill; not much, but it was better than nothing. She then pulled on the leggings that Allison had given her, moving her hips from side to side as she yanked the tight, stretchy material up her thighs and over her crimson-colored thong.

Grabbing her dress, Elena held it in front of her chest as she took a deep breath and exited the bathroom.

The lamp was off when she returned, and the room was quite dark but for the glow of the television. Elena let out an easy breath as she carried her dress over to Macy's bed and laid it out so that it would not wrinkle.

Allison, whose back had been turned to the bathroom while she loaded a DVD into the player beneath the television, turned at the sound of Elena shuffling around behind her. Her eyes instantly shot down the length of Elena's body in her clothes and then back up. Lips parted, she shook her head quickly and asked, "So, they fit, yeah?"

"Quite well, actually." Elena ran her hands a little self-consciously over the clothing, unable to recall a single time in her entire life when she had worn anything of the sort, at least, not in front of anyone outside her family. "Thank you."

"No problem. Make yourself comfortable."

Like before, Elena settled herself gingerly on the edge of the bed, and Allison took one look at her and rolled her eyes.

"Oh yeah. You look *hella* comfortable. Must be that rigid posture and the way your ass is hanging halfway off the bed." She crawled onto the bed, scooting all the way back until her back touched the wall, which she cushioned with a couple of pillows. "The bed's not going to swallow you, I promise. Loosen up a bit."

Elena inched slowly back until she was settled against the pillows next to Allison, who reached out and squeezed Elena's forearm. "Hey," she said softly. Green eyes glinted in the television glow.

"Yes?"

"I can tell that you're uncomfortable. You don't have to stay if you don't want to. I mean, you're not obligated to hang out with me just because you brought me my backpack. Okay? You don't have to stay."

Elena's heart clenched at the words and she quickly moved to place her own hand atop Allison's, which still rested on her forearm. "No, Allison, I'm sorry. I don't mean to be so awkward. To be honest, I am just feeling quite out of my element. That is all."

"What's your element?" Allison asked, grinning. "Fancy dinner parties and shit? Never had a friend like me, I'm guessing?"

Elena returned her smile as she nodded. "Something like that."

"Well, look, you don't have to be out of your element here. Just relax and be yourself. Pretend like we're back at your house, on your couch, bitching about shitty dates."

The tension in Elena's shoulders loosened at the mere reference, her body relaxing. She smiled at Allison's words and squeezed her hand. "Thank you."

Nodding, Allison retracted her hand and reached over to the bedside table to grab their beers. She handed Elena hers and then began to sip at her own. Between sips, she grabbed the remote. "I hope you like horror movies."

Elena's lip curled a bit. "Will there be much gore?"

"Eh, not *too* much. But really, it's your own fault that we're watching this."

"What? What do you mean?"

"You didn't get the lotion reference, and that means I am obligated to educate you. It's like an unwritten rule of life or whatever."

With the push of a button on the TV remote, the movie menu popped up, and Elena's stomach clenched in anticipation as she saw the title flickering across the screen.

The Silence of the Lambs.

Chapter Ten

TEETH DUG INTO HER LIP as Allison fought to keep from laughing at Elena. The other woman was coiled back against the wall next to her, body stiff and nearly rolled into a ball. Her lips pursed in disgust as her eyes remained fixed on the television screen.

The camera zoomed in on a man's lips, painted with bright red lipstick. Buffalo Bill's deep voice echoed through the speakers as he stared at his reflection, asking himself, "Would you fuck me?"

The scene flashed back and forth between those red lips and the man's young female captive shouting from her massive hole in the ground and desperately trying to capture his dog using a chicken bone and a bucket.

"I'd fuck me," that deep voice said again. "I'd fuck me hard. I'd fuck me so hard."

"This is positively *disturbing*," Elena whispered, and Allison just completely lost it. Elena smacked her on the thigh.

"Ow!" Laughter still bubbled in her throat as she rubbed the spot. "You don't have to beat me up, woman!"

"And *you* didn't have to laugh at me."

Allison could see how she had loosened up quite a bit since the start of the movie, relaxing into the cushion of pillows behind them, their shoulders frequently rubbing together. "Aw, come on. Your facial expression was pretty funny."

"Yes, well, you are *supposed* to be watching the movie, dear, not my face."

"Couldn't help it. You were just all balled up and horrified."

"Any respectable person would be horrified by the particulars of this movie."

"Yeah, I guess you've got a point there." But the shit-eating grin still hadn't fallen from her lips. "Now you know why I said what I said."

"Sorry?" Elena asked. "To what are you referring?"

"The thing about Vivian screening your dates. I mean, look at the chick in this movie. She was just trying to do a good deed, help a dude get his couch up into his van, and then, next thing she knows, she's in a damn hole with nothing but a chicken bone and some lotion and being referred to as an 'it' instead of 'she'. And they tell us that good deeds should be a priority. Psh! That shit gets you skinned alive so some dude can tuck his junk and dance around in your scalp."

Laughter shook through Elena's body. "This is the most disturbing conversation I have ever had."

Allison poked her in the ribs. "You just need to get out more then."

"I'm not sure I should if this is all I have to look forward to. Now you've caused us to miss a good portion of the movie. How am I to know what's going on?"

"Uh, good excuse for me to torture you with this movie again at a later date. Re-watches are a must with classics anyway."

"I see." Elena's gaze followed as Allison jumped off the bed. "Where are you going?"

"Well, since we've already missed a big chunk of the movie, I might as well take this opportunity to make a snack."

"Oh, let me guess," Elena said as Allison was digging through the contents of a small shelf near the foot of her bed. "Popcorn and candy?"

"Wow." Hand pressing to her chest, Allison gasped as she walked over to the microwave on Macy's side of the room. "When did you gain the power of foresight?"

"Some time ago. It's quite a lovely power to have, though I must tell you that it has also unfortunately predicted the many cavities your favorite snack will eventually cause."

"Ha ha. You're funny, you know that? So, so funny."

"Sarcasm is not your strong suit."

"Sure it isn't." Popping sounds began to echo from the microwave, filling in the small silences between the voices still spilling from the television.

Elena turned her mirth-filled eyes back toward the movie. "Hush," she said. "I'm trying to watch this movie."

When Allison plopped back down onto the bed, she shifted back until she was up against the wall and right next to Elena again. She shook her bag of popcorn at her and Elena glanced into the bag to see the little orange and brown candies floating around between the puffy kernels.

"You may as well give up. I'm not going to try it."

"No way. I'll never give up. I *will* convert you eventually."

Elena rolled her eyes. "It's not a religion, dear."

"It so is, though." Allison bumped her shoulder against Elena's again. "Popcorn and Reese's—guaranteed to save your soul."

They fell into silence after that, both of them getting sucked back into the movie as Allison munched happily. Elena was horrified at more than a few parts of the movie, but when Hannibal Lecter was transferred to a massive cell that looked more like a birdcage, she suddenly shouted at the television. "That cell is not even remotely safe! He can reach right through the bars!"

"I know, right?"

"You watch. Someone is going to get killed. I guarantee it. Idiots."

Allison decided then and there that she really needed to convince Elena to watch more horror movies, because her reactions were wildly entertaining, from her disturbed facial expressions to her random outbursts. It was far too amusing not to repeat.

Hannibal managed to make his great escape, and Allison bit her lip again to keep from laughing as she realized that Elena's face had gotten closer and closer to her throughout the entire scene. The woman had practically ducked behind Allison's shoulder by the time Hannibal had donned another man's face in order to get out of the building undetected. By the end, Elena was peeking over the top of Allison's shoulder, and, when Hannibal peeled the other man's skin from his face, a shudder rippled down her spine and shook through her body.

"Oh God, that is vile." Elena's words dissolved against Allison's neck in a puff of warm air.

"Uh-huh. And apparently scary. You gonna keep hiding behind my shoulder there?"

She torqued her head to the side so that she could look back at Elena, not realizing how close she was to her. Noses bumped roughly and both women instantly jerked backward, hands going up to their faces. They paused awkwardly for a moment as they stared at each other and rubbed their noses. "Uh," Allison mumbled. Then they both tried to speak at the same time.

"Sorry," they both said simultaneously. "I'm..."

Silence enveloped them again as small smiles slipped across their lips and then Allison broke. Her laughter started low and soft but built and flooded into the room as the awkwardness of it all cracked her up. Elena's own laughter soon followed, melding with Allison's as it danced in the air of the small dorm room.

"You're just beating the hell out of me tonight, aren't you?"

Elena smirked. "I believe it was *you* that just rammed your face into mine."

"Rammed? Don't you think 'rammed' is a little harsh, Elena?"

"If you say so, dear."

"Gentle, really," Allison said. "A gentle nudging of noses."

"Really?" The deadpan expression on her face did nothing to deter Allison.

"A nose nudge. A nose *hug*."

"Okay!" Elena grabbed one of the pillows and whacked Allison with it. "I get it."

"See? I knew you'd see things my way."

The movie was completely forgotten as they teased each other. When the soundtrack began to play loudly through the room and they turned to see the credits rolling across the small screen, Allison took that single moment of distraction to lunge across the bed and grab Elena's feet. She scraped her fingers across the sensitive skin, and Elena instantly screeched and began to flail. Allison only lasted about ten seconds before she took a hard kick to the gut.

Her breath slammed from her lungs in one loud rush of air, and she keeled over on the mattress, laughing even as she wheezed. But Elena was on her knees in seconds and reaching for her.

"Shit, Allison!" She placed a hand on Allison's arm as the blonde curled in a ball on her side. "Are you okay? Can you...can you breathe? Are you hurt?"

Allison coughed a few times before reaching for Elena's hand where it was still attached to her bicep. "It's okay." Sucking in a few deep breaths, she pushed herself upright once more. "I'm fine."

The sigh of relief Elena released quickly morphed into quiet laughter when Allison gave her a ridiculously wide smile and pointed to the visible pearly whites. "See? Still got all my teeth."

"So you do." Elena ducked her head. "I'm sorry, Allison. I didn't mean to kick you."

Allison could tell that Elena felt genuinely bad about it, so she shifted a little closer to her and rested a hand on her knee.

"Hey."

When Elena looked up and locked eyes with her in the glow of the television screen, she smiled at her again. "In all fairness, you did warn me, right?"

"I did."

"Well then, I totally deserved it." Allison squeezed Elena's knee. "I'm okay. Okay?"

"Very well."

"Good." She pointed toward Elena's feet. "By the way, those lethal fuckers are hella cold. You want some socks?"

Truthfully, Allison had noticed that Elena's feet weren't the *only* things that were cold. When the credits finished and the DVD menu had popped up on the television screen again, its bright glow cast over Elena, and that was when Allison noticed that her nipples looked hard enough to cut glass at that point and that she was definitely not wearing a bra. This caused strange tickly feelings in her stomach, but she quickly dismissed the sensation and did her best to avert her attention.

She hated that she was one of those people that couldn't *not* look. Any kind of weird or noticeable thing going on and Allison did double and triple takes. It wasn't that she found the fact that Elena wasn't wearing a bra disturbing or newsworthy for Christ's sake. Boobs were great, but it wasn't like she didn't have a set of her own, and everyone knows what happens when a woman gets cold. It was not a phenomenon. Still, that didn't stop her eyes from darting quickly down at least seven times before Elena seemed to notice her looking and tried to discreetly cross her arms over her chest to hide the perky little monsters. Allison was pretty damn grateful for that, because as soon as they were covered, she was no longer compelled to stare.

"I suppose," Elena agreed. "Thank you."

"I *suppose* you're welcome." Allison darted over to her dresser and pulled another pair of fuzzy socks from her drawer, identical to the ones she was wearing, except purple. She tossed them to Elena and sat back down on the bed.

"You are apparently intent on having us match this evening," Elena said. She slipped the socks over her feet while still attempting to keep her chest covered, using her knees to block them. From her expression, she seemed to be internally cursing her body and her decision not to wear a bra.

"True friends wear matching outfits when they watch horror movies," Allison said. "Everybody knows that." She cracked up at herself again. "I guess I am a fuzzy-sock hoarder."

"Oh?" Elena asked, amused. "You have an entire hoard of fuzzy socks?"

"Don't judge me!"

Smiling, Elena rested her chin against her knees which were still pressed to her chest, and Allison sat right across from her. Silence crept back in on them then, both of them just sort of rocking back and forth and staring at each other.

"So." Allison smacked and popped her lips, just to fill the void, but then quickly decided that words were a must. "Um, so, what's your favorite color?"

"Red."

"Mine's green." Allison beamed. "Together we make Christmas."

"Green is Lucas's favorite as well."

"I know." Knees lifted and pressed up against her chest so that Allison mirrored Elena. "He told me that first night I watched him. We bonded over our mutual love of the color green while he was dunking rubber boats under giant waves of bubble bath."

"Well, it sounds like you and Lucas had a better date than I that night."

"Oh yeah, it was pretty great. I was totally ready to see him again by the end of it."

Elena shook her head and sighed. "I suppose I should go soon." The blinking clock on the DVD player read 4:45. Her eyes widened. "It is quite late."

"Or you could stay." Allison's entire face went red as she realized what she'd just blurted out. She was having such a fun time with Elena, and once she left, Allison would be alone again and most likely bored out of her mind and unable to sleep. She cleared her throat, adding, "for a while."

Elena didn't say anything at first. Her eyes merely stared into Allison's, and Allison was so freaked out by her own word vomit that she almost missed the way Elena's lips were just slightly pulling up at the corners.

"I just meant that I, uh, I don't mind if you wanna stick around a while longer," Allison clarified, trying to fill in the silence. "I probably won't sleep for a while, and I'm…well, this has been fun."

Elena's smile fully blossomed then as she nodded gently against her knees. "It has."

Hope bloomed in Allison's chest in that moment, but then Elena exhaled. "However, I told Lucas I would pick him up first thing in the morning, so I really should be on my way."

"Oh, right. Sure, yeah. That's totally understandable."

They shared another awkward smile before Allison hopped off the bed, slipped on her house shoes, and busied herself with removing the DVD from the player while Elena slipped back into the bathroom to change back into her dress. When she re-emerged, she handed Allison the neat pile of clothes she had worn and slid her feet back into her red pumps.

The two women were silent as they shuffled slowly to the door. Elena turned and opened her mouth to say goodnight, but Allison urged her on. "I'll walk you down."

"Oh." Elena smiled. "Very well."

The elevator ride seemed to only last about a second, although Allison frequently felt the thing crawled. It landed at ground level way too soon, and then she and Elena took baby steps all the way out of the building.

When they stepped outside, the warm night breeze washed over them and both women breathed it in. "Uh," Allison muttered. "It's dark. Might as well walk you to your car, just to be safe."

"Are you sure?" Elena asked. "It is a bit far."

"Yeah. I don't mind."

They continued their shuffling crawl a few blocks over to Elena's waiting black Mercedes. Elena held her clutch tightly in her hands while Allison crossed her arms over her chest and they stood across from one another. Neither actually made any attempt to move or leave. The silence between them dragged on for quite some time before Elena finally cleared her throat and said, "Well, good night then."

"Yeah, good night." Allison smiled and gave an awkward little wave of her hand.

Elena placed a hand on her arm. "I really did have fun, Allison. Thank you."

Allison could do little more than smile and watch as Elena turned and lowered herself into the car. When the engine started, Allison let out a long sigh and turned to walk back to the dorm, wondering when Lucas might need a babysitter again.

Chapter Eleven

"Wow, you look terrible."

Elena rolled her eyes as she settled Lucas into a high chair at the restaurant table before dropping into the chair opposite Vivian. "Sometimes, I have to remind myself that I love you."

Chuckling, Vivian leaned over to kiss Lucas's cheek and place a small coloring mat and crayons on the table in front of him. "Thank you!" He latched onto her finger and held it tightly in one hand as he used his other to grab the green crayon and begin scribbling all over the paper.

"You're welcome, sweet pea." Vivian pulled her index finger from his grasp as she cooed at him. She watched as Elena ran a hand through her hair and reached for her menu. "So, are you going to tell me why you look like you had a wild party last night and woke up hung over?"

Elena glared. "Well, obviously, I did not have a wild party."

"Obviously. So, spill."

"I was out," Elena said. "Later than I expected to be."

"Oh *really*?"

Elena ignored Vivian's teasing tone, raising an eyebrow as she plowed right through and said, "And then of course my mother called me at six a.m. and put Lucas on the phone." She turned to Lucas. "And what did you say very loudly in Momma's ear, munchkin?"

"Momma!" Lucas quoted himself. "I'm awake! Where are you?"

"That's right," Elena said as Vivian laughed. "*Very* loudly."

"Uh-huh," Vivian said. "Let's get back to the 'out late' part. Where exactly *were* you, Elena?"

Elena cleared her throat and straightened her shoulders as she kept her eyes fixed on her menu. "I was at NYU with Allison."

"Alson!" Lucas never lifted his gaze from the paper where his little hand was still scribbling animatedly away.

"Allison, huh?" Vivian asked, smirking.

"Yes, Vivian," Elena snapped. "Allison, the babysitter. What is the big deal? *You* were the one who told me to take her backpack to her."

"Yes, but giving someone a backpack takes all of five seconds."

"And?" Elena asked. "Am I not allowed to make friends?"

"Well, I don't know why you would *need* any new friends considering the fact that you already have me and I am amazing." Elena rolled her eyes but smiled. "*But* yes, I suppose you're welcome to make new *friends*."

Vivian would not necessarily refer to the budding relationship between Elena and the babysitter as strictly friendship. But the fact that Elena was completely oblivious to the developing chemistry did not surprise Vivian.

The conversation was put on hold as Vivian and Elena gave the waiter their orders.

Elena reached down into the large bag she carried with her on her outings with Lucas and pulled out a small squeeze carton of organic apple juice. She pulled the little straw from the side and popped it through the hole on the top of the carton before setting it in front of her son. "Here you go, munchkin."

"Is it apple?" Lucas asked, reaching for the juice.

"Of course." Elena pointed to the picture of the apple slices on the front of the carton. "See the picture?"

"Oh." Lucas nodded as his little finger traced over the picture. "Thank you!" He brought the little straw up to his mouth to drink.

"You are very welcome, dear."

"So," Vivian said. "What did you and Allison do last night?"

"Oh nothing." Elena flicked her hand in the air.

"Oh, I see." Vivian laughed. "So, you were out late doing nothing. That makes complete sense. Nothing is one of my favorite pastimes as well. Boy, if I could count all the times that nothing has kept me out late."

Elena sighed. "Must you always be so frustrating?"

"Must you always give vague responses?"

"We watched a movie! There, are you happy? We watched a movie and then I went home. I had no intentions of staying when I took Allison her backpack, but she was kind enough to invite me up to her dorm room. She had no plans for the evening, and obviously, neither did I; thus, she asked if I would watch a movie with her and I agreed. End of story."

Vivian nearly bit through her tongue to keep from both squealing with excitement and laughing at her best friend's obviously flustered state. When she was able to control both urges, she cleared her throat. "So, you two really are becoming friends then?"

"Yes, I suppose we are." She smirked at Vivian. "I have to have *someone* I can complain about *you* to."

"Oh please," Vivian said with a dismissive wave of her hand. "So, what movie did you watch?"

"Ugh, some foul horror film featuring a cannibal and a psychotic man with a penchant for lotion and wearing other people's skins."

"*The Silence of the Lambs.*"

"You've seen it?"

"Of course. It's a classic." Vivian laughed at Elena's disgusted expression. "How did Allison talk you into watching that movie?"

"She simply asked me," Elena said with a light shrug of her shoulders. She took a sip of her water and ran a hand through her short, dark locks. "I *can* be adventurous, Viv."

"Uh-huh. Sure you can, babe."

The glare she received only made Vivian laugh harder. She reached across the table and patted Elena's hand. "Oh relax. I'm only teasing."

"I know." Elena squeezed her hand. "It seems that is something you and Allison have in common."

"What? Teasing you?"

"Teasing in general. She has quite the sense of humor. In fact, she is incredibly entertaining if you spend a bit of time with her."

"Is that so?"

"Yes. I can see why Lucas loves spending time with her. There is rarely a dull moment."

"So, you like her?" Vivian slipped the question in, hoping it didn't sound too suggestive.

Elena frowned. "Yes, I suppose I do quite like her. It's strange, really. Don't you think?"

"Why would it be strange?"

"She is so different from me, so free and relaxed."

"Mm," Vivian said, watching her friend closely.

"She is unrefined and sometimes has the mouth of a sailor, and she wears tatty jean jackets and fuzzy socks, for goodness' sake."

Vivian smiled as she saw how her friend's gaze darted all over the surface of the table, how her breath quickened as she spoke; it made Vivian's heart swell. *This is ridiculous,* she thought. But Elena's obliviousness to her growing feelings was overwhelming and if Vivian was being honest, somewhat adorable.

It made Vivian feel like a teenager again, just observing it made her want to shake Elena and scream, *kiss her already!* She couldn't bring herself to disrupt the organic development that seemed to be occurring between the two women, though. Sure, she would do everything she could to help nudge them in the right direction, but she wouldn't intervene on a grand scale. She knew this had to be natural, and Vivian honestly had no doubt that it would come to fruition on its own. She just hoped it would happen sooner rather than later.

If anyone deserved happiness and love, it was Elena. Vivian believed that.

"We could *not be* more opposite, but yes. I can't explain it, but I *do* very much like her. She makes me laugh. She makes me laugh all the time."

"That's nice," Vivian whispered. It was an important moment, a moment in which Elena Vega began to open her heart to someone who was beautifully both completely wrong and completely right for her. It was a moment that Vivian knew would change everything.

"Yes," Elena muttered. "It is."

She looked up at Vivian then and smiled warmly. "I think I'd quite like to be friends with her."

Vivian returned her smile. "Good," she said. But then she couldn't resist sticking her tongue out at her. "Despite how *utterly* jealous I am of your budding new friendship, it's true that you can never have too many good friends. And I, for one, think it's wonderful that you're both so different. It's good for you to branch out a bit. Your entire life revolves around being proper. Maybe Allison will loosen you up a bit."

"Alson!" Lucas's mouth remained still halfway wrapped around his straw while he scribbled with his crayons.

Vivian's shoulders bounced with her laughter, and Elena just shook her head and ran a hand through her son's hair. "That's right," she said. "Allison."

"Alson likes dinosaurs."

"What else does Allison like, buddy?" Vivian asked.

"Um..." His eyes widened and a smile stretched his lips. "Me!"

Allison barreled through the door of her dorm, tripping over her feet and tumbling to the ground. Grunting with the force of the fall, she crawled back to her feet. She was instantly greeted by her roommate and best friend's confused expression as the other girl lay in bed, drinking a beer and watching TV.

"Um, did someone die?" Macy asked in her thick Australian accent.

"No, why?" Allison tossed her backpack to the floor and began stripping.

"Because you just flew through the door like someone set your fuckin' pants on fire? Or am I the only one of us who noticed that?"

Allison laughed as she yanked her shirt over her head, left standing in only her green bra and bright blue boy shorts. "Just in a bit of a hurry. I've got to babysit tonight."

"Oooooh, that explains it then." Macy smirked. "Hot, rich, and fabulous calls, and you can't wait to get outta here. Does she know about your weird food obsessions yet? I'd wait a bit until she falls for you properly."

"You're one to talk." Allison rolled her eyes. "I'm surprised your dates don't run screaming when they find out about your obsession with Vincent Price. Besides, it isn't like that. Elena and I are just—"

"Just what? Just friends?"

"Yeah, we're *friends*." Allison changed into a fresh pair of skin-tight jeans and a three-quarter sleeve blue and green button-up. "And it's a job. You know I need the money."

"Uh-huh." Snorting with laughter, she took another sip of her beer. "Sure it is."

"It *is*." Allison stuffed some snacks into her backpack and removed a few of her textbooks.

"Whatever you say, mate. A tip though: when you finally bed her, don't be wearing the fuzzy socks. It's a moodkiller."

"*Anyway*," Allison hissed. "I'm late, so that's why I was running. I had Professor Rockford, and you know she rambles."

"That's the understatement of the year." Macy snorted. "The damn subject is twenty-first century American fiction, but the woman goes on about her fifteen cats half the time like she's a few roos loose in the top paddock, if you know what I mean."

"Nope, actually." Allison laughed. "I don't have a clue what you just said, but yeah, she rambles." She slung her backpack, which was much lighter now, over her shoulder and headed for the door.

"I'm headed out, but I shouldn't be home too late."

"Right, yeah. Best get a wriggle on then. You don't want to keep fancy pants waiting."

Allison rolled her eyes and waved before heading for the elevator.

"Uh, Elena?"

Allison had knocked on Elena's door several times but received no answer, so she had finally checked the knob and saw that it gave easily. She pushed the front door open just a crack and poked her head in.

She slipped inside and closed the door behind her. "Elena?" she called again as she took hesitant steps through the house. "Your door was unlocked, so I'm like, inside the house and stuff."

She walked cautiously toward the hallway, mumbling. "Please don't think I'm a robber and like jump out and shoot me or something."

Slinking down the hallway toward Elena's bedroom, Allison tapped on the door. "Elena?" she called through the wood but still heard nothing in reply. She slowly opened the door and poked her head in.

With a wave of relief, she heard the rushing sound of a shower. She was about to shut the door and head back toward the living room to wait for her employer when something caught her eye. She giggled as she realized what it was.

Lucas was fast asleep and sprawled out on his stomach on Elena's bed, halfway beneath the covers and halfway beneath one of Elena's pillows. Allison smiled as she darted over toward the bed and sat down. She reached over to rub small circles in the boy's back.

After a few minutes, Allison slowly stood up again and bent down and pressed a kiss to the bit of Lucas's head that was sticking out from under the pillow.

In that exact moment, Elena padded out of her bathroom, wrapped in nothing but a fluffy red towel. Her eyes went wide, and a screeching yelp escaped her as she saw someone bending over her bed. She grabbed the nearest thing to her, a bottle of perfume from the bathroom counter, and chucked it at the intruder. "Shit!" Elena exclaimed, clapping a hand over her mouth. The small, yet heavy perfume bottle smacked Allison square between the eyes with a sickening thud.

"Unnh," Allison groaned, her hand shooting up to her forehead as her eyes rolled back and she crashed to the bedroom floor, unconscious.

Dark blonde lashes fluttered slowly open, and Allison let out a deep groan, her head throbbing with a fury. She barely got her eyes open before she felt tiny hands press at her cheeks and then saw wide honey eyes hovering over her face, close enough to make her cross-eyed.

"HI!" Lucas shouted in her face.

Allison tried to laugh but it only caused her head to throb harder. "Hi," she croaked. Her side felt damp. Had Lucas peed on her?

She gently reached up and moved Lucas out of the way a bit. She was lying across Elena's lap, her right side pressed against the woman's body, which was still wrapped in a bath towel. That explained the dampness.

"Hi." She looked up into Elena's shimmering eyes.

"I'm so sorry." Fingertips rubbed gently at the space between Allison's eyes. "You are already beginning to bruise."

Allison's brow furrowed, which of course hurt like hell. "What, uh, what happened?"

"Momma tacked you with a fume bottle!"

"Lucas, don't sound so pleased about it." But a smile pulled at the corners of Elena's lips.

"Say what?" Allison smiled back up at her. "You attacked me?"

"Unfortunately, yes. I didn't know you were here. I came out of the shower, and there was a person leaning over my son. I suppose I just acted on instinct."

"And did what exactly?"

"Threw a perfume bottle at you." A vast amount of red flooded Elena's face. "I apparently have terrible aim, because I was aiming for your back as you were bent when I threw it, but then you turned around and it somehow hit you in the face. You blacked out."

"If you thought I stunk, Elena, you could have just *offered* me some perfume, you know? You didn't have to throw the whole bottle at me."

Elena laughed and pinched Allison's side. "Always making jokes."

Reaching up, Allison cupped a hand around Elena's cheek. "Keeps things fun, don't you think?"

Elena's breath hitched in her throat at the look in Allison's eyes, and she nodded against the blonde's hand. "Indeed."

Allison, realizing what she was doing, cleared her throat and quickly dropped her hand. She tried to sit up. Elena moved to help her, though she had to keep one hand tightly pressed to her towel to keep it from falling open. Allison wobbled a little even in only a sitting position.

"Whoa." She groaned. "Dizzy."

Elena frowned as she watched her. "Perhaps we should make a trip to the emergency room?"

"No, no way." She hated hospitals. "I'm fine. Just got a bit of a headache." That was a massive understatement, but Allison didn't want to make Elena feel any worse about what happened, given that it was really *her* fault for sneaking into the woman's bedroom without her knowledge. Plus, she didn't want Elena worrying too much over her.

"Are you sure?"

"I'm sure, yeah." Allison waved her off. "Could I just have some aspirin or something?"

"Of course, yes." Elena jumped to her feet. Allison couldn't help but stare at the woman. Water droplets slipped over her bare shoulders and down until they became lost in the fluffy material of the red towel. Anyone with functioning eyes would be unable to look away from *that*.

"Let's get you up on the bed, and then I will get some aspirin for you," Elena said, helping her to her feet. Allison wobbled again and quickly dropped down onto Elena's bed. The blankets were all pulled back from where Lucas had been sleeping, so Allison couldn't help but breathe in the scent from the exposed sheets.

Elena returned from the bathroom with a small bottle of pills tucked between her teeth and a small glass with water. Allison swallowed two pills and drained the glass. "Thank you."

Lucas crawled up on the bed and practically lay down on top of Allison. "Let her breathe, munchkin."

Lucas looked down at Allison. "Can you breathe, Alson?"

"Yeah, little man. I can breathe."

Sticking his tongue out at his mother, he collapsed on top of Allison once more.

Allison's hand moved to Lucas's back as he laid his head on her chest. Her eyes then locked onto Elena, who was watching them both. Silence and stillness filled the room as they stared at one another for a long moment before Allison's gaze slipped down to the fluffy red towel and back up again.

Flushing crimson, Elena cleared her throat roughly. "Well, I suppose I should dress myself."

Allison smirked. "Yeah, I suppose you should. You won't want to keep your date waiting."

"Oh Allison, no. I can't possibly continue with the night as planned. I should cancel and stay here to monitor you. You could have a concussion, for all we know."

Tingles buzzed lightly on Allison's skin at the concern in Elena's tone, but she just shook her head in response. "No way. I'm fine. You can't possibly miss this date."

"Oh?" Elena asked. "And why is that?"

"Because what if this guy turns out to be your Prince Charming or something?"

Elena snorted at that.

"He could sweep you off your feet and like, I don't know, wake you up from a sleeping curse or something."

"Allison, really. I think I should stay. I'm worried you might need to see a doctor."

"Elena, I'm fine. And you're *going*. End of discussion. Besides, the post-date ranting is my favorite part."

In truth, Allison was a little conflicted. She wanted Elena to go on the date, but she also wanted her to cancel. Elena really deserved to find happiness and love and all of that mess, even though it wasn't something Allison had ever imagined for herself. But for some reason, the thought of Elena out on dates didn't always sit right with her.

However, she was also a little worried that if Elena canceled the date, she would end up going home a lot earlier than usual. She really missed Lucas, even though it had only been a few days. She wanted to spend as much time with him as possible, even if she *did* have a raging headache.

"Go on," she said. "Go get fancy."

Elena rolled her eyes and disappeared into her closet.

Chapter Twelve

Elena slipped on her heels and took one last glance in the large full-length mirror that hung in her closet. She wore a light gray dress with a circle neck and a thick black belt around the waist. Her dark locks were perfectly coiffed and settled gently around her face, and the black pumps she wore accentuated her toned calves.

"How's this?" she asked as she stepped through the open archway of her massive walk-in closet and out into the main portion of her bedroom. "Allison?"

She stepped closer to the bed where the blonde lay with Lucas still atop her chest. Allison was sound asleep, as was the small boy lying on top of her. Her chin rested atop Lucas's head and one of her arms was hooked tightly over Lucas's back.

Elena couldn't bring herself to move. She stood beside her bed and stared down at the two sleeping people settled against her sheets. Something inside her warmed at the sight, little flames igniting in her stomach and chest.

Her gaze roamed over Allison, whose lips slightly parted and moved with each deep breath. She chuckled as Allison's nose twitched and wriggled, tickled by the flyaway hairs on her son's head. But then she focused on the darkening bruise now nearly covering Allison's entire forehead.

Guilt gnawed at her insides, causing her stomach to lurch. She could hardly fault herself for her actions, but it certainly did little to make her feel better about the outcome. She reached forward before she could stop herself and grazed her fingertips gently over the puffy, purpled flesh.

Elena could feel the fluid beneath the bruising as it squished beneath her fingertips, the skin swollen and pliant, and it only made that uncomfortable feeling in her gut grow. She pulled her hand away, suddenly conscious of causing the younger woman pain.

When she did, she was greeted by two, heavy-lidded but assuredly open eyes.

"Oh." The word was hardly more than a whisper between her teeth. "I'm sorry. Did I hurt you?"

Allison shook her head, her chin rubbing through Lucas's messy hair.

"Would you like an ice pack?"

Allison's forehead creased and she hissed in pain. "Right," she croaked, "for my head." She laughed at herself. "Sure, thanks."

"Okay." Elena turned to leave the room, but Allison's groggy voice called out to her again.

"Did we, me and the little man..." She frowned. "Have we been asleep this whole time? I mean, are you already back from your date?"

Elena patted her arm. "No, Allison. I haven't left yet."

"Wow. I guess that blow to the head really took it out of me."

Elena's expression crumpled, and Allison quickly shifted under Lucas's body to grab Elena's hand and lace their fingers together. "Hey, hey, I didn't mean anything by that."

Nodding, Elena squeezed Allison's fingers then pulled her hand free and turned toward the door again. "I will grab that ice pack for you."

She had barely taken a step, though, when the chime of the doorbell rang through the enormous house, catching both women off guard.

"I suppose my date is here."

"Yup." Allison smacked her lips and slowly pushed herself up. She carefully shifted Lucas off of her chest and settled him gently back against the sheets before rising from the bed. "I'll grab the ice pack myself."

They walked down the hallway together, their shoulders occasionally brushing. Before they made it to the end of the hall, where the path split to lead further into the house in one direction and toward the foyer in the other, Allison nudged Elena's arm with her elbow. "So, what do you think you'll get this time?"

Elena arched one perfectly sculpted brow. "What do you mean?"

"Oh, you know," Allison said, her smile only growing. "Could be another dude with bowel issues."

"Very funny." Elena bumped Allison's elbow with her own.

"Could be a big hairy Sasquatch. Or like, a guy with a lisp so bad that you can't even understand what he's saying, and, every time he asks you a question, he accidentally spits on you. Oh, or he could be totally sexist or something. That would be a quick way to piss you off. Oh, what if it's like one of those middle-aged men that still lives with his mother and talks about her all through dinner? Do you take issue with severe Momma's boys? What if Lucas turns out to be one? What if the guy is like a major horndog and just makes lewd comments the entire time or stares at other women the whole date? Would you b—"

Elena threw out a hand and cupped it over Allison's mouth. "That's quite enough, dear. I will never make it out the door if you continue to plant such horrid scenarios in my mind."

Allison laughed into Elena's smooth palm.

"What if it's not even a person?" she said when Elena moved her hand. "What if it's like an alien in a man suit and it tries to abduct you and take you back to its mothership to probe you and implant microchips in your brain and alien baby eggs in your ut—"

Elena's palm was back over Allison's mouth again. Elena turned full-bodied toward her as she tackled Allison, both of them wrapped up in their shared laughter—Elena's melodic and floating through the air and Allison's muffled against the heat of Elena's palm.

"Hush," Elena said. Allison's back was pressed against the wall of the hallway, with one of her hands gripping Elena's wrist and the other splayed across her waist. Their eyes locked.

"Are you going to stop now?" Elena asked.

Allison's shoulders shook with her muted laughter, but she nodded to show her surrender. When Elena's palm dropped from her mouth, it slipped down to rest on her shoulder. They continued to stare at each other, their laughter slowly fading, when the doorbell chimed again, and both women practically jumped out of their skins. They shot apart like their flesh was electric and they had just zapped the hell out of one another.

They smiled awkwardly at each other as Elena pointed toward the foyer. "I should get the door."

"Yeah." Allison nodded. "And I should get that ice pack."

"Indeed."

They lingered another moment before both women wordlessly sprang into action. Elena headed into the foyer and Allison moved into the kitchen, speeding like lightning to the freezer, and yanking a small ice pack from the back. It was shaped like a dinosaur. A little embarrassing, but it would get the job done.

Allison hummed in delight as she pressed the cold plastic to her forehead. "*Yes.*" For a moment, she forgot everything beyond the cool relief this frozen dinosaur offered her, but then she heard Elena's laughter spill in from the foyer.

She moved from the kitchen to get a better view, stopping at the opening of the hallway and bracing herself on the wall as she leaned back to see. She could see Elena standing in the open doorway, her hand moving as if in time to something she was saying, but Allison couldn't see the person on the other side. Since she couldn't even see the man's head poking up above Elena's, she assumed that the woman had gotten strapped with another shorty, but then Elena shifted: she turned to grab her clutch from the foyer table, and the person finally came into view.

Allison's jaw practically smacked into her chest. It wasn't a short man at all. It was a *woman*.

"What the—Shit!" Allison hissed, caught off guard by the presence of a hot lady on Elena Vega's doorstep. She momentarily let go of the wall and tried to catch herself, but there was nothing for her to grasp. She fell flat on her back in the mouth of the hallway with a loud grunt.

She soon heard the sound of heels clicking speedily toward her, and then Elena's hands were sliding under her arms to help her up.

"Allison? What happened? Are you all right? Is it your head? Are you dizzy?"

"Whoa, twenty questions." Allison's gaze shot right by Elena and back to the woman still standing in the open doorway and now staring back at her with a curious expression.

Pulling Allison to her feet, Elena whispered, "Are you all right?"

Bright green eyes jumped quickly back and forth between Elena and the woman in the doorway, and before she could stop herself, she blurted, "What is *that*?"

"I'm sorry?" Elena asked.

"I mean, who, I mean what...what is—" The words tangled as Allison was unable to keep up with her own rapid-fire thoughts. "That's a *woman*," she finally managed to spit out.

Elena glanced over her shoulder and offered her date a smile while holding up her index finger to indicate she only needed another minute. She turned back to Allison, her eyes locking hard onto her. She shuffled a bit under Allison's questioning gaze, but her voice was clear and confident. "Yes. Rather observant of you, dear."

"You're going out with a *woman*?" Allison stressed the word again as if she simply could not digest the shocking arrival of her own gender upon the doorstep. "Like on a *date*? A *date* date?"

"Yes, Allison. Why else would a woman be dressed like that and standing in my doorway?" Her gaze then grew conflicted. She lowered her voice to a whisper. "Is that...do you take issue with this?"

"Huh? What do you mean?"

"With my dating a woman. Do you take issue with my sexuality?"

"What?" Allison sputtered, choking on her own saliva. "Elena! *No*!"

Elena let out a sigh of obvious relief. "Oh," she whispered. "Okay then. Wonderful."

"I'm a little shocked," Allison admitted. "But no, of course I don't have a problem with it. I just didn't know you were into women."

I'm into women, Allison wanted to say. Wanted to shout it, even. *Exclusively into women!* The words were on the tip of her tongue, but Elena spoke before she could put them to voice.

"Neither did *I* for many years." She patted Allison's arm. "Now, are you sure I shouldn't stay?"

"No, no," Allison said. "Go. You should definitely go."

Elena narrowed her eyes for a moment before nodding. "Very well. Then you should probably wake Lucas to feed him. But if he wants to go back to bed afterward, that is fine."

"Oh right, yeah," Allison said. "Got it."

"Okay." Elena smiled and nodded. "I won't be home too late." She headed for the door, leaving an utterly astounded Allison in her wake.

Alexis was a gorgeous woman. Her dark braids fell over her exposed shoulders in a gorgeous wave, and her light brown skin was flawless, from what Elena could see. She had brown eyes so light that they were almost amber and positively mesmerizing. She was simply stunning.

The woman also practically oozed money, from her Jimmy Choos to her Cartier diamond earrings. She drove Elena in her new Ferrari to one of the most expensive restaurants in Manhattan.

"I hope you like sushi," Alexis said as she opened the door for Elena and let her step inside first.

"I do," Elena said, gaze roaming over the interior design of the restaurant.

Once they were seated, Alexis asked about her day and about her son, and Elena returned in kind with a few questions of her own. As the woman answered, Elena couldn't help but to check her phone under the table. She had kept it clutched tightly in her hand the entire drive to the restaurant in case it vibrated. Despite Allison's reassurances, Elena was concerned she could have a concussion. She could be in pain. She could pass out again, and no one would be there to help her, and there would be no way for Elena to know. Such possibilities were driving her mad.

Alexis cleared her throat pointedly and Elena's head shot up. "My apologies," Elena said, dropping her phone into her lap and forcing her hands away from the device. Alexis seemed somewhat perturbed, her lips pursing for a moment, but she then put on a smile and nodded. They placed their orders, and Elena did her best not to let her mind wander back to the babysitter.

When their sushi arrived, Alexis smiled at Elena. "So, how am I doing so far?"

Elena reached for her chopsticks. "Quite well."

"Fantastic. Because I am *quite* interested. I simply wanted to make sure that you were enjoying yourself."

"I am, thank you."

"So," Alexis said, taking a sip of her wine. "What is your type? Or, I suppose a better question would be to ask what you are looking for in a relationship. *Are* you even looking for a relationship?"

Elena took a sip of her wine and sighed. "Let's see."

"I mean, I just assumed that a person like Elena Vega would never be into women, you know?" Allison rambled as she tapped her fingers against the kitchen countertop. "She just seems so, I don't know, traditional? Conservative?"

"Now I'm just making assumptions, huh?" Allison shook her head. "Obviously, that is a dumb thing to do, because *obviously,* I was completely and utterly wrong, right?"

Wide honey eyes blinked at her as Lucas sloppily sucked and chewed on a dinosaur-shaped chicken nugget. Ketchup spotted his cheeks and mouth and the one hand he used to feed himself. He smiled around the nugget and nodded.

"Yeah, you're right. I'm never making assumptions again." She popped a few of her own dinosaur-shaped nuggets into her mouth. "But why wouldn't she tell me that she liked chicks too? We're friends, right? You'd think that that would be something you would tell your friend."

"Then again, I haven't told her that *I* like women, so I guess I really don't have any room to talk, do I?"

"Nope!" Lucas dunked a nugget into his ketchup, splattering it, and Allison chuckled at the kid.

"Do you even know what I'm talking about?"

He shook his head and reached for his juice cup. "Nope!" he repeated, and Allison laughed even harder.

"I just..." she started again. "I usually have awesome gaydar, even on myself. I mean, I knew *I* was gay by the time I was like four and Olivia Marks gave me her socks when mine got holes in them at the home. I totally worshipped the ground that toddler walked on."

"I'm a todder!" Lucas exclaimed.

"You totally are," Allison said, smiling at the happy boy. She sighed as she carried their now-empty plates to the sink and began to wash them. Allison wetted a washcloth and walked over to clean Lucas's face. He giggled as the cloth tickled at his neck, and Allison pressed a kiss to his forehead.

"You're such a good listener, kid."

"I honestly don't know if I am looking for a serious relationship at this point." Elena said. "I have been out of the dating game for quite a while now, as my son and my career are my priorities."

"That's understandable." Alexis nodded. "I ended a four-year relationship a little over six months ago, so I'm not sure if I am looking for something terribly serious just yet either. But then again, you never know. If something clicks, it clicks. I think..."

Elena's phone vibrated in her lap and she squirmed, fingers itching to grab it. She tried to force her focus onto Alexis as the woman went on about how she was mostly looking for a bit of fun, but she couldn't do it. Her mind kept racing with thoughts of Allison. What if she was feeling dizzy or hurt? What if she needed Elena to take her to the hospital? She reached for her phone and subtly tried to glance at it under the table.

When she saw it was merely an email update, Elena felt her stomach sink in disappointment, though she wasn't sure why. Why would she be disappointed not to receive an emergency text from Allison? It wasn't as if she *wanted* the woman to be injured.

It took a moment for Elena to realize that her date was no longer speaking, and then the silence suddenly seemed very daunting. She glanced up to find Alexis watching her, jaw set as her lips strained with a tight and obviously forced smile.

"Is there a problem?" Alexis asked.

"No, no problem," Elena said. "I was just—"

"Checking your phone." Alexis placed her chopsticks down on her plate and dropped her hands to her lap as she leaned back in her chair. "*Again.*"

Elena let out a long sigh and nodded. "I'm sorry, Alexis. I am concerned about my son's babysitter."

"May I ask why?"

"We had a bit of an accident earlier," Elena explained, "and she hurt her head. I simply want to be sure she is okay."

"I see." Alexis nodded.

"I *am* sorry," Elena said again. She could feel the heat rising in her cheeks. She was embarrassed by her own behavior. "I don't mean to be rude. Please, back to what you were saying."

"Do you *know* what I was saying?" Alexis asked, reaching for her wine, and Elena felt her chest flood with guilt. It must have shown on her face because Alexis nodded and said, "I thought not."

Elena shifted in her seat, crossing and uncrossing her legs under the table. "Alexis—"

"It is fine, Elena." The slightly sharp edge to her tone made it seem like it certainly was *not* fine, but Elena didn't argue. She simply nodded and let Alexis take the lead. "Let's start over."

Elena gave her a small smile, and she appreciated the effort Alexis made to plaster on a smile of her own despite the fact that things had become slightly tense between them. "Very well."

"What are you looking for in a relationship?" Alexis asked again.

"I haven't put much thought into it," Elena said. She swished her wine gently in her glass before taking a long sip. "I suppose there would be a number of things that would cause me to favor a person."

"Such as?"

"Well, he or she would obviously have to be good with children. Lucas would have to approve, of course."

"Of course." Alexis said. "Go on."

"Proper hygiene is a must." Elena shook her head. "And certainly no talk of restroom activities."

Alexis's lips parted as she stared at her. "I'm sorry. What?"

"My previous date," Elena said, and Alexis frowned.

"That is unfortunate."

"Yes." Elena nodded. "He carried on a full conversation about his IBS with the waitress. The poor girl was obviously uncomfortable."

"I hope you didn't plan a second date."

"Of course not." Elena chuckled. "The first made for quite the hysterical rant from Allison, though, so the night at least ended in a laugh."

"Allison?"

Elena blinked. She had not meant to bring up Allison, but she had slipped into the conversation regardless. Elena licked her lips and cleared her throat. "Allison is the babysitter I mentioned."

She was surprised when Alexis let out a sigh that bordered on a laugh. It sounded hard for a laugh, bordering on angry, and Elena stiffened in her chair.

"Is something funny?"

Alexis shook her head. "I'm sorry, Elena," she said. "It just seems like you are more interested in your babysitter tonight than you are in me."

The words hit Elena like a hard punch to the gut. Her heart began to pound against her ribcage, and a lump formed in her throat. Her head swam with thoughts of Allison, with looks and laughter and little touches, and, suddenly, it was as if something clicked firmly into place and Elena couldn't breathe.

"I..." She pushed up out of her chair, her hand clamping around her phone and clutch.

"Elena?" Alexis looked up at her, brows knitting together.

Elena's throat felt tight and dry and her eyes stung horribly. She could feel the heat in her face and knew it must be visible. "I need to go," she said. "I, I'm sorry. I should go."

Alexis gaped at her and Elena made quick work of pulling several large bills from her clutch and placing them on the table. "I will hail a cab. Dinner is on me. Thank you for a lovely evening, Alexis, and, again, I am terribly sorry about this."

She couldn't bring herself to wait for a response before speeding away, heels clicking loudly with every frantic step.

Chapter Thirteen

The slim stick heels of Elena's black pumps bounced rapidly against the taxi floor as she pressed the first number on her speed dial. Her heart was a flapping, fluttering mess, thudding into her ribcage in painful tremors as she waited through three agonizingly long rings before her best friend's voice finally drifted through the line.

"Elena?" Vivian said. "I thought you were supposed to be on a da—"

"It's Allison," Elena blurted.

Vivian snorted into the phone. "Really Elena? I've known you basically my entire life, okay? I know your voice almost better than my own. Plus, I've only had one glass of wine tonight. I know it's you."

"Of course it's me! That's not what I meant. I meant that it's *Allison*."

"That is literally exactly what you said the first time. So, you're telling me that you meant to say what you actually said? Because if so, then you have completely lost me."

Elena let out a trembling, frustrated sigh. "Will you shut up and listen, please?"

"Well, stop repeating yourself."

The ring of a doorbell echoed through Elena's phone, followed quickly by Vivian saying, "Oh, hold on, babe. There's someone at my door."

"I know."

"What do you mean?"

Vivian opened her front door to reveal a frazzled Elena, her phone still pressed to her ear and a taxi pulling away from the curb. She started to laugh, but the look in her friend's eyes caused the sound to die in her throat. Vivian nearly dropped her phone as she immediately reached out for her best friend and tugged her into the house.

"All right, big guy," Allison whispered. Lucas's head lay lazily atop her shoulder, his face buried into the crook of her neck as she carried him down the hallway. One of his fists curled into the neckline of her shirt and the other dangled limply behind them. He had fallen asleep in Allison's lap about fifteen minutes into a movie.

"Time for little boys with sneakily gay mommies to go to bed." She rolled her eyes. "Sneakily gay mommies who don't tell equally gay babysitters that they are ga-ay."

"Or bisexual." She lay Lucas in his bed. His fist clung to her shirt and she had to pry his fingers from the neckline before she could stand up again. "Or pansexual." She tucked him in tightly. "Hot-sexual. Dates hot people. Whatever."

Allison realized she was ranting. "Wow," she said as she leaned down and pressed two tender kisses to Lucas's forehead. "I'm so glad you're asleep right now, kid."

She then slipped from his room, closing the door behind her.

"You ran out on your date?" Vivian handed Elena a glass of wine, dropped onto the couch beside her, and patted her knee.

"Yes, I ran out on my date." Elena huffed. "*Politely*. I *politely* ran out on my date."

"How do you *politely* run out on a date?" Vivian chuckled. "And I still don't understand why."

"*Because!*" Elena nearly shouted at her. "Because I *couldn't* stay there, Viv! I panicked, and I couldn't stay there, because I realized..."

Elena trailed off, visibly swallowing. Vivian wanted to encourage her, but instead she kept quiet, waiting for Elena to say whatever it was she needed to say in her own time. She could only recall a few times in their lives in which she had seen Elena this genuinely disturbed. The first was in junior high school when Elena got her first ever period and bled right through her skirt and onto her chair in Keyboarding class. Vivian had chased after her after threatening to beat the shit out of Matthew Douglas, a snotty rich boy with an ugly bowl cut and a penchant for teasing all the girls. She bought a tampon from the coin machine in the girls' bathroom and helped Elena figure out how to insert it, and they hid out in there until Nora was called to collect them. The second time was when Elena lost her virginity to Preston McBride, a snobby heir to a multi-million dollar corporation, the summer before their senior year. Vivian had had to endure eight days of Elena crying over the possibility of being pregnant and cursing herself over the one time she actually allowed herself to be impulsive. The day her period came had been a relief to them both.

"Because I realized that it's Allison."

Vivian leaned a little toward her friend, locking gazes with her. She sincerely hoped that what she assumed was happening in this moment was *actually* happening, and her heart pounded in her chest.

"Honey," Vivian cooed, reaching out to lace her fingers through Elena's, "you keep saying that, but you are going to have to clarify what you mean, because I can't read your mind."

Like hell I can't read your mind, Vivian thought, her insides practically vibrating with the intensity of the moment. *I just want to hear you say it!*

Elena's lips parted as if she were about to answer, but then she merely reached for her wine and tipped it back. Vivian's eyes widened as Elena drained the entire glass in one massive strained gulp.

Oh yeah, Vivian thought, *this is totally happening.*

As soon as Elena choked her way through the swallow, she said, "I think I may be falling for Allison."

Vivian squealed like a giddy teenager on the inside but managed to keep her composure. She had to be the one to hold it together, because Elena certainly wouldn't. This one small yet major confession tore down the floodgates, and Elena launched into a massive, rambling explanation.

"I was on the date," Elena told her. "I was on the date with Alexis, and things were going well. Okay, actually, things weren't going so well. She was gorgeous and funny and well-mannered, but I was admittedly not the best date. Allison got hurt earlier this evening, nothing terribly serious, but I was concerned all throughout dinner and kept checking my phone."

"You would have been annoyed if someone did that to you," Vivian said.

"I know." Elena groaned. "I was awful, but I couldn't help myself. I kept thinking about her and worrying about her, and then Alexis suggested..."

"What?"

"She said I seemed more interested in the babysitter than in her."

Vivian pressed her lips together to keep from smiling, because Elena already looked nervous and embarrassed, and she didn't want to add to it, but it was a definite struggle.

"And then it just hit me," Elena said, taking a shaky breath as her heels tapped against the floor. "I realized that she was right. I was interested in Allison. I *am* interested in Allison."

Resisting the urge to clap was terribly difficult because Vivian was on cloud nine watching Elena's eyes grow distant yet warmer.

"I suppose it has been developing since the beginning." Elena twisted her fingers together in her lap. "Though I somehow never noticed it. We would spend time together after my dates, and she makes me laugh like I've never laughed. She is so wonderful with Lucas. He loves her, and she seems to genuinely enjoy spending time with him and with me, though I suppose I could be reading into that. I just feel so comfortable with her, Viv, which is shocking, I know, because she and I are so different. We come from completely different worlds, and there is nearly nothing that we have in common, but she somehow seems to understand me."

Vivian bit the inside of her cheek to keep the massive smile she was withholding from spilling across her face. She was *so* happy for her friend and that her plan had actually worked that she was afraid if her lips even slightly parted, she would burst into song or something equally over the top.

"I know that none of this makes any sense," Elena continued. "In reality, she and I hardly know one another, but when I'm with her, I feel like we've known one another forever. It feels easy with her when it shouldn't. It feels comfortable even when I am actually uncomfortable." She laughed, pressing a hand to her forehead. "And God, Vivian, the way she looks at me sometimes, and the way she holds Lucas, and th—"

"Oh my God, *stop*!" Vivian couldn't hold it in any longer. She squeezed Elena's hand as she groaned. "I am dying over here!"

Startled by her sudden outburst, Elena jolted from her reverie and stared at Vivian, completely bewildered. "I'm sorry?"

"This is just *too* good. You're spewing sonnets about the way your babysitter holds your son and makes you laugh, and it's like a freaking movie, and I'm *dying* from an overload of feelings."

Elena's face brightened with her smile, a disbelieving and breathless laugh escaping her. "Oh God, I know! I don't even know what I'm doing right now."

"Seriously! What *are* you doing? Why are you here?"

"What do you mean?"

"I mean, why the hell did you come here looking like you needed me to help you hide a body instead of rushing straight home to have hot lesbian sex with the babysitter?"

Blushing deeply, Elena smacked Vivian's hand. "Must you be so crass?"

"Uh yes." Vivian laughed. "Yes, I *must* be crass. This situation calls for it. Why aren't you off scissoring or whatever it's called? Do lesbians really do that?"

Elena's blush somehow managed to deepen, creeping down her neck. She swallowed thickly. "I'm terrified to go home."

"What do you mean?" Vivian asked. "I thought you were all fluttery and lovey and 'oh the way she looks at me'?"

"I am! I am, yes, but Vivian, I've never actually dated a woman. I've never actually *physically* been with a woman either, at least, not fully. I don't even know if Allison is gay!"

"I definitely wouldn't rule it out."

"She *did* seem awfully flustered when Alexis appeared on my doorstep," Elena pondered, tilting her head to the side.

"Mmhm. I bet she did. Look, babe, there's only one real way to find out, but that means you're going to have to go home and face her."

"I can't just outright ask her, Viv!"

"Why not? You've never been one to shy away from being direct."

"Yes, but truthfully, it's none of my business. Would it not be inappropriate for me to ask?"

"Well, I think it would be far more out of line for you to just attack her with your mouth, Elena. Asking a question is much more appropriate, though admittedly less hot."

Elena sighed heavily as she collapsed against the back of the couch and leaned over until her body collided with Vivian's arm. When Vivian moved to wrap that arm around her, it drew out another, quieter sigh.

"What am I going to do?" Elena groaned.

"Oh honey. It's just love. It's going to be all right."

Given the dull ache still throbbing in her purpled forehead, Allison thought she would be ready to crash after putting Lucas down, but she was wide awake. She didn't want to make a guess as to why. In fact, she didn't want to think on it at all, but her brain was determined. The issue kept shooting to the forefront of her mind.

Elena liked women. She *like*-liked women.

This one simple truth had seemingly devoured Allison's entire soul, and she could not stop obsessing over it. Allison didn't know why it bothered her so much that she hadn't known about Elena's sexuality, that she hadn't even *guessed*, but it did. It bothered her beyond words, and the only possible explanation she could come up with was one she wasn't willing to touch with a ten-foot pole.

Because in Allison's mind, there was no way, in the history of all worlds and possibilities, that Elena Vega would ever, *ever*, be interested in her.

Elena was rich, like really friggin' rich, and Allison was basically the complete opposite. Elena had an entire family that she was really close to, and Allison only had a roommate. Elena had a son. Allison was just a babysitter. Elena had class. She was poised and graceful and spoke like a fucking textbook. Allison didn't feel like she had any of that.

She was a smart person, and she knew how to speak well, but she rarely did. Sometimes she cussed like a sailor and she hardly ever took anything seriously, whereas Elena seemed to take *everything* seriously. Elena had a friggin' mansion and Allison lived in a dorm room. Elena was everything that Allison knew she would never be, so yeah. There was absolutely no way that a woman like that would ever be interested in a woman like her, not that Allison would ever approach Elena on that level. She was her *employer*, for starters, and what if Elena thought Allison just wanted her for her money or something? The thought alone made Allison's stomach turn.

"And why am I even thinking about this at all?" She spoke to the empty room. "It's not like I like her. I don't. I mean, I'm not *into* her or anything. Christ, I'm talking to myself again."

Allison took off through the house, deciding to explore a bit to keep her mind off the whole thing. The less she thought about it, the better and, apparently, the saner. There were whole portions of Elena's house that Allison had never ventured into. There was an entire second floor she had never even been on.

She wandered from room to room, taking in all the details. Elena's taste was impeccable. Every inch of her house was beautifully designed and decorated. It screamed style, class, and money. It somehow, though, still managed to feel homey. There was a toy box in every room and pictures scattered about the house—pictures of Elena and Lucas; pictures of Elena and some people that Allison assumed were Elena's parents, considering the physical likenesses; pictures of Elena and Vivian; and pictures of Lucas and Vivian. Elena even had framed colorings and drawings that Lucas had obviously done. Allison felt she was not just in a giant house. She was in a giant *home*, and that was a nice feeling.

Allison had not experienced that feeling too often in her life. She shuffled through too many homes as a kid and never quite felt like a real part of any of them. There had never been hallways littered with photographs or toy chests abundant with toys. She could only remember being in two houses that felt homier than usual, one because the mother liked to bake a lot and would frequently let Allison help. Something about the scent of baked goods filling the house made it feel more like a home. The other house was one she shared with two other foster kids, and the rooms were all decorated according to themes—an Americana living room, a kitchen adorned in ceramic roosters and rooster-covered wallpaper, and a bathroom made to look like a beach, with seashells and even a lifeguard ring hanging above the toilet.

Once she had wandered around for a while, Allison came across the only open room she hadn't yet been in. It was located at the very end of the long hallway on the second floor and was tucked just around the final corner. It was a fairly large room with custom hardwood flooring and bright white walls, and Allison was surprised to find it featured several different instruments.

No way, she thought. Was Elena a musician?

Allison carefully ran her fingers along the keys of a baby grand piano, but she quickly skipped past it to get to the part of the room that made her mouth water—a wall featuring several different acoustic guitars and even a banjo.

Pulling one of the guitars off the wall, Allison carried it over to a sleek black couch on the opposite side of the room. She sat down and plucked at a few strings, only to realize that the instrument was severely out of tune. She tuned it quickly by ear, a skill she learned while in one of her foster homes.

Although the father in that family had been a complete drunk, he'd been a pretty skilled musician. He taught her how to play guitar and even a tiny bit of piano, and she had loved playing ever since. It offered her an escape from life when her head was a mess of shitty memories or shitty circumstances, and so an old acoustic guitar was the first purchase Allison made with her first paycheck after leaving the foster system. She bought it from a lady at a garage sale for only thirty bucks, and she played the thing practically into the ground. It was the only one she had, though, and she didn't have a lot of money to spare for a new one.

Maybe she would look into it now, though, since Elena seemed to like paying her way too much.

Allison settled the guitar on her knee and got comfortable behind it. Once it was tuned, she played and played, her fingers dancing across the strings as she hummed or sang along through song after song, the perfect distraction from her toiling thoughts about her employer.

She played so long, her eyes closed and a smile pulling at the corners of her mouth, that she didn't notice the full hour that passed or the footsteps echoing through the house.

Elena shakily pulled Lucas's door closed after checking on him. A deep breath steadied her as she went on the hunt for Allison. She checked the kitchen and dining room first. Both were empty.

When she made her way into the living room, a soft sound caught her attention. Curious, she followed the sound through the house and up the stairs until she eventually found herself in the open doorway of her father's music room. She peeked into the room and saw Allison seated on the couch with her back to the door and an acoustic guitar tucked under her arm.

She could hardly help her surprise as she realized how skilled Allison was with the instrument, but when she began to hum and sing wordlessly to the sounds, Elena's eyebrows shot into her hairline and warmth spilled through her body, tugging low in her stomach. As tingles rippled down her spine, she found herself taking several steps into the room without even realizing it.

The click of her heels finally caught Allison's attention and the music stopped as the blonde whirled around and jumped to her feet.

"Shit, Elena," Allison said, her cheeks turning red. "I'm so sorry. I shouldn't have messed with your things. I just love music, and I saw these and I thought—"

Elena waved her hand to silence Allison. "Calm down," she said with an easy smile despite the fact that inside, she was positively screaming and on edge. "It's all right."

"Right, uh, do you play?" Allison asked as she stood with the guitar, shuffling from foot to foot.

"I don't, no. This is my father's music room. This is the house I grew up in. My parents bought a new place about five years ago, and I received this one as a graduation present. He never took his instruments with him. He likes to play for Lucas when they come to visit."

"Oh, okay, cool." Allison grinned. She scratched at the back of her head as they stood a few feet apart, staring at one another. "Hell of a graduation present."

"Yes. It was rather overwhelming to live here alone for the first few months. I even convinced Vivian to live with me for a short period, but we tend to get a bit catty if we are in each other's hair twenty-four-seven."

"Really? You guys seem really close."

"Oh we are." But Elena's words were quiet and lacking spirit. She was too busy indulging herself: her gaze roamed over Allison's body, taking in every detail. Elena could not believe how blind she had been. The more she looked at Allison now, the more beautiful she appeared.

Of course, Elena had always known Allison to be beautiful, but she had simply never realized how much that beauty affected her.

Allison clucked her tongue in the painfully tense and awkward silence that developed between them before holding up the guitar again and pointing at it. "Are you sure it's okay that I...you know?"

"Oh," Elena said, shaking herself back to reality. "Oh yes. It's fine."

Neither moved from where they stood. The silence began to filter between them once more, and neither seemed terribly comfortable with it. Elena found herself wanting to blurt out the revelation she had had earlier that night, but another part of her wanted to pretend like the revelation had never happened just so that she wouldn't have to try to figure out if Allison was even remotely interested.

Pointing at the guitar seemed to Elena like a really good stalling tactic.

"I heard you as I was coming up the stairs," she said. "You're rather skilled, Allison. How long have you been playing?"

"Uh, about eleven years now."

"Wow."

"Yeah, it took me a while to get the fingering down, but I eventually mastered it."

Their eyes locked hard, and, in that moment, a strange form of tension filled the space between them. Electricity practically crackled in the air as they took unconscious steps toward one another, the only obstacle between them the acoustic guitar in Allison's hand.

Elena's entire body vibrated. She didn't know what to do, but she knew she wanted to do *something*.

What if my feelings aren't reciprocated, though? I would hate to make things awkward and messy.

But her body seemed less concerned with repercussions than her mind as she leaned in. It was as if the tiny golden flecks in Allison's emerald eyes were beckoning her in, and she followed. A single word slithered across her lips before she could stop it.

"Allison?"

Allison sucked in a sharp breath. She shifted just slightly forward and whispered, "Yeah?"

Suddenly realizing what she was doing, Elena jerked back and cleared her throat. She blinked and refocused her gaze on the guitar, finding Allison's eyes too captivating to chance looking at again. She pointed to the guitar once more. "Would you like to play something for me?"

"Um, s-sure," Allison stammered, "if you want."

"I want," Elena answered. Her cheeks flushed a little at her tone, but before Allison could notice, Elena stepped around her and settled gracefully on the couch.

"Well, um, okay." Allison sat down. They glanced at one another a final time before Allison dropped her head to rest her chin on the side of the guitar, closed her eyes, and began to play a random melody.

Chapter Fourteen

Deft fingers moving effortlessly over tense strings, gliding gracefully from fret to fret, kept Elena utterly captivated. Her eyes tracked the movements of Allison's fingers, but what Elena was most drawn to was the expression of sheer bliss and peace that settled over Allison's face as she played. She was entirely serene in that moment, and Elena thought she had never seen her look more beautiful, even with the large bruise marring the skin between her eyes.

Chin resting atop the side of the guitar, Allison swayed gently as she strummed and hummed softly along. She didn't play any one song in particular but rather an amalgam of melodies.

Elena's lips parted, her fingers twisted together in her lap, and the more Allison played, the harder Elena's heart pounded against her ribcage. It was as if she could feel her rumbling pulse in every part of her body. It throbbed in her ears and quaked in her throat. She felt it fluttering in her chest, a steady, excited rhythm. It sent tremors down her spine and whispered between her legs like a purring plea.

She could not recall a time in her life that she had been more attracted to a person. It was completely overwhelming, as the realization seemed to only heighten the attraction, the new and wonderful sensations rippling through her cells. She was so mesmerized by it all, in fact, that she didn't even notice that Allison had stopped playing.

"Elena?"

Jolting, Elena blinked rapidly and realized that Allison was looking at her. Allison's fingers were still, settled neatly atop the guitar that was no longer producing gentle melodies, and a smile played at her lips.

"Yes?" Elena shook her head just slightly and cleared her throat. "Apologies, dear. I seemed to have gotten lost in the music. You play incredibly well, Allison. That was beautiful. Thank you for sharing it with me."

Cheeks flushing a beautiful shade of pink, Allison ducked her head a bit and shrugged as if to dismiss the compliment. "Yeah, it's no problem. I like to play."

"Yes, I could tell. You seemed quite peaceful."

Allison nodded and patted the guitar. "Yeah, there's something about playing that really mellows me out. It's like everything in my head just gets really quiet, and all I hear is the music, you know?"

Not waiting for an answer, she popped off the couch and carried the guitar over to the wall of instruments. She settled it back in its rightful place and walked back over to the couch. "So," she said as she plopped onto the couch much closer to Elena than before, "how bad was *this* date?"

As soon as the question slipped across Allison's lips, all of Elena's fluttering butterflies shriveled and died. Panic spilled through her cells as she tried to think of an appropriate answer. She didn't want to lie to Allison and say that Alexis was horrible, because she wasn't. She also didn't want to tell the entire truth, because she didn't want Allison to know that she had had a teenage meltdown. At the same time, Elena didn't want to make Allison think that she had been completely taken with Alexis either, because truthfully, Elena only wanted one person.

"Wow," Allison said. "Silence, huh? Must've been *really* bad." Allison reached over to poke at Elena's knee. "Was she like a total snob?"

Elena said nothing, merely shaking her head in answer.

"No? Okay, don't tell me. Let me guess."

"Very well," she agreed, knowing that Allison would never guess, considering Elena hadn't actually found anything wrong with the woman. Well, that wasn't entirely true. Elena supposed the only thing wrong with Alexis was that she wasn't Allison, but Allison certainly was not about to guess *that* either.

"Okay, so she wasn't a snob." Allison tapped her finger, as if ticking off the first of many options. "Did she have an issue with Lucas? You know, a lot of women don't want kids, despite the completely idiotic belief that that's all we're good for."

Elena chuckled. "No, dear." She shook her head. "Alexis seemed perfectly fine with my having a son."

"Yeah, well she should be," Allison said. "Because he is the cutest son ever."

A melodious laugh slipped through. "I am in perfect agreement with you there."

"Okay, so there goes that issue." Allison ticked another one of her fingers. "Oh, was she like overly sexual? You know, to the point of being inappropriate or whatever?"

"Not at all."

"Damn. Did she have bad grammar? You seem like the type of person that would be annoyed by terrible grammar. Speaking of which, you know I can actually speak really well, right? I just choose not to."

Elena smiled. "I gathered as much, yes, but no, she spoke well."

"Well, hell, Elena." Allison threw her hands up. "Just tell me then, because I'm starting to think that there wasn't anything wrong with this woman. She was hot. I know that much."

"She was rather attractive, yes."

"And she was definitely rich," Allison said, "because the jewelry she had on probably could've paid for my entire college education."

Elena tilted her head as if in reluctant agreement. "Yes, it likely could have."

The frown that touched Allison's lips bit at Elena's insides. "Was there *anything* wrong with her, with the date?"

"No," Elena whispered, her gaze never fully rising to meet Allison's. She decided to be at least partially honest and simply avoid the details. "It was actually quite nice. Alexis was a lovely date."

"O-oh," Allison stammered. "Oh, well...oh."

When she finally looked up, the completely devastated expression on Allison's face caused Elena's heart to rise into her throat. Flares of hope burned brightly as her thoughts went into overdrive. Did this mean that Allison was interested? Did it mean that Allison reciprocated her feelings? Should she just ask and get it over with, put herself out of her own misery?

Of course not, Elena reprimanded herself. There had to be cleverer, subtler ways to go about this than to have to put everything on the line and possibly embarrass the hell out of herself. Elena mulled that over for a moment, searching her mind for a slightly probing yet still safe question.

"Should I be worried about how disappointed you seem?" She let out a small laugh. "Were you hoping that the date would be another disaster?"

"What?" Allison shook her head. "Of course not."

"Are you certain? Because you seem rather less spirited now."

"Yeah. I mean, no. No. It's just, uh, I mean, nothing really to rant about if the date was awesome, huh?"

"Oh," Elena said, "I see. I suppose you are right."

"Yeah," Allison whispered. She raised a hand and pressed it to her chest, rubbing a small circle over the spot as if it hurt.

Elena tried not to put too much stock in the action. She didn't want to get her hopes up too high. "Well, shall we have a change of subject then?" she asked. "How was Lucas tonight?"

"So, you liked this chick then? *Alexis.*" Allison practically spat the woman's name, as she ignored Elena's question.

Elena reeled back a bit in shock at the sudden change in Allison's tone. Was that jealousy? Elena certainly hoped so.

Only a brief silence passed between them before Elena decided to test the waters. "I did, yes." She watched carefully for Allison's reaction.

Allison nodded roughly at the same time that she sort of shrugged and even inched away from Elena a bit. "Well, that's cool, I guess."

The tiniest jolt of excitement rippled through Elena's body. "Yes." She kept her eyes locked on Allison. "She was easily the best date I've had thus far."

Scoffing, Allison mumbled, "Well, you've only been on *three*, so that's not *really* saying anything."

"Allison."

"I mean, like you shouldn't just settle for the first good date that comes along, right? And yeah, Alexis was like really pretty and rich or whatever, but I mean, do you really wanna date someone who is basically *you* but in a different body?"

"Allison."

"If you wanted pretty and rich, you could just go look in the mirror, right? Maybe you should branch out or whatever and, like, date someone a little different."

"Allison!"

"What!" They both winced at the bite in Allison's voice, and Allison quickly shook her head. "Shit. I'm sorry, Elena. I didn't mean to snap at you."

"It's okay. I snapped first." Elena reached out to lay a hand on top of one of Allison's. "But are you all right? You seem flustered."

Allison sighed. "I just...my head hurts a little I guess. I, uh, I think I need to get some air."

Before Elena could utter another word, Allison jumped off the couch and ran out of the music room. Elena let out a heavy breath, her chin sinking to her chest. Her stomach churned uncomfortably as she whispered to herself, "What the hell just happened?"

Allison bolted down the stairs, through the living room, playroom, foyer, and out the front door without a second's hesitation. As soon as the warm evening breeze ghosted across her face, she sucked in a deep breath and began to pace the short length of Elena's stoop. "What the fuck was *that*?" She smacked her palm against her forehead. Her hand collided with the deep bruise between her eyes.

"Ow!" She clenched her teeth and blinked rapidly to hold back her tears as pain blasted through her forehead and face. "*Stupid!*"

Allison breathed heavily through the pain until it began to dwindle to a dull throb. Her brain felt like it was on fire. What the hell had just happened back there?

She had not only *completely* freaked out, but she had also snapped at Elena. That wasn't cool. Why was she even freaking out to begin with?

"Oh God," she whispered as she ran a hand through her tangled curls. "I'm *jealous*."

As soon as the words slithered across her lips, Allison knew they were true, and, in that moment, she wanted nothing more than to crawl in a hole and die. She could not, could not, could *not* be falling for Elena fucking Vega. It was positively *out* of the question.

And why was it out of the question? *Because*, Allison told herself, *you are a poor orphan student and she is a rich, successful businesswoman. She is way, way out of your lame little league!*

"Just let it go, Allison," she whispered. "Just let it go."

It wasn't like they couldn't still be friends, though Allison was going to have to get a handle on her jealousy, but yeah. She could do this. It wasn't like this was the first time she'd crushed on a girl she couldn't have. It would pass. She just needed a little time.

She took a deep breath and let it out in one long, easy sigh before cracking her neck to both sides, shaking out her hands, and walking calmly back into the house.

Elena was in the kitchen, pouring herself a glass of water, when she heard footsteps sound behind her. She looked up to see Allison standing just a few feet away, expression sheepish and feet shuffling in place. "Oh," Elena said. "I thought you might have left."

Allison shook her head. "No, I just needed some air."

"I see," Elena replied. She took a tentative step toward Allison and lowered her voice to a whisper. "Are you all right?"

Allison visibly swallowed. "Yeah, fine."

"Are you sure? Allison, have I done something to upset you?"

"No!" Allison took a step closer and reached for Elena's hands. She laced their fingers together. "No, Elena. You didn't do anything." She released one of Elena's hands and scratched awkwardly at the back of her neck as she then avoided the woman's gaze. "I guess pain just makes me a little grouchy."

Elena smiled and slowly reached out to graze her fingers across the puffy, purple flesh between Allison's eyes. "Would you like some more aspirin? Or an ice pack, perhaps?"

Allison shook her head gently back and forth against Elena's fingertips. "Nah," she whispered. "I should probably get going anyway. I'm sure you've gotta work in the morning, and I've got a nine a.m. class."

"You could stay," Elena suggested and nearly bit through her tongue the second the words escaped her. Had she *really* just said that?

"What?" Allison blurted. "Like overnight?"

Elena, realizing it was too late to take it back, choked down the quivering lump in her throat and nodded. "Yes. It's late, and you're in pain. I would offer to drive you, but then we would have to drag Lucas out of bed, and I'm still concerned about your head injury. Please, will you stay? I can drive you to school in the morning after dropping Lucas at my mother's."

"You'd do that?"

"Allison, of course." She squeezed Allison's hand, which she only just realized was still latched onto her own. "Will you stay?"

Allison smirked. "You sure you're not just trying to get me into your bed?"

Elena was absolutely aware that Allison was joking, but her entire body exploded, regardless, at the mere thought. She sucked in a sharp breath and before she could stop herself, she summoned her courage and whispered, "If you would like to be there, you are welcome to be."

"What do you mean?" Allison asked, her voice strained and her eyes practically boring into Elena's.

"I just meant that it would likely be best if I could monitor you overnight, considering you could still have a concussion," Elena explained, internally smacking the hell out of herself. *So much for courage*, she thought.

"O-oh. Right. Uh, I mean, I guess that'd be okay. Your bed *is* pretty huge anyway. Are you sure you don't mind, because I don't wanna inconvenience you or anything?"

Elena shook her head. "No, it's fine."

"Okay."

Elena wasn't sure who moved first, only that they had somehow gone from standing and staring at each other in the kitchen to walking slowly and silently down the hallway toward her bedroom.

Their shoulders brushed occasionally as they walked, and Elena was desperately trying not to overthink the fact that Allison still had yet to let go of her hand.

The air was thick and ripe with their silence as they entered Elena's bedroom. They stood inside the doorway for a moment, holding hands and staring at the king-sized bed before them, which now seemed terribly daunting. Elena was the first to move.

"Would you like something to sleep in?" She untangled her hand from Allison's and moved across the room to her dresser.

"Oh no, that's okay," Allison said. "But do you have an extra toothbrush?"

Elena pointed toward her bathroom. "There should be one in the second drawer to the right of the sink."

"Okay, thanks." Allison crossed to the bathroom, and Elena heard her open a drawer and rip open the package of a new toothbrush.

When she heard the faucet running, Elena quickly changed into a small silky nightgown and settled onto the edge of her bed to apply lotion to her legs, as was part of her nightly routine. She was rubbing down the length of her left leg when she glanced up to find Allison peeking around the corner, watching her hands move.

Their eyes locked and Elena felt a wave of heat roll through her lower abdomen. Seeing Allison immediately jerk back into the bathroom almost made her laugh out loud and gave her a flare of confidence. She finished with her lotion and then took a deep breath before sauntering into the bathroom.

Preparing her own toothbrush and popping it into her mouth, Elena stood opposite Allison. Their hips leaned against the counter, and they awkwardly stared at each other while they brushed.

Elena chuckled low in her throat when a long stream of toothpaste dribbled out of Allison's mouth and down her chin. She smiled around her toothbrush at her, but when she did, a stream dripped down her own chin, and that caused Allison to erupt into laughter as well. They cackled at each other as they each tried to catch their own minty drool, swiping at their chins and spitting their excess toothpaste into the sink.

The laughter helped to calm Elena's nerves—that is, until they re-entered the bedroom and faced the daunting bed once more. "Are you sure you don't want something to sleep in?" Elena asked again.

Allison nodded as she rounded the bed. "I usually just sleep in my boy shorts and a tank top. Is that okay?"

Heat sparked in Elena's body again, curling low in her stomach, but she did her best to appear casual and unaffected by simply nodding and slipping into the bed on her usual side. She tried to avert her gaze, but it was hopeless. Her eyes had other plans, and she found herself covertly sneaking glances in Allison's direction as she undressed.

First went Allison's boots and socks, then her belt. Elena clenched her fists tightly around her blankets as she watched Allison somewhat slowly unbutton her shirt before letting it drop to the floor, leaving her in only a thin tank top and jeans. Finally, Allison popped the button on her jeans and shimmied out of them with some difficulty, so that she only wore that thin tank top and boy-short panties.

Allison was quick to slide beneath the covers once she was exposed; so quick, in fact, that Elena barely got a glance at her long and muscled legs. Still, a glance was enough. Elena's entire body felt that glance.

They lay on their backs several feet away from one another, staring up at the ceiling. Elena reached over and clicked off her bedside lamp. Once the room was fully encased in darkness, she quietly said, "Goodnight Allison."

"Night," Allison replied.

Elena didn't close her eyes but continued to stare up at the ceiling. The air in the room seemed to grow thicker in the darkness. Allison shifted a few inches closer before rolling toward the center of the bed, and Elena turned on her side and inched over like a caterpillar until they met in the middle. They stopped when there was only about a foot of empty space between their bodies, and Elena's heart pounded.

She lay awake for a long time, long enough that it felt as if hours had passed, though she wasn't sure. She could have easily just rolled over and checked the time on her clock, but Elena couldn't bring herself to move. She was still on her side, facing Allison.

Elena slowly opened her eyes and it took a few seconds to adjust to the darkness so that she could see the woman lying beside her. Allison was positioned on her back, and Elena strained to see her better. She let out a sigh of relief when she noticed the way Allison's chest rose slowly, indicating that she was breathing deeply—a sure sign that Allison was fast asleep.

Her heart stammered and her stomach clenched as she reached across the small space between them, her fingers slipping slowly through the dark. She could barely make out Allison's serene features through the shadows, facing upward toward the ceiling. Elena tentatively grazed her fingertips over Allison's cheek as she whispered, "I wish I were braver, brave enough to have said this when you were awake." She let out a shaky breath. "Allison, I adore you."

Elena sighed as she then moved to retract her arm, but jolted in place when a hand shot out and wrapped around her wrist. Her heart blasted against her ribcage, panic spilling through her chest, as Allison turned quickly on the mattress to face her. She was awake. Allison's eyes locked onto her in the dark, and Elena's breathing grew fast and shallow.

"Do you mean that?"

"Yes."

The silence that followed seemed almost loud, and Elena's stomach rolled at the thought that she might have just ruined everything, but then Allison tightened her grip, and Elena felt a tug on her arm and followed the motion, shifting closer to Allison until they were a mere inch or two from one another. The warmth of their combined body heat quickly devoured the hair's width between them. Elena took in shallow breaths as their noses brushed and Allison's grip loosened, but only so her hand could slide up and tangle with Elena's.

It felt like electricity sparked in the dark, fueled by the energy flowing between their buzzing bodies as their noses bumped again and their fingers clenched tightly together. Elena could feel Allison's breath in hot puffs against her face, and then Allison whispered, "Elena?"

The breathy sound of her name sent tingles rippling down Elena's spine and pooling at the base of her back in a near-painful knot of tension. "Yes?" she breathed.

Allison nudged her nose against Elena's again. "Can I—"

Elena couldn't help the raspy moan that escaped her as she cut Allison off. "Please kiss me."

Allison closed the minute distance between them and tenderly pressed her lips to Elena's. Elena melted into her in a hard shudder, their bodies molding together beneath the sheets as shockwaves rippled through her at that first heated press of lips and breath.

Chapter Fifteen

That aching knot of tension at the base of Elena's spine exploded at the first gentle touch of Allison's lips. It burst open, sending ripples of pleasure in every direction. Rolling waves billowed up her spine, causing her back to bow and lurch forward. She released a deep moan, the sound vibrating its way up her throat, as those waves then crept down her legs. Prickling tingles tickled across the backs of her thighs and in-between, so that she clamped the flesh together almost unconsciously to assuage the sudden assault of sensation between her legs.

The softest of whimpers echoed just behind Allison's teeth as she sucked in a sharp breath through her nose and pressed further into Elena's heated form. Her palm was hot and slick, sliding over Elena's curves. She splayed her fingers over Elena's hip before slipping them down into the dip of Elena's side and around to her back, pulling her even closer.

Allison's exploration encouraged Elena, and she shot her own hands forward, eager to feel more. One hand wove its way into pillow-mussed curls and the other grazed over a defined bicep and a pounding pulse beneath a heaving chest. They touched one another tentatively, brushing so lightly that their touches were but fleshy whispers over shoulders and elbows, over hips and ribcages, over thin material covering quivering stomachs and twitching vertebrae in bowing backs.

Breath hitching roughly in her throat, Elena felt the tip of Allison's tongue flick gently at her bottom lip before sliding across its full length. She pulled back just a breath, her hand coming up to cup around the back of Allison's neck. Elena smiled as she slipped her lips over Allison's again and Allison's grip dug into her hip. She didn't hesitate another second as she claimed Allison's lips once more, letting her own tongue slip out and into Allison's mouth.

Both women moaned deeply as their tongues touched once and pulled back before tangling together. They explored one another with an achingly slow yet building hunger, their grip on each other soft but growing tighter by the second. Their gentle kisses deepened and turned faster and harder. Elena nearly came undone, her fingernails digging into Allison's back when Allison darted her tongue slow and deep across the roof of Elena's mouth—in and out, over and over, in a way that made Elena instantly imagine Allison's mouth travelling elsewhere.

Allison chuckled, low and raspy, against Elena's mouth as she took in a sharp gasp at the motion and tightened her grip to the point of pain. Their fingertips were lit candlewicks against taut, waxen flesh, searing, scorching, and melting their bodies further together.

Allison sucked on Elena's bottom lip before releasing it with a wet pop and whispering, "Elena."

Just that tiny introduction of voice into the space between them seemed to jolt both women out of the haze of their heady and overwhelming connection. They broke apart, just enough to look into one another's eyes in the dark.

"Elena," Allison panted. Her fingers ghosted over Elena's side, up the exposed flesh of her arm and neck, and then grazed across a heated cheek. "What are we doing?"

Elena breathed deeply through her nose and out through her mouth. Everything seemed cloudy, and she felt like she might burn alive at any moment, especially with the heat of Allison's body still pressed against her. "I," she said, a soft laugh bubbling up from low in her stomach, "I think that much is fairly obvious."

Fingers running through silken strands of hair and over flushed cheeks, Allison whispered, "Well, yeah, but I mean, what are we *doing*? What is this?"

Elena smiled against Allison's lips as she planted another tender kiss there. "I don't know," she answered. "Does this require a label?"

Shoulders shrugged under Elena's hands. "No, I guess not, but, like, you *do* realize that this is *me* you're kissing right now, right?"

"Allison, of course." Elena jerked back so that she could search the younger woman's eyes. "What is that supposed to mean?"

Sighing, Allison bowed her head forward and rested it gently against Elena's. "I don't know. I guess I just mean that you're *you*, you know? You're rich and powerful and, God, so gorgeous, and I'm just me."

She looked up and grinned at Elena through the dark. "Not that I'm not totally awesome, because duh." She laughed as she poked at Elena's sides, making her squirm. "It's just that even still, I'm nowhere near your league."

"I'm not a team sport, dear. I have no league."

"You know what I mean."

"I do," Elena conceded. She rubbed her thumb over Allison's bottom lip and cupped her cheek. "Allison, please don't put me on a pedestal. I am only a person."

A soft breath slipped through Allison's lips. "You *really* like me?"

Those familiar flutters returned to Elena's stomach as a slow smile slipped across her lips and she nodded against the pillow. "I *really* do."

Allison mimicked Elena's nod. "Okay. So then, I guess maybe I should go sleep in a guest room or something."

"What?" Elena asked. "Why?"

"Because I feel like if I stay, I might maul you or something."

One of Elena's eyebrows shot up as another wave of heat curled through her abdomen and pulsed between her legs. She blew out a slow breath as she laughed. "I never knew a mauling could sound so thoroughly appealing."

"Oh God, could you not?" Allison groaned. "My whole body already feels like it might explode, and I'm trying to be respectful here, woman—take it slow and all that."

With every word from Allison's mouth, Elena's confidence only grew, despite her lack of experience with women. She slipped her hand around the back of Allison's neck again before tilting forward and pressing her lips to the slender column. Allison sucked in a shuddering breath at the sensation.

"Or you could just make it so much worse," Allison said through gritted teeth. Elena's hot breath scorched up the length of Allison's neck, and when Elena's tongue dipped into the hollow of Allison's ear, her entire body jolted and she moaned.

"Oh my God, Elena. That is so unfair. Seriously?"

Allison grabbed Elena by the shoulders and pushed back, looking into the other woman's eyes. "What did I just say?" she teased, poking at Elena's stomach. "You're making it worse."

Elena smiled mischievously at her before moving to close the distance between them once more, but Allison quickly stopped her. "Wait, is that supposed to be a hint?"

"What do you mean?"

"I mean, is this your way of saying you *don't* want to take this slow?" Allison asked her. "Because I mean, I don't mind sex early on, except when I'm really invested, and I really am, so I'd like to take this slow, unless…Well, did you just want this to be about sex?"

"Oh," Elena whispered, her heart clenching at the tremble in Allison's voice. She cupped her cheek once more as she inched her body closer and shook her head slowly. She kissed Allison's lips. "No."

Allison let out an obvious sigh of relief that had a smile blooming across both of their faces. She leaned forward and kissed the tip of Elena's nose. "Well okay then. I need to go."

"Really?" Elena asked. "You are really going to leave me here alone?"

Gentle hands ran down Elena's body once more, then pulled back. "Yup, yup. Have to. I guess I'm just old-fashioned like that."

"Allison, we are both adults. I'm sure we can behave ourselves."

Allison narrowed her eyes in the dark. "Nah." She clucked her tongue. "I don't think you can control that devil mouth of yours."

"*Devil* mouth?" Elena gasped, arching a brow.

"Mhm. Devil mouth, as in hot as the fires of hell." Allison crawled off the bed and ducked down to feel around on the floor. When she found her clothes, she balled them up in her hands and held them against her chest. "So, I'm going, because—"

"Because my mouth is the devil." Elena was still laying on her side and peering up at Allison through the dark.

Allison shook her head and groaned. She shuffled a little farther from the bed, her eyes never leaving Elena. "Yup," she said, "and I gotta go because goddamn if it doesn't make me wanna be a sinner."

Another wave of heat rippled through Elena's body and burned between her legs. She clenched her thighs tightly to alleviate the throb as she watched Allison walk toward the door. "Are you sure?"

"Stop talking!" Allison hissed from across the room. "Your voice is the devil too. Right now, pretty much all of you is the devil. So, shh, and just let me go in aching, throbbing peace, woman!"

"Do you know where the guest ro—"

"There's gotta be like fifteen in this house," Allison grumbled. "I'll find one." She slipped out of Elena's bedroom, clicking the door closed behind her.

Elena rolled over and stuffed her face in her pillow. The butterflies in her stomach had grown and transformed into excited birds, crashing wildly around inside of her. She sighed into her pillow, the sound bordering on a soft squeal, before groaning and rolling her eyes behind her eyelids.

"I am behaving like a lovesick teenager." She rolled over and laid an arm across her eyes. Her entire body was thrumming with an excitement that simultaneously thrilled and embarrassed her. Flipping restlessly onto her side and bunching her pillow up, she wrapped one arm around it. "I *feel* like a lovesick teenager. This is ridiculous."

Still, the smile on her face never faded.

Elena jolted awake with a yelp as music blasted through her house. Jerking herself into a sitting position, she blinked rapidly through the lingering haze of sleep and glanced around her room. She could tell her hair stuck wildly out on one side, and her lips were swollen and sore.

As her sense of awareness slowly kicked in, Elena frowned in confusion. Lyrics spilled through the air and assaulted her ears. Why was The Jackson Five's "I Want You Back" echoing through her house like there was a live concert in progress?

Her blurry eyes widened as the events of the previous night came rushing back. She gasped as her body flooded with heat and she whispered, "Allison." Her fingers came up and touched gently at her lips. They were puffy and a bit chapped. Her cheeks flushed a deep crimson as she shook her head and smiled against her fingertips.

She glanced over at the clock on her bedside table and was shocked to see that it was barely six a.m. Typically, it would be another thirty minutes before she would be up and around on weekdays. The same was true for Lucas, who usually woke around the same time as his mother.

Slipping out of her bed, Elena grabbed her robe from where it hung just inside the closet door. She checked herself in the mirror and scoffed at her predictably wild hair. It was incredibly frizzy on the top. She grabbed her hairbrush and ran several fast strokes through it, taming it as best she could before returning the brush to the vanity. She ran her hands down the front of her robe, smoothing it out as if it were an elegant gown, before sucking in a steadying breath.

Elena crept down the hallway as quietly as possible. She peeked into Lucas's bedroom and was unsurprised to see that his bed was empty. There was no way her child, who was both a light sleeper and an early riser, would be able to snooze through the blaring tunes spilling through the house. No, he was assuredly with Allison, wherever the two were.

She found them soon enough, and Elena remained tucked partially behind the corner as a smile blasted across her face at the scene playing out in her kitchen. She quickly brought a hand up and cupped it over her mouth, containing the laughter that threatened to spill forth as she watched Allison, clad in her jeans and tank top from the previous day, dance all around the kitchen with a spatula held to her lips like a microphone. Lucas sat in his chair, bopping excitedly up and down and giggling and clapping as Allison danced around him and sang into her spatula.

Even though Allison was singing several octaves higher than what Elena would guess was her natural register, it was still startlingly beautiful. God, Elena thought, how was it that literally everything about this woman seemed so incredibly attractive to her?

Elena felt her insides turn to mush as she watched Allison hold the spatula out toward Lucas and let him babble senselessly before turning back toward the stove and grabbing the skillet. With a flick of her wrist, a pancake soared high into the air. Elena snorted with laughter as Allison barely caught the pancake again, nearly letting it tumble to the floor.

Lucas clapped happily as Allison then returned the skillet to the stove and resumed her dancing. Elena watched every second of it, completely absorbed in this precious moment. Thought after thought spiraled through her mind, too rapid to pinpoint any particulars, except for one. Elena was quite certain that she wouldn't mind waking up more often to find Allison Sawyer dancing around her kitchen.

It was in that moment that Elena's darling son happened to glance over and see her. He threw his hands into the air and squealed. "Momma!"

Elena's breath hitched in her throat and Allison, red-faced, whirled around at Lucas's cry and nearly dropped the spatula in the process. Her heart jumped into her throat and stuck there as Allison's eyes glittered in the sunlight streaming through the kitchen window and her lips parted just slightly.

"Good morning," Allison whispered so quietly that Elena had to read her lips to understand her over the loud music.

"Hi." She mouthed the words with a smile as she leaned her head gently against the wall.

"Hi!" Lucas screamed at his mother, waving his arms dramatically.

Allison's eyes widened, and then she shook her head and shot over to the stove to check on her now-burning pancakes. "Crap," she muttered as she threw one in the garbage and poured another dollop of batter onto the skillet to start anew.

Elena laughed as she finally tore her gaze away from Allison.

"Good morning, munchkin!" She crossed the kitchen and bent to kiss Lucas's forehead. "You are up bright and early."

"Can't hear you!" Lucas shouted.

"Oh!" Allison exclaimed, shooting past them. "I got it. Just a sec." She ran into the living room, and the volume of the music went down. She then shot back to the kitchen to finish cooking the pancakes.

"Sorry," she said when she returned. "Lucas said that it was time for you to wake up, so we figured music would be a good replacement alarm."

Lucas beamed up at Elena as she ran her fingers through his soft and wild hair. "What you say, Momma?"

"I said you are up bright and early."

Lucas nodded. "Momma, did you know Alson had a sleepover?"

Moving to grab a glass from the cabinet to the left of the sink, Elena chuckled. "Yes I did." She crossed to the refrigerator to retrieve the apple juice.

"Yeah," Lucas sighed. "She didn't sleep with me."

"No?" Elena asked, biting her lip as she stood in the open door of the refrigerator and poured her apple juice. Elena's breath caught in her throat when Allison placed a hand on her hip before leaning slowly around her to grab the butter from the side door. Turning to put the juice container back just as Allison straightened from the door, their chests brushed gently, and they both breathed sharply at the contact, their eyes locking again.

"No," Lucas said, snapping Elena and Allison back to attention. He let out a dramatic huff as he popped the straw of his juice box into his mouth.

Elena smiled teasingly at the woman in front of her. "She didn't sleep with me either, dear."

Allison turned a playful glare onto Elena before returning to the stove so that she could transfer the final finished pancake onto a plate. "Ha. Ha." She shook her head.

"You're sposta sleep with someone when you have a sleepover, Alson," Lucas said. "Like when Gram sleeps with me."

"Yes, Allison." Elena smirked. "You are *supposed* to sleep with someone."

Allison's cheeks burned a lovely shade of pink as she carried Lucas's plate over to him. "Sorry, little man," she said. "I didn't know the rules."

A bright smile greeted her as she set two small silver-dollar pancakes in front of him. "Thank you!" He then jumped right back to the topic of sleepovers. "Next time you gotta sleep with me or Momma, okay?" Lucas looked over to his mother as he picked up his syrup-less pancake and bit off a piece. "Right, Momma?"

Elena pinned Allison with a smoldering look. "Absolutely, darling." She tilted her head and added, "Whichever you prefer, Allison."

Placing a plate of pancakes in front of Elena, Allison shook her head. She lowered her voice to a whisper as she said, "Just eat your pancakes, woman."

Chapter Sixteen

"SEE THAT!" LUCAS CRIED, POINTING out the window of the moving vehicle. Allison looked over her shoulder so she could look out Lucas's window. She didn't have a clue what he was pointing at, but she still gasped and pretended to be thrilled.

"Whoa! Yeah!"

"And that!" Lucas shouted again, still pointing.

"Yeah, what *was* that?"

"I don't know!" He shrugged his shoulders and grinned like he was on top of the world. He seemed even more pleased with himself as both his mother and babysitter laughed loudly.

"Is he always like this in the car?" Allison asked Elena.

Elena shook her head and kept her eyes fixed on the road. "Not typically, no. He has occasional mornings when he is more energetic, but he usually sleeps or repetitively sings the dinosaur song."

"What?" Allison asked, her grin widening. "There's a dinosaur song?"

"Oh yes."

"Like from a TV show or something?"

"No." Elena rolled to a stop at a red light. "It's *his* song."

"*His?*" Allison glanced back at Lucas again. "As in he made it up?"

Elena confirmed with a proud nod. "He is rather creative, that son of mine."

"Heck yeah he is." Allison turned in her seat again and faced the back. "Hey Lucas!"

"Hey!" Lucas's gaze snapped away from the window and back to Allison in the front seat.

"Sing me the dinosaur song. Please?"

Lucas didn't hesitate to nod. "Okay!"

He kicked his legs in an absentminded way against the front of his car seat as he began to sing loudly, and Allison had to cup a hand over her mouth in order to keep from laughing or squealing or some strange combination of the two. The song came out in shifting rhythms with no set pattern, and none of the lines rhymed. Lucas didn't seem to notice, though, bopping his head as if the rhythm never altered and made perfect sense.

"Dinosaurs are big.
Dinosaurs are green.
They eat plants and other dinosaurs.
Dinosaurs have big teeth.
And big claws too.
Dinosaurs are my friends.
Dinosaurs, dinosaurs, dinosaurs."

Lucas held out the last word for a long time, raising his voice an octave and throwing a small fist into the air dramatically, and Allison just completely lost it. She had been biting her lip behind her hand the entire time, trying her best not to ruin the moment, but she couldn't hold it in anymore. She burst into laughter as she clapped her hands and cheered for Lucas. Elena joined in the cheering and Lucas beamed from the backseat, clapping his hands as well.

"That was a great song, little man!" Allison reached back to pat his exposed knee. Elena had let him choose his outfit for the day, and he had chosen khaki shorts, a green-and-white striped polo, green socks, and solid white tennis shoes. There was no denying that the kid had style, much like his mother.

"And a superb singing voice," Elena added as she glanced at her son in the rearview mirror.

Allison nodded enthusiastically. "Totally!"

"Want me teach you?" Lucas offered.

"Do I want you to teach it to me?" Allison raised her brows and bugged out her eyes. "Well *yeah*! Of course!"

"Perhaps next time, munchkin," Elena said before Lucas could begin another loud round of the dinosaur song. "We are here."

Allison whirled around in her seat and her jaw instantly dropped.

"Holy Cracker Jack!" Her eyes widened as she leaned forward in the passenger seat of Elena's car and stared up through the windshield at the massive home looming in front of them. "This is where your parents *live?*"

Elena glanced up as well as she parked the car. "Yes. It is rather ostentatious, I know."

A teasing smile painted Allison's lips. "Like you have any room to talk about *other* people having ostentatious houses."

"Ah-ah," Elena said, clucking her tongue. "You forget that my home first belonged to my parents before it belonged to me."

"You're right. I forgot. Fair enough."

"Thank you." Elena unlatched her seatbelt and exited the car.

"You want me to help?" Allison asked, unlatching her own seatbelt. "I can get Lucas."

"No, that's all right dear. I only have the munchkin to carry, since he has duplicates of nearly everything here. There is rarely a need for me to pack anything for him."

"Oh." Allison pouted. "Well, you want me to walk with you to the door?"

"You *could*. But only if you wish to subject yourself to my mother's interrogations."

"Interrogations?" Allison asked. "What about?"

Elena opened the back door and went to work unbuckling Lucas from his car seat. "Oh, a variety of topics, I'm sure."

"Ow, Momma," Lucas squeaked and lifted his leg. "Don't pinch."

"I'm sorry, baby," Elena cooed, readjusting her hand around the base buckle. "It was an accident."

Allison's hand shot to the door handle. "Need some help?" she asked, ready to exit the car and run around to assist Elena.

"No, it's fine." Elena shook her head. "This one is frequently a hassle, but if I can just get enough pressure on th—" A click sounded as the buckle released, and Elena glanced up at Allison with a smile. "There."

Lucas threw his arms out for his mother to pick him up. She propped him on her right hip and bent to look back into the car at Allison. "I'll just be a moment."

"No big." Allison shrugged and watched Elena close the door and make her way up the walkway. She didn't get very far, though, before Allison heard Lucas shout through Elena's cracked open window.

"Momma wait!"

Elena stopped and patted his thigh. "What is it, Lucas?"

"Alson!"

"Yes." Elena nodded, and Allison waved from the car. "Allison is waiting in the car."

"No," Lucas told her, shaking his head. He started waving his arm wildly, motioning for Allison to join them. "She has to say bye."

Elena sighed and freed her left arm to mimic Lucas's beckoning motion.

Allison reached out and turned the key back in the ignition to shut the car entirely off. She pulled the key out and stuck it in her pocket as she jumped out of the car and jogged over to where Elena and Lucas waited.

"Apparently, your presence is required." Elena chuckled as Allison stepped up to them and Lucas dove toward her.

She caught him mid-dive and transferred the small boy from Elena's hip to her own. "Well, I'm cool with that," she said, shrugging her shoulders and bouncing Lucas atop her hip.

When they turned to continue their short trek up the walkway, the door opened and out stepped an older brunette woman that Allison had seen in several pictures around Elena's house. The resemblance was striking if you knew what to look for, and Allison had spent plenty of time studying Elena's features, whether consciously or not, so she could definitely see the similarities. This woman was most certainly Elena's mother.

"*Gram!*"

"Hello, my sweet boy!" Nora called to him from the porch, but she wasn't looking at Lucas. Her gaze was locked onto Allison. Her eyes narrowed as she stood in the doorway with her arms crossed over her silken robe.

As Elena, Allison, and Lucas reached the door, Lucas dove forward again without warning, practically leaping from Allison's arms to Nora's. His grandmother caught him easily. She kissed his cheek as she held him at her side before leaning forward to kiss Elena's cheek as well. "Good morning, darling." Her narrowed gaze never left Allison as she greeted her daughter. It made Allison squirm.

"Good morning, Mother," Elena replied, pressing her lips to her mother's cheek as well. "He is rather excitable today, so he may be a handful."

"Oh, he's fine, dear." Nora waved a hand dismissively. She then pointed at Allison. "Who's this?"

"Mother, this is Allison. Allison, this is my mother."

"Allison," Nora repeated, smiling at Allison as she held out her hand. "Lovely to meet you."

Allison shook her hand firmly. "You too, Mrs. Vega."

"Oh dear, please call me Nora."

"Okay, Nora," Allison replied. That was a good sign, right? Allison relaxed a bit and smiled. "Nice to meet you."

"Allison is the babysitter that I told you about," Elena said.

"Of course. Of course," Nora said, nodding. "I knew the name sounded familiar. Lucas goes on and on about you. So, how do you like our darling boy?"

Shuffling in place, Allison's shoulder brushed gently against Elena's. "He's the best kid I've ever worked with," she said.

Elena beamed, as did Lucas, who was now twirling Nora's hair around his fingers. "Alson likes green, Gram."

"She does?" Nora asked, bouncing the boy on her hip.

"Yup!"

"Well then I suppose Allison is a keeper, isn't she?"

Lucas nodded.

"So," Nora said after a beat, "why might the babysitter be needed this morning? Am I being replaced?"

Allison felt her face flush with heat as the boy exclaimed, "Alson had a sleepover!"

One of Nora's eyebrows arched impossibly high, much as Allison had seen Elena's do countless times. The resemblance between them in that moment was almost uncanny. "Is that so?" Nora asked.

"Yeah," Lucas told her, "but she didn't sleep with me."

"She didn't sleep with me either!" Elena added in one long, frenzied stream of words. She then cleared her throat and straightened her back. Her mother's face erupted into a knowing smirk, and Allison was fairly certain they were screwed. She glanced to Elena and noticed that her face was as red hot as Allison's felt.

"I see." Nora hummed. "And were you disappointed by this?"

"Mother!" Elena hissed.

Nora completely ignored Elena. Her eyes locked onto Allison and she asked, "So, I take it your position has surpassed babysitter then?"

"Uh." Allison glanced back and forth between Nora and Elena. "Uh, y—"

Elena subtly shook her head, and Allison quickly changed her course of speech. "...No. I mean, uh, nope. Just a babysitter."

"And a poor liar." Nora chuckled. "So, may I ask—"

"No, you may not, Mother." Elena snapped at her. "We have neither the time nor the desire to endure a classic Nora Vega Inquisition."

"Inquisition is a bit harsh, don't you think, Elena?"

"Not at all," Elena said, moving in to press a kiss to Lucas's cheek. "I stand by my word choice. Have a good day, munchkin, and I will see you this evening."

"Lickstick, Momma." Lucas stuck out his tongue as he wiped at his cheek where a perfect imprint of Elena's lips remained. He giggled as she stuck her tongue back out at him.

"I love you." Elena ran a hand through his hair lovingly.

"Love you," he said right back.

Elena shot her mother a glare even as she leaned in to kiss Nora's cheek. "Bye Mother."

"Have a good day at work, dear." Nora smiled smugly. "Lovely to meet you, Allison. I look forward to our next visit."

"Uh, yes ma'am," Allison said with what she was sure was an awkwardly lopsided smile. She reached out and patted Lucas's back. "See ya, bud."

He waved at her as he laid his forehead against his grandmother's temple. "Bye Alson!"

Elena hooked her hand around Allison's elbow and tugged her along. "Come, Allison," she implored, leading them hurriedly back toward the car.

"Holy shit," Allison muttered but managed to hold in her laughter until they made it back inside the car.

"It wasn't that bad," Allison said as Elena drove them through the busy New York streets.

"Yes," Elena agreed, "and that is *only* because I put an end to it before it even began."

"Would she really have interrogated me?"

"Oh, most certainly." Elena nodded. "Ranging a number of topics, I'm sure."

"Well, I guess we dodged a bullet then, though I'm wondering if..." She hesitated, drumming her fingers on the console as she stared at Elena. "Nah," she said after a minute, shaking her head. "Never mind."

"What is it?" Elena asked, glancing over at her.

"It's nothing. Never mind."

"No, tell me," Elena said. "Please."

Allison sighed as she picked at the frayed parts of her holey jeans, her head ducking down a bit. "Fine," she muttered. "It seemed like you *really* didn't want your mom to know about us, not that I think that there is an *us*, but I guess that's kinda what I'm hoping for. Anyway, I'm just wondering if you want me to deny it too, because—"

Confident in where this was headed, Elena laid a hand on Allison's knee. Her voice was soft and quiet as she filled in the gaps. "You were wondering if it was because I am ashamed of you?" she asked.

Allison nodded without looking at her. "I mean, it would make sense."

"Absolutely not." When she stopped at a red light, she reached over and tucked her index finger beneath Allison's chin. She lifted Allison's head and turned it to face her. "Please believe me."

When she felt Allison nod into her hand, Elena offered her another small smile before dropping her hold and turning back toward the road. As she drove them nearer and nearer to Allison's dormitory, Elena explained, "I simply did not want my mother drilling us for answers that we have yet to even possess. This, whatever this is between us, is very new."

"Yeah. You're right. Sorry I asked."

"You don't have to be sorry, Allison," Elena told her, driving around the block from Allison's dorm to find parking. "I can understand why you would ask, but I will have you know that status and wealth have never mattered to me. They are unimportant where my love life is concerned."

"Really?" Allison asked. "Because it was pretty obvious that all the dates Vivian set you up on were hella rich."

Sighing, Elena pulled into an open spot and shut off the engine. She and Allison relaxed back into their seats, turning to face one another. "Yes, well, that was Vivian. She gave me no say in the matter, though she does know my feelings on that particular issue. It is simply that she and I have little extended or personal exposure to people outside of our own social class. She likely chose people from her daily life and work."

"Yeah, I guess that makes sense," Allison said.

A tender silence developed between them as they continued to stare at one another. Allison's gaze very obviously raked slowly up and down Elena's body, and Elena smiled and shifted in her seat. She leaned over the console, Allison meeting her halfway, and nuzzled her nose against Allison's. "I suppose we should talk about last night," she whispered.

"Yeah." The word was hardly more than breath as it floated from Allison's lips and faded in the inch between them.

Elena's heart raced, and both women's breathing audibly quickened as they drew together like magnets. The air inside the car turned thick and hot as the heat radiating off of them filtered through it and caused small droplets of sweat to bead at their temples and on their palms.

Allison nodded as she scooted a little closer, her nose brushing Elena's again. "Yeah," she whispered again. "We should—"

Elena devoured Allison's words before the sentence could ever be finished. They both moaned softly, little whimpers escaping their throats as they met in a kiss, just as fiery as the first. Fingers itched against moist palms before finding their way up arms and slender necks and twisting into hair.

Their lips slid together in perfect harmony as they touched one another gently, almost reverently. Their hands explored tentatively and the press of their mouths cycled experimentally from soft to hard to something that was somehow both. Elena reveled in it, in the innocent heat of that moment.

When they parted, a shy smile played at Allison's lips. "I thought you wanted to talk."

Elena smirked. "Among other things."

Shaking her head, Allison laughed and said, "So, I know you gotta go, but can we talk soon? I mean, will I see you again soon?"

"I would like that," Elena agreed.

Their hands slipped down one another's arms before slim fingers laced together.

"Me too." Allison waggled her eyebrows and poked Elena's side. "I guess I should go then before my sheer animal magnetism has you dragging me into the backseat."

"Oh yes. Do relieve me of the terrible temptation, dear."

"I'll see you soon," Allison said. She pecked Elena's lips once more before hopping out of the car and bending down to wave through the open window.

Elena nodded. "You certainly shall."

"We kissed," Elena blurted as soon as Vivian answered the phone. "Twice. Well, more than twice, but basically twice."

Vivian squealed like a thirteen-year-old girl, needing no further information to know what Elena was talking about.

"Do try not to burst my eardrums, Viv."

"Sorry. I freaked out, but I am drowning in my excitement over here! It actually worked!"

Vivian smacked a hand over her mouth, realizing what she'd said, but it was too late to take it back.

"*What* actually worked, Vivian?"

"Uh, that's not important right now." Vivian waved a dismissive hand, even though Elena couldn't see her.

"*Vivian*," Elena hissed, and Vivian let out a heavy sigh. She knew there was no distracting Elena or getting her to drop the issue. She assumed she would eventually have to tell her anyway.

"Fine. But please keep in mind that all of what I am about to tell you led to this wonderful lesbian love you're feeling right now."

"*Vivian*!"

Vivian confessed in one rushed exhalation: "I may have purposely set you up on specific dates to steer you in Allison's direction."

"*Excuse me*?" Elena asked. "What *exactly* do you mean?"

Chapter Seventeen

"Uh, well, how much time do you have?" Vivian asked.

"I am headed into the office," she said. "You will meet me there and explain yourself."

"What?" She glanced around her office. "Elena, I can't. I have to work too, you know." This was not the entire truth. Her team was more than capable of handling her responsibilities in her absence.

"Is that supposed to deter me from demanding your presence?" Elena's voice drawled over Vivian's phone. "Because honestly Vivian, I believe you can do much better in the way of excuses."

"You're probably right." Vivian knew it was pointless to argue or deny anything. "But I haven't been awake that long, so my creativity is lacking."

"Then shall we bypass the nonsense and simply agree that you will be in my office within the hour?" Her tone of voice made it obvious that her words were more of a command than a request.

"Uh, well, let's see," Vivian began but was quickly cut off by a loud and enduring sigh. She could hear the anger in that sigh.

Elena was not the type of person to hash things out over the phone. She liked to be face to face, if for no other reason than that she could be much more intimidating in person—what with her power suits and her authoritative stances, her sharp enunciations and her icy glares.

"Vivian Abigail Warren, do *not* test me. I haven't a clue as to what *exactly* you have done, but I believe I can safely assume from your willingness to avoid me at all costs that I am not going to like it. As such, I suggest you be more agreeable, because I can guarantee that if you are not in my office within the next hour and with a perfect explanation for whatever it is you've done, you shall surely be sorry."

Vivian snorted with laughter even though she could tell Elena was seriously angry. Her friend's speech got even more severe when she was angry—long, harshly enunciated sentences and a threat or two tossed in. Still, Vivian couldn't help pushing her buttons sometimes. "Oh? What are you going to do to me, Elena? Disinvite me from Christmas dinner this year?"

"Worse." Vivian could hear Elena locking her car and making her way toward the elevator. "I doubt you would even want me to say it over the phone."

"Damn." Vivian sighed, tapping her nails against her desk. Give me a hint." They had a tendency to play horribly embarrassing pranks when they were upset with each other. "Like, would it be worse than the time you abandoned me at that gala with the buck-toothed guy that kept spitting on me when he spoke and so I lied and told everyone that you left because you had diarrhea?"

"I still cannot believe you did that." Elena groaned. "And yes, much worse."

"Shit. I'll be over in around twenty minutes depending on traffic."

"Wise choice."

As soon as the elevator jolted to a stop and the metal doors pulled apart, Elena tore through the office, her heels clicking furiously as she went. Various workers flitted around the busy environment, several ducking out of her way as she lit a fire through the room with her pace. They had all seen her in a mood, and none wanted to provide her any reason to direct her fury at one of them.

They peeked over their cubicles or gawked at her from behind papers, printers, and coffee cups. Some even whispered behind their hands as she passed, likely wondering what had set her off. Elena had a reputation for being a bit of a hard-ass at work, though she knew her employees respected her completely; well, most of them did.

She was demanding. She liked to assert her authority but she was also fair. She offered her employees massive bonuses during holidays, an adequate number of sick days, constructive feedback on their ideas and designs, even if they were of a poorer quality, and enduring respect. She rarely stooped to verbal blows with an employee, though it was common knowledge to stay out of her way if she entered the office with steam practically spewing out of her ears—much like today.

"I suggest you all stop gawking!" Elena snatched a cup of coffee from her personal assistant, who shot to her side as soon as she came off the elevator. "These shows do not run themselves, nor do the lines design themselves! I want sketches on my desk within the hour and pitches scheduled before lunch! This is a place of business, people, not a goddamned zoo. Get to work!"

Elena rarely cursed, but she was hardly in the mood for people's staring or whispering today. She had begun her morning in complete bliss, only to have it possibly shattered by whatever it was her best friend would soon be confessing.

The entire floor exploded into activity at her words. Nearly every walking, breathing creature in the room spiraled into action—running back to their desks and jumping into their work. The place was like a swarming cloud of bees, all of them spilling back into their hive.

A few attempted to wish her a good morning, to which she merely nodded, and then, of course, Wendy, the resident suck-up, popped in front of her.

"Good morning, Ms. Vega!" she said. "You look wonderful today. I'm loving this ensemble. Classy yet spicy. It's fabulous."

Elena arched a brow at the woman. "A spicy Latina? How original of you, Wendy."

Wendy deflated on the spot before slinking off to her desk.

Elena paid the hive no further mind as she glanced over the various papers handed to her by her assistant. When they reached her personal office, Elena crossed to her desk and dropped the files onto its surface, along with her coffee. She handed her jacket to her assistant, who hung it on the rack in the corner and closed the office door.

"Bad morning?"

"Strangely enough, Darla, no," Elena replied, "but possibly worsening by the second."

"Would you like an aspirin?"

"No, no, dear." She shook her head as she moved to stand in front of the massive transparent wall of windows. She propped her hands on her hips and sighed as she gazed out on the enormous city she had always called home. The view calmed her.

"Vivian will be dropping by within the hour," she said. "She and I will need a bit of time to discuss a rather important and private matter. Thus, I will need you to secure the pitch board by the time she arrives, and make sure I have no pitches scheduled before ten. Rearrange them if you have to, and if Elliot fights you on it, which he undoubtedly will, tell him that I have already reviewed his designs and have sent him an email with my thoughts. Then, schedule *his* pitch last."

Darla smirked as she made a note in her pocketbook. "He's not going to like that."

"Precisely," Elena replied with a wicked grin. "I could use the amusement today."

Darla chuckled. "Shall we review your messages now then or would you like to wait until after Vivian leaves?"

"Let's hold off." Elena dropped into her cushy black chair and tapped her mouse to wake her computer from hibernation mode. "I have several emails to attend to first, unless there is anything pressing?"

"Nothing pressing, ma'am," Darla told her, which instantly earned her a pointed look from her boss. "Sorry. Nothing pressing, *Elena*."

Elena smiled. "Six months, and I still have yet to break you of that habit."

"I'm working on it." Darla laughed and turned to leave Elena's office, then whirled back around. "Oh wait."

"Yes?"

"There was a message about the newest model for the Spring Social line," Darla informed, tapping her pen against her pocketbook. "Her agents would like confirmation that her new contract will be sent over with the included adjustments that were agreed upon prior to her first formal fitting and shoot."

"When is the fitting?"

"In two weeks."

"Very well, yes." Elena nodded as she clicked to open her email inbox. "Have legal send the adjusted contract, and, Darla, have them double-check to ensure that the particular caveats we discussed are included and clear prior to sending."

"Will do," Darla said, making another note in her pocketbook. "I'll head down to legal then. I should be back within the hour."

"Thank you, dear." Elena scanned through her emails as Darla quietly exited her office.

As soon as the door closed, Elena's eyes shot to the clock on her desk. She had been in the office only fifteen minutes, which meant Vivian would hopefully be arriving soon. Not knowing was driving Elena mad.

Allison was surprised to discover her roommate's absence when she finally tore herself away from Elena's awesome car, and Elena's intoxicating scent, and Elena's soft hands, and Elena's perfect mouth, and returned to her dorm. Then she remembered that Macy switched from her evening literature course on Fridays to the early morning time-slot on Wednesdays. She liked going out on Friday nights too much to spend those evenings trapped in a three-hour class that did nothing but bore her to tears.

Allison grumbled, disappointed. She needed someone to dish to but resigned herself to getting ready for the day. After a quick shower, she threw on some clothes, grabbed her books, and headed out into the quad. She had a nine a.m. seminar she would actually be early for. However, when she reached the auditorium where the seminar was held, she found nothing more than a stark, white piece of printer paper taped to the door and marked with a bold-faced notice:

Dr. Warner's Integrated Seminar,
SW 443, 9 AM, CANCELED

"For reals?" Allison groaned. She had walked all the way across campus for this class. Great. She pulled out her cell and checked to see if she had gotten an email notification of the cancellation and had simply overlooked it, but there was nothing—her inbox was empty. "The hell, Dr. Warner?" She glared at the notice. "This is what friggin' *email* is for!"

She trudged back to her dorm and collapsed onto her bed. She had a good four hours before her next class, so she closed her eyes and tried to force her brain to quiet long enough for her to get a good nap in. Only about thirty minutes passed, though, before the door burst open and Macy popped into the room, kicking the door closed behind her so that it slammed, all loud enough to wake Allison. She jerked up with a snort, wiping at her mouth.

"Oh, sorry mate." Macy laughed and tossed a red-and-white paper bag onto Allison's bed. "Didn't know you were sleeping."

"What's this?" Allison asked, reaching for the bag.

"Stopped by the Maccas. Got like fifteen of those burritos you like. I already ate like six of them."

Allison chuckled and rubbed at her eyes. Despite having already eaten, her stomach rumbled at the mere thought of breakfast burritos. They were her favorite.

"Thanks." She pulled one of the burritos from the bag, unwrapped it, and took a huge bite. "How is it possible that we eat as much as we do and yet neither of us weighs more than 130 pounds?"

"Haven't got a bastard clue, but I'm not complaining."

"Neither am I." Allison cracked up. She was quite proud of her figure. She had worked hard for it after all—running and working out as often as possible, and Allison knew she attracted quite a bit of attention because of it. She didn't care much for the gawking, though, unless of course it was a certain brunette doing the gawking.

The thought of Elena had Allison choking in her effort to swallow too quickly so she could speak, which caught Macy's attention.

"You all right?"

"Oh my God, Mace. I have *so* much to tell you."

"Ooh." Macy grinned as she settled more comfortably atop her bed. "That sounds juicy."

Before Allison could say another word, though, Macy continued. "Oh wait, lemme guess. You and hot-pants waited 'til the kid was out like a light and then you did the do on every surface in her enormous fancy house. Am I right?"

Jaw practically smacking into her chest, Allison gaped at her roommate.

Macy barreled over with laughter at Allison's reaction. "Your face, Alli! Your face is killing me!"

Snapping out of her trance, Allison reached for her pillow and chucked it across the room at her best friend. It smacked into the side of Macy's head. "You are an ass."

"Yeah, but was I right?" Macy asked. "Did you get naughty with the boss lady?"

"Well…"

"Explain yourself," Elena stared her best friend down from across her desk.

Vivian ran a hand through her hair, sighing as she nodded and resigned to spilling her little secret. "It's really not as bad as you're acting like it's going to be. Like I said, anything I did is at least partly responsible for the fuzzy love feelings you've got going on with the hot babysitter right now. So, just keep that in mind."

"Stalling will win you no points with me." Elena sat back in her chair, resting her elbows on the armrests, and steepling her fingers just under her chin.

Vivian rolled her eyes and launched into her story. "Okay, so the first date was completely natural. I didn't have anything planned. I hadn't even met Allison at that point."

Elena nodded, signaling for her to continue.

"Admittedly, he was an ass, but that was all his own doing."

Both she and Elena smiled despite the fact that one was mad at the other. "Then I met Allison that day at the museum with you and Lucas, and well, it was obvious."

"What was obvious?"

"The chemistry between you two." Vivian sighed. "It still astounds me that you were completely oblivious to it."

"Was it really?" Elena whispered.

"Uh yeah. I've never seen you act with a stranger—or anyone, really, for that matter— the way you did with Allison. The way you spoke to her and about her and even your body language. You two looked like a couple, and, from the way some of the people in the museum looked at you, I'm guessing they thought you were. It was adorable."

Elena tried to keep her expression stoic, but she couldn't help herself. A smile tugged at her lips, slowly growing the longer Vivian went on. Had the connection between her and Allison truly been that obvious from the beginning? How had she missed it?

"So, anyway, it was obvious that neither of you had clued into what the rest of the free world had already picked up on, and I was afraid that nothing would develop if I didn't intervene at least a little. So, you see Elena, I was doing it for *you*, because I'm such a wonderful friend. You can't *really* blame me for that, can you?"

Though Elena's anger quickly leaked away, she did her best to remain stern as she cut her eyes back to her best friend and pursed her lips. "That would depend on what *exactly* you mean when you say you 'intervened'."

"Nothing major," Vivian swore. "I simply coached the next two dates you had, and only a little."

"*Coached*?"

"I told them how to act," Vivian said, biting her lip. "Admittedly, Garrett went overboard; though in my defense, I didn't tell him to wear a toupee. He actually has hair, so I'm not even sure how he managed to get the thing to stick in place. He apparently thought it was a hilarious addition, though. He even sent me a selfie with an all-caps 'LOL' when he was on his way to your house."

"Vivian!" Elena couldn't even believe what she was hearing.

Vivian laughed. "I know! I know. I'm sorry. Listen, I only told him to be clingy and crass. Again, in my defense, I never said he should bring up anything even remotely related to his bowels. I said crass. He chose how to fulfill those requirements."

"Vivian!" Elena reached for the box of tissues on her desk and chucked it at the blonde. "I can't believe you! Do you have any idea how *embarrassing* that entire ordeal was for me?"

"Well yeah," Vivian mumbled. "I can imagine. Look, I'm sorry. I didn't know he was going to take it that far."

"What was the purpose of even doing such a thing? How would that have any bearing on my relationship with Allison?"

"Allison mentioned at the museum that you complained to her about the first date. I thought that if the dates were bad enough, it would not only show you the stark contrast between those horrible dates and the good-looking, funny babysitter waiting for you at home, but that it would also give you a chance to bond with her over ranting about each date."

"But Alexis was—"

"I know," Vivian interjected. "I originally planned to set you up on a string of bad dates, but then, the day of the show, you joked that you thought I was setting you up on bad dates on purpose, and well, I panicked. So, I decided to set you up on a good date instead, and I coached Alexis on the topics of conversation."

"Meaning?"

"Meaning I told her to ask you what you were looking for in a partner," Vivian explained. "I hoped it would help you realize *on your own* that you had already found someone who fit the bill, but, even if it didn't, I was at least ninety-seven percent sure that the mere sight of Alexis on your doorstep would make Allison jealous. I wasn't positive she had figured out her feelings for you yet, but then I thought she might not have even known that you are into women, so then I—"

Elena waved a hand for Vivian to stop. She heard all she needed to hear.

She could not believe that Vivian had concocted this elaborate, and actually rather genius, plan for no other purpose than to bring her and Allison closer together, to give her a real shot with her. As angry as Elena wanted to be, she had to admit that she found her friend's actions endearing. In fact, it was undoubtedly the sweetest scheme Elena had ever heard of and, furthermore, the plan *had* actually worked.

She and Allison had found their way to one another, and Vivian's actions certainly aided in the journey; that much was undeniable.

"Please don't be angry with me, Elena. I know I shouldn't have gone behind your back, but I know how you are. If I outright mentioned the possibility of you and Allison, you would have dismissed it, and then you would have overanalyzed everything to the point of panic. I didn't want you to give up on the idea before you ever even gave it a chance. I just wanted you to be happy. That's what I still want."

Elena sighed as she shook her head and looked up to meet Vivian's eyes. They stared at one another for a long time, Vivian's eyes cautiously mirthful despite her worry that Elena was actually upset with her. Elena held her serious expression a bit longer just to toy with her before she finally dropped the act and let a smile spread across her lips.

Vivian mimicked the expression as Elena said, "You are a complete pain in my ass, Vivian."

"But you love me." She jumped up from her chair and rounded Elena's desk, wrapping her arms around Elena from the side. "Right?"

Elena tilted her head to rest it against Vivian's. "Right."

Chapter Eighteen

"That's it?" Macy boomed. "You're seriously *this* excited over a bit of pashing?"

Allison rolled her eyes. "You weren't there, okay? It was hot. It wasn't just a kiss, okay? It was *the* kiss."

"No way it was *that* good," Macy laughed, shaking her head.

"It *was* though!" Allison threw a wadded up burrito wrapper at her roommate, falling back into her pillows, her cheeks red. She rolled her eyes again as she threw an arm over her flushed face. "God, I sound like a friggin' tween with a crush."

She rolled on her side to face Macy again. "One of my last homes before I left, I had a foster sister that was almost twelve, and she totally freaked out about this boy at school. She talked about the kid nonstop—his spiky hair and eyebrow ring. I thought it was so lame, you know? I used to tease her a lot when she'd fill up whole pages of her notebook with 'Mrs. Marcus Walsh'. But weirdly enough, that's how I feel right now, every time I think about it."

"Well, fuck me dead! You're starting to sound like you're *in love* with her, Alli."

Allison jolted up in shock. "No!" she protested. "What? No, of course not! I hardly even know her yet. I mean I *know* her. I just don't really *know her* know her. But no, not in love. Hell, I don't think I'd know what that whole 'in love' thing was even if it bit me on the ass. I just like her. I like her a lot. She's awesome. I mean, she's stunning, really, and nothing like what you would expect, you know?"

If Macy was honest, watching Allison speak about this other woman was enough to make her feel giddy, and that was rare. She had been privy to a few of Allison's childhood stories, how they had weathered her, and she knew that her friend rarely, if ever, got her hopes up about anything. She seemed hopeful in this moment, though. She seemed happy, almost like she had found something she had been searching for, for quite some time.

But rather than say any of that, Macy mocked gagging, sticking her middle finger in her mouth.

Allison smiled as she said, "Shut up."

"No, go ahead, mate. Keep on with the gross gushing. I love it."

Allison collapsed back on her pillow. "I mean, she can be totally awkward and stiff when you throw her out of her comfort zone, but who's not like that, right? But when she gets comfortable, she's so funny and smart and always so fucking pretty. Seriously, I think she might be an alien in a person suit, because who the hell is *that* pretty all the time?!"

"You," Macy said. She then grinned goofily at her friend and added, "And me, of course."

"She's in a completely different league." Allison laughed when Macy gasped, pretending to be offended. "Seriously, you should see her."

"Well, good on ya if she's *that* fine, but I'll reserve judgment 'til I see her myself."

"Oh yeah? And when exactly were you planning on seeing her?"

"Whenever you bring her home to meet the family, of course." Macy grinned and shrugged behind the pillow still wrapped in her arms.

"The *family*?" Allison cackled. "Are you talking about *yourself*, or have you forgotten that I don't have any family?"

Macy scoffed. "Of course I'm talking about me. *I'm* your family, and so you're obligated to bring this Elena chick by to meet me."

Allison sighed. "We'll see."

"That's it?"

"What do you mean?" Elena asked, frowning. "It was quite heated."

"Still," Vivian said, "you had her in your bed, and you were making out, and you were both apparently groping each other, and then you just *stopped*?"

"There *is* such a thing as taking it slow, Viv. Some people prefer to move quickly. Some don't."

"Yes, but—" Elena waved her off.

"I know you wanted me to 'let loose'." Elena clucked her tongue as she leveled her best friend with a playful glare. "But I think we both know that that simply isn't *me*. I'm not saying it won't happen or even that it won't happen soon, but we only *just* realized our feelings for one another. I'm actually glad we stopped, because I—"

"You what?" Vivian had an inkling she knew where this was headed.

Elena swallowed and sighed. "I care for her, more than I expected I would."

"Oh Elena, I know you do." Melting, Vivian grinned and resisted the urge to clap her hands. She felt like a cupid, a badass and entirely successful cupid. "And I *know* she cares about you, too."

"Oh?" Elena asked. "And how is that?"

"Because she got up and walked away in the middle of a make-out session that easily could've led to hot sex." Vivian made a show of waving her finger over Elena's face and upper body. "I've seen you, okay? I'm looking at you right now, babe, and you're way too gorgeous to walk away from."

Elena blushed, her head dipping slightly. "Yet she went."

"Yeah, she did." Vivian nodded. "Maybe she's more like you than you realize. Maybe she's just a take-it-slow kind of girl. If it's me interpreting her actions, I would say it's a clear sign that Allison is invested in at least seeing what could possibly develop between you two."

"Is it strange how much that excites me?" Elena asked. "In truth, I barely know her, but I find myself thinking about her all the time."

Vivian shook her head as she propped her elbow on her knee and settled her chin into her open palm. She smiled at Elena, her insides positively squirming with her excitement. This was the most hopeful, and the most thrilled, that she had seen Elena in quite a while, though she obviously reined it in better than most would. Elena Vega was nothing if not composed.

"It's not strange," she replied. "It's good. You will get to know her the more time you spend with her. It's *good*, you hear me? I know you like to overanalyze everything, but just this once, try not to, and just let it be good, okay?"

Elena gnawed softly at the corner of her bottom lip. When she nodded, Vivian practically jumped for joy. "Okay, so we have to plan a date."

"Date?" Elena whispered, eyes widening. "I hadn't even thought of that. Oh God, Vivian, what the hell am I supposed to do with Allison on a date?"

Vivian watched Elena's eyes flit steadily back and forth, panic brewing in their depths. "Okay, okay," she said, snapping her fingers at Elena, "let's just take a breath, okay? It's all fine. It's just a date."

"Yes," Elena snapped, her knee bouncing rapidly under her desk, "a date with someone who has very little in common with me! How are we even interested in one another? Vivian, I haven't the slightest clue how to plan a date with her. I don't even know if she would want to go on a date with me."

"Now you're just being modest, Elena," Vivian said. "It doesn't suit you. Let's go back to the I'm-sexy-and-I-know-it Elena. She's fun, and she knows for a fact that anyone would be lucky to date her, and Allison Sawyer is no different."

"Right," Elena croaked, clearing her throat.

"Okay, work on your delivery next time. That was the poorest vote of self-confidence I've ever seen. I can't believe this has you so rattled. Nothing rattles you."

"Right." Elena tried it a little more firmly this time.

"That's better." Vivian smiled at her and opened the notepad application on her smartphone. She poised her fingers over the keyboard once she opened a new note. "Now, let's plan this date."

"Shit!" Allison hissed, swiping a hand down the front of her face. "*Shit!*"

Macy snorted with laughter. "You said that already."

"This warrants repetition. In fact, I'll say it again. Shit! Shit! Shit!" Allison ran her fingers through her ratty blonde hair that was in desperate need of a wash.

"Stone the flamin' crows, Alli!" Macy groaned, wrapping her pillow around her face and sighing into it. "It's just a damn date! Take a breath and calm down. You're driving me crazy."

"It's not just a date," Allison argued. "It would be like the *first* date, and that's the most important or something. I don't know, really, but it has to be good, right? I don't even know what to do with Elena. I mean, I don't have much money, and I wouldn't want her to pay for everything. You have to help me, okay?"

"Fine. I'll help."

"Okay," Allison said. "Do you think she'd want to go somewhere fancy?"

"I'm guessing she does fancy on the regular," Macy said. "Take her out *your* way."

Allison's expression crumpled and Macy pushed herself up and out of her bed and over to Allison's. Plopping down, she placed a hand on Allison's knee. "Hey, no worries, okay? We'll plan the perfect date."

"We will?"

"Definitely. Now, she's all about that little rascal of hers, right?"

Chapter Nineteen

ELENA SMOOTHED HER HANDS DOWN the front of her shirt as she stepped from her closet. "Okay, munchkin, what do we think?" she asked as she motioned to her outfit.

Lucas looked up from his place in the center of Elena's bed, a giant coloring pad in his lap and a green crayon pinched between his fingers. He smiled at his mother and nodded firmly. "Pretty, Momma!"

When Lucas was a little over two years old, Elena came down with a terrible stomach virus and spent two full days in baggy sweatpants that no one knew she owned and a ratty Harvard T-shirt. He told her she was pretty more than once in those two days; Elena was convinced his opinion was biased by the fact that she gave him life and regular meals.

She offered him what she knew was a strained smile. She was more nervous than she was willing to admit aloud, but she couldn't miss the way it showed in her body: her expressions were tight, and her movements lacked their usual finesse as she flitted around her bedroom and bathroom, readying herself for the date she had been both looking forward to and dreading.

The past three days had been utter torture. The stress over what to wear on a first date—to the *zoo* of all places—to which her toddler would be accompanying her was hell enough. Her brain had taken it a step further, though, and kept her spiraling through a constant mental cycle of questions, both hopeful and worrisome. What if the date went splendidly? Would they have a second date? A third? Would this actually develop into a relationship? Was Elena ready for a relationship? Was *Allison*? What if their social statuses got in the way of their relationship? What if they kissed at the end of the date? Would it lead to anything? Wait, no, Lucas would be there.

What if the date went poorly? What if they ran out of things to converse about? What if things were awkward? What if Lucas monopolized the conversation as he was prone to do? What if they had to eat zoo food? Elena didn't know if she could eat a hot dog elegantly. What if someone fell into the gorilla pit? Okay, admittedly, that last one was a bit of a stretch, but Elena's mind was a complete mess after three days of what-ifs. They had gotten more ridiculous by the hour.

After checking her reflection once more in the mirror above her vanity, she put on a few pieces of jewelry, two white-gold bangles her mother had given her, and a simple circle-pendant necklace. She then touched up her lips and crossed over to her bed.

Full lips twitched with a smile as she looked down at Lucas, his little face hidden by the overhanging brim of the light green and gray newsboy hat he had chosen to pair with his white polo, light green shorts, and white sneakers. The natural curl of his hair caused it to flip up just behind his ears and under the hat in a few places. It had tamed a bit in almost four years, but when he was first born, Elena had had quite the time with his headful of dark kinky curls, much like her own when fresh out of the shower. His hair now, though, was more like his father's. It had lightened in color and was finer, less coarse than Elena's, though her own was soft enough.

"Are you ready?" she asked. He tossed aside his coloring pad and jumped to his feet on Elena's bed.

"Yeah!" He leapt onto Elena.

Elena chuckled as she caught him, letting out a soft grunt. He wrapped his thighs around her sides as she settled an arm under his bottom, and his right hand instantly found its way to the small hairs at the base of her head, hidden beneath her thick locks. "Are we gonna see monkeys?"

"We just might, my love." They headed out of her bedroom and down the hall. "What else would you like to see?"

"Um." Lucas tilted his head in thought, but then his eyes widened. "Dinosaurs!"

Elena laughed heartily at that. "I'm afraid there won't be any dinosaurs, Lucas." She grabbed her purse and car keys. "They are extinct, remember?"

"No bones?" Lucas pouted.

"No bones," she confirmed. "We have to go to the museums to see the bones, remember? Zoos are for living animals."

"Oooh," Lucas said, wiggling around on Elena's hip before she bent to settle him into his car seat. "Algators?"

"I'm not sure, Lucas." She buckled him in. "Would you like to see the reptiles?"

"Yeah! Does Alson like algators?"

"She may, love."

"Where is she?"

"We have to go pick her up," she said as she loaded Lucas's stroller into the trunk. There was no way he would stay on his feet the entire time, and she preferred him protected from the sun anyway. She also wouldn't have to worry about him wandering off, or letting go of her hand, or being picked up by a stranger and whisked away.

"For our date?" Elena could hear him bouncing in his car seat. Since the moment his mother had picked him up on Wednesday evening and informed him of the weekend date, it was all he could talk about. Not a day went by that he didn't ask her if it was time to go to the zoo with Allison.

Elena closed the trunk and moved around to close Lucas's door as well. She leaned in before doing so and kissed his temple. "Yes, Lucas, for *our* date."

Allison glanced down at her phone, her palms sweaty as she gripped the device tightly between her hands. She didn't know why she was so nervous. They were just going to the zoo after all. Still, though, the moment she received the "we're here" text message from Elena, Allison's heart began to thunder so loudly in her chest that she was surprised people weren't dancing around the dorm to the erratic beat.

"Okay, they're here."

"So go," Macy laughed. "And Alli, don't look so terrified. No worries, remember?"

"Right." Allison nodded and took a deep breath. "Right." She brushed her hands down the front of her white tank top before pulling at the open edges of her blue-and-white pinstriped button-up shirt. Running a hand through her hair, she glanced back at Macy.

Macy sighed. "Will you stop? You look great."

"But like *date* great?" Allison asked. "I mean, I know we're going to the zoo and I should be comfortable, but I still want to look, you know, presentable or whatever."

"The ripped jeans are really working for you," Macy said. "How you look isn't going to matter, though, if you don't stop yabbering and just go already."

"Okay, okay," Allison groaned. She grabbed her phone and sent a quick reply. "I'm going."

"Good."

Allison stuck her wallet in her back pocket and then headed for the door. Just as Allison opened it, Macy called out to her again. "Oh, and Alli?"

Allison turned back. "Yeah?"

"Try to relax. Use a little of that Sawyer swagger." She reached over and grabbed something off of her bedside table and tossed it through the air. "And eat that."

Allison caught the small item in midair and cracked up when she saw that it was a peppermint. She pulled the wrapper off and popped the mint in her mouth. "Thanks Mace. I'll see you later."

"Hopefully *much* later."

Allison slipped out of the dorm, closing the door behind her.

"Sawyer swagger," Allison muttered as she passed the elevator and shot straight to the stairs. She took them two at a time and did her

best to take Macy's advice and just relax. "It's all good," she told herself as she finally made it to the ground level. "She likes you. It's good."

Before exiting the building, she took a deep breath. She cracked her neck to both sides and smoothed her hands over her shirt once more, whispering "Sawyer swagger" to herself over and over. She then shook out her nerves and pushed open the door, stepping out into the bright sunlight of the late morning.

Allison only managed about ten seconds of her cocky little strut before she glanced up and stumbled to a stop. Elena was parked a short distance from the dorm and stood beneath the glimmering sun, leaning against the passenger door of her car. Allison's breath caught so forcefully in her throat that she nearly choked.

Her heart hammered away as her eyes tracked the length of Elena's body. The woman was practically painted into dark-wash skinny jeans, a simple white V-neck T-shirt that she somehow made look like a royal fucking gown, and black pumps with a shorter heel than Allison was accustomed to seeing Elena wear.

It was obvious that Elena had gone for that classic sexy look, while Allison had went more the route of effortlessly hot, and it almost made her want to laugh. They were so different. It was apparent in everything—their manners of dress, their manners of speech, their body languages, and their individual demeanors. They were in stark contrast, and, yet, they somehow always found a way to fit easily together; at least, they always had before. Allison was hopeful, and now maybe a tad confident, that it would be much the same this day.

"Hi," Allison said when she reached the car.

"Hello." They stared at one another for another long moment, until Allison finally just shuffled awkwardly forward. She wrapped an arm around Elena, hugging her, and was pleased when she felt Elena's arms come around her a moment later to return the embrace.

"You look great," Allison said as they pulled apart again. "I mean, really. Wow." She glanced down Elena's body again. "I'm surprised you even own jeans, but now I'm thinking that you should probably *only* ever wear jeans from now on."

Elena smirked. "Thank you. You look wonderful as well."

"Eh, I've got basically nothing goin' for me but these abs, so I figured if nothing else, I couldn't go wrong with a tight tank." Allison blushed at her own words, wishing she hadn't even said them. She cleared her throat and laughed awkwardly, expecting Elena to join in. Elena, however, merely continued to smirk at her.

Her eyes tracked back down to Allison's abs, the indentations between the muscles clearly visible through the thin material of the white tank top. Her voice lowered an octave when she said, "You figured right."

Allison swallowed thickly, heat ripping through her body at the sound of Elena's voice. Before she could reply, though, a loud sigh sounded from inside the car and they both heard Lucas shout, "I'm here too!"

They laughed, and Elena surprised Allison by turning and opening the passenger door for her. "Uh, thanks," Allison said. "No one's ever opened the door for me before."

Elena smiled and waited until Allison was seated before closing the door and leaning down through the open window. "You're welcome," she replied. "Oh, and you have much more going for you than just your abs, dear, though they are rather nice." She winked and made her way around to the driver's side.

Allison bit her lip and shook her head as Elena disappeared from the window. That woman was seriously going to be the death of her. She took a deep breath, and as Elena slipped into the driver's side, Allison turned in her seat and smiled back at Lucas. "Hey little man!" she greeted. "You ready to see some animals?"

"Yeah!" he shouted. "You like algators?"

Allison sucked in a hissing breath and tilted her head. "Ooh, I don't know, Lucas. They're a little scary."

The small boy giggled. "Me and Momma will hold your hand! Won't we, Momma?"

"Absolutely," Elena agreed as she pulled into traffic. She glanced to the woman beside her and added, "If you would like, dear."

"What if there aren't any alligators? Do I have to be scared in order for you to hold my hand?"

Elena kept her eyes on the road, but Allison could see the pink tint on her neck and cheeks. When Elena shook her head, Allison grinned like a fool.

Elena unbuckled Lucas from his car seat with only a bit of difficulty, and, as soon as she pulled him from the car and set him on his feet, Allison whistled loudly. “Whoa, Lucas, you look handsome, buddy.”

He beamed up at her and waited for Elena to prepare the stroller. “Thank you!” A faint blush touched his cheeks, making him somehow look even more like his mother than he already did.

“Who’d you get all dressed up for?” Allison asked, squatting down to be eye level with the kid. She poked his sides playfully, and he giggled and pushed her hands away. “The monkeys?”

“No.” Another giggle burst forth. “Our date.”

“Aw, really? You got dressed up for our date?”

“Yup!” He nodded. “I’m a gennlemen, right Momma?”

Allison swooned as Elena laughed. “That’s right, Lucas. You are a perfect gentleman.” Elena wheeled the stroller around and motioned for her son to climb inside. He happily took his juice cup from his mother as Allison buckled the strap around his waist.

“All right,” Allison said with a clap of her hands. “Are we ready, Vega family?”

“Ready!” Lucas boomed, and Elena laughed from behind the handles of his stroller.

“Lead the way.”

They took off as a unit into the zoo.

Lucas squealed and pointed every few minutes as Elena and Allison wheeled him from exhibit to exhibit, animal to animal. She made easy conversation with Elena about random things as they strolled along. They talked about everything from Elena’s lack of comfort clothes to Allison’s strange habit of brushing her teeth in the shower every morning. It was easily the most comfortable date Allison had ever been on, though there hadn't been many.

They took a break after about an hour of walking to eat. They ate simple—chicken fingers and fries shared among the three of them. Allison cracked a joke about how Elena looked like she was eating escargot in a fancy restaurant and was pleasantly surprised when Elena teased in return that Allison looked like she had never eaten before in her life.

Once finished, Allison insisted on buying everyone ice cream. Lucas wanted chocolate, so she ordered him a small sugar cone with a single scoop of chocolate. Elena asked for mint pistachio, which earned her another teasing smile from Allison, and Allison went for plain old vanilla.

"I love ice cream!" Lucas cheered halfway through his cold snack, his cheeks, chin, and nose already covered in chocolate.

"Yes, we see that, dear."

"I don't know what you're talking about, Elena," Allison said, her eyes glinting with mirth. "He doesn't look to me like he's enjoying that ice cream cone at all."

"Oh, didn't you know?" Elena asked. "You simply cannot enjoy ice cream unless it's covering at least half of your face."

Allison grinned wickedly. "Oh, well, in that case, you're not enjoying your ice cream at all, are you? I don't see a single bit of—oh wait." She popped her hand over and jostled Elena's wrist just as she went to take a lick, and Elena gasped when green ice cream smeared across her chin.

"Allison!" Elena's hand instantly went up to cup around her chin as Allison buckled over laughing.

Allison couldn't help herself. Elena's expression was priceless, and she couldn't stop the laughter as it bubbled up and out of her. She expected Elena to instantly go for the baby wipes in the stroller, ridding herself of the cold evidence of Allison's betrayal, but, instead, Elena thoroughly surprised her.

"Well, I suppose you're not enjoying yours either," she said and launched forward, smashing the globe of her ice cream cone against Allison's lips and nose. "Perhaps you should try some of mine!"

Allison's gasp was even louder than Elena's, but she needed hardly any time to rebound before she burst out laughing again. Green ice cream decorated her face. She could feel it freezing against her nose and smeared across her lips, and she couldn't believe that Elena went there, but she was so glad. It was incredible to see this playful side of the usually tightly bound woman. Allison wanted to unravel her entirely and see all the quirky parts that she kept hidden.

Lucas's high-pitched giggle echoed around them like a warm embrace as Allison glared at Elena's mocking smirk and asked, "Oh, you think that's funny, do you?"

"Quite."

One fair hand shot out and latched onto Elena's arm. Allison jerked Elena flush against her and asked, "First date kiss?"

Elena sucked in a sharp breath as their eyes locked, but laughed, the sound muffled, when Allison then pressed her ice-cream covered lips to hers. She nuzzled Elena's nose with her own, covering its dainty tip with sticky green, all to Lucas's great amusement.

"Alson! Don't 'tack Momma!"

Both Elena and Allison chuckled as they pulled apart. Allison smiled down at him. "Sorry, buddy. But she got me first."

"Oh, I did no such thing! You started it."

Allison shifted a little closer to her. "Fair enough." She laughed.

Elena grabbed the wipes and passed Allison a few. She cleaned her own face and hands quickly, tossing the rest of her melted and destroyed ice cream cone in the nearby trashcan, and cleaned Lucas's face as well. "What do you think, Lucas? I think Allison might like me a little."

He nodded vigorously and smiled up at Allison who hovered over Elena's shoulder. "Yup!"

When Elena peered over her shoulder, Allison mimicked Lucas's response, nodding just as vigorously. "Yup!"

Chapter Twenty

"HEY LOOK!" ALLISON POINTED TO a large stand near the front of the zoo where dozens of stuffed animals hung from racks and lined shelves.

Elena laughed. "I never would have pegged you for the type to sleep with a stuffed animal, dear."

Allison nudged her with her elbow as she leaned atop the handles of Lucas's stroller and pushed it along, Elena walking leisurely at her side. "Ha ha. I meant for Lucas."

"You have been in my son's room." Elena glanced at Allison with a pointed sigh. "I'm sure you are aware of the already excessive number of stuffed animals he owns. They are impossible to miss after all."

That was true. A large shelf lined the corner of Lucas's bedroom and was covered in books and stuffed animals of all kinds, mostly dinosaurs. Allison thought it was cute but yeah, a little excessive. Still, she wanted to get the kid *something*.

"Well why do you keep buying him stuffed animals?" she asked, poking Elena's side.

"I haven't bought him a single stuffed animal since before he was two. There is no need. My mother buys every one she comes across."

"Aw. That's kind of sweet that the kid's grandma wants to spoil him."

"It's not sweet, dear, it's detrimental to discipline." Elena chuckled. "Lucas has both my parents wrapped around his little finger, and they don't even deny it. If I refuse him something, my mother is always there to swoop in and buy it for him anyway. It's maddening."

"Your mom sounds like a trip." Allison shook her head, remembering her short encounter with Nora Vega. "Scratch that," she said. "I *know* your mom is a trip. Within about five seconds of meeting me, she was basically asking you if you were mad that we didn't sleep together."

Elena groaned at the memory. "My mother has no filter." She then amended herself. "No, actually, she *does* have a filter. She simply chooses not to exercise it where my personal pride is concerned."

"Yeah." Allison cracked up. "I swear I thought your face was gonna explode. It was bright red."

Elena poked Allison's side. "Yours was not much better."

"Yours was worse."

"How can you possibly know that? You couldn't even see your own face. I assure you, Allison. It was red."

"Yeah, but yours was redder," Allison teased.

"It was not."

"Was so."

"It was not."

"It totally was."

"This is childish," Elena snapped, though the edge of her words was softened by the growing smile on her lips. She tilted her head back, poking her nose into the air as if she was much too classy to participate in such childish banter. Allison laughed, though, when she heard Elena murmur, "Yours was redder."

"Ha!" Allison croaked. "No way. Had to be yours, because it was *your* family doing the teasing."

Elena glared at Allison. "Fine." She released an overly dramatic sigh. "You have a point." She inched a little closer to Allison, seeming to enjoy the way their shoulders brushed together as they walked. A contented sigh escaped her.

"My mother *does* quite like to see me squirm. I suppose it's merely a maternal thing, though. I'm sure I will tease Lucas once he is old enough to date. It's a rite of passage for mothers. Don't you think?"

Allison shrugged, her laughter crumbling in her throat. For only a moment, her eyes grew distant, but then she snapped back to the present and said, "I wouldn't know."

Elena's gaze shot to Allison. "Allison, I …"

"No, don't," Allison said, turning toward Elena. "I'm sorry. I don't know why I said that. I didn't mean to make things uncomfortable."

Elena looked at her, and Allison was surprised to find that it was not pity she saw reflected back at her, but something akin to admiration. It made her feel stronger somehow, better. She was so used to avoiding topics or making comments that in any way related back to her upbringing, or, rather, the lack thereof, because she hated the way people always reacted—sympathetic, pitying. She had even had a few people pretend they had not heard her and just change the subject. She hated the look people got in their eyes, like she was some kind of stray puppy that hadn't eaten in weeks. It made her feel weak. It made her itch in all the worst ways until she just wanted to peel her fucking skin off.

Elena was different. She did not look at Allison with pity in her eyes, even when caught off guard by a comment. She appeared startled, sure, and maybe a little unnerved, but not pitying. Instead, she looked at Allison like she was some kind of hero, and, well, Allison didn't quite know how to respond to that. Still, she couldn't deny that it was an incredible difference, one that made her feel like so much more than the lost, lonely girl she had always been.

Elena took a tentative step closer to Allison and placed a hand on her bicep. "Don't apologize, Allison. You never have to apologize for who you are or where you come from, not to me and certainly never for speaking your mind."

Allison let out a heavy breath. "You're like crazy perfect, you know that?"

A smile bloomed across Elena's supple lips. "Crazy or perfect, which is it?"

Allison laughed, her hands inching out from her body and toward Elena's as if they were magnets, constantly straining to touch. She wrapped her arms around Elena's waist and pulled her a little closer. "A crazy amount of perfect."

They breathed in the heat of the building tension between them. It was electric, sparking higher and brighter with every passing second, and Allison asked, "Is this okay?"

Elena watched the way Allison's mouth moved as she spoke, her tongue unconsciously peeking out to moisten her bottom lip. "Is what okay?"

"That I'm, you know, holding you like this? I mean, I kind of just grabbed you."

"Allison, we nearly slept together only a few nights ago."

Allison cleared her throat. "Right, yeah. You're totally right."

"You are welcome to touch me, dear," Elena whispered, reaching up to trace a finger along Allison's bottom lip. "But thank you for being respectful. You are quite the gentlewoman."

"Yeah, that sounds weird. But 'lady' doesn't really seem very fitting either. There should be a better word."

"There should," Elena agreed. They seemed to regain their senses some in that moment, both taking a deep breath and stepping slightly away from one another. Space allowed more air, and air allowed oxygen to actually reach their brains, which was a good thing, because it seemed like the closer they were to one another, the more likely they were to simply short-circuit and implode. Or they would end up making out in the middle of the zoo, scarring children and animals left and right. Allison seriously considered it anyway.

"So." She cleared her throat to get the dirty thoughts out of her voice. They never left her brain though, not for a second. "Which stuffed animal are we getting for the little guy?"

Elena groaned. "Must we?"

"Alas," Allison said dramatically, nodding, "we must."

A snort escaped Elena with her small burst of laughter, an entirely undignified sound that Allison wanted to squeal over, but, instead, she just smiled and kept her cool. "Note to self," she said, "talk fancy more often. It results in snorts."

Elena smacked her arm. "I did not snort."

"Elena! You *so* did. Now you're just blatantly lying."

"It isn't a lie if it never happened. *I* do not recall a snort, therefore it never happened."

"Oh, is this you getting all existential on me now?" Allison asked. She pinched her face and pressed a hand to her chin. In a nasally voice, she asked, "If one snorts and then lies about it, does the snort really exist?"

Elena burst into loud laughter as Allison slung an arm around her and kissed her cheek. Even when things were awkward, a comfort always existed between them, as if they had been laughing together for years, or as if they would.

When the laughter quieted, Allison pointed toward the stroller in front of her. "Why don't we just ask Lucas which one he wants?"

"Oh, dear, Lucas is fast asleep," Elena told her.

"How do you—" Allison bent around and peered down into the stroller. Sure enough, Lucas was out like a light, like a broken light. He looked like he hadn't slept in days, chin pressed hard to his chest and his head lolled over to one side. A large stream of drool fed a growing spot on his polo. "Wow, he is like *really* sleeping. How'd you know?"

"We have been walking for nearly thirty minutes now and haven't heard a peep from him," Elena said. "I'm sure the excitement of the day has merely worn him out."

"Yeah, there's a river running from his mouth."

"I suppose our conversation wasn't entertaining enough to keep him awake." Elena smirked at Allison. "Although, *you* certainly seemed to find it titillating considering you didn't notice his silence."

Allison leaned in and lowered her voice. "You totally only said that word so you could say 'tit' on our first date, didn't you?"

Elena gaped as Allison doubled over in laughter. Allison wrapped an arm around her and joked, "Geez, Elena. First date, and you're already bringing up tits. Your gay is showing."

Allison only laughed harder when Elena hilariously glanced down at herself without thinking. They then both erupted, poking at one another and forgetting entirely where they were and what they were doing. They jumped apart, startled, when a throat cleared loudly behind them.

They turned to see the teenager running the merchandise booth staring pointedly at them. "You guys have been standing there for like ten minutes."

"So?" Allison shrugged.

"So, you're kinda blocking the stand."

It was obvious the kid hated his job, or maybe his life, Allison didn't know; all she knew for sure was that he had a bad attitude. Not really the best person to be working in a place teeming with children.

"Are you gonna buy something or what? 'Cause if not, then you should move already."

Just as Allison was about to retaliate, she felt Elena's hand slip around her wrist and squeeze. "Don't bother, dear," she said. "Let me handle this."

Elena stepped over to the counter of the stand. Allison was a little intimidated just watching the way Elena moved, her spine straightening, her body somehow growing taller, larger, more imposing. How she could just turn it on like that, just go from laughing and adorable to the larger-than-life head bitch in charge in a snap, was completely beyond Allison. It also completely turned her on.

Elena narrowed her eyes at the nametag on the teen's shirt. "Hello, Seth. It appears you aren't having the best of days."

"Lady, come on," Seth said. "I don't need any kind of weird reverse psychology or lecture or whatever. I'm just trying to do my job and you're blocking the stand."

"Mm." Elena glared at him. "I would inquire as to who taught you your manners, Seth, but it appears you have none. Quite a shame when one works in the service industry. You see, in a job such as this one, you need to be able to maintain a polite demeanor and attitude with any and all potential and paying customers."

Seth let out a dramatic sigh as he rolled his eyes at Elena and tapped his fingers against the counter. "Like I said, I don't need a lecture."

"*Because*," Elena bowled right over the boy's words, "you never know with whom you might be speaking."

That got the kid's attention. His eyes narrowed as he looked her over. His gaze then flicked over to Allison and back to Elena. Allison could see Elena had him then; that tiny flicker of panic in his gaze was all she needed to work with.

"Ah yes." She was perfectly composed and poised, her hands clasped neatly in front of her. "Now I have your attention."

"Should I know you?" he asked her.

"Oh no, dear." Elena never dropped that strangely cold smile that painted her luscious lips. "You wouldn't know me; however, you should have thought to be a bit kinder before speaking to my girlfriend and me in such a rude manner."

Allison perked up at the mention of 'girlfriend', her stomach flipping and her heart kick-starting into a drumming rhythm. Did Elena mean that? Surely not. It was only their first date, after all. She probably just said that because it was convenient. She couldn't decide, though, if she was happy or disappointed about that.

"You see," Elena told Seth, "some of us have quite a bit of power. In fact, some of us might even own this very zoo you are working in."

Seth's eyes practically bugged out of his skull, and Allison even had to turn her head to hide her own reaction. She could hear Seth stammering out an apology, obviously afraid he would lose his job.

A few minutes later, Allison felt a tap on her arm and turned to see Elena holding a green stuffed monkey with long lanky limbs. She wore a satisfied smirk. "Shall we, dear? I believe it may be time to get Lucas home."

"Uh, y-yeah, yeah. Of course." As they moved away from the merchandise stand and toward the zoo's main entrance, Allison asked, "Do you seriously *own* this freakin' zoo?"

Elena chuckled. "Of course not," she said, nudging Allison with her elbow, "but Seth didn't know that."

Chapter Twenty-One

Elena didn't ask if Allison wanted to go home with her, and Allison didn't ask if she could. It was apparently a silent yet mutual understanding that neither wanted the date to be over, so instead of driving toward campus, Elena headed home, bringing Allison along.

Lucas hadn't stirred once, not even when Elena lifted him out of the stroller and settled him into the car seat. That didn't change when they finally made it back to Elena's house. He curled around his mother like a koala bear as she hoisted him out of the car seat again and carried him into the house, Allison following closely behind.

After following Elena down the hallway, Allison watched her settle the boy into his bed, having to unclench his fingers from around the hair at the base of her head. She pulled his shoes and socks from his feet, popped off his hat, and then stripped him down to his pull-ups. The kid only mumbled a few times throughout the whole process but then settled right back into his sheets and drifted off again.

Allison stepped in and handed Elena the green stuffed monkey. "Here," she whispered. "He can sleep with it."

"Are you sure you wouldn't rather save it so that *you* can sleep with it?" Elena tucked the toy in beside Lucas. "You were rather adamant about getting a stuffed animal after all."

"I don't need to sleep with monkeys if I've got you."

When Elena pulled the door shut behind them, the two women stood staring at one another. That painfully familiar electricity sparked between them again, and Elena cleared her throat, letting her gaze fall away from Allison's. "Would you like something to drink?" she asked, moving past Allison and heading back down the hallway toward the kitchen. Allison shrugged and followed, laughing internally at herself because it seemed like every time she was in this big, beautiful house, she followed Elena around like a puppy. In fact, she realized she had been doing it since her very first visit. It seemed the draw between them had always been there despite the fact that, foolishly, neither had noticed it.

"Uh, like alcohol?" Allison asked. "Because I'm not big on wine. I'll take some tea or something if you've got it."

"Juice?"

"Yeah, thanks."

Elena went about readying a couple of glasses, filling half of one with wine and the other to the brim with apple juice. She turned to see Allison leaning up against the kitchen counter and watching her. They looked at one another, and both women sighed, completely affected by only a glance. Elena handed the juice to Allison, their fingers brushing in the exchange and causing a delightful shiver to ripple down Allison's spine. Retreating until her back nudged the counter on the opposite side of the kitchen, Elena stared at the woman across from her as both took long sips from their glasses.

"So," Allison said, setting her glass on the countertop. Her entire body felt like a coiled snake, tense and practically vibrating with energy as she watched Elena's tongue slip across her bottom lip to capture a bit of escaped moisture.

Elena mimicked Allison's action, placing her own glass down behind her. "So," she repeated, the word barely a whisper. The pull between them was magnetic, and neither said another word. Both women shot off of their respective sides of the counter and collided in the middle.

Hands landed anywhere they could, *everywhere* they could. Elena's fingernails dug into Allison's scalp as Allison's gripped tightly around Elena's hips. The kiss was hot and rough, desperate and hungry, tongues slipping together, tasting, exploring. Their teeth knocked together with the frantic motion, but neither paid any mind to the messy state of the kiss. They only wanted more.

Elena pushed her body into Allison's, backing her up until they slammed into the counter again, the cabinets shaking and the glass of juice nearly falling from the edge.

"God, you're hot," Allison whispered as she ran her hands around from Elena's hips and cupped them over jean-clad cheeks. Allison moaned into Elena's mouth, echoing a similar sound that bubbled up from Elena's throat. "Your ass."

Elena smiled into the kiss as she slid her tongue along Allison's bottom lip. "Mm. Your mouth."

Her hands slinked down from Allison's hair, down the column of her slender neck, down over collarbones, down until they were cupped around—

"Momma?"

Allison and Elena sprang apart fast, bodies whipping in the direction of the sleep-laden voice.

"L-Lucas." Elena's hand shot up to wipe at the corner of her mouth where her lipstick had smudged. She righted her shirt, which was only slightly askew. "What are you doing up, darling?"

Naked but for his pull-ups, Lucas rocked on his heels a few feet from them. His messy hair stuck up on one side and his eyes drooped. He held his green monkey in one arm, tucked atop his round belly, and he used his other hand to rub at his eyes. "Hot," he mumbled, too tired to even attempt a full sentence.

Allison tapped her fingers atop the counter nervously as she stood a bit away from Elena, putting some distance between them. It was the only way to keep her hands to herself. She could feel the heat in her cheeks, entirely mortified at having been caught macking on Elena by none other than Elena's son.

Awkward and uncomfortable.

Lucas didn't seem to mind, though. In fact, he didn't even seem fully awake—just a partially naked zombie baby, too tired to function.

"Oh," Elena sighed, the blush on her own cheeks prominent, even as she tried to pretend like they hadn't just been doing what they had totally just been doing. She crossed over to her sleepy child and hoisted him up into her arms. "Let's go get your fan, okay? Then you can nap some more."

He laid his head on her shoulder and nodded into her neck. Elena glanced back at Allison and offered an apologetic smile before carrying Lucas back to his room.

Allison scrubbed a hand down her face and let out a heavy breath that quickly evolved into quiet laughter. What a day.

When Elena returned to the kitchen, she found Allison leaning against the counter and sipping her apple juice. They smiled at one another before Elena said, "He apparently required a story."

"Ah. I wondered what was taking so long. I was starting to think that maybe you had crawled into bed with the kid and had fallen asleep in there, too."

"No, of course not." Elena chuckled.

"Wouldn't blame you. The kid is pretty snuggly."

"True." Elena cleared her throat, her cheeks flushing a soft pink as she added, "However, I highly doubt I would be able to nap after..."

"Yeah," Allison breathed. Her body still buzzed from the impromptu kitchen make-out, and she couldn't help but grin like an idiot at Elena, basically confirming that she felt the same way.

They shared a small, almost shy laugh, both blushing. Their gazes flicked between eyes and lips, hearts pounding in unison. When Allison pushed off the counter and took a step forward, though, Elena took a step back and put up a hand. "Allison, I think we should talk."

Allison's heart sank into her stomach. Every single time she had ever heard those words, disappointment or heartbreak followed—news that she was being shuffled off to another home, that she wasn't what the family wanted, that she simply wasn't enough. Every single cell in Allison's body rioted against those words, because, if they meant what she expected them to mean, that Elena was about to tell her that all of this had been a terrible, impulsive mistake, then Allison didn't think she could handle that.

This thing with Elena, whatever this was, had been such a reprieve from the loneliness Allison often felt. It had been a patch for the dark, gaping hole inside, the part of her that still felt so unlovable. It had been exciting, refreshing, and riddled with hope. To lose it before it even truly began made Allison feel like she couldn't breathe. Her whole body was a pin cushion, pricked over and over by the possibilities ripping through her mind, and, within seconds, she talked herself into believing that whatever it was Elena wanted to talk about would result in nothing but utter disaster, and that made Allison sick to her stomach.

She wanted to run. She wanted to get as far away from that house as possible, wanted to pretend like those words had never come out of Elena's mouth at all. Maybe she could go home and sleep and wake up to realize that it was all a dream and it was still the day before their date. Allison didn't care, as long as she didn't have to live in this one moment, this one moment that would undoubtedly prove to be yet another disappointment in a long list of disappointments that colored her life.

"That came out wro—" Elena tried, but Allison shook her head and took another step back.

"It's, uh," Allison said, her voice strained as if her throat had collapsed, "it's okay. I get it. You don't have to say anything, Elena. I'm actually pretty used to this."

"Allison, no." Elena tried again, but Allison was already moving around her and toward the foyer, desperate to escape.

"Don't," Allison said through gritted teeth. Tears built up in her voice. "You don't have to explain or whatever. You think we made a mistake, and that's, uh, that's okay. I'm just going to go. I should go."

She raced to the door, Elena hot on her heels, and then whirled around at the last second. "Can I at least still see Lucas sometimes, though? Because I care about him, and I—"

Elena launched herself into Allison's personal space, hands shooting up and cupping around her cheeks to silence her. She looked directly into her eyes. "Allison! Stop."

The words died in Allison's throat, her gaze captured by Elena's. The woman looked at her so lovingly, so intensely that it threw Allison's balance. Was she or was she not being rejected?

"I *don't* think this is a mistake." Elena stroked her thumbs over Allison's cheeks.

Allison's mouth went dry. Her heart clenched in her chest. Her flesh tingled beneath Elena's fingertips. "You don't?"

"Of course not," Elena whispered. She lowered a hand and poked at Allison's side. "Are my kisses that unconvincing?"

Allison let out a sigh and muttered, "No."

"Good," Elena told her, smiling. "I would hate to think my kissing was inadequate."

Allison snorted, shaking her head and taking a deep breath. "Your kisses are the best I've ever had."

"I'm sorry for my wording, Allison," Elena said. "I realize now how ominous that sounded, but I assure you it's nothing worth running from." Her brows furrowed. "At least, I hope it isn't."

"*I'm* sorry. I freaked out. I should've let you finish, but I've just heard that a lot in my life, and it's never been followed by anything positive, you know?"

She nodded. "I am not turning you away, Allison. I simply thought it best that we discuss a few things. Will you stay, please?"

Latching onto Elena's hand, Allison let her lead them back through the house and into the living room. They settled on the couch, a fair distance from one another, and an awkward silence developed between them—one woman unsure of how to begin and the other still completely wary of whatever was coming. "So," Allison croaked, unable to take the silence any longer, "what was it that you wanted to talk about?"

A soft sigh slithered across Elena's lips. She sat across from Allison, her hands clasped atop her knees and her legs crossed elegantly at the ankles. "I think it's obvious that you and I are *quite* attracted to one another," she said, "considering the fact that we seem to be unable to keep our hands to ourselves."

"We seem to be doing a pretty good job of keeping our hands to ourselves right now."

Elena's deadpan stare made them both laugh. "Thank you for that keen observation, dear.

"Sorry," Allison said. "Go ahead."

"As I was saying, the attraction between us is obviously intense, and I hate to be presumptuous, but I believe it is apparent where things are headed."

Allison bit her lip and cleared her throat. "Sex, right?" she asked. "I mean, just clarifying that we're talking about sex here, yeah?"

Elena smiled, shaking her head. "Yes, dear," she replied with a throaty laugh. "We are talking about sex."

"Yeah, okay. Thought so." Allison waggled her eyebrows and slipped her foot across the floor to bump Elena's crossed ankles. "So, you wanna have sex with me, huh?"

She liked the way she could make Elena squirm sometimes by just being forward, but when Elena nodded firmly and said, "I do, yes," Allison nearly fell off the couch.

"Uh, um, well." She tried to orient herself, and Elena burst into a teasing smile.

"Oh see, you can dish it out, but you can't receive." She bumped Allison back with the toe of one high-heeled shoe.

"Good God, woman! Are you trying to kill me?" Allison wheezed. They laughed together and shifted closer to one another on the couch. Allison relaxed back into the cushion, and Elena leaned on the couch arm. "Seriously, though. Were you being serious?"

"Yes."

Allison felt like a teenager again, like she was crushing so hard on Elena in that moment that she was surprised the woman wasn't flat as a pancake. "Um, well, that's good." Her cheeks flushed and she wiped her sweaty palms on her jeans, hoping Elena wouldn't notice. "That's *really* good."

"Yes," Elena whispered again, moving closer to Allison. "Only, like I said, Allison, I think it's best if we discuss a few things first."

"Okay," Allison agreed. "I don't have any STDs or anything like that if you're worried. It's been a while since I've been with anyone, and I've had my yearly exam since then, but, I mean, I can go get tested again if you want, like, proof or something."

Elena shook her head and smiled. "Thank you, but I trust you. However, I'm glad you mentioned that it has been some time since you have been with someone; because that is one of the things I wished to speak with you about. It has been a very long time since I have been with anyone, sexually or otherwise."

"Is it okay if I ask how long?" Allison whispered.

Elena nodded, head ducked. "Over four years."

"Wow." Allison breathed. "That is longer than I expec—Oh."

Suddenly, it clicked in her mind. Lucas was three, and likely nearing four, but the timing was clear enough.

"Lucas?" Allison asked quietly.

"Yes," Elena sighed. "His conception, actually."

Allison tapped her fingers together. She felt incredibly awkward, and not because Elena was sharing with her but because she had so many questions; but she *really* didn't want to cross a line.

"Um, was it an accident? The pregnancy, I mean?"

Elena nodded again. "Yes, it was rather jarring to discover. I had never planned on being pregnant at twenty-three, barely out of college. It terrified me. Such an experience in itself can make one wary of sex, especially someone like me. I like things calculated. I like plans. I like structure. I don't typically care for surprises, and Lucas was certainly a surprise, but..."

"But, it was more than that? More than the pregnancy that scared you off sex?"

Brown eyes grew distant, colored darker by some painful memory dancing through Elena's mind. "Yes," she whispered, and Allison's stomach lurched.

Allison gripped her knees, nails digging into her jeans. "He didn't, Lucas's dad..." The mere thought made it difficult for her to breathe. "Was it not consensual?"

"Oh no, Allison." Elena reached over to latch onto Allison's arm. "It was nothing like that, dear. It was consensual, yes—foolish, but consensual."

The tension in Allison's body faded as she turned more fully toward Elena and took her hands. She stroked Elena's knuckles with her thumbs. "Okay."

They were silent for a long moment, both just staring at their laced fingers, before Elena whispered, "I met him at Harvard."

Elena's eyes focused on her, sad and soulful. "His name was Jonathan." Allison didn't miss the past-tense verb. "He was a year ahead of me, but we had two classes together. He pursued me relentlessly, always complimenting me and asking me to lunch or dinner or breakfast even. I turned him down many times, because I didn't want any distractions from my studies. In fact, I turned him down the entirety of the time we were in school together, though we did develop a rather fulfilling friendship, frequently studying together and occasionally meeting for coffee. It remained that way for over a year."

Allison squeezed her hand and Elena took a deep breath.

"He was kind and incredibly intelligent," she continued. "We began dating after I left Harvard. Sex wasn't something that was ever a prominent part of my life, nor was it a prominent part of my relationship with Jonathan for a while; not that I never had sex, because I did; it just wasn't often. I had always been cautious about activities in which the risk factor was relatively high. Honestly, you should have seen my reaction to losing my virginity. I was a mess until my period came."

Allison chuckled and squeezed Elena's hand again."I've always assessed risks and determined whether the activity was worth the possible consequences," Elena said. "As such, I've rarely 'let loose' as Vivian puts it, especially where sex and relationships are concerned. It's not that I think sex can't be wonderful. I know it can be, in more ways than one, but as I said—risks. I hardly felt that a ten-second orgasm was worth a lifetime commitment to an unplanned child, or worth a lifetime struggle with an incurable disease. You see what I mean?"

"Totally. I can get that you would be cautious about it, especially since you already had specific plans for your life and everything. And don't take this the wrong way, because, obviously, Lucas is the best thing ever, but I guess you were totally right to be wary. I mean, you *did* end up pregnant."

"Exactly." Elena sighed. "It's amazing how so many people can have unprotected sex countless times and never have it result in a pregnancy, and then others only once, and surprise—a baby."

Allison squeezed her hand again. "So, is that how it happened? One time, and then say hello to Lucas?"

Elena laughed wetly, her voice strained. "Mm." She hummed, nodding. "Only once with Jonathan, and I ended up pregnant. Of course, I absolutely have no regrets about it now, because Lucas is the light of my life. He is *everything*. But when I found out, I was devastated. It felt like my life had ended before it even began."

"And Jonathan?" Allison asked. She hesitated, scratching at the back of her neck and averting her gaze. "I mean, did he like leave you or something?"

"He never knew."

"You didn't tell him?"

"I never got the chance." A lone tear slid down the smooth expanse of her cheek. "He was in a car accident three days after that night. They said it was instant, that he died on impact and didn't feel any pain. It was weeks before I even discovered I was pregnant."

Allison's chest felt uncomfortably tight, and she squeezed Elena's hands until both their knuckles turned white. "I'm sorry, Elena" she whispered.

"I never talk about it. My parents and Vivian avoid the topic like the plague because they know how painful an experience it was for me. The pain lessened with time, but it never fully faded. It is just difficult to discuss."

"Yeah," Allison muttered. "I don't talk about a lot of the hard shit either. Sometimes, just saying it out loud is too much, like it somehow makes it feel too real again, too close."

Elena looked up at her, eyes wide and deep. "Yes," she gasped. "That's exactly it."

Allison offered her a sad smile. They stared at one another, holding hands and nodding in the weighted silence. It seemed like hours passed before either spoke again. "Did you love him?"

"Who's to say? I'm not sure I even knew what romantic love was at the time. My entire life had been about growth, ambition, achievement, success. Of course, I know what *love* is. I've lived a happy life, filled with love, but *romantic* love? That's different, isn't it?"

Allison smiled tenderly at the way she walked circles around her question. She did this often herself, so that the weight of certain truths never settled fully upon her. She squeezed Elena's hand again. "Elena," she said, ducking to capture her gaze, "did you love him?"

Fresh tears escaped down Elena's cheeks as she finally nodded and whispered, "I certainly thought I did."

Pale fingers moved over damp cheeks as Allison wiped away Elena's tears. "I'm sorry," she breathed, and Elena leaned into her touch. It made Allison ache in a thousand different ways.

"I get it. At least, I think I know what you're trying to say. You haven't let anyone in in a long time, and maybe you're a little nervous about it, yeah?"

Elena straightened, her body tightening, and exhaled deeply. She cleared her throat and nodded firmly as she coiled her posture back into her typically composed self.

Respecting Elena's space, Allison pulled back a bit. "I am too," she said. "Nervous, I mean. It's been a while for me too, and I don't let people in easily, you know? I mean, I don't really get close to people. I don't usually do emotions, relationships. I just don't trust people not to, you know, hurt me or whatever."

"Do you trust *me* not to hurt you?"

Allison swallowed. "I think so. I want to. It's hard for me."

A firm nod was all she received as Elena simply accepted her answer, respected it. Allison saw no disappointment in the woman's eyes, only understanding. She closed the distance between them and pressed her lips to Elena's.

The kiss was soft, tender, and almost hesitant at first, but then grew and deepened. It was everything Allison had always thought a kiss should be—powerful yet gentle, deep yet light, emotional, and communicative.

Fingers wove gently into tangling hair, brushed over cheeks and necks, behind ears, and down backs. Chests pressed together, hearts thumping rhythmically beneath. Breath quickened. Heat spread.

Allison pulled back, breath rapid on her tongue, and smiled. Elena returned the smile, her supple lips kiss-swollen and wet.

"So, maybe we don't try to rush anything," Allison said. "Maybe we just do whatever feels right and try not to overthink anything."

Elena cupped Allison's cheek and leaned forward to kiss the corner of her mouth. "Okay," she whispered against flesh.

"Good. So, if we have sex, we have sex. If it's a while before we do, then it's a while before we do. Hell, if we don't, then we don't. Whatever feels comfortable and right."

"Would this be a proper time to mention that I have never actually been with a woman?" Elena blushed.

Allison's lips parted as if surprised, but then she merely shook her head and laughed.

Elena scoffed and smacked her arm. "Don't make fun," she snapped, and Allison reached for her.

"I'm not making fun." She slipped her arms around Elena. "I'm just...you're full of surprises, Elena, you know that?"

Elena narrowed her eyes. "Is that a bad thing?"

"No. I love it."

"Well then, excellent," Elena said. "I'm quite the overachiever, though, you know. I'm sure I'll learn quickly."

A ripple of heat rolled through Allison's lower abdomen and burned between her legs, so that she had to close her eyes and bite her tongue to keep from moaning. The mere thought of Elena being an "overachiever" in the bedroom was riveting.

"I'm sure you will." Allison focused her gaze again on Elena. "But for now, let's start with something simple just to take the pressure off. What do you think?"

"What did you have in mind?" Elena's fingers twitched over the tight denim material encasing Allison's thighs.

Allison grinned like a fool as she threw her arms out wide. "Hug?"

Elena laughed and sank into Allison's embrace.

Chapter Twenty-Two

"You sure you don't think this is totally lame?" Allison shuffled through the contents of a cabinet in Elena's kitchen.

"I'm sorry?" The question put a halt to Elena's wine-selection process. "To what are you referring, dear?"

Allison stopped her own rifling as well. "This," she said, waving a hand through the air.

"Perhaps you could be a bit more specific." Elena chuckled. "I'm afraid I can't read your mind."

"Damn, and here I was really hoping we were going to have one of those sweet telepathic connections or whatever like all the weirdoes in movies."

"Has that ever actually happened in a film?"

"Eh, I don't know. But tell me that wouldn't be sweet. Lovers who can communicate with their minds? Pretty awesome."

"Lovers?" Elena arched a brow and leaned against the counter.

Allison winked. "A girl can dream, Elena."

Turning back to the cabinet, Allison began shuffling things aside again. She could still feel the heat of Elena's gaze on her back, though, and knew she had yet to look away from her. Her stomach flipped and her skin began to tingle, and all from only a stare.

"She certainly can," Elena said. Her voice was an octave lower than before, and Allison felt those words in every part of her body. Her pants suddenly felt tight and uncomfortable. The few kisses the two women had already shared had been enough to nearly transform Allison into a puddle of goo; Allison thought she and Elena might *actually* explode if their hands ever moved below the waistline. *What a way to die.*

Allison laughed, the sound strangled as she cleared her throat. “You seriously have to quit with the devil voice.”

“You seriously have to quit with the references to sex.”

And then suddenly Elena was behind her, the heat of her body radiating over Allison’s body and making her shudder.

“What *are* you looking for, dear?”

“Uh, nothing. I was *trying* to look for something, but now I’m just fiddling with random stuff in the cabinets because *somebody* keeps distracting me.”

Elena chuckled as she moved a little closer to Allison, her hands extending toward her. She grabbed Allison’s hips and squeezed. “I have been busy with my own tasks, Allison.” Her breathy whisper skirted across the back of Allison’s ear. “It’s hardly my fault that you can’t keep your focus long enough to complete your own.”

“You are so mean.” Allison hoisted herself up on the kitchen counter to reach the back of the cabinet, because she had apparently hidden her stash farther back than she originally thought. Elena’s hands never moved from her hips.

The new position put Allison’s ass right in Elena’s face. Elena sighed. “And you say *I’m* the mean one.”

“Got it!” Allison’s hand finally latched around the Reese’s Pieces and microwaveable popcorn she had stuffed in the back of the cabinet for safe keeping. “Sorry, I apparently hid the things in Narnia.”

“What things?” Elena asked as Allison pulled back from the cabinet and started to turn to jump down.

“Momma!” a voice suddenly shouted from behind them, and Allison jumped so hard that she lost her balance. “Whoa wh—” Toppling down from her precarious perch on the edge of the kitchen counter, she barreled right into Elena. Elena’s back hit the tile floor with a hard thud, a loud rush of breath expelling from her lungs in an echoing grunt, and Allison landed right on top of her, her own knees cracking loudly against the floor.

“Ow.” Allison groaned as she forced herself up and off of her. “Elena?” she asked, one hand on Elena’s stomach and the other on her shoulder. “You okay?”

Elena finally sucked in a sharp breath and nodded, and Allison let out a sigh of relief. "Why didn't you catch me?" She couldn't resist the urge to rib her a little, even as Elena wheezed and pushed herself up into a sitting position.

"I believe I am the one who broke your fall, am I not?"

Allison grinned at her. "Good point, hero."

"Momma."

Elena and Allison turned to see Lucas standing just a few feet away, a giant smile on his face and still clad in only his pull-ups even after having been awake for a few hours. He clutched his new stuffed monkey like his life depended on it.

"Yes love?" Elena asked.

Lucas bounced on his heels as he giggled. "Alson falled."

Allison burst into loud laughter as Elena chuckled and nodded. "Yes, Lucas, I am well aware that Allison fell."

He just continued to offer his cheesy, adorable smile as he swayed from side to side and made his request. "Spicamal me?"

"Despicable."

"Spicamal," Lucas repeated.

Allison literally had to bite her knuckle to keep from laughing as Elena calmly repeated herself. "Despicable."

Lucas narrowed his eyes at her as if mulling it over in his mind before slowly saying, "Spicamal." Allison's shoulders were shaking with silent laughter. She almost lost it entirely when she felt Elena's elbow nudge her side.

"Okay, baby." Elena began again, smiling at her son. "Listen to Momma very closely, okay?"

Lucas nodded and his gaze remained firmly fixed to his mother's lips as she then slowly and carefully sounded out the word. "*Deeee*-spick-uh-bull."

Both Allison and Elena watched as Lucas's eyes narrowed again and the kid's mouth moved wordlessly, as if he was working it all out before speaking. "*Deeeeee.*"

Elena had to nudge Allison again to keep her from giggling.

"—spicamal."

Allison's face practically turned blue.

"Well," Elena said, tilting her head and reaching out to poke her son's belly. "Perhaps we should work on that one another time, munchkin."

"Okay!"

"Now, can you go wait on the couch like a big boy? Allison and I will be there in just a few minutes to start the movie."

Lucas shrugged and ran off toward the living room.

Once he was out of sight, Elena and Allison slowly turned to look at one another. The moment their eyes met, the silence between them burst wide open with their shared laughter.

"That was the best thing ever," Allison said as they sat next to each other on the kitchen floor. "Seriously, how is that kid so adorable?"

Elena's playful gasp feigned overdone shock. "What do you *mean* how is he adorable?" She waved a teasing hand down the length of her body.

"Oh right," Allison said, "must get it from his Mom."

Elena arched a brow. "You disagree?"

"Not at all."

They helped one another to their feet, and Elena rolled her eyes as soon as she saw what Allison had been looking for all along, items that had led to the likely bruise on her ass. "How many stashes of that vile concoction do you have hidden in my house?"

"More than you would think," Allison said, sticking her tongue out. "And again, don't knock it until you try it."

"I truly loathe that saying." Elena moved to the counter to uncork her wine selection.

"What saying?" The flat bag of popcorn kernels landed in the microwave with a thud as Allison tossed it in. "Don't knock it until you try it?"

"Yes. It's a poor motto."

"How so?"

"Apply it to more than one topic, dear. Many have never tried murder, and yet it is still widely considered vile. Furthermore, do we not typically know ourselves well enough to have an established idea of what we will likely enjoy?"

"Touché."

"Thank you."

"So, I guess that means that I'm not going to get you try this stuff then, huh?" Allison asked as she pulled the now fully-popped popcorn from the microwave, dumped it into a large bowl, and then poured in her favorite little candies.

"I'm afraid not." They walked toward the living room.

"Allison," Elena said as they swept through the dining room and past Lucas's playroom, "what were you talking about earlier when you asked if I thought this was lame?"

"Oh. I just meant like this whole me-being-here-all-day-long thing. I don't want to overstay my welcome or anything, and this date has technically been going now for like a century."

"On the contrary," she replied, "it's been a lovely day, and I'm glad you stayed."

"So, *not* lame?" Allison chirped as they entered the living room.

"Not lame at all, dear."

They began the movie with Lucas smashed between them, Allison chomping on her popcorn and candy, and Elena sipping wine while absentmindedly running her fingers through her son's soft hair. Allison laughed every time she caught Elena trying *not* to laugh at the little yellow minions.

"It's so funny how they just speak constant gibberish." Allison said.

Elena smiled. "They sometimes speak Spanish."

"Seriously. When? I thought it was all nonsense."

"Various points. When they give Agnes the little unicorn stick is one."

"So, you speak Spanish?"

Elena nodded. "My father wanted to pass along the language; that, and my grandparents, his parents, speak very little English. I've been bilingual since I was Lucas's age."

"That's so cool." She then silently mouthed over Lucas's head, *And hot.*

Elena laughed and shook her head. "I'm glad you think so."

"Have you taught Lucas any?"

"Some. My father teaches him more than I do. It's a wonderful bonding experience for the—"

The sound of the doorbell chiming interrupted her.

"That's strange," Elena whispered. She then slowly eased off the couch, moving Lucas over a bit from where he was half on her lap. "I will be right back."

"Want me to pause?"

"No dear, go ahead."

Allison sighed as she leaned back into the couch and glanced down at Lucas. The kid was entirely unfazed by all things happening around him—his mouth hanging wide open, his hair stuck up where Elena had been playing with it. His eyes remained glued to the screen. It had always amused Allison that no matter how many times kids saw the same movie, they could still be so enraptured by it.

Muffled voices filtered in from the foyer, but she couldn't quite make out any words, and then she heard one loud exclamation. "Oh, nonsense!"

Lucas didn't seem to hear any of it. Even when the sound of multiple sets of heels clicking in their direction reached their ears, Lucas merely continued to gape at the large television screen. Allison, though, grew nervous.

The sound of heels clicking toward the living room was followed by the form of Elena's mother whipping around the corner. A wide-eyed and obviously highly annoyed Elena followed right behind.

"Allison darling!" Nora said. "How lovely to see you again!"

"Uh." Allison scrambled to get out from beneath Lucas's weight where he had unconsciously shifted over and halfway onto her lap once Elena left the couch. She finally scooted him aside and stood to take Nora's hand. "Uh, Mrs. Vega. Hi…uh, hi. Wow, I wasn't expecting…uh, hi."

Nora smiled at Allison's babbling as they shook hands. She pulled Allison into a shallow hug, adding a few quick pats to her shoulder. With eyes a little panicked, Allison glanced over her shoulder at Elena, who mouthed *I'm sorry!* As soon as she pulled out of the embrace, though, Allison forced herself to school her features and relax.

"Do take a breath, dear. I'm not here for your firstborn."

Allison sucked in a breath and let it out in an awkward, strained laugh. Glancing at Elena, she saw her fighting a smile, and Allison glared before turning back to Nora, who moved past her to get to the little boy on the couch.

"Pumpkin!" Nora lowered herself elegantly onto the couch. Lucas only continued to gape at the television. He did, however, shift his body over and onto his grandmother's lap without a word. He leaned back into her chest as he continued to watch the movie and then he tugged on her hand as he exploded into a fit of high-pitched giggles at another minion moment.

Nora glanced up at the other two women. "Apparently I am only useful as a piece of furniture."

Elena and Allison stood several feet apart. Allison didn't have a clue how to respond to this entirely unexpected interruption of their date, and, given Elena's complete lack of action, it seemed she didn't either. Allison felt nervous as hell, because, unlike the first time she met Nora Vega, she was now actually *dating* the woman's daughter. The words Elena had spoken that day outside of Nora's house kept echoing in Allison's mind. *Nora Vega Inquisition. Nora Vega Inquisition. Nora Vega Inquisition.*

"So, Allison," Nora began as she bounced Lucas lightly on her knees, and Allison felt her stomach clench as her mouth went dry. She didn't know what was coming, but if her first meeting with Elena's mom was anything to go by, she had half the mind to expect it wouldn't be a standard "How have you been?"

"My daughter informs me that today is your first official date," Nora said. "So, I assume this means that you are interested in more than a one-night stand?"

"Mother!" Elena hissed.

"Daughter!" Nora rolled her eyes.

"Must you do this?" Elena groaned.

Just then, the credits of the movie began to roll, and it was like an instant trigger snapping Lucas back to reality. He looked around and grinned at them all as he bounced on his grandmother's lap. "You having a sleepover, Gram?"

"No, my sweet boy," Nora replied. "Gram can't have a sleepover tonight, but perhaps soon."

Lucas looked in Allison's direction. "You having a sleepover, Alson?"

Allison froze as Lucas stared at her expectantly. Pressing a hand to her temple, Elena let out a soft sigh, and Nora merely arched a brow, clearly waiting to hear Allison's answer.

"Erm, I don't think so, kid." She glanced over at Elena, who looked just as lost for an answer as she did. All she could think to do was to shrug and repeat herself. "I don't think so."

"My, my." Nora stood and lifted Lucas up into her arms. "Let me just take my grandson to bed, and then we shall discuss this further."

"We *shall*?" Elena's expression turned even more incredulous. "Mother, honestly—"

"Say goodnight to Momma, pumpkin." She drifted past Allison and toward Elena. Lucas waved at Allison over Nora's shoulder, already rubbing sleepily at his eyes, then turned to Elena. She sighed as she leaned over and pressed a kiss to his cheek.

"Goodnight, munchkin. Sweet dreams."

"Night Momma." He yawned, and then they were gone.

Elena and Allison shot across the gap between them, both grabbing the other's hands.

"Oh my God, Elena, I'm tripping out."

"Allison, I am *so* sorry. I had no idea my mother had any plan to visit."

"Is she gonna interrogate me?"

Elena hesitated. "It is likely," she admitted. But then, an idea struck her. "Unless!" She darted away to grab her cell phone before returning. A moment later, the device was pressed to her ear.

"Daddy!" she said into the phone. "Yes, yes, listen: I need you to call mother and ask her to return home at once. Daddy, I'm not kidding. This is serious. She is imposing on my date and is being entirely inappropriate. You have to—what? *Vivian*?"

Allison hadn't seen that one coming. The dread pooling in her gut only intensified.

"Vivian, what are you doing at my parents' house?" Elena shook her head. "It doesn't matter. Put Daddy back on the phone. He has to convince Mother to return home before she interrogates Allison about God only knows what."

"It's not funny, Viv!" Elena's eyes went wide. "Oh no! No, no, no, no, you are *not* coming over here. No! You will not add to this! Vivian, don't you da—hello?"

Elena cursed as she slammed the button to hang up her phone. She looked at Allison. "This is about to get ten times worse."

Allison's heart pounded. Was she seriously about to get a tag-team interrogation from both Elena's mother *and* Elena's best friend? "Elena, I'm too young to die!"

Snorting with laughter, Elena pulled her closer. "You can escape now. I will cover for you."

A smile spread over Allison's lips, lopsided and tense from her buzzing nerves. "Will that automatically make me a coward in your mom's eyes?"

"Likely yes," Elena admitted, and they both sighed, pressing their foreheads together.

"Well, shit. I guess we're doing this then."

Elena pressed a quick, small kiss to Allison's lips. "I guess we are."

Chapter Twenty-Three

Sitting on the small loveseat across from the couch, Allison's spine was like a steel rod. She was pretty sure she had never exhibited better posture in all her life. Her fingers tingled, that feeling of borderline numbness, as they danced nervously atop her knees. Her stomach rolled with every breath, and she was certain that her heart had not stopped pounding since the moment she heard Nora returning from Lucas's room.

Elena, seated beside her, leaned over and bumped Allison's shoulder with her own. "Take a breath;" she whispered.

Realizing she had been holding her breath to the point of pain, Allison took Elena's advice and sucked in a mouthful of air. Her shoulders sagged an inch as he exhaled and she smiled at Elena. "Thanks."

Nora swept into the room with a calculating look in her eyes. She dropped onto the couch opposite her daughter and Allison and inspected them. "My, you two look as if you've seen a ghost."

Elena leaned back into the cushion of the loveseat, her shoulder resting warmly against Allison's. "Stop taunting us, Mother, and let's get this over with, shall we?"

"Oh, Elena, I haven't the slightest idea as to what you are referring." The sparkle in her eyes, so like Elena's, gave her away, though.

An annoyed, pointed stare was all she received from Elena. Allison, though, chuckled awkwardly and scratched at the back of her neck as she said, "You're a bad liar."

Elena whipped around, eyes wide, as she stared at Allison with a mixture of shock, worry, and something akin to admiration.

"Pardon?" Nora asked, her face hard.

Chest clenching tightly, Allison internally screamed at herself for opening her big mouth in the first place. She swallowed thickly before she answered. "I said that you're a bad liar." Her voice shook just slightly.

Nora's lips parted as the woman made to respond, but Allison cut her off. "I didn't mean any disrespect," she said.

That earned her another brow raise, which made Allison's stomach roll. "Not that I'm calling you a liar or anything. I figured you were teasing or whatever. So was I. But if we're being real here, I think we all know we wouldn't be sitting here like we're facing a firing squad if you weren't intending to have a little fun at our expense, right?"

Elena, smile tugging around her pearly white teeth, stared at Allison as if she was a revelation of sorts.

"Well, well," Elena said, turning to offer her mother a smug expression. "It seems Allison here has you pegged rather well, wouldn't you say?"

Silence grew between them then as Nora narrowed her eyes at Allison. She allowed that silence to grow and fester in Allison's soul until Allison was so freaked out that her insides squirmed.

She held her breath as Nora and Elena looked at one another, and then Nora began to smile. As soon as Allison saw that slight upturn, she let out a slow, silent breath of relief. Perhaps she would live to date Elena Vega another day after all.

"She certainly seems to match you in boldness, Elena."

"So, that's good, right?" The words rushed out of Allison. "I mean, I haven't failed already, have I?"

"Failed what, dear?"

"The, uh, Inquisition?"

Allison felt Elena's shoulders next to her shake with laughter.

"Sorry?" Nora asked.

Clearing her throat, Allison tried to covertly dig her elbow into Elena's side as payback for the laughter. "The uh, the Nora Vega Inquisition."

Nora smirked and tilted her head. "Ah, I see Elena has made you properly afraid."

"Oh, I've done no such thing," Elena said.

Allison, though, merely gulped. "Properly?"

"Hmm?"

"You said 'properly'. So, I *should* be afraid?"

"No," Elena said quickly. But her mother's voice competed with hers. "Perhaps," Nora said.

"Oh Mother, stop it."

"Yeah, you'll probably end up more mortified than scared."

A voice chimed from behind them, and all in the room turned to find Vivian standing in the open arch of the doorway.

"Vivian, dear!" Nora turned toward Vivian and waved the woman over. "This is a lovely surprise."

"Yes, Vivian." Elena's voice drawled the words out with maximum irony. "What a *lovely* surprise."

Vivian grinned as she bent down and pressed a kiss to Elena's cheek. She nodded at Allison, who offered her a half smile that she was pretty sure came off more as a grimace, and then Vivian turned to kiss Nora's cheek as well before dropping onto the couch beside her.

"So spill," she said. "How was the first date?"

Elena's tone deadpanned. "The level of enjoyment just hit a sudden and rapid decline."

"Oh come on, Elena. You didn't actually expect me to miss this, did you? It's been way too long since the last Nora Vega Inquisition."

"You girls," Nora said. "You act like I'm going to water-board the poor girl for government secrets."

"Well, I don't have any government secrets," Allison said, the heel of her foot tapping rapidly against the floor. "In fact, I don't have any secrets at all, so we could probably just, you know, skip this whole thing and it'd be totally fine."

"Uh-huh." Vivian leaned back and put her arm around Nora's shoulders. "We'll see about that."

"Or we could see both of *you* to your vehicles." Elena pinned her best friend with a glare.

Allison smiled. At least she wasn't in this alone. She could only imagine the embarrassing crap that Nora and Vivian might ask her.

"In my defense," Nora said. "I'm only here because I *assumed* the date would be over by now. I wouldn't have come otherwise."

"Yeah, and stop acting like you don't want us here," Vivian said with a grin.

"I *don't*. Why were you at my parents' house anyway?"

Vivian shrugged and patted Nora's shoulder. "I was taking Mom's dishes back from that lasagna she sent me home with."

"That was over a month ago. You just *now* decided to clean those dishes and return them? How convenient."

"*Anyway*." Vivian barreled right through Elena's snide remark. "I was there when you called, and of course, I wasn't about to miss this."

"Elena?" Nora gave a melodramatic gasp. "Were you calling your father to try to get rid of me?"

"Yes."

Nora pressed a hand to her chest. "I'm hurt."

"Oh please, you are not."

Elena laughed, and then, before Nora or Vivian could respond, Allison cleared her throat and leaned forward.

"All right, look," Allison said, locking gazes with Nora, "I don't really know how this is supposed to go down, but this whole dragging-it-out business is driving me nuts. You've got me here. I didn't run even though I knew you were probably going to ask me embarrassing things, because, hey, I can respect the fact that you're curious and maybe even cautious about who your daughter chooses to date. But I seriously can't take this build-up anymore. So, can we just get on with it? Ask me what you need to ask me, and then this can be over with."

Vivian laughed. "Oh yeah, she's definitely a winner."

Elena pressed her shoulder closer to Allison's and offered her mother and Vivian the smuggest expression she could manage without contorting her face. "Excellent," she said with a smack of her lips, "then perhaps we could skip this entirely."

"Such confidence," Nora said. "That's good. You will need it if you want to keep up with my daughter."

"I don't doubt that." Allison let out a relieved breath. "I mean, she's always pretty sweet around me, but I'm guessing that's not the entire picture."

Elena's smug expression fell away as she gaped at Allison, while Vivian snorted with laughter. "Well, she's got that right."

"I didn't mean that in a bad way." Allison squeezed Elena's knee. "I just meant that you're crazy successful already and you're only twenty-seven. You're smart and can obviously handle yourself. I mean, the way you dealt with that guy at the zoo made it seem like that came pretty naturally to you. I'm guessing you can be a shark when you need to be. It's not a bad thing."

"Yes, well." Elena sighed. "It is sometimes necessary and has served me well on several occasions."

"I don't doubt it."

"You two haven't slept together yet, have you?" Nora asked, catching everyone off guard. "*That* is certainly surprising."

Vivian burst into laughter again, while Elena's face flared crimson and Allison gaped.

"Mother." Elena groaned, shaking her head and pressing a hand to her temple. "Can we not?"

"Oh my God," Vivian gasped. "*Have* you?"

"No, they haven't." Nora answered before Elena could.

"You cannot possibly know that," Elena snapped. Nora merely smirked at her.

"Oh dear, I've been around a long time," she said. "You two still have that doe-eyed innocence about you—the sweet, timid compliments and the sideways glances and the blushing. Neither of you act as bold as you are, or in Allison's case, as bold as I imagine you to be."

"So?"

"So, that sort of behavior dies quickly after having seen one another naked and exchanging fluids."

"Ew, Mom, really." Vivian gagged and shook her head. "That was not an image I needed in my mind."

"Not to mention the fact that Elena's bedhead could scare the hair off a cat," Nora said.

Elena's blush only deepened while Vivian nodded in agreement, and Allison's lips stretched into a small smile, even as her cheeks burned brightly. The image of Elena's wild bedhead somehow eased

Allison, made those little butterflies that sometimes lived in her stomach when she was near Elena fly madly around.

"Mine can get pretty crazy too," Allison said. "So no judgment here."

"Is there a point in there somewhere?" Elena asked, glaring at her mother. "Or are we merely segueing into embarrassing me for no reason whatsoever?"

"I'm only saying." Nora reached across the small gap between the two pieces of furniture to pat Elena's knee. "It's now quite obvious that you two haven't yet slept together."

"Does that matter?" Allison asked, taking a steadying breath before slipping her right hand over and onto Elena's thigh. She squeezed it, hoping to offer her a bit of comfort.

"Not at all," Nora answered, "though it *is* rather telling."

"Of what, Mother?" The blush on her cheeks crept down her neck even more. "Do enlighten us with your apparent omniscience."

"Nothing negative, dear. It merely implies that one or both of you has prioritized an emotional connection over a physical one."

"Or it just means that you're both a couple of cowards who have been too afraid to sow your sweet, sweet lesbian oats."

"What does that even mean?" Allison chuckled.

Elena rolled her eyes. "I'm beginning to think that *you* would enjoy sowing a few lesbian oats of your own, Vivian."

Vivian shrugged and grinned at Elena. "That would depend on the woman, but I definitely wouldn't rule it out."

"Of course you wouldn't."

"Well," Allison said, "just to clear the air, I've already sown my lesbian oats or whatever, so for me, it's just about an emotional connection. I mean, not that you can't have that when starting a relationship with sex. I just didn't want to rush anything."

Elena smiled at her, and Allison returned it, squeezing her thigh again, which provoked a conspiratorial smirk between Nora and Vivian. Nora cleared her throat then and asked, "So, do you identify as a lesbian then, dear?"

"Yup," Allison answered, popping her lips together. "I knew by the time I was like four. Came out to a few kids at school when I was fifteen. They were the only ones I told."

"Really?" Elena asked, and Allison nodded.

"And how many of these lesbian experiences have you had?" Nora asked, and Elena groaned.

"Um, you mean like girlfriends?"

"I mean sexual experiences." Elena suddenly looked like she wished she could melt into the couch and disappear. "Elena herself is lacking in experience."

"That doesn't matter," Allison said, trying not to smile at the abashed expression on Elena's face. Nora Vega seriously had no reservations about getting personal. "It's an instinctual thing for a lot of people anyway."

"I agree," Nora said. "So, how many? One never knows what one might pick up from others."

"Oh, uh, I'm clean, if you're concerned about that, and, to answer your question, I've had a few." Allison was feeling a little unnerved by the topic, but she told Elena she wasn't going to run, so she might as well suck it up and get this over with. "Not a lot, though. My first was a little before my sixteenth birthday, with a girl I went to school with."

"Ooh." Vivian waggled her eyebrows. "Please tell me it was your tutor or something, or that it was in the school library or the janitor's closet."

Allison shook her head. "I think you've been watching too much television or reading too much kinky lit."

"Guilty." Vivian winked at Allison. "But seriously, tell us about it. Is this your coming out story?"

"No," Allison said. "Or maybe. I guess. What even *is* a coming-out story, because every one I've ever heard was never actually about when they *came out*. It's always about the first sexual experience or I guess the person just realizing that she's a lesbian."

"How are we supposed to know?" Vivian asked. "*You're* the lesbian here."

"Well, Elena," Allison started to say, but Vivian cut her off.

"Elena has been half in the closet, half out of it since college," Vivian said. Elena scoffed and rolled her eyes at that. "She's not a reliable source for all things lesbian."

"Okay." Allison sighed. "This isn't my coming out story, I don't think, but no, the girl was not my tutor and it wasn't in a library or a janitor's closet. It was at my house at the time. She *was* over to study with me, though, so does that earn me some points?"

"A few." Vivian grinned. "Keep talking."

"Dear, your rainbow is showing," Nora said, nudging Vivian with her elbow, and they all laughed as Vivian shrugged and urged Allison on.

"It's really not that interesting," Allison told them. "She came over, and we were studying, and then she said that she really liked my hair—"

"I like your hair," Elena said, and Vivian snorted.

"It's not a competition, babe. This was like, what, seven years ago?"

"I was only saying," Elena mumbled, and Allison patted her thigh and smiled.

"Thank you," she said, before turning back to the others. "Anyway, she said she liked my hair and then she started playing with it, and then I don't know. Somehow we ended up kissing, and then there was some touching, and then—"

"And then?" Vivian asked, on the edge of her seat.

Allison sighed, scratching at the back of her neck. "And then my foster mom walked in and caught us."

Both Elena and Vivian grimaced at the image of a parent walking in on such activities. It clearly wasn't a pretty one. "Yeah." She nodded. "That was my reaction, too. It didn't go over too well."

"I see," Nora said. "You *are* an orphan then?"

Elena winced at the question. "Mother, that isn't really any of your business."

"It's okay." Allison patted Elena's thigh again. "I mean, I pretty much walked into that one with my comment about the foster mom, so it's fair game. Besides, I'm guessing that your mom already knew that somehow." Allison looked expectantly to Nora, who merely arched a brow and tilted her head respectfully forward.

"Quite the perceptive one, aren't you? I will admit I looked into your background once I realized Elena was developing an attachment to you."

"You did?" Vivian and Elena said at the same time.

Nora gave them both a deadpan expression. "Are either of you *really* surprised?" She then turned back to Allison. "So, yes, I was already aware that you are an orphan, or that you *were*, whichever you prefer."

"Well, I wouldn't have preferred either. But hey, it wasn't like I could do anything about the fact that my parents apparently didn't want me."

Elena blanched at that, her body stiffening and the crimson quickly draining from her face. As Vivian sank back into the couch, looking highly uncomfortable, Elena let out a hissing sigh and turned an icy gaze on her mother that told Nora to back off or else. Nora met Elena's gaze with understanding, her eyebrows drawing together and her lips pressing thin with a sad smile, but she made no sign of dropping the subject. "I can imagine that would be difficult," she began, "but—"

"But what?" Allison cut her off. Her knees bounced beneath her sweaty palms as she fought the urge to jump to her feet and walk out before she could be turned away. "Is this the part where you tell me that because I'm a poor kid with no family or money really to speak of, I'm not good enough to date your daughter?"

"Ac—"

"Because I don't really need to hear that. I know I don't have the best past, but I won't apologize for that. I'm a good person, and I care about Elena. I wouldn't hurt her intentionally, and I'd never try to take advantage of her. I respect who she is and how she lives her life. I don't care about money or upbringing or any of that, and I never got the impression that that mattered to her much either considering she chose me despite knowing that I have never had much of either. So, if *she* doesn't want me around, then I won't be around. But, as long as she chooses me, then I plan on being here."

Nora cleared her throat roughly and said, "*Actually*, had you given me a chance to finish, I would have said that that must have been difficult, *but* you seem to have truly turned things around for yourself quite nicely. That is something to be admired."

Allison's chest clenched tightly, her heart rocketing up into her throat and sticking there like a piece of hard candy. Her face flushed bright red, and she felt like the biggest asshole in the history of all assholes. She had practically just given Nora Vega a verbal smack-down for no reason whatsoever. *Way to go, Sawyer*, she reprimanded herself. "I'm—"But Nora shook her head and waved it off.

"It's fine, dear," she said. "I come from poorer beginnings as well, and so I recognize that instinct to assume the worst and to jump to defend oneself. I assure you that I have nothing but respect and admiration for the life you've lived. It is, however, quite comforting to know how much you seem to respect my daughter."

"I'm sorry," Allison whispered. "I just...I need a moment." She then raced from the room.

Elena sighed, shook her head, and rose to follow Allison. "I wish you two could have simply minded your own business," she croaked before taking off after her girlfriend. Was Allison her girlfriend now?

She found Allison in the kitchen, buckled at the waist. Hands on her knees, she was taking deep breaths, very obviously to keep the tears in her eyes at bay.

"Allison?" Elena whispered as she entered the kitchen, and Allison whirled around.

"Hey," she choked out. "I just needed to catch my breath."

"I'm so sorry about this."

"Don't be," Allison said as they gravitated toward one another. "I'm not upset." Their hands created a perfect puzzle, fingers lacing together between their bodies, as Allison shook her head. "I'm a little embarrassed at the way I went off, but I'm not upset." She laughed and wiped at her eyes. "It's just that no one's ever said anything like that to me about the way I grew up. That they understood or that they respected...it's just a lot for me."

Elena placed two fingers under her chin to lift Allison's gaze. "Some people are quite capable of seeing how strong and magnificent you are, dear."

"I'm gonna kiss you," Allison whispered, and Elena had barely begun to smile before Allison covered her lips with her own.

It was chaste but somehow just as intoxicating as all the others. When they broke apart, Elena teased, "You only pulled that whole 'I-need-a-minute' scene so that you could get me alone, didn't you?"

"I wish I was that quick on my feet, babe." Elena's flesh tingled at the term of endearment. "But I'm definitely not complaining about how this is turning out. Wanna just stay in here and make out while they wonder if we're ever coming back?"

Elena chuckled, leaning forward to rest her forehead against Allison's. "As tempting as that sounds, I guarantee my mother wouldn't let us off that easily. She would come looking."

"She'd get an eyeful."

"Oh, would she, now?" Elena asked, a wave of heat rolling through her lower abdomen.

"Maybe." Allison shrugged, winking. "I've got to admit that I'm pretty interested in seeing your famous bedhead now."

Elena rolled her eyes. "It's not a pretty sight."

"It's *you*. So yeah, I'm sure it's the *prettiest* sight."

A throat cleared from behind them, and both women turned to find Vivian standing in the doorway of the kitchen, a smile playing at her lips as she observed their tender moment. "Sorry to interrupt, love birds. But Nora still requires an answer to the what-are-your-intentions-with-my-daughter question."

Allison squeezed Elena's hand. "I think I can handle that."

"You're lucky," Vivian said. "She must really like you, because she's being way less embarrassing than usual."

"That's true," Elena said.

"How many times has this happened?"

"Oh, too many to count," Vivian said.

"Damn." Allison looked at Elena. "How many people have you dated?"

"Oh, it's not just for me." Elena shook her head. "She does this to *everyone*—potential employees, drivers, maids."

"Yeah, she's thorough like that," Vivian laughed. "She just likes it best when it involves Elena somehow, because then she gets to watch her squirm. You should have seen some of our teachers at prep school. It was hilarious."

"Yes." Elena cleared her throat and shook her head. She gently patted Allison's arm. "So, as Vivian said, consider yourself lucky."

Allison took a deep breath and motioned for Elena to lead her back to the living room, mumbling, "Yeah, but it's not over yet." The two of them followed Vivian out of the room, their fingers still laced together.

Chapter Twenty-Four

When Allison, Elena, and Vivian returned to the living room, they found Nora poised on the edge of the couch cushion, just as they left her. Allison caught her eye, and they smiled at one another.

"Better?" Nora asked.

Allison tightened her grip around Elena's hand. It was comforting but also addicting—that feeling she got when Elena's fingertips slipped across her own and their gazes met, when they laughed together, when Elena's breath whispered across her lips, and when their bodies molded together in a gentle embrace. It was like waking up and falling asleep all at once—a hazy stirring that somehow managed to be both gentle and jolting, numbing and yet teeming with sensation. It was powerful and heady, and it was something that Allison couldn't even begin to comprehend yet already cherished.

She was in this, even if it felt fast, even if it felt somehow unreal. She was in this.

"Yeah," she breathed. "Thank you."

Nora licked her lips as if preparing for a long speech. "Allison, I won't apologize for being cautious or even curious. I know that, at times, I can be rather invasive, and I am more than aware that much of what I ask is truly none of my business. As such, you are always free not to answer; however, I assume you do so, regardless, because you worry that I will reject you."

"Well, I d—" Nora waved a hand to stop her again. Allison clamped her mouth closed and nodded, letting her continue.

"It is true that I may form particular opinions about whomever my daughter chooses to become involved with."

Vivian snorted and Elena's lips tilted up as Nora rolled her eyes at the two of them and raised her voice just a bit. "At the end of the day, though, all I truly want is for Elena to be happy and to be with someone who makes her truly happy. Her father and I have always told her as much."

Allison smiled at the soft pink tint of Elena's cheeks and the way her eyes lit with affection as Elena stared at her mother. Allison's own eyes stung with tears. It moved her to see something like this firsthand, to literally be able to feel the love radiating between Elena and her mother. She had never known that kind of love, but was glad that Elena did. The sting of her teeth biting into her tongue kept any tears from falling as she squeezed Elena's hand and laughed softly when Elena scoffed, "Mother, it's only our first date. Stop acting like she asked your permission to marry me."

"You never know." Nora turned back to Allison. "I do, however, apologize if I have managed to dredge up painful memories for you, Allison. That was certainly not my aim. I am merely trying to get to know you a bit better, and I don't like to skirt around touchy subjects."

Allison nodded. "Yeah, I get it. I mean, it's a little invasive, yeah, but I've honestly got nothing but respect for how much you obviously love Elena. I never got to have that, so it's really nice to see that *she* does."

"Mm." Nora hummed as Elena squeezed Allison's hand and moved a bit closer to her.

Allison smacked her lips together with a loud pop. "So, does that about cover everything, Nora," she asked, "or do you want some more sticky information like maybe my bra size? It's not very impressive, I'll warn you."

Vivian and Elena burst into laughter, while Nora merely shook her head. "Well," Vivian said, clapping her hands together, "I think you just got owned, Mom. *I'm* sold, anyway." She bumped Nora's shoulder. "She had a way better attitude about her Nora Vega Inquisition than I had about mine."

"I thought you and Elena were practically sisters?" Allison cut in. "Why would you get one?"

"Oh, it didn't have anything to do with Elena." Vivian leaned over to lay her head on Nora's shoulder. "It was when I lost my virginity. She grilled me for like an hour, and then she grilled Elena about whether or not she had done it as well."

"Which, of course, I hadn't." Elena said, smug smile in place.

"Oh Elena, don't even. There's a lot that your mom knows, but there's a lot that she doesn't. I could change that pretty easily, you know."

Elena narrowed her eyes. "You wouldn't dare."

"Oh, darling." Nora patted Vivian's knee. "You know she is easily swayed. Don't tempt her."

"Good point. She would roll on me in a heartbeat with the right persuasion."

"Loyal when it counts though!" Vivian grinned. "Nah, you know I've got your back, babe."

"I wish somebody had *my* back right now," Allison sighed, her mouth slanting up in a half smile.

Elena released Allison's hand to slip her arm around her back instead. "There, dear. I've got it."

"God, you two are sickening." Vivian rolled her eyes. "Just have babies together already. I need more nieces and nephews."

Allison flushed.

"Cállate," Elena groaned, throwing a small pillow at her best friend.

"Manners, dear." Nora's reprimand had Vivian poking her tongue out at Elena.

Elena merely rolled her eyes. "Por favor."

Suddenly feeling entirely lost, Allison cleared her throat and said, "Uh, I guess I'm the only one in the room who doesn't speak Spanish."

"She told me to shut up," Vivian said, "though *why* she couldn't have just said that in English, I don't know. Oh, wait. Maybe she just didn't want you to know that she's a lot more sensitive than she lets on."

Tilting her head back against the couch, Elena sighed as she stared at the ceiling, and groaned again.

Allison chuckled, leaned into Elena's side, and whispered, "Will you teach me?"

Elena looked at her, eyebrows curving upward. "Spanish?"

"Yeah. Is that weird, you know, for me to ask?" Allison paused at Elena's silence. "I mean, you don't have to if you don't want to."

"No, no," Elena said. "I am just a bit surprised. Why do you want to learn?"

Allison shrugged. As if simply talking about the weather, she said, "It's a part of you."

"Yes…?"

"It's important, right? It's an important part of who you are, so why wouldn't I want to learn?"

"Oh hell, Mom," Vivian said. "You may as well just get your purse and come on. If *that* didn't win you over, I don't know what will. I'm swooning over here. Jesus."

Nora smacked Vivian's knee as if to tell her to shut up.

With more affection in her voice than she rarely ever offered anyone other than Lucas, Elena whispered, "Thank you, Allison. I'm touched that you would even consider learning another language simply because it is important to me."

Allison, feeling that stirring in her chest and stomach that she now associated with Elena, caught herself leaning forward before remembering that they had an audience and quickly jerking back. She cleared her throat. "Yeah, uh, no problem. I mean, it's not like it wouldn't do me some good anyway. Like I said, I'd get to share in an important part of who you are, and it would definitely benefit me where social work is concerned. So, it's a win-win really, though I think we both know I'm probably just gonna sound really lame and…I don't know, *white*, trying to speak Spanish."

"Join the club, girl," Vivian said.

"*You* sound awesome, though," Allison told Elena.

"You've only heard me say one word."

"Yeah, but that one word sounded…" She squirmed a bit before licking her lips. "Well, let's just say I really liked it."

Elena cleared her throat and crossed her legs. "I will have to keep that in mind, dear."

"I think that's our cue to leave." Vivian nudged Nora with her elbow and both women rose from the couch.

Scrambling to her feet, Allison held out a hand. Nora stared at it for a long moment before offering her own. With a firm shake, Allison said, "I don't really know how you feel about me, but thanks for taking the time to ask, even if it *was* a bit embarrassing."

Nora chuckled as she squeezed Allison's hand. "I don't believe you have anything to worry about, dear." She winked at Allison before turning to press a kiss to her daughter's cheek.

Elena and Allison walked the inquisition squad to the door and bade them goodnight. Hands scrunched into her pockets and blonde hair cascading over one shoulder, Allison leaned all her weight on her right foot, the left looped around the back. She smiled at Elena as they stood just inside the door together, their gazes each devouring the other.

"Some first date, huh?" Allison whispered.

"Yes it was."

"Would you change anything about it?"

Elena smiled slyly at her. "Would *you*?"

"Maybe just this part," Allison said, grinning.

"Which part?" Elena asked, cocking her head to the side.

"Just the leaving part."

"You could stay."

"Yeah?" Allison asked, taking a step forward. Her gaze shifted back and forth between Elena's steadily darkening eyes and her supple lips. "And do what?"

She took another step forward, and Elena's breath caught tightly in her throat. Without another word, her hands shot out and latched onto the front of Allison's shirt. She yanked Allison flush against her and molded their mouths together, her back pressing firmly into the door.

Allison shuddered as Elena's tongue slipped through her lips and teased at her own. She groaned as she pulled back just enough to part the kiss. Their breathing had already spiraled out of control, both panting hotly against the other's lips as Allison whispered, "That's why I have to go."

"Perhaps that is why you should stay."

Allison leaned forward to rest her forehead against Elena's and brace a hand against the door. "I know, I know," she said against Elena's lips. "I want to, but in this one sense I guess I am just a little traditional. No sex on the first date, not when I plan on sticking around for a while, and I do."

"You do?" Elena asked, smiling into a brief kiss.

"I do." Allison ran her hands down Elena's arms. "The second date, though…"

Elena laughed, the sound raspy as it floated over Allison's ears. "And when will that be?"

"Oh soon. Definitely soon. I don't think I'll be able to stay away for more than a couple days, tops."

"Perhaps I could plan this one?" Elena ran her fingers down the length of Allison's sides, making her tremble.

"Whatever you want, babe."

Eyes fluttering closed, Elena whispered, "I like that."

"Yeah? Good, because it just sort of slipped out, so it'd be hard to avoid it."

Elena wrapped her arms fully around Allison. "Thank you for the date."

Smiling against the heat of Elena's neck, Allison returned the embrace. "Thank *you*." When she pulled back, she pressed a gentle kiss to Elena's lips and then another to her forehead. She then slipped out the door.

Chapter Twenty-Five

"Wait, wait." Macy waved her hands to stop her roommate mid-story. They lay on their beds across from one another with their backs up against the opposite walls and tossed a ball back and forth. Macy's auburn hair, pulled up in a messy bun, squashed against the wall, and she wore only a baggy gray sweatshirt and neon pink panties. Her attire mostly matched Allison's, except for Allison's boxer shorts and fuzzy socks. "So you're telling me that you couldn't even get through one date without her mum showing up?"

"No," Allison said. "That's not what I'm saying at all. I mean, our actual date was supposed to just be the zoo thing, so we *did* have our entire date in full, uninterrupted, and it was awesome. I just happened to, you know, hang around long after the date was over."

Macy made a loud whip-cracking sound, snapping her right hand down at her side. "One date and you're already hooked. The odds aren't in your favor, mate. You're whipped."

"Oh shut up." Allison chucked the ball at her roommate a little harder than usual. Macy caught it with an *oof* and a loud laugh. "Aren't people supposed to be a little more obsessed with each other than usual at the beginning of a relationship or whatever? I mean, it's that whole new-and-exciting thing, right?"

"Uh-huh." Macy tossed the ball back. "I'll just go out and buy the booze for your wedding next week." She leaned up to stick her tongue out at her roommate. "Tell hot-pants I've got it covered."

"You've never even seen her pants."

Macy rolled over laughing at that one. When she finally caught her breath, she said, "Oh, you're right. She probably wears skirts."

Allison rolled her eyes, chucked the ball back at her friend. "*Anyway*!"

"Right, right, back to whatever the hell it was we were talking about." Macy rubbed at her eyes with a snort, letting the ball fall to the floor. She glanced toward the window and saw the first bits of morning light streaking the sky. *Christ, we've been up all night.* She didn't mind, though. She enjoyed teasing Allison about the date, but, most of all, she was genuinely overjoyed to see her best friend so giddy about something.

"Nora." Allison wiggled around to get more comfortable, curling up around her pillow and turning on her side to face her roommate.

"Right." Macy yawned. "Anyway, not the Mum's fault that you're too obsessed with her daughter to leave once the date is actually over."

"Hey! It's not like Elena ever actually tried to take me home or even mentioned anything about wanting me to go. She never even hinted. So, I'm pretty sure she wanted me to stick around."

"I'm pretty sure she wanted you to stay the night." Macy made her point with waggling eyebrows.

"Seriously." Allison groaned. "I think we might both explode if we don't sleep together soon; then again, we might explode if we *do*."

Macy snorted. "You're the one who keeps putting it on hold."

"It was the *first* date! You know how I am about this stuff. I mean, I'm trying to be like a gentleman, uh, woman or whatever."

Macy laughed and shook her head. "Yeah, well, be a gentleman and give the lady an orgasm, why don't you?"

Allison flushed from her ears to her collarbones.

The butterflies that relentlessly assaulted Elena's stomach throughout her entire date survived into the next day. As she and Lucas made their way through various art galleries for their Sunday outing, they found themselves talking about Allison more than once. Lucas pointed out all the works that incorporated bright splashes of various shades of green and how much 'Alson' would love them.

Elena's smile grew with each mention, those butterflies stirring, and she had to force herself not to text Allison to join them.

Surely it would seem a little too eager to want to spend yet *another* full day with her after having just done so the day before. Yes, Elena told herself, it would be better to wait. She didn't want to come across as too desperate or obsessed. Elena was not about to take any risks. What they had was new and delicate, and God help her, she really wanted it to work. It certainly didn't stop her from babbling on with her son about Allison, though. They talked about having her around more often, to which Lucas clapped and agreed.

"I share my dinosaurs with Alson," he told her more than once, nodding firmly as if such an offer was sure to keep Allison coming back to see them time and time again.

Given how much Allison seemed to love Lucas, Elena wouldn't be surprised if it did. She kissed her son's head. "That's very generous of you, munchkin. I'm sure Allison would enjoy that."

"She can have sleepovers," he added.

Elena's stomach flipped and she smiled. "She certainly can."

They visited two more galleries before lunch. They had plans to meet Elena's father at a nearby restaurant, and Lucas was ecstatic.

"Where's Pop?" he asked on the way.

"We're not there yet, Lucas," Elena laughed.

"Oh," he sighed. He waited only about ten seconds before asking again, "Where's Pop?"

"She asked me if she could plan the second date." Allison yawned. "I'm a little nervous that it's gonna be something fancy and I'm not going to have any clothes that are appropriate to wear."

"That doesn't matter," Macy told her, hating the insecurity lacing Allison's voice. She knew Allison was a bit unnerved about dating a woman who was socially and financially the complete opposite of her. "It's obvious Elena doesn't care about any of that, Alli. She would've ended up with one of those rich blokes if that was the case."

"Yeah, I guess that's true," Allison whispered, but her facial expression remained warped with concern.

"Hey," Macy said, "stop worrying. She obviously saw something in *you*, exactly the way you are. Whatever kind of date she chooses, it will be fine. Just be yourself."

"Myself is a broke orphan with secondhand clothes and not a damn clue which fork is the salad fork and which one is the dinner fork," Allison told her, laughing despite the fact that her voice cracked.

"Who the fuck cares about fork etiquette?" Macy scoffed, rolling her eyes.

"Elena might."

"No," Macy argued. "Elena cares about *you*, and even if you *are* a broke orphan with secondhand clothes, you're a wonderful one that any damned woman would be lucky to hook. Understand?"

Allison smiled, eyes glossed with tears, and nodded against her pillow. "Yeah, I hear you."

"Good," Macy replied, grinning over her blanket. "Though again, let me just reiterate that a good orgasm can only increase your chances."

Allison burst into loud laughter, tears finally breaking at her lids and slipping down her cheeks.

"Look Lucas! There's Pop!" Elena pointed across the restaurant as she patted Lucas's bottom where he was propped on her hip.

"Pop!" Lucas squealed, waving so dramatically that he nearly tipped Elena over. She held him a little tighter and made her way through the maze of tables to the small window table where her father waited for them.

Lucas Sr. offered them both a wide smile, wrinkles forming around his eyes and mouth, and stood to greet them. Lucas gave no warning before launching across the small space and into his grandfather's arms. The elder man laughed heartily. "Whoa, there's my big guy." He squeezed the toddler and patted his back.

Lucas hugged his little arms around his grandfather's neck and happily squealed. "Hola Pop!"

Lucas Sr. chuckled again. "Hola." He leaned over to wrap Elena in a one-armed embrace around the toddler still clinging to him. "Mija," he greeted. "You look beautiful."

Elena kissed her father's cheek and patted his shoulder. "Hi Daddy. Thank you." She smoothed her hand over the arm of his suit. He had always been a very well-dressed man. "You look pretty dapper yourself."

"What 'bout me, Momma?" Lucas asked, pulling his face away from his grandfather's neck. "Am I dapper?"

Elena reached out to pat his cheek. "Yes, munchkin. You look very handsome today."

Lucas, who had insisted on dressing to match his mother, had ended up in a dark purple button-up shirt with khaki shorts. It went quite well with the deep purple of Elena's dress.

"I ordered some stuffed peppers for an appetizer," Lucas Sr. informed them. He settled Lucas into a high-chair before he and Elena dropped into their seats. "How does that sound?"

Elena hummed in delight. "Delicious."

"Delicioso!" Lucas chirped from his high-chair. His pronunciation was a little off, but it made Elena proud nonetheless.

Once seated, Elena pulled a few of Lucas's dinosaur figurines from her bag as well as a juice box and placed them on the high-chair. He began crashing the toys together while Elena looked over her menu.

"Where's Mother?" Elena asked after she placed her order with the waiter.

"Meeting with one of her many organizations."

"You don't know which one?"

Lucas Sr. ran a hand over his short gray hair and then over his trim goatee. "Of course not. She is involved with far too many charities and organizations for me to keep track of them. You know she only keeps me around to be her arm candy at all the banquets."

Elena laughed loudly at that.

"So, your mother seems rather smitten about your new love interest," Lucas Sr. said, smiling. "That's rare. I take it you are just as smitten?"

"Almost sickeningly so." Elena ducked her head a bit and smiled. "I've hardly been able to think of anything else." She then tilted her head in her son's direction. "It seems Lucas hasn't been able to either."

"There is nothing wrong with that, dear. Love is a beautiful thing."

"I don't know about love." Elena sighed. "I think it might be a bit early for such terms."

"An open mind is as important as an open heart, dear. Love can be fast or even immediate. It's us who have to catch up to love, not the other way around." He laughed when his daughter blushed and reached over to pat her hand. "So, when will I get to meet this young lady?"

"Respectfully, Daddy, I would rather spare her having to meet yet another parent, at least for a while. Mother caught us both completely off guard, and Vivian certainly didn't help. I'm surprised Allison even agreed to a second date after that."

"Well, from what your mother said, she seems like a resilient young woman. I'm sure she's more than up to the challenge."

"That is true." Elena nodded. "I'm sure you will meet her soon, but let's at least wait until after the second date. You will love her though. She loves music as much as you do."

"Ah, well, there's my vote." Lucas Sr. chuckled. "Does she play any instruments?"

"Mhm." Elena took a sip of her water. "She plays guitar incredibly well, and she hasn't even fully performed for me. But, from what little I have heard, I think it would be safe to assume that she has quite the voice as well."

"Oh, well, in that case, we will have to have a concert." At Elena's cautious look, he put his hands up. "I know, I know. You want to wait on the family matters."

"I don't want her to feel rushed. I'm already toiling over when to contact her about the second date. I want to have an idea in mind, though, before I do. I haven't a clue where to take her."

"No ideas?"

"Not even one. You know I abhor the cliché dinner dates. I doubt Allison would enjoy something like that either."

"Then what do you think she *would* enjoy?"

"I'm unsure. I hate that I feel so nervous about planning this date. The mere thought of messing this up makes me sick to my stomach."

"Well, you've always been a perfectionist, Elena."

"Is it so wrong to want to plan the perfect date? I just want this to go well. Do you think I'm being ridiculous?"

"Not at all, dear. It is natural to be a little nervous when you want things to work with someone new, but I think you will be fine. You just need to relax."

"That is easy for *you* to say. You aren't the one attempting to court someone who is entirely your opposite." She rested her head in her palm as she leaned her elbow on the table and reached for her water.

"Elena, do you know how it is that your mother and I have remained so strong all these years?" Lucas Sr. reached across the table to pat her hand. "We have always shared everything with each other. We share our likes as well as our dislikes with one another. We share our passions. We share the things we love most with each other."

"Like your music," Elena offered, grinning. She always found it so endearing to listen to her father talk about her mother and their marriage.

"Yes, like my music. And your mother's passion and eye for art, our love of travel, our interests in business and politics, our complete lack of trust in the government seventy percent of the time."

Elena chuckled and shook her head back and forth. She melted, though, when her father added, "And our love for you, Elena."

"And me!" Lucas dropped his plastic triceratops to look up at his grandfather.

Lucas Sr. laughed, the sound booming out from their corner of the restaurant. He reached over to ruffle his grandson's hair. "That's right, Lucas. Gram and I love you very much."

"Love you, Pop." Lucas ducked his head, grabbing his dinosaurs. He crashed his triceratops into his pterodactyl while making shrieking sounds that made Elena's eye twitch. She placed a hand over Lucas's arm.

"Not so loud, munchkin."

"Sorry Momma." He lowered his voice and whisper-shrieked as he continued to bash his dinosaurs together.

"So, what exactly are you suggesting then, Daddy?" Elena asked, turning back to her father.

"I'm suggesting, dear, that you don't overthink it."

Elena grunted. "Easier said than done."

"If you want something real to develop, mija, then stop thinking in terms of wooing the girl and just be yourself. Show her your passion instead. It's part of what makes you so special. Show her the things you love and why. Share them with her."

A bright smile painted itself across Elena's face when she looked up a moment later and said, "I think I have an idea."

Chapter Twenty-Six

Allison woke up with her stomach completely in knots. She had expected time to drag, but even with the anticipation of the second date, the week had flown by. She had been grateful for the distraction school provided, keeping her mind off her buzzing nerves.

She rubbed bits of crust from her eyes as she rolled over in bed and glanced at the flashing red digits on her alarm clock. Elena had told her to be ready by nine in the morning, so she still had plenty of time. Allison had never been invited on a morning date before. She wasn't even sure if a morning date was an actual thing that couples did, but whatever. She was fairly certain she would show up anyplace at any time Elena asked her to. The woman was quickly becoming an addiction.

Sheets rustled as she slid her arm across her mattress, seeking her cell phone. She frequently lost it in her bed after staying up late reading e-books on the device until the words all began to blur together. She let out a soft hiss as her fingers finally slipped over the cold device where it was stuffed under the upper right corner of her pillow.

Allison tapped out a text to Elena and pressed *send* before tossing her phone back onto her pillow and sitting up to stretch out her back and limbs.

Hey, good morning. I just wanted to make sure we were still on for today.

A soft groan escaped her as her back bowed forward and burned with the delicious stretch. Before her arms had even extended fully over her head, though, her phone chimed with Elena's response.

Allison glanced at Macy's bed to make sure the chime hadn't disturbed or woken her, but it was empty. She likely went home with someone the night before or crashed at a friend's place. After sending a text requesting confirmation that Macy was alive, she then switched over to Elena's messages to read her reply. She rolled her eyes at herself when she realized she was holding her breath as she clicked on Elena's name.

"Chill out, Allison." She needed to just relax. There was absolutely no possible way that Elena would cancel on her on the morning of their actual date, right? *Right!*

A smile snuck across her lips, though, quelling that tiny spark of apprehension as she read Elena's reply.

Of course we are. Why? Is today no longer good for you? I know it's early, but I promise there is a reason.

No, I'm totally still down. I don't mind that it's early, though I still have no clue what we're supposed to be doing at nine a.m. because SOMEBODY is being stubborn.

Patience, dear. ;)

Allison grinned as she bit her bottom lip and clutched her phone. The little winky face at the end caused a wave of tingles to ripple down her spine.

Yeah, yeah. I'm being patient, she typed back. *So, should I meet you somewhere or are you picking me up? What's the plan?*

A black town car will be there to collect you at nine sharp.

Laughing, Allison shook her head. That was some *Pretty Woman* shit right there, except Allison wasn't a hooker or a ginger, but hey, whatever. It was fancy stuff nonetheless. Before she could inquire further, her phone chimed again.

I apologize that I cannot pick you up myself, but you will quickly discover why.

That's cool, Allison replied. *I trust you. Is there any specific way that I should dress or something?*

No, dear. Wear whatever you like.

Awesome. I guess I'll see you in a few hours then?

Allison smiled at Elena's quick response. *I very much look forward to it, Allison.*

Me too.

Jumping off her bed, Allison headed for the shower, her entire body buzzing with excitement.

Allison approached the black town car cautiously. She was about halfway from the dorm building to the vehicle when the driver's-side door opened, and a tall, balding man in an extremely expensive suit stepped out. Allison eyed him warily as he stepped around the nose of the car sporting a wide smile.

"You must be Miss Sawyer. Good morning."

Stopping a few feet away from the man and car, Allison narrowed her eyes as, in a clipped manner, she asked, "How did you know?"

The driver moved toward the rear door of the town car. He opened it as he answered her. "Nine a.m. sharp. Long blonde hair, striking green eyes, and an attitude." He smirked. "Miss Vega's description was certainly on point."

Allison laughed. "Hey, watch it."

The driver motioned once more toward the now-visible back seat of the town car. When she didn't make a move, he cleared his throat and asked, "Shall we?"

She shook her head. "Look man," she said, holding up a hand, "I'm not trying to be rude or anything, but when you've lived the life that I've lived, you don't just trust people because they smile and know what to say, okay? It's one thing to go into a nice stranger's house or something, because at least I can still make a break for it if I need to, but if I get in your car, you could friggin' take me anywhere you wanted and the only option I would have would be to like either jump out or try to wreck the car, and neither one of those options bodes well for my physical well-being. Know what I'm saying?"

Chuckling, the man scratched at the back of his head. "You've put a lot of thought into this, haven't you?"

"Yup," she replied with a loud smack of her lips.

"Well, if I was a kidnapper, how would I know your name and the name of the woman who sent for you?"

"Psh, please. There are lots of ways to find out easy information like that. You could've been stalking me for days or something. You could've hacked into my phone and read my texts and knew what kind of car I'd be waiting for. I mean, come on. Tons of serial killers have had way more elaborate schemes than that for just getting a person into a car, let alone all the stuff that comes after. I mean, Ted Bundy dressed up like a police officer to get potential victims to trust him and get into a car. He had all kinds of schemes and even faked different accents. That shit was elaborate. How do I know this whole 'I'm-your-driver thing' isn't just a scheme?"

"I suppose you have a point." A new, small smile pulled at his lips. "Though I think maybe you need to lay off the documentaries and crime shows."

"Hey, those shows could be saving my life right now." The man's smile only grew.

"Fair enough." He tilted his head. "You're a smart girl; I'll give you that. So, what can I do to gain your trust?"

"Simple." Allison shrugged as she pulled her cell phone from her pocket. "First, what's your name?"

"Rick," he said. "Rick Adkins."

"Okay, Rick. Just stay right there." She opened her camera app and held her phone up. When she angled it just right so that the sun wasn't glaring on the lens, she snapped a picture of the driver. "Okay, just give me one sec."

She inserted the photo into a text message to Elena: *So, before I get in some stranger's car, can you confirm that this Rick Adkins dude is your driver?"*

A moment later, her phone rang.

"Elena?" she asked as she clicked to accept the call.

Amusement adorned every note of Elena's voice. "Yes, dear, that is my driver. He is trustworthy. Get in the car."

Allison rolled her eyes. "Stop laughing at me, woman." She didn't wait for an answer before she ended the call.

"Thanks Rick," she said as she slid onto the seat, and the driver closed the door.

Slim, calloused fingers drummed against the leather seat as Rick drove Allison through the teeming traffic of Manhattan. After a while, she couldn't handle the silence any longer.

"So, Rick. You got a second job, or are you just a driver?"

"This is my only job, ma'am," he said. "Why do you ask?"

"It's Allison or Alli, and, well, your suit looks hella expensive. I didn't figure drivers made quite enough to afford those brands."

Rick glanced at her in the rearview mirror. "You would be right, Alli. However, there are certain perks to being a loyal driver of those in the fashion industry. I've been with Miss Vega's company for many years, long before she even took over."

"Whoa, whoa, whoa," Allison said, eyes widening. "*Fashion* industry? Elena works in fashion?"

"You didn't know? We are headed for the fashion district as we speak."

"Wow. I figured she was a CEO of one of those big Fortune 500 companies or something, but I thought it was just business, you know?" Allison sat up a little straighter. "Wait. Did you say that we're headed for the fashion district? Are we going to her office or something?"

"She didn't tell you *anything*, did she?"

"Not a damn thing." Allison craned her neck as she stared out at the buildings now swooping by and the enormous sewing needle and button sculpture in the heart of the district.

"Then I had better keep my lips sealed, hadn't I?"

"Nah, come on, Rick." Allison tilted her head and smiled in the rearview mirror. "You can tell me."

"Not a chance, kid. Besides, we are nearly there, and you can find out for yourself."

When Rick pulled up to the curb outside of a massive building, Allison's breath caught roughly in her chest. The concrete building towered high above them, casting an enormous shadow over the street, and there were more windows than Allison could count. She opened the door and stepped out of the car just as Rick was about to grab the door for her.

"Well, it was a pleasure to make your acquaintance, Alli," he said as Allison stood by the car and continued to stare up at the building. "Perhaps I will be seeing you again soon."

"Yeah." Allison's jaw hung slack. She then shook her head and refocused on the man beside her. "Yeah. Sorry. It's just a *huge* building. Um, thanks for the ride, Rick." She stuck her hand out, and the man shook it. "You wouldn't happen to know what I'm supposed to do now, would you?"

"I would wager that going inside might be a good first step." He winked and then headed back around the car. A moment later, he pulled away and left Allison standing at the curb, still staring up at the building with her heart hammering in her chest.

It took her a few moments to work up the nerve to go inside, but she finally forced her feet to move. She walked a little timidly toward the front desk, where a pale, red-headed woman whose face seemed to be frozen in a pinched sort of scowl while she repeated the same two lines over and over pressed various buttons on a call board. "Yes, I can transfer you. Please hold."

Allison stood in front of the desk for several minutes, but the woman refused to even acknowledge her. Finally, Allison rolled her eyes and cleared her throat loudly. "Excuse me."

The receptionist looked up then, arching a brow as her gaze scanned down Allison's body and back up. It was as if Allison's attire completely offended her. "Yes?" Her voice dripped with her disapproval and annoyance.

Allison flushed red with her irritation.

"I'm here to see Elena," she snapped. "Can you tell me where to go?"

"*You* have an appointment with Miss Vega?"

"I don't need an appointment, lady," Allison bit out. "She's expecting me."

The receptionist laughed mockingly and shook her head. "I'm sure," she said.

"What is that supposed to mean?"

"Mm." The woman hummed disbelievingly, rolling her eyes and ignoring Allison's question. "Name?"

"Allison Sawyer."

The receptionist's eyes widened, brows disappearing into her ginger hairline. "*You're* Allison Sawyer?"

Allison took a deep breath to keep herself from outright hissing at the woman before answering through gritted teeth. "Did I stutter?"

The woman pursed her lips almost to the point that the damned things nearly disappeared, but she didn't respond to Allison's comment. Instead, she glared at Allison and said "Miss Vega is currently in shoot. Fifteenth floor."

Allison huffed and stalked off toward the elevators.

On the fifteenth floor, she stood slack-jawed, taking in the busy scene before her. The room she found herself in was quite large, and the majority of it was covered in intensely white sheets. The sheets blanketed the floor, the walls in places, and provided a massive backdrop behind a gorgeous woman that Allison could only assume was a model. A man flitted around her with a large camera, the rapid clicking sound of the device's shutter like a swarm of birds all taking off for flight at the same time.

Several people hovered around the edges of the shoot—makeup artists wearing aprons splotched with color stains and sporting cosmetic tools in hand. Other makeup artists were off to the side in a somewhat separate portion of the room, applying face and body touches to other, mostly nude, models. The models were then shuffled over to have their hair picked at by stylists. Some were slipping carefully into various clothing items.

The entire scene was much busier than Allison had ever imagined a photo-shoot to be.

"Are you lost?"

Allison jerked out of her daze and focused on the woman standing in front of her. She was tall and thin, clad in a skin-tight black dress. Her blonde hair fell in neat waves around over her shoulders, and she stared at Allison through her black-rimmed glasses like every second she had to wait for an answer was a year off her life. "What?" Allison asked.

"*You.* Are you lost, or do you always look like you just landed on another planet?"

"Uh, n-no, no. Sorry. I've just never been to one of these before."

The woman's eyes scanned down Allison's body. "Clearly. And you aren't actually allowed to be in here unless you have business. No Starbucks, so you're not the coffee girl. No messages, so you're not the mail girl. No style, so you're clearly not a model. I'm thinking a call to security is in order."

Allison took a deep breath and let it out in a long sigh. "Seriously?" She groaned. "This shit again? Look, lady, my name is Allison Sawyer. I was invited here by Elena Vega, and I—"

"Sawyer." Recognition painted the woman's features. "Right, yes. My apologies."

Without another word, she scurried away, and Allison was left staring after her, half-stunned, half-pissed. Did anyone in this building have an ounce of decency in them, a modicum of respect? She felt raw and vulnerable, and she couldn't help but be defensive. These people looked at her like she was a cockroach, and it made her skin crawl. It was a harsh reminder of the two very different worlds she and Elena lived in, and that made Allison feel a little sick to her stomach. She did her best, though, to swallow down the feeling and shake those people off.

As Allison took a moment to collect herself, a voice drifted her way that instantly had a wave of tingles rolling down her spine and pooling at its base. *Elena.*

Allison's eyes followed the sound and saw the stunning woman just across the room, her back to Allison, and heatedly discussing something with a man in an olive-toned tweed suit. A smile began to creep onto Allison's face as she made her way quietly over, ignoring the stares she could feel picking her apart. As she approached, she overheard the conversation Elena was having; well, it was more like a lecture.

"I honestly don't *care* about the reason, Monroe," Elena said. "I have absolutely no time or patience for anyone's incompetence. We have precisely this one chance to get this right; thus, I want what I asked for, and I want it yesterday. Is that understood?"

The man swallowed thickly before nodding and muttering, "I will call again, and if I have to, I will go over there myself."

"See that you do." Elena waved a hand to dismiss him.

He scurried off, and Allison had to force herself not to chuckle at the loud, dramatic sigh Elena let out once the man had disappeared.

"Man." Allison cleared her throat. "Remind me to always give you whatever it is you want." Elena's body stiffened before the woman whirled on the spot and their gazes locked.

"Allison." A smile touched Elena's lips. "You made it."

"Yup," Allison said. "Big fashion head, huh?"

"I suppose so, yes." Elena propped a hand on her hip with a smirk and tilted her head toward a small room a few feet away from them. Allison followed her into what she discovered was a massive closet. It was packed with various pieces of clothing. A few women lingered in the room, but Elena dismissed them as well.

"We're in a closet, Elena." Allison laughed once the others were gone. "Insert lesbian joke here."

Elena smiled even as she rolled her eyes. "I'm glad you are here, Allison."

"Me too, though some of the people here are really hard to like." She shrugged and shook her head. "Just sayin', babe. That receptionist lady downstairs is a real bitch."

"What happened?" Elena asked, stepping closer and running a hand down Allison's arm. "Did she give you trouble?"

"Only if you call her judgmental face and voice and body language 'trouble'." A spark of anger flashed through Elena's eyes. "And then I got up here, and some lady asked me if I was lost and said I had no style. She threatened to call security on me."

Elena fumed. "I will have them both fired."

Allison nearly choked.

"Uh, no, that's okay," she said with an awkward laugh. "They're probably just not used to people coming in here in clothes from the Goodwill and asking to see *you*." She chuckled again as she scratched at the back of her neck. "It's okay. I mean, it sucked, but it is what it is. No need to fire anyone. Thanks though."

Elena didn't appear even remotely convinced. In fact, Allison thought she looked downright murderous, so before the woman could go on a firing spree, Allison cleared her throat and nudged Elena's arm. "Hey, it's okay."

"It's not." She let out a long sigh. "I don't ever want you to feel like you are, in *any* way, lesser than me or that you somehow do not fit into my life. So, no, it isn't okay for anyone to make you feel that way."

"I'm okay, Elena."

Elena nodded. "You are now," she said. "But you weren't. I saw it in your eyes."

Allison sighed and relented with a nod. "Yeah," she admitted, "it got under my skin, but only for like a second, okay? I'm good now."

"And you know I …" She trailed off, shifting her weight from one foot to the other.

"You what?" Allison asked. "Do I know that you don't give a damn about where I buy my clothes or how much money I've got in my pocket?"

Elena nodded, glancing to the floor.

"Yeah," Allison whispered, stepping even closer to kiss the line of Elena's jaw. "I know, Elena. I just don't want *you* to ever feel, you know, embarrassed or something by me."

Wrapping her arms around Allison, Elena nuzzled her nose against her ear. "Never," she whispered. "I promise you that, Allison."

Allison held Elena tightly, breathing in the scent of whatever perfume the woman was wearing. It was rich but not overwhelming, and Allison inhaled it eagerly. She kept her face buried in Elena's neck as she mumbled, "So, for our second date, you decided to bring me to work with you?"

A light scratch of Elena's nails along Allison's scalp made Allison purr. "For our second date, I wanted to share something with you that I am passionate about, which just so happened to entail bringing you to work with me, yes."

Allison pulled back, smiling as her stomach flipped and her heart stuttered in her chest.

"Stop," Elena said, blushing.

"Stop what?" Allison asked, her smile only growing.

"Smiling like that." She chuckled.

"Why?" Allison poked at her ribs. "Is it creepy? Is my smile like totally eating my face right now?"

"Yes." Elena squirmed under the tickling touch. "You've nothing left but eyes and teeth."

"Oh good! I always wanted to be a living, breathing emoticon. Thanks for that."

Elena caught Allison's hands to still the tickling pokes. "It isn't my fault."

"It so is. You're over there being all cute and wanting to share important things with me. Totally worthy of a giant, creepy smile."

Elena rolled her eyes, shaking her head as she stepped over to the door and motioned for Allison to follow. "Come along, dear. I've much to show you."

Allison followed her out, feeling on top of the world again.

"That was pretty incredible," Allison said as she stuck her fork into the small white box of lo mein. She spun the fork several times until it was basically a noodle popsicle and then shoved it into her mouth, moaning at the taste.

She hung out with Elena throughout the entire photo-shoot, learning about the process and Elena's role in it. It had been incredibly intriguing, entertaining, and also rather arousing to see Elena in her element. The woman was a powerhouse—intelligent and cunning and a force of nature. She knew exactly what she wanted, and people genuinely respected and damn near idolized her opinion. It was pretty amazing to witness.

Once the shoot was over, Elena had taken Allison up to her office on the thirtieth floor where they ordered Chinese delivery for lunch.

"Have you always been into fashion?" Allison asked.

Elena chewed her chicken and swallowed. "My job lands more on the business aspects of the industry, but you really must have a passion for the intricacies in order to appreciate it fully."

"Like what?"

"Many things, honestly. It is much more complex, more layered than most people realize. It isn't only a group of size zeroes and twos prancing around in heels and name brands. That is merely what you see on the surface. The process behind it, though, is intricate, and, when you know that process, you come to appreciate the art of fashion. It isn't merely about clothing, Allison. It's about creating an image from the ground up or, rather, from the page up. It's about creating a medium through which people can truly express themselves."

Allison swore she could listen to Elena Vega talk about fashion all day long every day for the rest of her damned life. The way the woman's eyes lit up was enough, but it was more than that; it was the way she dug into it. Elena was passionate about the entirety of fashion, not just the finished product. She was invested in it. Her heart was in it, and that was beautiful to witness and to hear her openly express.

"What many don't realize is that a great portion of fashion lies not with the designs but with those wearing the designs," Elena said. "For shows and shoots, we bring in people to complement the designs, true, but the designs are *created* to complement people. That's what fashion is all about—people. Individuals. It is about finding what makes you *you* and adorning yourself with the outward expression of it. It is about confidence and self."

"Confidence?" Allison asked, intrigued. "I always just kind of thought it was about brand. If you've got the right brands, people assume you're fashionable, right?"

"Some people, yes," Elena answered, taking a sip of her tea. "But frankly, *few* people know as much about fashion as they like to think they do. Certain labels will gain respect in this industry, that is true, but a label means nothing without the confidence to support it. *You* must wear the outfit. You mustn't let the *outfit* wear you. You can walk down the street in the most ridiculous attire, but if you carry your confidence in your stride, it resonates. That ridiculous outfit becomes fashionable because of *you,* not because of the design."

Allison chuckled. "Yeah," she said, a little in awe of the woman across from her. "Yeah, totally. I've never even thought of it that way, but that is so true."

Elena grinned as she popped a bite of steamed vegetables into her mouth. "I'm sure you have seen some of the positively ludicrous or even horrid designs on the red carpet deemed fashionable or positively to-die-for by the media. Those designs do not, *could not,* sell themselves. It is the wearer selling the design, not the other way around. That, of course, isn't to say that some pieces aren't truly stunning, because the majority of them are, but anyone who believes high-waist shorts and pants are gorgeous designs is severely misguided. Those designs never should have been revived; however, they work. They work because of the confidence carrying them down the runway or down the city street. One can often learn much about another person by his or her attire—the colors, the material, the angling, the patterns, the fit, the style. *That,* to me, is fashion, Allison. Fashion isn't clothing. It is people."

"Fashion is people," Allison said with a smile.

"Indeed. And people matter; thus, fashion matters as well. It is more important than many ever realize."

Allison stared at her as if she was some sort of revelation. Elena's passion for her work was awe inspiring and beautiful to witness.

"What?" Elena blurted.

"Nothing," Allison said. "You're just...you're pretty amazing, you know?"

Elena sucked in a soft breath. "Thank you," she whispered.

They stared at one another, the air of Elena's office thickening around them and growing hot. Several moments passed in heated silence before Elena pushed her mostly empty food cartons away and rose to her feet. "Now," she said, "what do you say we have a little photo-shoot of our own?"

"Are you sure about this?" Allison asked, glancing nervously around the studio. It was now empty but for herself and Elena, the latter having dismissed all her lingering subjects. "I mean, I'm not very photogenic."

Elena scoffed. "That is a blatant lie."

"True," Allison laughed, joking to enforce a false sense of bravado. "I *am* pretty cute." She stood in the middle of the solid-white set, wearing light-wash skinny jeans and a black tank top Elena had provided from the closet. Her feet were as bare as her soul felt in that moment, and she chewed on her bottom lip as she waited for direction from the other woman.

Elena smiled as she stepped over to her, a camera strung around her neck. "Allison," she cooed, running her hands down Allison's bare arms, "I would love to photograph you. I'm not much of a photographer, but I know a few things. If you are uncomfortable, though, we certainly do not have to do this. I thought it would be fun."

"No, it's cool," Allison assured, sucking in a steadying breath. "I mean, no harm, right? Plus, you must be pretty attracted to me if you wanna take my picture, right?"

Elena leaned in to press a feather-light kiss to Allison's lips. "Right."

"Well then, I'm fine with it," Allison told her, shrugging. "But don't expect me to like be good at posing or anything. I think we both know how awkward I am."

Elena walked slowly backward and away from her. "You aren't awkward, dear," she said as she lifted the camera to her face. "*You* are *stunning*."

Before Allison even realized what was happening, Elena began to snap photo after photo. Allison just sort of stood there awkwardly at first, unsure of what to do. She refused to even look at the camera, keeping her head down or simply looking away from Elena. Her hands were stuffed down in her pockets, and one of her knees was bent as she kept her weight steadied mostly on one foot.

"Take your hands out of your pockets, dear. Look toward me." Elena's voice called from behind the camera.

Allison did as she was told, still feeling incredibly awkward. She expected Elena to then give her more motion or posing direction, but the woman surprised her.

"Think of your most embarrassing moment."

"Huh?" Allison asked.

Elena laughed from behind the camera. "I want to shoot your expressions as certain emotions or experiences touch your features." She crouched a bit and pulled the camera back to her face. "Now, think of your most embarrassing moment."

Allison had way too many embarrassing moments to think of only one, but as soon as the collective memories began to flood her mind, she heard Elena chuckle again and she assumed that her face was likely bright red.

The more they shot, the more comfortable Allison became, even playfully dramatizing a few of her reactions to Elena's directions. Elena played along with her.

"Yes, love!" "The camera ADORES you!" "Give it to me!" "Yeeees, yeeees, NO!"

Allison cracked up at her. She flexed her biceps, posed ridiculously like a tiger, and reveled in the way Elena's voice croaked when she lifted the tank top and flexed her abs for the camera.

"Now, imagine me naked."

Allison's brain completely short-circuited. Her mouth went dry, her body quaked, and her flesh heated to an almost unbearable degree. "What?"

Elena carefully set the camera down and began to slowly make her way toward Allison. As she walked, she began to pop open the buttons at the top of her gray silk blouse. Patches of creamy flesh were revealed, and Allison's body began to throb, a flood of moisture pooling between her legs.

"Elena." Her voice squeaked, her face flooded in crimson. Elena gazed at her with dilated pupils, her lips slightly parted. She reached Allison just as the final button slipped free and opened to reveal a smooth expanse of flesh—a beautifully toned stomach and full, round breasts cupped deliciously inside a charcoal-colored lace bra. Allison's head swam dizzily at the sight, her senses overloaded.

"Allison," Elena whispered in return, drawing so close that Allison could feel the static on her skin.

Their eyes met for one gloriously charged moment before they simultaneously dove into one another, lips smacking together roughly. It was fast and hot and messy—teeth and tongues and noses clashing as they tried desperately to get closer to one another. Allison's hands wasted no time in exploring the exposed flesh of Elena's stomach, her fingertips making patterns over heated skin. They both moaned at the sensation and pressed harder still.

Allison suddenly pulled back, just an inch, and locked eyes with a very flushed Elena. "Elena, you sure? You sure you don't wanna wai—"

"No." Elena dug her hands into Allison's long golden hair. Her lips were practically molten as she slid them up the length of Allison's slender neck and hovered over her ear. "No more waiting."

Chapter Twenty-Seven

THOSE THREE LITTLE WORDS BURNED in Allison's cells like the red tips of matchsticks held between Elena's teeth and stricken across the salt of Allison's skin.

No more waiting.

The smell of the heat from the flames that burst instantly between them burned in her body down to her bones. Elena's eyes seemed to grow wider and darker like beckoning tar pits pulling her in and drowning her in the sweet stickiness of a promise that throbbed beneath her ribs and between her legs.

No more waiting.

This was the moment, the culmination of heated gazes and timid touches, of wet kisses and ghosting breath over lips and lashes, of waiting and wanting, of distance and closeness and the timid yet eager steps in between. This was the moment when the rolling wave of desire that had been building between them finally crested and crashed, melting down into fingertips that sought to discover new worlds in trembling limbs and sighs.

Allison almost didn't recognize her own voice as her words came out in a strangled whisper, ragged and raw from Elena's intentions alone. "Yeah." She breathed into Elena's hair, the thick silky strands slipping across her lips as Elena's breath turned her neck loose and fluid. Her head fell back at the press of Elena's scorching kisses. "Yeah," she uttered breathlessly again as she grabbed Elena's shoulders and gently pushed.

When their eyes met, she whispered, "I think we've waited long enough."

She dove forward then, swallowing Elena's expelled sigh of relief and melding their lips together again in a wet press that made them both only long for more. Allison's itching fingers dipped into Elena's naked flesh, sinking into the quicksand draw of her warmth and dimpling fissures along her exposure. Every press evoked delicious whimpers that vibrated against Allison's own tongue and teeth as they kissed.

Allison followed the path from Elena's hips to her waist, up to the lace-clad swells of her exquisite breasts and felt her gasp as it pulled the air from the depths of her own lungs. She hovered there a moment, an ache building at the base of her spine that was nearly unbearable as she splayed her fingers over the rough pattern of the lace before letting her touch travel higher. She traced over the goose-pimpled flesh adorning delicate collarbones until her fingertips met the material of Elena's open blouse.

Her lips slipped from Elena's, and Allison held the other woman's gaze as she caught onto the edges of the gray silk and slowly slid the material down two slender arms. She held Elena's gaze a moment longer before letting it drop to take in the sight below.

Allison's eyes tracked over the entirety of Elena's torso and arms, seeking out every detail and absorbing each slowly. She didn't move to unclasp her bra and further expose her. Her hands didn't jump to grab at the full swells and hardening peaks beneath the lace. Instead, she moved slowly, her fingertips following the trail blazed by her burning gaze. She traced her fingers down the length of Elena's arms with feather-light whispers of flesh on flesh and pressed gently into the pad of each of her ten fingers before tickling across her palms and circling her wrists.

"Elena, you are *so*..."

Their eyes met. She swallowed thickly as she tried to put her thought to voice. When her lips parted again to finally finish the sentence, all she could manage was a single word. "*Everything.*"

Elena's breath expelled in a rushing sigh that quickly evolved into a guttural moan as she latched onto the front of the black tank top and jerked Allison forward. They collided roughly, melting into a heated kiss that was wet and hard and made no further room for slow exploration.

Their arms became a tangled mess as they each struggled to fulfill the same needy objective—the removal of all barriers. Within seconds, they abandoned their separate tasks and moved to work together, both pulling at the hem of Allison's tank top and damn near ripping it off of her as they yanked it over her head to reveal the small designer bra Elena had pulled from the studio closet. Elena's fingers then found their way to the waistband of Allison's skinnies, and as soon as the soft pads dipped below and out of sight, that trembling knot of tension at the base of Allison's spine exploded.

She moaned loudly as her back bowed forward, and the raw, throaty chuckle that escaped the woman who was wrapped partially around her was heated enough to evoke yet another. As soon as the button popped open and Elena's fingers pushed at a zipper that easily gave, Allison was practically itching to get out of her jeans. She pushed desperately at the tight material while trying to keep her lips locked onto Elena's, sucking at the woman's bottom lip like her life depended on it. When her jeans were at her ankles, Allison managed to almost get one bare foot free. She kicked the other frantically and, in her struggle, took one miscalculated step backward and completely lost her balance.

Allison stumbled, her hands wrapping tightly around Elena as she attempted to steady herself, to no avail, and down they went, barreling to the floor in a jumble of jean-tied ankles and nearly naked torsos. Allison's back hit the sheet-covered floor with a hard thud, the air expelling from her lungs in one loud rush of breath, and Elena landed atop her with a raspy grunt.

Heat burned in Allison's face the instant her breath returned, and she closed her eyes against the mortification of the moment. A second later, though, her heart burst beautifully with the sound of Elena's melodic laughter as it drifted up to her. She opened her eyes to see the glint of mirth in Elena's own as she let out another loud, bubbling laugh and crawled up Allison's body to press kisses to her lips and eyes and chin.

Face still hot, Allison grinned as her hands found their way once more to Elena's sides. "Sorry," she muttered, rolling Elena onto her back. She hovered over her, a hand planted on each side of Elena's head. "Guess I got a little eager."

Elena's hands ran the length of her sides and spine, and Allison thought she might simply melt when Elena reached up to cup her cheek and whispered, "Don't be sorry." She lifted her head to press her lips to Allison's again. "The jeans were my idea after all."

"Good point. Still, I'm guessing that ending up in a laughing fit on the floor probably wasn't how you pictured our first time going, right? Not exactly sexy."

"Except that it *is*," Elena told her, her voice low and melodic. "It *is* sexy, Allison." She took a deep breath, holding Allison's gaze, and whispered, "You make me feel so alive."

Allison smiled down at her, breathless and aching from the confession. "This is crazy, right?" she murmured as she held Elena's sparkling gaze.

"What?" Elena asked. "Sex on the floor of the studio in my work building, or our inability to remain upright?"

With a small laugh, Allison shook her head. "Falling for each other this way," she whispered, the words so quiet that they were hardly more than breath that dusted gently over Elena's kiss-swollen lips. "So fast?"

Elena's breath caught, and she swallowed heavily.

"So intensely?" Allison said. "I don't think I've ever felt like this before. I mean, it's crazy, right?"

Letting out a shaky breath, Elena nodded. "Yes," she said. "It is absolutely crazy." She hesitated only a moment before adding, "And wonderful."

Allison's eyes stung at the sincerity in Elena's soft voice as she nodded in return. "Yeah, it really is."

Threading her fingers through Allison's cascading hair, Elena pulled her closer. Allison's body blanketed over Elena's, pressing in and fitting perfectly as they met in a kiss much slower than before, so slow that it was nearly torture as they explored one another's mouths.

They ran their hands along the lengths of each other's sides, letting their fingertips become acquainted with newly bared flesh. Elena's back arched upward as Allison's right hand slid beneath her and, a moment later, the tension in Elena's bra released as Allison unfastened the clasp at the back. Allison held her breath as she pulled the lacy material from Elena's body and let it fall to the floor beside them.

Allison swallowed thickly as she took in the sight of Elena's plump breasts. She leaned her weight on one elbow as she brought up a hand to caress the soft mounds. Elena's chest heaved, her breathing becoming rapid as Allison's fingertips tickled over the pebbled peaks of hardened nipples, pinching slightly, before Allison cupped each breast fully one by one. She kneaded the flesh and watched as her touch caused Elena to tremble, her teeth digging into her bottom lip as her dark eyes watched her every touch.

With Elena's eyes on her, Allison dipped her head to draw one tight nipple between her lips. As soon as the wet tip of her tongue caressed the flesh, Elena's back shot off the floor and she let out a low moan that had Allison clenching her thighs. She grazed her teeth over the sensitive flesh, circling her tongue slowly, before sucking in long, deep pulls. She then released her hold and switched, paying some much-needed attention to the neglected breast. Elena writhed beneath her, a hand cupping the back of Allison's head.

Allison was already addicted to Elena's body, and she hadn't even seen all of it yet. The sheer softness of her skin was enough to warrant addiction in Allison's opinion. Whatever damned moisturizer the woman was using had to be infused with pure magic. She ran her hands along the quivering plane of Elena's stomach before releasing a now-reddened and wet nipple from between her lips and sitting up. She smiled as Elena whimpered with the loss but then gaped as Allison reached back and snapped open the clasp of her own bra. The overwhelming desire to feel her flesh pressed against Elena's had simply become too much.

Elena's hands were on her in an instant as Allison dropped the bra away to reveal what lay beneath. Allison's head rolled back on her neck, her eyes closing as a soft moan escaped her the moment Elena's fingers pulled gently at her nipples and cupped her small breasts. She followed eagerly when Elena urged her back down, and when their chests pressed together, nipples grazing and flesh dipping into flesh, both women trembled and let out throaty moans that echoed around the studio.

"Fuck," Allison whispered as she slipped along the static of Elena's skin, the ache between her legs growing with the friction; and then Elena's mouth was on her again. They kissed roughly, messily, their breathing ragged against teasing tongues and teeth digging into full lips. They nipped at one another as they touched.

Elena's thighs clenched tightly when Allison's tongue began a rhythmic dance at the roof of her mouth, slipping in and out and stroking her in a way that was all too similar to another action she could be performing with her tongue. She pinched Allison's side and muttered, "Tease."

Allison laughed, her breath hot and wet as she dropped to suck at Elena's bottom lip again. "It wasn't a tease, babe. It was a promise." She slid down from Elena's mouth, her tongue and teeth carving a scorching path down Elena's throat and over her collarbones. Just before Allison sucked one taut nipple into her mouth, she added, "And I always keep my promises."

"Oh God," Elena moaned, back arching up and out. When Allison's fingertips pulled at her waistband a moment later, her breathing grew shallow and she whimpered.

Allison toiled with the fastener of Elena's black pencil skirt, and Elena became visibly agitated in the wait. She smacked Allison's hands out of the way and made quick work of her skirt, kicking it off over her heels and not even bothering to send the shoes flying away with it. Allison certainly wasn't complaining. The sight of Elena laying naked beneath her but for bright red pumps and gray lace panties nearly caused her brain to explode inside her skull.

Slender fingers slipped up Elena's thighs, teasing close to her throbbing center before backing away again. Allison's entire body felt like it was on fire just from touching Elena. The woman wasn't even touching her in return. She didn't think she had ever been so turned on in her life, except maybe that one time that she was talked into taking Ecstasy at a house party her sophomore year.

Allison could feel the heat radiating from between Elena's legs, and it made her pussy throb almost painfully. When she finally sucked in a breath and ran her fingertips over the soaked lace covering Elena's dripping core, Elena cried out beneath her and latched onto Allison's wrist, urging her to stay right here, to press harder, to never stop.

"Fuck, Elena, you're so wet," she groaned as she ran her fingers up and down over the drenched lace and then slipped them under the material, pushing it to the side and letting her middle finger glide through Elena's molten slit.

A guttural moan rumbled up from Elena's chest and slithered across her lips as her hips bucked up and she ground into Allison's hand. That one sound drove Allison over the edge. She yanked Elena's panties down slender legs and nestled between trembling thighs, her breath puffing hotly against Elena's pulsating need. The scent of Elena's arousal filtered through her nostrils, and Allison's head bowed forward, her forehead resting against Elena's lower abdomen. She moaned as she pressed her lips to Elena's core in a gentle kiss that had her bucking and jumping once more.

Allison wanted to tease her further, wanted desperately to take her time, but she also needed some relief. And when a hand dug roughly into her hair a moment later and pressed her face further down, she knew she could wait no longer. She licked roughly up the length of Elena's slit, applying as much pressure as she could, and the volume of Elena's cry made it clear the woman had just come dangerously close to orgasm already.

Her name became a mantra on Elena's lips as the woman panted it with each swipe of Allison's tongue. She circled the tip around the throbbing bundle of nerves that begged her attention. When she wrapped her lips fully around Elena's clit and sucked it roughly into her mouth, the entire world went mute as Elena's thighs clamped around her head. Allison rode out the orgasm with Elena, sucking and licking as a rush of fluid coated her lips and chin.

Elena's grip in Allison's hair loosened, and then her hand fell away to the floor as her body went limp with the last, dying embers of that explosive climax. Her thighs fell open so that the sounds of her breathing and gentle whimpers returned swiftly to Allison's ears, but she remained between Elena's legs.

Allison nuzzled her nose against Elena's still-soaking slit, alternating kisses between the woman's inner thighs and sensitive clit. Elena jumped with the first few presses, too sensitive to enjoy the sensation, but, within seconds, her body began to tense again. Allison smiled when Elena lifted her head to look down at her and breathily asked, "Again?"

"Mm." Allison hummed, the sound vibrating deliciously against Elena's aching core. "Abso-fucking-lutely."

"Oh God." Her fingertips curled into the white sheet beneath her when Allison's mouth latched around her again and that skilled tongue pressed at her throbbing entrance.

Allison's tongue teased at Elena's opening for only a moment before thrusting in, causing Elena's body to rocket upward as the woman clung to Allison's head and ground her sex against her mouth. "Yes," she moaned. "Fuck, don't stop."

Allison nearly came undone from hearing that word slip across Elena's lips, the woman's voice so deep and ragged, strained by her arousal. She had no intentions of stopping. She brought her right hand up to Elena's sex and slid her two middle fingers up and down the woman's slit, thoroughly coating them with her own juices before pressing the tips at Elena's entrance. Allison pressed in slowly, letting Elena adjust with each gentle thrust, and then she amped up her pace. She wrapped her lips around Elena's clit and sucked vigorously every time her fingers curled back on the down-stroke, pressing against the ribbed patch of flesh that had Elena practically jumping off the floor, her legs wrapping fully around Allison's head and holding her there.

Her own body trembling with the need for pressure and release, Allison pulled her mouth from Elena's core and slid up the woman's body, keeping the pace with her fingers still buried deep inside her clenching sex. Elena grabbed at Allison's hair and yanked the woman's face down to meet hers. They kissed hungrily and Elena moaned at the taste of her own arousal on Allison's tongue—salty and rich.

Allison used her one free hand to push at her underwear until she could kick them off. Throwing one leg over to straddle Elena's thigh, she slid her sex up the length of Elena's thigh and back down, coating the flesh with her arousal. Elena's breath slammed out audibly.

"Allison," she husked.

Allison used her free hand to reach for Elena's. She pushed it between her legs where she balanced on the woman's thigh. "Touch me," she begged.

One swipe down Allison's drenched slit, and Elena thrust into her, her palm cupping her sex and pressed firmly between Allison's grinding rhythm and her own thigh. They bucked against one another, both trying their best to maintain a rhythm with their hands while seeking climax.

Allison rode Elena's hand and thigh with absolute abandon, panting hotly against Elena's neck, barely able to press kisses to the woman's skin as she fought for air. She gritted her teeth as she ground down and worked her fingers steadily inside the woman beneath her.

Elena moved just as frantically, thrusting up into Allison's hand while she made delicious circles against her inner walls.

"I'm close," Allison breathed against her ear, and Elena nodded, unable to say anything.

Allison knew that it was because Elena had been holding off her own orgasm, waiting for her. She could feel it in the way Elena's inner walls clenched around her fingers to the point of pain. But she had barely realized this when she felt her own pussy clamp down around Elena's fingers as her climax crashed over her like a tidal wave. Both women cried out as Elena's quickly followed, and they froze in place for one solid second before rocking back into motion and riding out the tremors together.

Allison's arms trembled as she tried to hold herself up and then gave out entirely. She collapsed, half on top of Elena and half on the floor beside her. Their breathing was sporadic and shallow, their chests heaving and slick with a light coating of sweat.

"That was..." Elena began once she caught her breath, but then simply let the sentence trail off into silence.

Allison understood. She chuckled breathlessly and nodded against Elena's shoulder. "Yeah," she agreed.

They lay there in a heap of limbs, and, a moment later, without any obvious reason, they both burst into loud laughter. Elena rolled to the side and pressed laughing kisses to Allison's lips, managing to say in between, "We just had sex on the floor of my studio."

"I believe your sentence needs a bit of an adjustment."

Elena wrapped one leg around Allison's hip. "How so?"

"See," Allison said, grinning, "I think what you *meant* to say was that we are *about to* have sex on the floor of your studio."

A wide smile stretched Elena's lips as Allison grabbed her and pulled her on top of her and added, "again," before lunging upward for another kiss.

Chapter Twenty-Eight

"I can't believe we didn't get caught." Allison leaned her back against the elevator wall. Elena stood next to her, their shoulders brushing, as the doors of the elevator slid shut and they began the long ride up to Elena's office.

Elena smirked, watching her next to her in the reflection cast upon the door opposite them. "There are many perks to my job, dear, but one of the best is that when I say something is off limits, no one dares go near it. I made sure my assistant knew that the studio was to be left alone before you and I ever even left the office. I'm sure everyone avoided it like the plague, though I *did* lock the door to be safe."

As they laughed, their shoulders brushed again, and Elena's fingers twitched at her side. She itched to touch Allison again. There had been embers burning between them since they met, but after their little escapade in the studio, a fire now blazed, bright and overwhelmingly hot. Elena didn't know if she wanted to throw a bucket of water on it to offer herself some relief or fan the damned flames and make them grow higher.

The fashion industry was a hive of homosexuality, so it was likely no one would care beyond a little water-cooler gossip. It was more that Elena prided herself on being professional and collected at all times, especially in front of her employees and colleagues. As such, she and Allison were dutifully, *excruciatingly,* keeping their hands to themselves.

"You think anyone heard us?" Allison asked, nudging Elena's arm with her elbow. A goofy grin painted her lips. "I mean, you *were* pretty loud."

Elena let out a staggered breath, the air stuttering over her lips. She closed her eyes and sucked in fresh air through her nose, her stomach stirring and flipping. She wanted to deny the claim, but she knew that it was true. She had hardly been able to contain herself with Allison's head between her legs, with her making Elena feel things she hadn't felt in a terribly long time, if ever. Elena had no shame, but it would be rather embarrassing if others in the building overheard her moans and cries of pleasure.

Allison rubbed her pinky finger against Elena's hand where it dangled between them. "I'm just kidding. I mean, I guess it's possible that someone heard us, but they would have heard *us*, not just you."

Elena took another deep breath as images flashed through her mind and the sounds of their lovemaking filled her ears like it was happening all over again. Her stomach fluttered pleasantly, and a deep throb sparked to life between her legs. Clearing her throat roughly, she clenched her thighs as she leaned her back against the wall and cursed herself for not masturbating more often. Surely she would not be so flustered and easy to excite if she had indulged in a little self-play more often during her four-year stint of abstinence.

Her goofy and adorably blunt lover was not making matters any better. Allison's mere existence in such a small space, occupying the same air as Elena, made her spine tingle. It didn't help that Allison seemed to want to continuously make mention of their earlier activities in the studio.

"Hey, come on," Allison whispered, snapping Elena back to the moment. "I wasn't trying to embarrass you or anything. I was just teasing. I'm sorry."

Elena, again, said nothing. She sucked in another sharp breath and shook her head, but Allison didn't seem to get the hint.

"I actually thought the sounds you made were really sexy." Allison grabbed Elena's hand and squeezed it before letting go. "Like *really* sexy. I seriously almost got off on those sounds alo—"

Allison's back slammed into the side wall as she stumbled from her position, Elena's mouth suddenly devouring hers. Her hands claimed her flesh, nails digging into the back of her neck and the curve of her hip. A guttural moan escaped her as Elena sucked the breath right out of her lungs, the woman's tongue teasing hotly at her own. Allison latched onto Elena's sides and yanked her even closer, so close that any third party witness would have thought them desperate to be one.

Itching fingers slipped down from Elena's sides to the woman's thighs. Allison's hands dug into the backs of Elena's thighs almost viciously when Elena's teeth sank into her bottom lip and ripped a trembling moan all the way up from Allison's toes.

In that moment, Elena was fairly certain that Allison Sawyer would, at some point, be the death of her. She thought this crazy and nearly unbearable tension between them would at least *slightly* abate after their first time together, but it only seemed to increase and intensify. That first incredible physical connection between them was passionate and heated and beautiful, and Elena didn't even care that it happened on the floor of a studio because it was the most intimate she had ever been with another person. The way Allison looked at her and touched her was riveting, and Elena was still reeling from how perfect their first time had been for her.

The only issue was that she didn't want to stop. She now wanted Allison more than ever. Just the smell of the woman surrounding her was enough to make her blood boil. Apparently, scratching the itch only made the itch worse. That had never happened to her before, but Elena didn't want to fight it. She wanted to dive into those heated waters head first and never come up for air.

Allison kneaded the soft, pliant flesh of Elena's thighs, drawing little whimpers from her slender throat. Elena sucked roughly at Allison's bottom lip before releasing it with a pop and hotly whispering, "You still taste like me."

Elena let out a soft yelp that quickly evolved into a moaning shudder of pleasure as the hands at the backs of her thighs suddenly jerked upward and jolted her feet right off the elevator floor. Allison lifted her with ease and spun them so that now Elena's back was the one thudding against the wall with a bang. Elena's head swam dizzily as the action caused a wave of heat to roll right through her before flooding at the apex of her thighs.

"Oh," she hissed, "*yes.*"

Elena's legs wrapped tightly around Allison's waist, and Allison shuddered. Her back lurched forward as Elena's skirt rode up and the heat between her legs met with the trembling plane of Allison's stomach, separated only by the thin materials of Elena's underwear and Allison's shirt. Their kisses were passionate and scorching as they panted into one another's mouths and Allison used her hips to make gentle rocking thrusts between Elena's legs that had her almost whining.

Allison sprang away from Elena so quickly that Elena nearly hit the floor as the elevator chimed its arrival on the thirtieth floor, both caught off guard given that neither had felt the machine rock to a gentle stop. Elena caught herself, heels smacking roughly against the elevator floor. Both her face and Allison's were heavily flushed as they quickly patted at their hair and smoothed down their clothes.

The elevator doors slid open to reveal a single person waiting. As soon as she saw him, Elena stiffened her spine and kept her jaw rigid, determined to show that she was nothing if not completely composed. The man stared at them for a moment, his eyes tracking over the slight wrinkles in their clothes, especially those marring Elena's skirt. His lips pursed as he stepped onto the elevator. "Afternoon, Miss Vega."

"Elliot," she replied with an acknowledging tilt of her head before practically shooting out of the elevator. She heard Allison choke out a quick "Sup?" before darting out of the elevator to follow her.

As soon as Allison closed Elena's office door and looked at Elena, they both burst into loud laughter.

"Oh God," Allison said, "that was so damn awkward."

Elena held her stomach as she laughed and nodded her agreement. "I think he knew."

"He definitely had an idea," Allison said. "He probably would've asked if he wasn't so afraid of you."

"He has always been afraid of me," Elena gloated. "He honestly cannot stand me, but he is the type who prefers to let that be known behind closed doors and behind my back."

"Yeah, typical," Allison grunted. "There are way more people like that in the world than there are people willing to say stuff to your face." She sighed as her laughter waned, but then the image of the awkward elevator exchange drifted through her mind again, and she burst into loud laughter all over again.

"What?" Elena asked.

"It's nothing," Allison said. "I just keep seeing it in my mind. Your face was so red."

"Yours was just as red," Elena countered, wiping at the tears that had developed in the corners of her eyes.

"And you were just like, '*Elliot*,'" Allison said, mimicking Elena's rigid posture and cold voice before cracking up all over again.

"Oh yes, dear," Elena drawled, "because '*Sup?*' is so much better."

Allison grabbed her phone from her pocket. "Wait, wait. Say that again. I *have* to get that on camera."

Elena smirked and shook her head. "No."

"Come on," Allison whined, offering the woman her signature charming grin. "Please?"

"Not a chance. That crooked smile of yours has no sway over me, dear."

"Yeah, right," Allison said as she strutted over and wrapped her arms around Elena's waist. "Don't deny it, Elena. You find me totally adorable."

Elena's eyes practically sparkled as Allison danced her around. "Is that right?"

"*So* right."

"Hm." Elena narrowed her eyes, pretending to contemplate the claim.

Allison winked at her and waggled her eyebrows ridiculously. Elena rolled her eyes in response but said, "You may not be *entirely* wrong."

"See?" Allison bragged, leaning forward to kiss the slender column of Elena's throat. "That's what I thought."

"Allison."

"Hm?" Allison hummed against her throat.

"We have to stop."

"No we don't."

"Oh, but we do." Elena sighed. "I actually have a bit of work to do, and I, unfortunately, cannot put it off any longer."

Allison groaned into Elena's neck as she squeezed the woman tighter, breathing her in. A moment later, though, she relented and pulled her face from Elena's neck. "Okay," she said, "but if you expect me to be able to help you out with anything, then you're going to have to stop smelling so good and looking so good and tasting so good and sounding so g—"

Elena pressed an index finger to Allison's mouth to quiet her. "I get it, dear."

Allison snorted with laughter and kissed Elena's lips. "So, what can I do to help?"

"I don't actually believe there *is* anything," Elena replied. "It's mostly paperwork and a meeting that I need to be present for. You are welcome to stay and wait for me, Allison, but it will likely be incredibly dull and we won't have much opportunity to interact."

Allison sighed as she scratched at the back of her neck and pondered what to do. She didn't want to leave Elena, because she was still on one of those clingy highs after the bonding and the sex and then the almost-sex and all the little playful moments and laughter. She pretty much wanted to crawl inside this date and live in it. At the same time, she didn't want to be in the way or anything, nor did she want to just be chilling on the couch in Elena's office, twiddling her thumbs.

"Well, damn," she said. "I don't really have anything else to do."

She pulled her phone back out and glanced at the time only to see that she had a text message from Macy, likely just checking in. She opened it and read the short message.

Still alive. Bit dusty. Tired. The hell are you?

Allison snorted at the typical hung-over-Macy text. Though Allison couldn't hear her voice or see her expression, she knew Macy was grumpy. She had never seen anyone as grumpy when not feeling well as Macy.

"Macy just texted me," Allison informed Elena, turning the phone around to show her the message.

Elena arched a brow, confused, and Allison laughed.

"Yeah, I know. Just wait until you meet her."

"And when will that be?" Elena asked, brows knitting together and eyes widening. It somehow managed to make her look both nervous and excited about the idea.

"Do you actually *want* to meet her?"

"Of course," Elena replied. "It's the least I could do after unleashing the storm that is my mother and Vivian on you."

"Well, really, it was more like they unleashed themselves."

"True."

"I get that you think you *should* meet her," Allison said after a moment, "but I mean do you really *want* to? Because I won't make you; at least not so soon."

"No, no," Elena told her, shaking her head and pulling Allison close again. "I *want* to. She's important to you, so this is important to me."

Allison hated the burning sensation in her throat as Elena's words actually managed to choke her up. She bit the inside of her cheek to keep any tears from welling up in her eyes, but they came anyway. She sucked in a cool breath and nodded, not wanting to say anything, for fear that her voice would crack. But when Elena stroked her cheek, Allison's chest practically concaved, and she knew she had to get away for a minute. She moved quickly and wordlessly away from Elena and into the private bathroom attached to the woman's office, closing the door behind her.

Allison cursed at herself in the mirror of Elena's office bathroom as the woman's words echoed through her mind over and over. She blamed her stupid post-sex hormones or whatever for the sudden urge to cry, but Allison knew it was really just because it was incredibly nice to have someone who cared about the things and the people that *she* cared about simply because she cared about them.

She glanced around the bathroom and was surprised to see that the room was fully stocked, and not just with the typical items. There were two complete makeup kits, the top-dollar stuff of course; makeup cleansing wipes; face and body lotions and exfoliating washes; various nail polishes and remover; cotton swabs; Q-tips; nail clippers; toothbrushes; toothpaste; mouthwash; and more. Allison was pretty impressed. She reached for the makeup cleansing wipes and pulled one out. Her makeup was a little smudged from the sweating in the studio and now the watery eyes that Allison refused to deem as crying. She contemplated simply cleaning away the smudged bits and touching up her makeup afterwards but decided to just wash her face bare and leave it that way until later. It wasn't like she ever wore very much makeup anyway—foundation, a thin layer of eyeliner, a bit of eye shadow, and some mascara.

Allison scrubbed her face clean and took a deep breath before heading back into the office where Elena was busy typing away on her computer, a thin pair of crimson-rimmed glasses perched on her nose. Allison's stomach bubbled and fizzled pleasantly at the adorable sight.

Elena glanced up at the sound of the bathroom door opening and smiled at Allison. She pulled the glasses off her face and laid them on her desk before swiveling in her chair to face Allison. "Hi."

"Hi," Allison murmured.

"I see you utilized a few of my many supplies."

Allison nodded. "Yeah. You have a whole arsenal in there."

"I used to spend many nights here when I first took the position," Elena said. "The restroom is actually quite tame. I used to have an entire section of my office blocked off with a crib and changing table for Lucas."

"Yeah? I bet that was cute."

"I don't know about 'cute'." Elena said. "*Convenient*, though, yes."

Allison crossed the distance between them and dropped to her knees in front of Elena's chair to be more level with her; that, and it made it easier to slip her hands over Elena's thighs.

Elena smiled at her, eyes roaming over Allison's face, and Allison felt full of so much in that moment that she could hardly breathe.

Elena reached out, and Allison felt her brush her fingertips over the faint bruise between her eyes.

"Almost completely gone," Allison said. "I keep bruises for a long time. I guess because I'm so pale. I don't know."

"I still feel terrible about that." Elena rubbed over the flesh again.

"Don't," Allison said. "It's a funny story that we can tell people one of these days."

"One of these days," Elena whispered. "Do you plan on being around for a while?"

Allison reached up and caught Elena's wrist. She pulled the woman's hand down from her forehead and pressed a kiss to the center of Elena's palm. "Is that what *you* want?"

Elena was silent for a long moment, her gaze intense as she held Allison's eyes. "In this moment, Allison," she whispered, rubbing her thumb gently against Allison's chin, "it is *all* that I want."

Allison let out a gentle sigh, relieved. She had always been a runner. The system had taught her how to detach, how to remain at a distance. It taught her to love only the sounds of things and people fading into the distance as she moved forward, moved on. It taught her to be on her own, but with Elena, it felt easy to stay. It felt natural. The woman had come blazing into her life like a wildfire in a sensible pantsuit, and Allison had been willing to burn ever since.

Allison leaned her head into the soft flesh of Elena's palm and nodded. "Then yeah," she whispered, "I plan on being here."

"Are you sure you don't wanna walk me down to the first floor?" Allison asked, offering Elena a mischievous little grin. "Another loooooong ride on the elevator." She waggled her eyebrows.

A loud laugh left Elena's lips. "I think it is best if we avoid the elevator for the time being."

"True," Allison said. She rocked on her heels, stalling. She wasn't quite ready to leave. "I should probably take the stairs. Last time I rode in that elevator, some hot brunette attacked my mouth."

Elena pinched Allison's arm. "Rumor has it that you did not resist."

With a cluck of her tongue, Allison shook her head. "I don't know who told you that, but they were totally telling the truth."

Elena smiled and pulled Allison into a gentle embrace. "Thank you for today."

Allison shook her head in answer. "Thank *you*, Elena. This was *all* you, and I loved every second of it."

"I did as well."

"Well, good."

They pulled apart and stared at one another a moment longer before Allison said, "All right. I'm gonna go hang with Macy, but when you're finished up here, give me a call, yeah? I'd like to see you again before the night is over, if that's okay with you."

Elena nodded. "I will call you."

"Okay good." Allison pressed a quick kiss to Elena's lips before turning to go. She turned back just before she stepped out of the woman's office and said, "Oh, and Elena?"

"Yes dear?"

"We should visit your studio more often." She winked as a wide smile stretched between Elena's crimson cheeks, and then slipped out of the office.

Chapter Twenty-Nine

"You did what?!" Vivian hissed through the phone, and Elena winced as it echoed loudly in her ear.

"Vivian, I am not going to repeat myself," Elena said, glancing up and around her office nervously. Despite knowing that no one could hear her, Elena still felt as if every ear in the entire universe was currently tuned in to her very private admission of secret studio sex with her lesbian babysitter-turned-lover.

"Oh my God!" Vivian exclaimed. "Elena!"

"Feel free to stop shrieking in my ear any time, Viv."

"I will not sto—*What*?" Midway through Vivian's response, Elena heard another voice echo from the other end of the line. She couldn't be sure, but it sounded like Vivian's assistant, which meant that Vivian had gone in to work today as well. It didn't surprise Elena. She and Vivian both were workaholics, though Elena herself had slowed way, way down in the last two years in order to spend as much time with Lucas as possible. "Jeanine, I don't give a damn about that right now, because my best friend just got laid for the first time in four years, okay? *Four* years, *and* it was with a woman. Okay? Do you see the importance of this conversation now? The new spread can wait."

Elena's entire body felt like it caught fire in that moment as she fumed. "Vivian Warren! Shut your mouth this instant!"

"What? It's true, and besides, I didn't say your name, so relax."

Elena rolled her eyes as she pressed her fingertips to her temples. "Everyone in your office knows exactly who your best friend is, you idiot," she said.

"Oh." Vivian laughed. "That's true. Sorry, but hey, don't be embarrassed. It's something to celebrate not something to be embarrassed about."

"Thank you for that encouraging pep talk, dear."

"You are quite welcome. So, spill. I need details, and when I say I need details, I mean details along the lines of trashy-romance-novel details. Catch my drift?"

"Go buy a book then, Viv, because you won't get any details out of me, and you know it."

Vivian sighed heavily into the phone. "I'm demoting you. You no longer hold the position of best friend, because best friends share everything with each other. I even tell people that Lucas is my son sometimes."

"Oh, you do not," Elena said. "And I can't be demoted. It's in the contract."

"We wrote that stupid best-friend contract when we were seven, Elena."

"Yes, and it still stands," Elena told her. "It clearly states that none but me can hold the position of best friend in your life and none but you can hold it in mine."

"It also says that you will always share your gummy bears with me, and I will always share my Milk Duds with you," Vivian countered.

"Yes, well, have I ever broken that sacred covenant? I do believe I have always shared my gummy bears with you."

"True, even though you hardly ever eat candy anymore." Vivian sighed again. "I love gummy bears."

Elena chuckled as she leaned back in her office chair and twirled a pen between her fingers. "I know you do."

"So, you're not going to tell me anything?" Vivian asked. "Not even a little bit? Are you at least going to tell me if it was good?"

"Very well, but this is all you get," Elena said.

"Spit it out already!"

"It was amazing."

Vivian giggled like a little girl. "I want to squeal again."

"Please don't."

"So how amazing are we talking here, Elena?"

"Nice try, Viv."

Vivian huffed out a breath. "What kind of best friend calls just to say that sex has occurred but then refuses to share any details of the occurrence?"

"The evil kind." Elena let out a low, playful laugh to suit the statement. "Besides, I am still in the office."

"Oh, so you can have sex in the office, but you can't talk about sex in the office? I call bullshit, but I will let it slide for now. You do realize, though, that you will likely end up telling me more at some point, right?"

"Most likely," Elena admitted, knowing the chances were pretty high. They had never been good at keeping things from one another, and Elena would likely feel the need to gush to someone at some point, given how incredible the sex with Allison had actually been.

They stayed on the phone with one another for a long time, even after they both fell silent. It was something they had done many times in their lives. After a long silence, Vivian quietly asked, "You really like her, don't you?"

Elena sighed. "I really do, Vivian," she whispered. "I really, really do."

Hey gorgeous! You up for an adventure tonight, or do you have to pick the little man up?

Elena's body erupted in tingles as she read Allison's text. It amazed her how easily all things Allison Sawyer seemed to do that to her. She contemplated her mysterious offer as she stared at her phone, her thumbs stilled over her keypad. She had already informed her parents and Lucas that it was likely he might have to spend the night there, thus it would be easy for Elena to simply use that to her advantage and take Allison up on her offer.

What sort of adventure?

You'll see. The next text sent an address and told Elena to meet her there at nine that night. Elena laughed softly when she read the end of the message. *Oh, and wear jeans, Elena, because damn. Just damn.*

Elena didn't have a clue what adventure the other woman had in mind, but she found she hardly cared. She just wanted to be there, wherever Allison was.

The night air was warm and wonderfully breezy as Elena stepped out of the cab and onto the curb. The address Allison had given her was that of a small bar; it was small, but from the looks of it, lively. A large poster plastered across the window right next to the door read *OPEN MIC-NIGHT!* Intrigued, Elena made her way inside, her black pumps tapping as she walked.

Patrons packed the place, filling tables in front of a large stage at the far end of the building as well as standing around the bar waiting for drinks. She took a moment to glance around for a flash of wild golden hair, but it was useless. There was no way Elena would find Allison in this crowd, so she made her way to the bar instead.

Weaving through the bodies, Elena felt several people brush against her, and some in ways that obviously could not be deemed as accidents. As always, she shuddered at the contact and did her best to weave through the crowd a little faster. When she found a thankfully empty stool at the bar, she plopped down and waited for the bartender to take notice of her. Familiar with the routine of being a well-dressed woman sitting alone at a bar, she counted in her head, avoiding the urge to roll her eyes:

And in 3, 2, 1…

"Hey there, pretty lady."

Elena didn't even bother making eye contact with the man who approached her nearly as soon as she sat down. Anyone who started with "pretty lady" was doomed from the beginning. She avoided his gaze, straightened her back, and said, "No, thank you."

"Oh come on. Don't be like that."

Elena did make eye contact with him then. "Don't be like what?" she asked. "I said 'No, thank you'. Would you prefer I *rudely* turn you down?"

"You're a sassy one." He let out a nervous laugh and pulled a bit at the collar of his wrinkled navy button-up shirt.

"No. Currently, I'm being quite polite. You, on the other hand, are not."

He ran a hand over his buzzed dirty-blonde hair and offered up what Elena assumed he considered to be a charming smile. It came off as more predatory than anything. "Don't like compliments?"

"I don't care for men who don't understand the meaning of the word 'no'."

His eyes hardened as he simply stared at her for a moment.

She thought he might actually try another pass at her before he finally just sneered "whatever" and walked off.

The bartender showed up a moment later. "What can I get ya, ma'am?"

"Absolut neat." She was going to need something with a little kick to start her off, especially if it was going to take a while to find her date. As she waited for her drink, she pulled her phone from her clutch and typed out a text to Allison, letting her know where she was.

"Well, well." Another voice spoke from behind her, and Elena closed her eyes and sighed at the deep register. "Beautiful woman alone at the bar?"

The man stepped around her and into view. "That's a crime."

Elena arched a brow as her gaze scanned down his body. He was a younger guy, barely out of high school from the look of him, and Elena was appalled to see that he was actually attempting to rock the circa-early-2000s frat-boy look of khaki cargo shorts, a bright pink polo with a popped collar, and a white ball cap only partially on his head. Her lip curled as she shook her head. "So is your attire, dear."

The guy had a typical "psh" reaction before muttering that she was a bitch and stalking off.

The bartender arrived with her drink, and Elena took a sip, reveling in the slight burn as the vodka slithered down her throat.

It wasn't long before she was approached again. This man, at least, was dressed well. He wore a lovely dark gray button-up and black slacks. His face was nicely groomed, and the soft blue of his eyes paired beautifully with his dark hair. "Hello." He greeted her with an incline of his head.

Elena narrowed her eyes and did her best to appear confused as she stared at the man's lips.

"Something in my teeth?" he asked.

She did her best to appear even more confused at that, and then she let out a sigh and shook her head. She offered him a strained smile and said, "Lo siento. No hablo inglés."

The guy stared at her for a moment, as if contemplating whether or not to believe her, but then he just nodded, mumbled a "sorry" and wandered off.

Elena had a few moments of merciful peace before she noticed a woman with auburn hair and strikingly bright eyes making her way toward her. She wondered for a moment if she truly was the intended target of the other woman, but given the way those bright eyes were pinned on her, Elena would bet almost anything that she was. While Elena wished that she could avoid come-ons entirely, she did prefer those made by women. She had encountered a few women who had seemed to take on that whole *playa* persona, but for the most part, Elena had much more respectful encounters with women than she did with men. They typically accepted a "No, thank you" with much more grace and ease than the men did.

A moment later, those striking eyes were right in front of her, taking in every detail. "Evening," the woman said, her smile bordering on a smirk. "Can I buy you a drink?"

Elena was surprised by the thick Australian accent but found it lovely. She smiled at the woman and shook her head. "No, thank you."

The other woman nodded. "Fair enough," she said. "Already have a date?"

"Yes, actually," Elena told her. "I am meeting my…my girlfriend." It felt so strange to say that. She had only said it once before, at the zoo, and it had felt weird then. But just as it had that day, saying the word had also sent a jolt of excitement rippling through Elena's gut.

"Yeah?" the Aussie asked. "Sounds nice. What's she look like? Maybe I can spot her for you?"

Elena smiled. "Blonde, bright green eyes, a stunning smile, and undoubtedly wearing some kind of tank top or three-quarter-sleeve button-up." She paused for a long moment as she looked out into the crowd before sighing and adding, "Beautiful."

The other woman smiled. "Excellent description, Elena, and given that lovey-dovey look you had in your eyes while you said it, I'd say Alli's done quite well for herself."

Elena startled, eyes wide and confused. She blinked rapidly, her mouth opening and closing, but then the other woman just laughed and stuck her hand out.

"Macy Davis." Her eyes scanned over Elena's figure. "It's nice to finally meet the woman who's turned my best mate into a puddle of goo."

Clearing her throat, Elena smiled and reached out to shake Macy's hand. "Macy," she said. "It's wonderful to finally meet you. Allison speaks quite highly of you."

"You too. Really, *really* highly, if you know what I mean."

Elena's cheeks flushed heavily as she cleared her throat again and nodded.

"I'm not so good with censorship." Macy laughed at herself.

"I thought you were hitting on me when you first walked up," Elena said, and Macy nodded, grinning.

"I was." She leaned her elbows on the bar and settled in beside Elena. "But only as a test."

"A test?"

"Yeah. To make sure you were loyal. It's my duty as her best mate."

"I see," Elena said. "I'm glad she has someone looking out for her in such a manner."

"Always have, love," Macy told her. "Always will."

Elena could hear the sincerity in Macy's voice and the fierce protection of Allison that shone in her eyes and posture as she spoke of her. It was heartwarming, and reminded Elena greatly of her own best friend.

"Speaking of Allison," Elena said. "Have you seen her? I sent her a text, but she never responded."

"Sure she did," Macy said. "That's why I'm here."

"Oh, I see. So, is this the part where you tell me that if I break her heart, you will break my face or something along those lines?"

"Something like that."

"I thought as much." Elena took a sip of her drink. "Well, dear, you needn't worry."

"I know." Macy shrugged.

"You do?"

"Oh please. I only just met you, I know, but you two are so bloody in love with each other, it's borderline disgusting."

Elena's heart shot into her throat as those words sank into her. She couldn't think of anything to say in response, because her brain felt like it was on fire as she closed her eyes and pondered her feelings for Allison. Was it love? It definitely *could* be.

An image of Allison playing with Lucas flitted through her mind, and a smile tugged at her lips. It definitely *might* be.

"Relax," Macy said. "Before your face overheats and explodes."

Elena's eyes fluttered open again. She swallowed and smiled at Macy, who leaned over and nudged her with her elbow. "But just so you know, if you *do* hurt her, I'll have to come after you, and I used to wrestle dingoes in Oz. So you would be lucky to live to tell the tale."

Elena started to laugh but fell silent and gaped when Macy simply stared at her, serious as ever.

"Is that...are you being serious?"

Macy stared at her only a moment longer before she grinned and shook her head. "Your face, love. That was priceless."

Elena inclined her head and pointed at the woman. "You had me for a moment."

"Americans think Australia is literally just a ton of blokes in board shorts, shrimp on the barbie, and dingoes stealing our babies or something. Thanks, Meryl Streep, for that last one, even if it *was* based on a true story." Macy barked out a loud laugh. "So, it's easy to pull one over on most of you."

"I would imagine so. I would love to visit Australia."

"Alli wants to go too. I'm thinking of asking her along after graduation."

"Oh?" Elena was about to inquire for further details when the lights in the bar dimmed considerably and the static sounds of a woman tapping on a microphone distracted her.

"What's this?" Elena glanced up at the stage.

Macy grinned and pointed to a very familiar blonde walking onto the stage behind the woman at the microphone and sitting down with an acoustic guitar. "Your date just arrived," she said, and Elena's heart began to race.

Chapter Thirty

"How's everyone doing tonight?" asked the woman at the microphone, and the patrons of the bar erupted into an echoing chorus of hoots and hollers. Elena just barely registered that one of those hooting people was Macy. She was so focused on Allison's long blonde hair pulled back in a low messy bun. It was incredibly sexy and made only more so when paired with the radiant smile stretched over Allison's lips as she looked out on the bar crowd.

"All right! That's what we like to hear. We're gonna go ahead and get this open-mic night kicked off with one of our regular performers. You all know her. You all love her. You all can't wait to buy her album when she finally decides to get her ass into a recording studio!"

Elena smiled as she watched Allison chuckle and shake her head as several in the bar cheered once more. Her heart's racing had yet to cease or even slow, and Elena's entire body felt electric. She had heard Allison play and even hum a bit once before, but she had never actually heard her sing. She was on the edge of her barstool.

"You're in for a treat, love," Macy said.

"Is this for me?" Elena asked and Macy only winked.

She sucked in a deep breath and turned back to face the stage.

The woman at the microphone had taken a moment to remind everyone of half-priced pitchers at the bar before she clapped her hands together and said, "All right, everyone! Give it up for the one and only Allison Sawyer!" The woman then turned and patted Allison on the shoulder before walking off the stage.

Once she was gone, Allison stood and reached for the microphone stand. She wore a white button-up shirt, mostly open to reveal a bit of her chest, adorned with a silver chain necklace, and a bit of her lower stomach. The sleeves of her shirt were rolled up above her elbows, and her dark jeans were practically pasted to her flesh and tucked into black motorcycle boots. Elena found her positively irresistible.

Allison pulled the microphone stand over to her chair and lowered it so that the microphone hung right in front of her when she sat back down. Once she was settled, she offered the crowd an awkward little wave. “Hey everyone.”

Allison tapped her guitar. “I know I usually do a few songs, but I’m only going to do one tonight, because I’ve got a hot date waiting for me at the bar.”

The bar erupted in another round of hoots and hollers, including a particularly loud one from Macy, who even fist-pumped into the air.

“Yeah,” Allison said, grinning. “So, I’m gonna take you back to 1999 with this one. I hope you guys like it.”

Allison began plucking at her guitar, a melody that sounded familiar to Elena but a bit different on acoustic. Elena completely forgot the guitar, though, when Allison actually began to sing. Her voice was soft and even a bit raspy, and it blasted right through Elena’s flesh and straight to her soul.

Mouth hanging slightly open, Elena stared up at the stage, mesmerized. There was a natural effortlessness about Allison’s singing that only added to the beauty of it, and it blew Elena away.

Macy nudged Elena’s side with her elbow. “She’s great, right?”

“She is magnificent.”

Allison put her own little spin on Tal Bachman’s “She’s So High”, which only made it better in Elena’s opinion. It was softer, slower, and somehow more romantic than anything, which surprised Elena, given that the lyrics weren’t terribly deep. That raspy lilt in Allison’s voice made it sound like a lullaby, gently rocking Elena’s heart into submission.

“I think she might like you a bit there, fancy-pants.”

Elena arched a brow at Macy. “I’m wearing jeans,” she countered. “Hardly fancy.”

"Yeah okay."

Smiling, Elena held a finger to her lips. "Shh. I'm being serenaded."

As Allison led into the chorus a final time, Elena watched her close her eyes and sing the final bits of the song, plucking her fingers expertly over the strings of her guitar until the music faded into silence. The bar erupted in cheers as Allison's eyes fluttered open again. She smiled and nodded before rising from her chair and making her way off the stage.

She disappeared behind a door just off from the stage, and a moment later, Elena felt Macy tugging on her arm.

"Come on, love."

"Where are we going?"

Macy called over her shoulder. "Alli reserved a table for us."

She led her around the bar to a table tucked into a corner with hardly any view of the stage at all. Elena slid into the small booth, and Macy took the seat opposite her. When the waitress came around, Macy ordered two beers and Elena requested an apple martini.

"Appletini," Macy said. "You are *definitely* fancy."

"I have a feeling you would say as much if I ordered *anything* other than a beer."

"True." Macy tapped her fingers against the table top. "So, when is the wedding?"

"Pardon?"

"You and Alli."

Elena smirked. "Very funny."

"It's only a matter of time." Before Elena could respond to the teasing, Allison's shadow clouded over their table.

"Allison," she murmured, a gentle smile touching her lips. She stood up quickly.

Allison grinned at her. "Hey."

They stood a few inches apart, just staring at one another for a moment, before Macy sighed. "Just kiss already," she said.

Leaning in, Allison planted a soft whisper of a kiss to the corner of Elena's mouth before pulling the woman into an unexpected embrace.

Elena went willingly, wrapping her arms around Allison's waist and sighing into the embrace. It felt nice to be in Allison's arms again, even though it had only been a few hours since they were last together. It seemed like much longer.

"What did you think?" Allison whispered into Elena's ear as they hugged.

"You were incredible. Thank you for singing to me." They slipped out of the embrace, and Elena kissed Allison's cheek. She then smiled and reached up with her thumb to wipe away the evidence of her lipstick. "But I am not high above you, dear."

"Yeah, actually, mate, it looks like she might be a bit shorter than you if she took those monster heels off."

They laughed as Elena and Allison slid into the booth, Elena's hand finding Allison's under the table. Their fingers laced together as they settled in, and Macy rolled her eyes.

"You two and your lovey looks are gross."

"Jealous," Allison sing-songed.

"Agreed," Elena said.

"Maybe a little," Macy said, like it was an admission.

The waitress arrived with their drinks, and Macy handed one of her beers over to Allison. "So, Alli, you'll be happy to know that your lady here passed my test with flying colors."

"Your test?"

"She hit on me," Elena said, and Allison cracked up.

"Did she call you 'Elena-r'?" Allison asked.

Macy glared.

"I can't help it, you arse!" Macy laughed as she slid her moist hand from her sweating beer bottle and flicked the cold water droplets at her best friend.

"She did, but only once," Elena said. "She mostly called me 'love'."

"Oh yeah," Allison said. "She called me that a lot when we first met."

"But she didn't like it," Macy said. "She likes 'mate' better, so it's been that for years now."

"So, you two met at NYU?" Elena asked as she sipped her martini. Both Allison and Macy nodded.

"And we've been inseparable ever since," Macy said.

"Pretty much."

"That's nice," Elena said. "My best friend Vivian and I are much the same."

With Allison by her side, Elena felt incredibly at ease, and she was quite pleased with how well she and Macy clicked. There wasn't an awkward moment the entire night, and Elena found Macy charming and amusing, much like Allison. She could only hope that Macy liked her as well.

Elena passed a wad of cash to the cab driver as the taxi came to a stop in front of her house. Allison stepped out first and reached for Elena's hand to help her exit the vehicle.

They walked silently toward the door, Allison's pulse racing and her skin prickling with the tense anticipation that seemed to live in the air around them. She trailed a bit behind Elena, led by the other woman as the fingertips of her right hand barely dusted through the spaces between those of Elena's left.

Elena pulled Allison into the house and down the hall. Allison's heart thundered in her chest as she followed Elena into her bedroom.

The air felt electric as Elena opened the door to her bedroom and, leaving the light off, pulled Allison inside. Their free hands found their way together so that they were connected like shy little girls on the verge of singing "Ring Around the Rosy".

They stood at the foot of Elena's enormous bed, and Allison could just make out Elena's features as her eyes began to adjust to the dark. Elena released one of Allison's hands and let her fingers trail slowly up the length of Allison's arm, dusting along her collarbone through her shirt, and up her slender neck to rest around Allison's cheek.

Elena took a deep breath and whispered, "I am so crazy about you."

Allison's breath escaped her in a rush. "Really?" she asked, her voice strained with the magnitude of all that she felt in that moment. She was astounded by the way this woman could make her feel so much with so few words, with a gentle touch, with a quiet connection in a dark room.

Elena nodded. Her hand slipped down from Allison's cheek to rest on her chest, just over her heart. "And I think I deserve this," she whispered. "I think *we* deserve this."

"This?" Allison asked, her own hands settling on Elena's waist.

"This," Elena repeated, tapping her index and middle fingers lightly over Allison's heart. "Whatever this is."

Allison swallowed, her breath coming out in a shaky whisper. "Feels like..."

She hesitated as she searched for the right word. Her throat felt like it was on fire, her eyes stinging just as horribly as Elena's, but for the first time in her life, Allison didn't fight the tears that sprang up and spilled over. They were soft, like a release, because she wasn't running. She was standing still. Finally, she was standing still, and Elena was standing with her. "Feels big."

Elena's eyes shimmered in the dark as the small bit of light shining through the window caught them in fractured movement. Allison's fingertips slipped beneath the hem of Elena's shirt and danced across the flesh beneath. "You don't think it's too fast, all of this?" she asked as she began to slowly lift the garment, slipping it up the length of Elena's torso.

"Yes," Elena whispered, and Allison's hands halted on her flesh. "It feels fast, but it feels right as well, to *me*, at least." She brought her own hands back to rest over Allison's just under her bra. "I am so tired of being afraid, Allison." She slipped her fingers under Allison's and latched onto her own shirt. She lifted it the rest of the way up and over her head before letting it fall to the floor. "I'm so tired of being afraid of reaching for something that I know I deserve, something that I have denied myself for such a long time now."

"Me too," Allison choked out as Elena's fingers then slipped over the buttons of her shirt and slowly began to pop them open, one by one. "I just...I'm not used to being..." Her voice cracked as she let out a shaky breath. Her hands came up to cup around Elena's wrists and halt the other woman's task. "Elena," she whispered. She hated the feeling of being vulnerable. She had hated it her entire life, but, in this one moment, Allison didn't care. She could be vulnerable with this woman. She could be afraid. She could be honest. She trusted Elena to remain. "I'm not used to being wanted, not like this."

"Like what?" Elena asked, turning her wrists in Allison's hands so that she could tangle their fingers together.

Allison took a deep, steadying breath and squeezed Elena's hands. "Like you might actually want to keep me."

Elena pulled Allison to her, releasing her hands, and wrapping her arms around Allison's neck. She peppered kisses along Allison's jaw and then pressed two soft kisses to her lips. "I do," she promised, and those quiet words blasted through Allison's heart.

Allison let out a shaky sigh as she dove forward to capture Elena's lips again.

"Stay, Allison," Elena whispered. She kissed Allison again, hands returning to the buttons on her shirt. "Stay with me."

Allison knew she would. She would stay forever if Elena asked her.

Allison's brows furrowed in her sleep as the distinct feeling that she was being watched trickled in through the haze of dreaming and brought her to the surface. She rubbed at her eyes before opening them, and then yelped as she came face to face with the wide eyes of a toddler.

"Hi!" Lucas's face was so close to hers that their noses brushed.

She chuckled and shifted back in the bed, the memories of the previous night flooding back to her in a rushing wave. She was in Elena's house, in Elena's bed with Elena's son sprawled out next to her and smiling so big that it looked like it had to hurt, but Elena herself was nowhere in sight. She then realized that under the thin blanket and sheet covering her, she was completely naked.

Well, this is awkward, she thought.

"Hey buddy," she said, pulling the covers a little higher. "Where did you come from?"

"Gram's!" He kicked his legs up and down on the mattress as he lay on his belly next to Allison. "What you doing in Momma's bed?"

"Uh." Allison mulled that one over. "I had a sleepover."

"Oh," he said, drawing out the word. "Where are your clothes?"

A soft pink dusted Allison's cheeks as she said, "Um, on the floor, I think."

"Why?"

"Because I took them off."

"Why?"

"Uh, because I was hot."

"Why?"

"Because it was hot in here." Lucas's goofy grin made it clear that he was enjoying this little game.

"Enough questions kid," she said and ruffled his hair. "Did you have a good time at your Gram's?"

"Time to get ready for my birthday."

"Huh?" Allison asked. "What? Your birthday?"

"Yeah!" He leaned on his elbows and held up four fingers. "I'm gonna be four."

"Wow," Allison said, doing her best to sound super excited. "When is your birthday?"

Lucas's face scrunched. "Uh, um..." He then shrugged and said, "I don't know."

Allison chuckled, the sound still a bit raspy from having just woken up. "I see. So why are we getting ready then?"

"Gram's taking us shopping!" He cheered, but Allison's stomach dropped.

"Your, um, your Gram is *here*?" she asked. "Right now?"

"Uh-huh." He resumed kicking his legs on the mattress, smiling. "And Pop!"

"Shit," Allison muttered. Lucas didn't hear her, though, as his mother arrived in that moment to distract him.

Elena slipped into the room, dressed in a silken robe. She smiled apologetically at Allison before catching Lucas as he jumped to his feet, hopped on the bed twice, and then leapt at his mother. She swung him around before setting him on his feet on the floor and patting his bottom. "Baby, why don't you go play dinosaurs with Gram and Pop while Momma gets dressed, okay?"

"Okay!" He ran out of the room and down the hall.

Elena closed the door behind him and let out a sigh. "I'm sorry," she said. "I completely forgot that I made plans with my parents to take Lucas shopping today for party supplies."

"Oh." Allison sat up and held the sheet to her chest. "It's cool."

"I didn't remember until the doorbell woke me up. I didn't tell them that you were here, but apparently Lucas snuck off while I was talking to my parents and discovered it all on his own."

"Yeah, I woke up to his nose pressed against mine. Thankfully I was covered up."

Elena leaned her back against the door as silence developed between them, and then a smile broke over both their faces.

"I had a great time last night," Allison said, and Elena nodded.

"I did as well."

"Good." Allison pointed to Elena's hair. "Your bedhead isn't bad at all."

Elena ducked her head. "I brushed it."

"Cheater." Allison laughed as she threw aside the covers and climbed out of the bed. She stood up, stark naked, and stretched her arms over her head, coming up on her tiptoes and groaning with the stretch.

"My God," Elena whispered.

"What?" Allison asked, bending to grab her clothes from the floor. Thankfully her shirt was only slightly wrinkled. She didn't want to look like Elena's sloppy one-night stand when she inevitably encountered the woman's parents.

"You are beautiful."

Allison smiled and tucked a rogue strand of hair behind her ear. "So are you."

Elena stared a moment longer before asking, "Would you like to join us today?"

"Shopping for birthday supplies?"

"Yes. With my parents, Lucas, and I."

Allison hesitated. "Would your parents be cool with that?"

"I believe so, yes," Elena replied. "I'm sure Lucas has already informed them that you are here, and you know my mother will insist. She has taken quite the shine to you. Lucas will insist as well, I'm sure."

"All right," Allison agreed. "As long as you don't mind me wearing the same clothes I wore last night. Otherwise, I can catch a cab back to campus and change. I'm sure I probably smell like a bar."

Elena crossed the room and wrapped her arms around Allison's waist. She sniffed her shirt and shook her head. "You smell fine. But you can borrow some perfume if you would like."

"Thanks." Allison bent and pressed a kiss to Elena's nose. "Wanna take a quick shower with me anyway?"

Elena kissed her neck. "Absolutely, but we have to hurry."

"Okay. You can start the shower and set the temperature. I'm gonna brush my teeth first, though."

"Good plan." Allison laughed and smacked Elena on the ass.

"So when is the kid's birthday?" Allison asked as they entered the bathroom and she grabbed a spare toothbrush from the drawer.

"Not for another month." Elena slid back the shower door and reached for the knob, "But we're having his party in two weeks, because Vivian will be out of state on his actual birthday, and she insists on being at his party."

"Oh, okay," Allison said, her words muffled from the toothpaste now foaming in her mouth. "Makes sense."

They showered and readied themselves quickly, Allison in the same clothes from the night before but otherwise fresh. She knotted her damp hair in a tight bun at the base of her head and watched Elena, looking as immaculate as ever, slip into a set of heels. Allison admired her from across the room until they were ready to go out and face the family together.

When Elena and Allison stepped into Lucas's playroom, Nora instantly stood from the small chair she was seated in and made her way over to them.

"Allison, dear!" She leaned in to kiss Allison's cheek, which made Allison blush, before Nora pulled her into a quick embrace. "It's lovely to see you again."

"You too," Allison said, patting Nora's back. "I hope it's okay if I tag along with you all today."

Nora pulled out of the embrace and squeezed Allison's bicep. "Of course it is, dear. Of course." She then led Allison over to where Elena's father was playing with his grandson. The man's gray hair was a bit ruffled from Lucas climbing on him, and he patted it down as he stood and offered his hand to Allison.

"This is my husband," Nora said.

"Lucas Vega." He shook Allison's hand, and it was gentler than Allison expected, more of a soft squeeze than anything.

"Allison Sawyer. It's nice to meet you, sir."

"Oh, there's no need for formalities. You can call me Lucas."

"Okay then, Lucas."

The toddler on the floor looked up. "What?"

"Uh-oh. That might be a bit of a problem."

Lucas Sr. laughed as he nodded. "Good point."

"You can call him 'Dad'," Nora said, a knowing smile decorating her lips. "Vivian does."

"Vivian's known him since she was six, Mother." Elena said.

"I'm almost four!" Lucas shouted.

Elena rested a hand on Allison's back. "You don't have to call him 'Dad'. Lucas is fine. We will figure something out."

A strange mixture of nerves and excitement swirled through Allison's gut. The thought of Elena's family becoming *her* family flitted through her mind, and Allison couldn't deny how good it felt even inside her head, though she said nothing of it aloud. Maybe someday, though.

"Can we go now?" Lucas asked, jumping to his feet and tucking one of his dinosaurs to his chest.

"Yes we can, munchkin," Elena said. "Do you want to ride with Allison and me or with Gram and Pop?"

"Alson!"

Nora gasped. "I think you may have replaced me as his favorite, Allison."

"Nah." Allison patted the top of Lucas's head. "I'm just a novelty."

"Oh my dear," Nora said. "You are *much* more than that." She squeezed Allison's arm before turning and heading toward the door. "Come along, dears. We have much to do."

Allison turned to look at Elena, and Elena smiled at her before reaching out to cup her cheek, sliding her thumb over the smooth skin. She motioned for Allison to go ahead as she hoisted Lucas up onto her hip.

Lucas Sr. surprised Allison by stepping over and putting his arm around her shoulders to lead her toward the door. “So, Allison,” he said. “I hear you are quite the musician.”

“Uh, yes, sir.” She cleared her throat. “Sorry, yes. I play guitar.”

“That’s what my darling daughter tells me,” he said. “You’ve seen my collection, yes?”

“Oh yeah.” They made their way toward the front of the house, Elena trailing behind them. “It’s incredible.”

Chapter Thirty-One

Lucas had to see *everything* available in *every* party-supplies department in *every* store that Elena, Allison, and Elena's parents visited. He wanted square plates, not round plates or divided plates, and he wanted the hard plastic ones instead of the Styrofoam ones, because the former felt better when he squeezed them between his small fingers. He wanted napkins with dinosaurs on them and tablecloths that matched, but at least one of the dinosaurs shown had to be a T. rex. He wanted streamers and party horns, but the horns had to make the right sound, which meant testing a few sample horns to the annoyance of other shoppers.

He wanted a bounce house, despite Elena claiming they had no room for one, which meant their house could no longer be his party venue. He decided they would have to have the party in a park or some other open space large enough for a small bounce house. Nora was on her phone within seconds making arrangements.

Lucas wanted a dinosaur piñata, but three different stores had three different dinosaur piñatas, which meant three piñatas at Lucas's party, because although Elena said, "No, dear, three is too many," Nora responded with a resounding "Of course, darling. One can never have too many piñatas." Apparently, Gram's approval trumped Momma's disapproval.

He wanted balloons as well, tons of them, but not just any balloons.

"Green balloons, Momma," he said as he bounced on Elena's hip and pointed at all the different greens available. He had been alternating between walking on his own while holding someone's hand, and throwing his arms up so that he could be toted around on someone's hip. He had just rotated back around to Elena's hip after she scolded him for his daring attempt to climb on top of Allison's shoulders with the speed of a baby cheetah, a move which took Allison completely by surprise.

"This green?" Elena asked, pointing to the nearest one. It was a vivid green, a *grass* green as Allison put it.

"Reminds me of the park," Allison said, and Elena smiled, remembering the day her son barreled over Allison in Central Park.

"It does me as well," she said, bumping Allison with her side.

"No." Lucas shook his head with certainty. "Too green."

"*Too* green?" Allison gasped. "There's no such thing, kid."

Lucas stuck his tongue out at her as he continued shaking his head. "Too green." He giggled around the words.

"Perhaps a nice chartreuse, dear?" Nora asked, pointing to one of the balloons that was a much yellower green.

"Too yellow." Lucas shook his head while Allison nodded in agreement.

"What about this one, munchkin?" Elena pointed to a teal balloon. "This is lovely."

Lucas sighed dramatically. "Too blue."

"It really is." Allison said.

"It is," Nora said as well.

"Excuse me, *chartreuse*," Elena teased, rolling her eyes at her mother. It wasn't as if her mother's choice had been any more successful.

"Mi nieto quiere verde, mija." Lucas Sr. grinned as he came around to poke Elena's side, before patting her back.

Elena rubbed her temple and sighed. "Tu nieto está siendo difícil."

Allison cleared her throat and stepped a little closer to Elena. "So, I know that 'nieto' is grandson," she whispered, and Elena turned to her, surprised. "And 'verde' is green, so I think I got what your dad said, but can I ask what *you* said? Something about Lucas…"

Allison's pronunciation was a little bland and slightly off, but Elena's heart swelled all the same. "Being difficult," she said. She squeezed Allison's hand. "I thought you didn't speak any Spanish."

Allison shrugged and scratched awkwardly at the back of her neck. "Yeah, well, I don't, but I told you I wanted to learn."

"Yes, and I agreed to teach you."

Allison nodded. "I just wanted to know a little before we started so that I wouldn't sound like a total dork. So, I've just been reading on the Internet some."

"Skilled guitarist," Lucas Sr. said before his daughter could speak a word. "And now learning Spanish for my Elena?"

Allison blushed as the man stepped around Elena in the store aisle to place a hand on Allison's shoulder. "Dear, if you haven't yet won my daughter's heart, you have certainly won mine."

"Winning over my grandson, my daughter, and now my husband." Nora winked at Allison. "You are quite the charmer, Miss Sawyer."

Allison chuckled, still red-faced. "Uh, I think you're forgetting someone."

"Oh, am I?" Nora asked.

"Yeah," Allison told her. "Don't you remember when I won *you* over? I charmed you with all my confidence and Elena Vega adoration."

"I believe I can clearly recall that as well, Mother," Elena said, positively giddy that Allison was joking around with her *mother* of all people and gaining her father's approval as well.

Despite the vast differences in social status and lifestyle, Allison seemed to fit so easily into the family; and watching that fluid integration happen right before her eyes was a privilege Elena cherished deeply. It felt simultaneously like a rush of adrenaline and a soothing bath—both thrilling and comforting, and beautiful in its simplicity and delicacy.

Pure and easy and beautiful—that was it. That was she and Allison since the beginning. In fact, Elena found it breathtaking just how easy it had actually been and continued to be with Allison. Even when it should have been hard, it was easy. They connected instantly, even if there had been a bit of awkwardness throughout. The transition from strangers to friends had been fast and fluid, which was rare for Elena. The transition then from friends to confidants had been faster and even easier, and the transition from confidants to lovers had felt like the most natural progression in the world.

"Mhm. I distinctly remember charming you, Nora. It definitely happened."

"I believe I remember you mentioning something about how charming 'that Sawyer girl' was as well, dear," Lucas Sr. said, and Nora offered him a playful glare.

"Oh, see there," Allison said, nudging Nora with her elbow. "You can't deny it any longer. May as well 'fess up."

"Never," Nora replied, making them all laugh. She then surprised Allison by nudging her back and whispering, "*Quite* charmed, my dear."

Allison smiled. "Same."

Elena cleared her throat, bringing the attention back to her. "Does no one here find *me* charming?" She looked over at her mother. "Are you going to throw me out and adopt Allison instead, Mother?"

"Of course not, darling," Nora told her. "How would I ever see my precious grandson?"

"Oh ha ha." Elena bounced Lucas and squeezed his hand. "You hear that, baby? Gram only keeps me around because of you."

Lucas completely ignored her, still staring up at the selection of balloons, his mouth hanging open.

Stepping over, Allison kissed Elena's temple. "Well, *I* think you're charming."

Elena leaned into her touch when Allison wrapped an arm around her, her hand coming up to rest on Lucas's warm back.

"This feels good," Allison whispered against Elena's ear. "All of us together, like a family."

The sincerity in Allison's voice made Elena's chest ache in the best way. "I—"

"Miss Vega?"

Elena startled, turning to face the end of the aisle. Her blood ran cold as she saw Elliot standing there, watching her.

"Elliot." She tried to offer him a courteous smile, but she knew it likely looked as tight and forced as it felt. "How are you?"

Elliot didn't answer her as his sharp gaze narrowed and flicked back and forth between her and Allison, zeroing in on Allison's arm where it was still wrapped around her body. One thick eyebrow rose as his gaze tracked the length of Allison's body, obviously taking in her attire, and Elena didn't miss the subtle way the man shook his head in disapproval.

"Family outing?" Elliot asked, eyes locking onto Elena's.

Elena felt her anger begin to boil beneath the surface. She could see the calculating glint in Elliot's eyes, the near-glee at gaining more dirt to spread around her own office about her. She had never had much patience for people like him.

"Yes, actually," she replied, and, had it been anyone else, she might have actually moved to introduce everyone, but this was Elliot. She knew the man did not care beyond gaining more gossip material, which meant he was only interested in one of Elena's companions—Allison.

"I see," he said, smirking. He then pointed to Allison. "And who's this?"

Elena sucked in a sharp breath through her nose. Her jaw remained rigid as she grit her teeth before straightening her back, readjusting Lucas on her hip, and moving closer to Allison. "This is Allison," she said, hesitating only a moment before adding, "my partner."

She felt Allison stiffen beside her, and Elena bit the inside of her cheek. She hoped the term wasn't too much too soon.

"Partner." Elliot's eyes flicked back and forth between them again. His gaze scanned down Allison once more, and then Elena nearly burst into flame as the man snickered softly.

Her stomach lurched and then bottomed out when she felt Allison practically concave beside her. She saw her shoulders slump out of the corner of her eye, deflating. Elena wanted to scream, mentally damning Elliot to all kinds of hell.

"Well," Elliot said. "I won't hold you up." He nodded at Elena. "Miss Vega."

He disappeared around the end of the aisle.

Silence flooded the aisle for several long moments before Nora smacked her lips and drawled, "Well, he was *quite* the delight."

Elena's jaw hurt from clenching her teeth. She placed a hand on Allison's arm but it was gently shrugged off as Allison took a shaky breath and quickly walked off.

"Allison, wait!" Elena quickly passed Lucas off to her mother before chasing after her.

She caught Allison a few aisles over. "Allison, please don't go." She grabbed her hands.

Allison avoided her eyes. "I wasn't going to leave," she said. "I just needed a minute."

Elena's eyes stung when before she could get a word out, Allison looked up at her and whispered, "It's always going to be like this, isn't it?"

"I'm so sorry," Elena whispered.

"So am I." Allison sighed. "People are always going to think you're crazy for being with me. I mean, you saw the way he looked at me. You look like you just stepped out of a magazine. I mean, your clothes and your jewelry...everything about you screams money, but I look like I just walked out of the thrift shop, and that's never bothered me. Not once in my life has that ever bothered me, but it did just now." A quiet strangled sob escaped her, and she wiped hard at her eyes. "He laughed at the idea of us together, Elena. He laughed!"

Elena's throat burned, and no matter how many times she swallowed, she never found any relief. Her chest felt tight. Her eyes welled with tears as she let go of Allison's hands and cupped her cheeks instead. "I don't care what he thinks," she said. "That man is not worth your emotions or even a second thought. That was not about you. It was about me. I told you the man despises me."

"But it's not just him," Allison argued, pulling Elena's hands from her face. "Those people at your office looked at me the same way. People are always going to look at us like that, because you're, you know, *you*, and I'm—"

"You are every bit as good as me." Elena latched onto her again. "Look at me, Allison."

Allison struggled against her hands for a second before sighing and relenting.

"You are every bit as good as me," Elena repeated when Allison looked into her eyes. "Every bit, and please don't ever let anyone make you feel otherwise." She wiped at the tears escaping Allison's glossy green eyes. "I don't give a damn what he or *anyone* thinks. Do you hear me?"

Allison huffed and leaned into Elena's palm, her hands coming up to gently grip her wrists. "Yeah, I hear you."

A smile slowly stretched Elena's lips. "I am so proud to be with you, Allison," she said. "*So* proud."

"Really?"

Elena nodded and kissed her lips. "Really."

When Allison and Elena reentered the balloon aisle, Nora wrapped an arm around Allison's back and squeezed her. "I believe Lucas has made a decision," she said, and Allison appreciated that she didn't bring up what happened with Elliot.

"Oh yeah?" Allison asked, leaning into Nora's embrace as Lucas dove from his grandmother's hip to Allison's. "Which one, buddy?"

"That one!"

Everyone followed his finger, and Allison burst into laughter upon seeing it while Elena merely sighed and shook her head. It wasn't a green balloon at all. It was a white balloon with a green dinosaur on it.

"Son, that balloon is not even green," Elena said.

"Uh-huh! I want it."

"Kid, I showed you that same green a minute ago and you said it was too dark," Allison said.

"But *this* green is a dinosaur!" Because apparently that made all the difference in the world. "I want it!"

"Very well, Lucas." Elena looked to her mother. "We should thank Vivian for beginning this obsession of Lucas's."

"Eh," Allison said, shrugging. "The kid loves dinosaurs. Don't most little boys?"

"Alson likes dinosaurs too," Lucas sang, a large smile spreading over his lips.

"*Yeah* I do." Allison high-fived him. "We play dinosaurs together a lot, don't we buddy?"

"Yup!"

"Were you one of those young girls who preferred G.I. Joe's to Barbies, dear?" Nora gave a small laugh. "Elena loved her Barbies."

"I didn't really get into either," Allison said. "I didn't have toys when I was a kid."

"None?" Lucas Sr. asked. "Were your parents strict?"

Nora nudged him with her elbow, hard, and Allison chuckled as the elder woman pinned her husband with a glare. Face purpling, he cleared his throat.

"My apologies, Allison," he offered, and Allison shook her head to dismiss the apology.

"Don't worry about it. It's not something you guys have to tiptoe around, you know. People always seem to do that, and maybe it's just because I don't really talk about my time in the system, but you don't have to. If you want to know things, just ask me. I'll tell you."

"You don't have to do that," Elena whispered, reaching over to squeeze Allison's hand that was wrapped around Lucas's leg.

"It's okay," Allison said, shrugging and giving Lucas a small bounce. She took a deep breath and let it out in a soft sigh. "Anyway, there's not a ton to tell. Like I said, I didn't have toys. I never really had *anything* of my own. I remember a few stuffed animals but that's it. The few group homes I spent some time in had toy chests, but most of the toys were broken. And I rotated families pretty often, so I never got much there either."

Everything in the aisle drew her eye as she spoke, unable to really hold anyone's gaze. Her throat felt too tight to speak but she labored through it. She wanted to share with these people, even the parts that were hard to talk about and even harder to recall.

"I had nine different families just by the time I was sixteen. They never felt like families to me, though. Family is supposed to be permanent, and they were all so temporary. No one ever kept me for long, because either they ended up having a baby of their own or I was too much of a troublemaker or the house was just overcrowded." She swiped a hand down her face, lingering for a moment under her left eye. "So, yeah, anyway, I never really had any toys or a family, for that matter. I guess I was never very good at finding one."

Nora's fingers pressed tightly against Allison's shoulder as she was pulled even closer to the woman. "You have found one now, dear."

Eyes glossy but alight with affection, Elena stepped closer and wrapped her arm around Allison from the other side, Lucas tucked snugly between them. Her voice was slightly choked as she said, "You have."

"Absolutely," Lucas Sr. said with a firm nod.

Allison closed her eyes a moment and let those words sink in so deep that she knew they would always remain. Her breath released in a staggered sigh before she whispered, "Thank you."

"Of course," Nora said, giving Allison one last squeeze before stepping away and clapping her hands together. "Now, how about we place an order for some balloons? We are going to need more than what is available here."

"Yes," Elena said, clearing her throat and sniffling. "Could you and Daddy take care of that with the clerk, please?"

Nora nodded before she and her husband took off for the front of the store. Once they were out of sight, Elena slipped her hand into Allison's and smirked. "So, tell me, what else have you learned in Spanish?"

"Uh, a few things. Mostly simple stuff like colors and some items and then, like, family terms. But there is one sentence I learned that I want to say to you."

"Oh? And what is that, dear?"

Allison ducked her head. "I, uh, maybe now isn't the best time or place."

Smile widening, Elena's tone turned lascivious. "Well, well, Miss Sawyer."

Allison nudged her shoulder. "It's not like that."

"That's a shame." Elena clucked her tongue.

They stepped around the corner and into the next aisle. "Momma, I need these!" Lucas pointed to a package of green invitations.

Allison laughed. "Yeah, Elena, surely all the toddlers coming to the party would love some invitations that none of them can read."

"I can read!" Lucas crossed his arms over his chest.

"Yes, dear, you have already learned to read many things." Elena pointed to a word on one of the packages. "Tell Allison what this says."

Lucas eagerly leaned forward so that Allison had to tighten her arm around him to keep him attached to her hip. "Um," he said, scrunching his face up as he stared at the word.

"Sound it out, munchkin."

"Ha—Hhhha...p...Happy!" He clapped his hands and turned wide eyes to his mother. "Is it *happy*, Momma?"

"It is! Well done, Lucas!"

He beamed at her before sticking his tongue out at Allison. "See?" Allison grinned despite Elena telling Lucas that it wasn't nice to boast.

"I see, buddy," Allison said. "Good job!"

Lucas leaned his head over and rested his forehead against Allison's, one of his hands curling into her bun. "Alson, am I heavy?" He stared into her eyes from less than an inch away, pressing his face against hers.

Allison kissed the tip of his nose and shook her head against his. "Not at all."

"But I'm a big boy."

Allison and Elena both glanced to one another, sharing a smile that somehow felt intimate. "Yes, you are," Allison agreed.

"So why I'm not heavy?"

"Why *am I not*, Lucas," Elena said.

"Right," he said. He then looked back to Allison, waiting for her answer.

"Um," Allison muttered, contemplating what to say. She didn't want to call the boy scrawny or skinny, because he might not like that. She patted a hand over his chest. "Because you're a big boy in *here*, and big hearts aren't heavy."

"Why?"

"Because they're full of love, kid." She caught Elena's eye for a moment and couldn't help but blush a bit. "And love doesn't weigh anything."

"Even if there's a lot?"

"Even if there's a ton."

Lucas quickly looked over at his mother for confirmation. "No matter how much love you have in your heart, it is always light as a feather," Elena said, and Lucas narrowed his eyes.

"You sure, Momma?" he asked. "I got lots."

"I know you do." Elena tickled his belly and he giggled and squirmed in Allison's arms. "You love Momma, don't you?"

"Yup!"

"And Aunt Viv."

"And Gram and Pop," he said.

"That's right."

"That's a lot of love, kid," Allison said.

She then practically swooned as he leaned in and rested his head against hers again and said, "And Alson."

Allison's eyes instantly watered. She squeezed Lucas.

Elena smiled. "Yes, you love Allison."

A tear slipped down her cheek. Wiping it away quickly, she smiled at Elena. "It's crazy how that gets to me so easily."

Elena stroked Allison's cheek and nodded. "It does me as well, dear."

Allison kissed Elena's palm where it rested around her cheek before squeezing Lucas again. "I love you too, kid."

"Well, this looks cozy."

Nora and Lucas Sr. both stood at the end of the aisle watching them. Nora rolled her eyes, despite her smile. "My daughter is canoodling in the middle of the party supplies."

"No one is canoodling, Mother." Elena rolled her eyes in just the same fashion.

"Nah." Allison laughed. "I was totally canoodling."

"I like her," Lucas Sr. told Elena.

Allison and little Lucas beamed while Elena smirked at her father. "So you've said, Daddy."

"Well, some things need to be said more than once." His voice was deep and cheerful. He then clapped his hands together and asked, "So, who is ready for lunch?"

Chapter Thirty-Two

ALLISON BURST INTO THE DORM room, and Macy winced as the door slammed behind her. She was barely inside the dorm before she began to pace over the short length of the room.

"Uh," Macy muttered as she watched this strange and slightly amusing behavior, "something on your mind there, mate?"

"I love her," Allison blurted out, shaking her head and alternating between planting her hands on her hips and tugging at the bottom of her shirt.

"Come again?" Macy asked. She wasn't quite yet fully awake, having slept a good part of the day away after a late night at the bar, post meeting Allison's girlfriend. She sat up in her bed and reached to mute her rerun of *One Tree Hill*. Macy rubbed at her eyes and yawned as she asked, "Do I need coffee for whatever this is? Are you having a complete panic or just a partial one? Because it's already almost five, so we can skip the coffee altogether and go straight for shots if we need to."

"Elena!" Allison snapped, eyes wide but distant as if she was in some sort of trance or somewhere else entirely; most likely, she was just stuck inside her own head. "*Elena*," she repeated. "I *love* her."

"Yeah," Macy said, shrugging. "I don't mean to sound like an insensitive twat here, Alli, but well, *duh*."

"No, no, no," Allison babbled as she crossed over to Macy's bed. She plopped heavily down onto the mattress and pinned her with wide emerald eyes full of both panic and thrill. "I mean, I *love* love her, Mace. Like, I'm 99.999...oh hell, I'm *one hundred* percent sure that I am *in love* with her."

"Yup," Macy said, popping her lips loudly.

Allison's eyes bugged as she exclaimed, "That's *it*?" She threw up her hands. "I tell you that I'm actually in love, repeat *in love*, with Elena Vega, and *all* you have to say is 'yup'?"

"Um," Macy said, "please refer to my previous answer of 'duh'. It's more suited to this situation anyway."

Allison stared at her, blank-faced, and Macy burst into laughter. "You knew?" Allison asked, smacking her roommate's shoulder roughly. "You knew how I felt even before *I* knew how I felt? How is that even possible?"

"Well, Alli, that would be because I have functioning eyes," Macy teased, "as well as common sense and excellent deductive reasoning skills."

Allison smacked her shoulder again.

"Ow!" Macy pushed playfully at Allison's arm and leg in retaliation. "Don't beat me up just because I know you better than *you* know you."

"How long have you known?"

Macy grinned as she scooted backward and bundled back under her covers. "Oh, let's see?" she said. "I would say that I've known ever since you were like, 'Elena and I are *just friends,* Macy!'"

Allison smacked a hand to her face. She then slid her hand up and cradled her forehead in her palm. "Oh God," she groaned. "What the hell am I gonna do?"

Through the covers, Macy nudged Allison's thigh with her foot. "What do you mean?" she asked. "You're going to keep doing what you're doing, and just *love* the woman."

"But—"

"No," Macy said, shaking her head against her pillow. "No *buts*, Alli. I know your automatic response to those gross and terrifying things known as *feelings* is to completely freak out and run away, but you don't have to. You don't have to do anything, okay? Just because you love Elena doesn't mean you have to suddenly change or act differently. You don't have to *be* anything or anybody but yourself. That's kind of the whole point, mate."

Allison stretched out on Macy's bed, throwing her legs over the blanketed lump of Macy's own and resting her back against the wall. "You're the best friend ever."

"I know," Macy said. "So, I'm guessing you had some wicked sex last night since you burst in here with frantic declarations of love spewing out of your face."

"Yes, yes I did," Allison admitted. "And then we went out with her parents today to shop for party supplies for Lucas's birthday party."

Macy shifted so she could see Allison's face better. Smirking, she quirked a brow at Allison. "A family outing, eh?"

"Yup."

"I see, and how was that?"

Allison stared off into the empty space of the room for a moment, and Macy watched as a smile worked its way onto Allison's lips. "Weirdly amazing," Allison finally answered after a moment.

"Wow," Macy said. "I feel like I should be documenting this moment."

Allison snorted with laughter and smacked Macy's thigh. "Probably," she agreed. "It's true, though. I mean, her mom is tough, but she's also…I don't know. She hasn't ever looked at me or talked to me like I was less than her or less than her daughter. They just accept me, you know? They called me *family* today."

Macy's instinct was to tease her best friend, but she knew how big this was for Allison. She could actually see tears glistening in Allison's eyes. Family was everything Allison had always searched for.

"So," Macy said. "That's good, right?"

"Yeah," Allison whispered. "Yeah, and it felt genuine, you know? Like when they said that to me, I didn't have any doubt that they meant it."

"So, why all the panic?"

Allison groaned and dropped her forehead back into her hand. "Because I'm no good at this stuff, Macy," she said. "I'm not good at being part of a family. I'm not good at loving people."

Macy's stomach clenched uncomfortably as a wave of sorrow rolled through her, and she sighed and nudged Allison with her foot again. "I would argue otherwise."

Keeping her head down, Allison picked at Macy's blanket. "I need popcorn," she grumbled, "to help me *deal.*"

Macy snorted and rolled her eyes. "And *I* need coffee in order to help you deal, but you don't hear me whining about it."

"You should make me some popcorn," Allison said, smiling slyly. Her smile then quickly morphed into a well-practiced pout. "*Please.*"

"You go make your own popcorn," Macy said. "What am I, your maid? Does being in love mean your limbs suddenly no longer work?"

"Yes, that's exactly what it means," Allison told her. Her pout then deepened. "Please, Mace? Can't you see I'm in a crisis? I need comfort food made by my best friend."

"You're not in a crisis, Alli. You're in love."

"Same thing," Allison said.

Macy laughed out loud at that one. "Not quite, mate. Last time I checked, crises don't come neatly packaged with a smokin' hot millionaire and an adorable three-year-old."

Allison pinned her with a playful glare, and Macy just shook her head and rolled her eyes. "Fine. I'll make you some bloody popcorn, but don't think this conversation is over. I want full details on this birthday party you mentioned."

Nodding, Allison sighed and sank down further on Macy's bed. "Yeah, yeah. I hear you."

"Oh," Macy added as she climbed out of bed, "and I want full details on the awesome sex you had last night, too."

"Not a chance," Allison said as Macy disappeared into the kitchen that joined their room to another.

"Do you want the popcorn or not?"

"Hello?" Allison answered the phone but quickly jerked her head away from the device when random loud tones went off in her ear. She glanced at the caller ID again to be sure she read it right. "Elena?"

"Alson?"

Allison smiled, surprised to hear Lucas's voice. "Hey buddy!"

"Is this Alson?"

"Yeah, kid." Allison let out a soft laugh. "This is Allison."

"Alson!" He squealed. "What you doing?"

"Well, I'm talking to you," she told him.

"Oh. When you coming home?"

Allison closed her eyes at those words, letting them sink in and swirl around. It was amazing how children could say the simplest yet equally monumental things.

"I don't know, buddy."

"Now?" he asked. "It's dinner time."

"I don't think so, Lucas. I just saw you earlier today."

Lucas whined. "But me and Momma miss you!"

Ah, hell, Allison thought. He was laying it on strong. She could imagine the pout he likely wore, his puffy bottom lip poking out as far as it would go.

"I miss you guys too."

"Okay!" Lucas cheered. "See you at dinner! Bye!"

Allison blinked and looked at her phone to see that the call had been disconnected. She thought about calling back to see if Elena actually intended for her to come over again so soon, but after a moment's hesitation, she simply decided to go.

When Elena pulled open the front door fifteen minutes later, in fresh clothes, and grinned at her, Allison knew she had made the right decision. "I see my son has conned you into devoting more of your day to us," Elena said.

Allison shrugged. "He told me to come home." She stepped over the threshold and pulled Elena against her. Allison nuzzled her nose against Elena's before pressing a tender kiss to her supple lips. "So I did."

Chapter Thirty-Three

When they were finally able to get Lucas to sleep after a wild temper tantrum that resulted in the boy barring himself behind a coffee table and refusing to go to bed, Allison grabbed Elena's hand and pulled her from Lucas's room.

"Where are you dragging me off to?" Elena asked once they were in the hallway.

"Living room," Allison said. "I figured we could watch a movie or something."

Elena tugged on Allison's arm to pull her to a stop at the end of the hall. "I thought we were going to bed." She pulled her a little closer. "That *is* what you told Lucas after all, and we would not want to violate his precious trust, now would we?"

Allison wrapped her arms around Elena's waist. "I won't tell him if you won't. Come on, don't you wanna couch-cuddle with me?"

"Can we not cuddle in bed?"

"Totally, *but* I'm pretty sure that we can't be an actual official couple until we've cuddled on a couch at least once."

"Oh, is that so?"

"Yup. It's in the official, um, manual of couple things."

"I see." Elena looped her arms around her neck. She then tilted her head toward the living room. "Then by all means, darling."

Allison didn't hesitate to scoop her up, bridal-style, and take off toward the living room.

"Oh God," Elena whispered as Allison's hands slid up her thighs, her hot, wet mouth leaving a scorching trail along Elena's collarbone. "I thought we were supposed to be cuddling."

"We are," Allison said. "This is advanced cuddling."

They sank further into the couch cushions as Allison shifted to position herself between Elena's thighs, her hands sliding up the lengths of Elena's legs and onto her sides. She anchored herself there, holding tight. Mouths melded together, Allison and Elena became a tangled knot of passion as the heat between them grew into a roaring flame and Allison almost began a gentle yet rhythmic thrusting motion with her hips.

Her pelvis pressed firmly against Elena's clothed sex with every forward thrust, and the friction drove them mad. Her pace quickened as Allison felt Elena's nails dig into her back, the woman's ankles locked firmly above her ass. Their breathing became ragged, staggered, and shallow as Allison ground down into Elena's sex, craving the pressure. They moved together easily, naturally, as if they had been lovers for years, had known one another's bodies for a lifetime.

Allison chuckled hotly against Elena's throat, and Elena pushed at her chest so that she could see Allison's face. "What is so funny?" she panted.

Allison grinned at her, the motion of her hips slowing but never stopping. "I feel like a teenager," she said.

"What do you mean?"

"We're grinding, fully clothed, on the couch," Allison said. "It feels like we're teenagers, you know? Like we're dry-humping in your parents' house and might get caught any minute or something."

Elena laughed out loud and pulled Allison down to swallow the sound. She nibbled at Allison's bottom lip before whispering, "There is a certain appeal to getting naked with the babysitter, I suppose."

"You *suppose*?" Allison asked, raising her eyebrows.

"Okay," Elena said. "There is *definite* appeal to getting naked with the babysitter; then again, I am beginning to wonder if we are actually going to get naked at all."

A sly grin crept over Allison's lips as an idea sprang to mind. She made a show of glancing around the room before lowering her voice to a whisper and asking, "Are you sure we should? What if your parents come home early? We could get caught."

Elena's brows knit together for a moment before realization seemed to kick in and she blushed. Allison worried for a moment that she wouldn't go along with it, but then Elena bit her lip playfully and said, "Don't worry. Daddy's work galas always go on for hours. They're never home before midnight."

"Okay," Allison whispered. "Well, can I, um, can I take your shirt off then?"

Elena pushed herself into a semi-sitting position. She nodded shyly and let Allison pull her top up over her head and drop it on the floor. She giggled as Allison dropped her mouth open dramatically and whispered, "Wow."

Allison cupped both hands around Elena's breasts, feeling their weight and rubbing her thumbs over the stiffening peaks beneath the soft fabric. "You're beautiful," she breathed.

Elena kissed her deeply. "So are you."

The kiss quickly turned feverish, both women panting into each other's mouths and breathing sharply through their noses so that they could remain latched together. Elena groaned her disappointment when Allison finally did disconnect. Allison yanked her own shirt over her head and tossed it. She wasted no time popping open her bra either, and Elena's mouth was on her flesh before the material even hit the floor.

"Fuck," Allison gasped as Elena's teeth grazed her nipple. Her hips jerked forward, and both women moaned as the motion sent Allison's pelvis colliding into Elena's clothed clit once more. Elena latched onto Allison's hips, digging her nails in, and jerked Allison forward and against her again.

Allison began a steady rhythm between Elena's legs again, pumping forward with absolute abandon. She shoved up Elena's bra and sucked one nipple roughly into her mouth as she continued to grind down into Elena's sex with her own. She moved hard and fast until her flesh began to feel too hot and her jeans too tight and constricting.

Panting, Allison pulled back and popped open the button on her jeans. She emptied her pockets, too, just to give herself a little more comfort. Her wallet dropped to the floor with a soft thud, and then she reached for the hard knot where her keys were shoved down in the front right pocket of her jeans. She yanked them free and then chuckled as she held them up for Elena to see.

"Look," Allison told her. She held up the small bottle of pepper spray attached to her keychain. "I brought protection."

Elena laughed out loud before slapping a hand over her mouth. She shook her head as she laughed into her hand before taking a breath and saying, "You are such an idiot."

Allison just grinned at her and dropped down to kiss her again. "But a lovable one, right?"

Elena pressed laughing kisses to Allison's lips and chin and cheeks. "Yes, dear," she answered. "Now, finish what you started before my parents come home and catch us."

"Oh right," Allison said. "I can't believe you're gonna let me take your virginity on your parents' couch."

"Oh, now I'm a teen virgin?" Elena asked. "Does this make you the experienced senior? Because, considering the fact that I am older than you, I think I should get to be the experienced senior, and you can be the hot, young freshman."

"Good point," Allison said. She then cleared her throat and slipped back into character. "You don't know how long I've wanted to do this, Elena. I used to watch you in math class and write your name in little hearts all over my notebook. This is like a dream come true!"

Elena giggled so adorably in that moment that Allison actually pulled back. "What?" Elena asked. "What's wrong?"

"Nothing," Allison said, shaking her head. "I just…I never thought you would be the giggling type. You surprise me sometimes."

Elena pulled her back down so that their chests rubbed together. "I never was before," she whispered against Allison's mouth. "I suppose you bring it out in me."

They smiled into their kiss, and then Allison whispered, "Let's see what else I can bring out, shall we?"

Elena yelped as Allison suddenly and swiftly jerked her up off the couch and pulled her onto her lap. Peppering kisses over Elena's chest, she wrapped her hands around the brunette's hips and slowly began to rock her back and forth on her lap. Elena's hands tangled in Allison's hair as Allison sucked at her nipples, one after the other, and then licked her way back up to Elena's neck and then her mouth.

As their kisses grew deeper and hotter, Elena's hips surged forward faster and faster, until she was panting and riding Allison's lap, grinding against the rough material of Allison's jeans. When she couldn't take it any longer, she reached down to unclasp her slacks. "I need more," she whispered. "Touch me, Allison."

She reached for Allison's hand and pulled it to the top of her pants. Allison slipped her hand down into the thankfully loose material, and both women moaned deeply as her fingers slid through Elena's soaked slit.

"God, you feel good," Allison panted against Elena's open mouth as the woman gasped and slammed her hips forward so that Allison's fingers slipped even further south.

Allison positioned two fingers at Elena's opening and teased it, dipping in and out with just the tips, just enough to drive Elena positively mad. "Is this what you want?" Allison whispered, and Elena nodded against her forehead.

"Yes," she said. "Yes, please."

"You want me inside you?" Allison husked, still only teasing. She felt a new rush of fluid as Elena moaned at the words and her sex clenched tightly around Allison's fingertips.

"God yes, Allison," Elena pleaded. "Do it."

Allison teased her only once more before plunging her fingers upward and inside, loving the way Elena's breath slammed from her lungs and she instantly began to ride her hand. Allison pumped in and out of her the best she could in this position, Elena's knees digging into the couch on both sides of Allison's thighs.

Elena had one arm wrapped around Allison's back, her fingers pressing into Allison's side. The other hand was still tangled in blonde hair. Her grip tightened as Allison drove her to the edge of orgasm, and she bit into Allison's shoulder when she came, coating Allison's hand in her pleasure. She rode out the last waves of her orgasm, jerking with each movement of Allison's fingers inside her before expelling a massive sigh of relief and going limp in her lap.

"Mm," she hummed against Allison's neck. "Thank you."

"Thank *you*," Allison said. "That was sexy as hell."

Elena chuckled hotly against the sweat-slicked flesh of Allison's neck. "You must be dying," she said after a moment. "Let me touch you."

Allison kissed Elena's shoulder. "Whatever you want, Elena."

"That's what I want," Elena told her, leaning back to look into Allison's eyes. "I want to touch you, and I..."

"What?" Allison asked.

Elena blushed beautifully in the semi-dark. "I would like to taste you as well."

Allison's limbs all turned to jelly in that moment as an image of Elena's head positioned between her thighs sprang instantly to mind. She moaned before she could even stop herself, her clit throbbing almost painfully inside her jeans.

Elena smiled. "I take it you are amenable to this?"

"Oh my God, Elena." Allison groaned, shifting her legs so that Elena bounced on her lap a bit. "I'm so fucking amenable I should change my damn *name* to amenable. Amenable Sawyer."

Elena laughed so hard in that moment that she actually snorted, the sound only causing Allison to adore her more. She blushed again as she bit her bottom lip and said, "Very well then, Amenable Sawyer. Shall we take this to the bedroom?"

Allison jumped to her feet with an excited grunt, taking Elena with her.

They tripped their way down the hall, Allison shuffling along with Elena in her arms. When they finally made it to the bedroom, Allison practically tossed Elena onto the bed. She took just a moment to shut and lock the door before leaping onto the mattress. They wasted no time in divesting themselves of their remaining clothing before their mouths melded together once more and Elena's fingers dipped into the molten heat between Allison's thighs.

"Yes," Allison hissed as Elena touched her eagerly, the *s* sound carrying on for what felt like forever. She writhed beneath Elena's touch, realizing that Elena was intent on teasing her just as much as she herself had been teased. Allison didn't care. Worked up as she was, she was fairly certain she could get off on Elena's teasing alone.

She was right, because a moment later, Elena's fingers slipped up and pressed against her clit. "Oh God," Allison gasped. "Elena, I'm gonna come."

Elena pressed her clit again and then ran a circle around it with her thumb, and Allison's hips surged up off the bed as she came with very little urging.

"Wow," Allison panted as she trembled. "Wow."

Elena ran her fingers through Allison's slit again, collected the juices and then brought her fingertips to her lips.

Allison propped her head up just in time to see the woman's fingers disappear between supple lips, and when Elena moaned at the taste, Allison thought she might just orgasm again.

"Fuck, that's hot." She gulped. "Do you like it?"

"As if you can't tell," Elena said. She leaned down then and licked along Allison's bottom lip before kissing her deeply. "Are you ready for more?"

"So ready." Allison moaned as she slid her hands over Elena's heated flesh and then up into her hair when Elena began to kiss her way down Allison's body.

Elena hovered over Allison's sex, breathing her in. She hesitated only a moment before dipping down and pressing a firm kiss to Allison's wet outer lips. Allison jerked at the touch but urged Elena to continue with a gentle press to the back of her head.

Elena slipped her tongue down through Allison's slit and pressed at the soaked opening that begged for her attention. She sucked at every inch of Allison's sex, obviously enjoying learning the places that made Allison moan the deepest or jerk the hardest, and when she sucked Allison's clit fully into her mouth, Allison rocketed over the edge with a sudden cry. She clamped her thighs around Elena's head and rode out the orgasm on her tongue.

Elena continued to kiss and suck between Allison's legs until Allison's thighs went slack. She pressed a final kiss to the sensitive flesh before crawling back up to rest just to the side of Allison's heaving chest. She smiled down at her, looked quite pleased with herself.

"So, I take it I did well?" she asked, kissing Allison's shoulder and tracing a finger around a taut pink nipple.

Allison, unable to even speak, nodded and patted Elena's thigh. She then rolled over and pulled Elena against her chest, and they lay there, wrapped around one another, sharing soft kisses and slowly regulating breaths until they both drifted off to sleep.

Allison woke to Elena's soft lips brushing over her naked shoulder and down her side. She smiled into the plush pillow she was partially wrapped around as she lay on her stomach and tried not to jerk with each kiss. They made her body feel electric, her spine tingling to the point of pain. When Elena slipped the sheet from Allison's hip and bit softly into the flesh just above her hip bone, Allison couldn't hold still any longer.

"Mm," she moaned as her hip jerked forward just a bit.

Elena laughed quietly, the sound ragged from sleep and sexy as hell. She licked over the area she had just bitten before pressing a soft kiss there. She then crawled up Allison's body and lay on top of her back. "Good morning."

"*Best* morning," Allison said, her own voice low and raspy. She rolled, Elena rolling with her, and then resettled with the woman now resting on her chest.

Her vision was blurry from sleep, so she quickly rubbed at her eyes and then blinked. When Elena came into focus again, Allison's chest clenched so hard, it hurt. She thought it was the best pain she had ever felt, like a physical jolt from all she felt in that one breathtaking moment of seeing a bare Elena partially wrapped in a white sheet, hair wild and eyes glimmering in the streaks of early morning sunlight spilling through the window, and wearing a smile so small but so intimate and so radiant that it seemed impossible that it could actually be directed at her.

"You see," Elena whispered, "my bedhead is horrible."

Allison didn't say a word. She simply continued to stare at the woman, her breath completely gone and her heart racing.

Elena sighed. "How do you do that?"

"Do what?" Allison choked out, barely able to form words as she lost herself in Elena's eyes.

"Look at me and make me feel as if the entire world has disappeared." The words barely touched the air before fading in another gentle sigh.

Allison licked her dry lips and swallowed thickly before saying, "Maybe..." Her voice cracked on the word, and she closed her eyes to settle her soul. She felt so much in that moment that it was hard to keep her shit together. She felt like she was on the verge of cracking open and letting everything spill out. There was so much she wanted to say, so much she felt like she needed to say, and so much that she didn't have a clue *how* to say.

She knew how she felt about Elena. She knew it so intimately that the knowledge seemed to thrum in her veins. It was a feeling she had spent her life thinking she would never know, and yet, here it was. It was embedded in her cells as if she had *always* known it, as if all the days of her life that she spent feeling unlucky and unloved and alone were eradicated by its presence, and all that remained was Elena and Lucas. Family. Love. Belonging.

She took a deep breath and tried again. "Maybe because when I look at you, it sometimes feels like the world actually does disappear. Sometimes, it feels like you're the universe and I'm just lucky to be here. I'm just lucky to exist here, to be a small part of your world."

Elena's eyes watered, and she took a shaky breath. She reached up and traced her index finger over Allison's bottom lip as a tear escaped her eye and slipped down her cheek. "You are so much more than a small part, Allison," she whispered. "You are so much more."

Allison could see Elena's love so clearly in her eyes, and it made her heart beat heavy and hard in her chest. This was the moment, she thought. This was the moment to say it, to say everything; this was it. She took a deep breath and opened her mouth, the words dancing on the tip of her tongue.

"Momma?"

Both Elena and Allison leaned up to glance at the bedroom door. Lucas's soft voice echoed through it, followed by a gentle knocking against the wood. Allison cursed herself for letting the moment pass as she watched Elena slip from the bed, pull on a robe, and move to the door.

"Time to return to the rest of the world," she said with a soft laugh, wiping at her eyes.

"Yeah." Allison sighed. "I guess I should head out soon."

Elena hesitated before opening the door. "Already?"

"I wish I didn't have to," Allison said, "but I really do have a lot of homework that I need to get done before class tomorrow, and I've got finals coming up soon. I should study."

Elena frowned but nodded anyway before opening the door to see her son.

As she made her way to the nearest subway station, Allison was still annoyed with herself for not having told Elena how she felt. Her stomach was unsettled by it, almost like she felt guilty for not having put the feelings to words. It ate at her, though she wasn't entirely sure why. Maybe it was because she knew that other days and other times weren't always guaranteed. Maybe it was because she was afraid she would lose her nerve altogether if she didn't just do it as soon as possible. Maybe it was because she had never felt this way before, and she was bursting with the feeling. She just had to say it.

It didn't really matter the reason, because that uncomfortable feeling was enough in itself, and, before Allison even realized what she was doing, she turned around and took off at a sprint. She needed to say all the things swirling around inside her. She wanted to. She wanted Elena to know, and she wanted to know if Elena felt the same way about her.

So, in true Allison fashion, she ran; only this time, she ran *toward* the hope of love instead of away from it.

Allison entered Elena's house quietly and made her way toward the living room. She stopped just outside the room, though, when she realized that Elena wasn't there. Lucas sat on the couch, mouth open as he stared at the television, watching cartoons. He didn't hear or even notice Allison, so she quietly turned and made her way back toward the kitchen. It was empty, so she hurried down the hall to Elena's room.

"Elena?" she called as she stepped inside, but she received no answer. That was when she noticed the sound of the shower running in the bathroom.

Allison darted over to the bathroom door and opened it just enough to poke her head in. "Elena?" she called. She wanted to make the woman aware of her presence before Elena could startle and chuck the nearest object at her head.

The foggy shower door slid open just a crack, and Elena's face came into view, her hair slicked down around her cheeks. "Allison? Did you forget something?"

Allison swallowed around the massive lump that had suddenly taken residence in her throat and nodded.

"Oh," Elena said. "What was it?"

Allison's entire body felt like it was on fire, her nerves sparking electrically under her flesh. She sucked in a deep breath and moved, not even bothering with her clothes or her shoes before pushing back the shower door and climbing into Elena's shower.

"Allison!" Elena exclaimed, stumbling backward under the spray. "What are you doing?"

"I…" Allison began, water droplets streaming down her forehead and over her eyes. They clung to her lashes, making her blink rapidly, but she never closed her eyes. She continued to stare at the beautiful bare woman before her. All of those feelings bubbled rapidly to the surface again, and a surge of confidence ignited in Allison's heart. "I read a lot," she finally managed to say and then immediately wanted to smack herself when she saw Elena's brows furrow.

"I don't understand," Elena said. "You climbed into my shower, fully clothed, to tell me that you read a lot?" She laughed awkwardly, the sound croaky and weak, but her eyes deepened with concern. She reached out and cupped a hand around Allison's cheek. "Are you feeling ill, dear? You're behaving strangely."

"Just listen," Allison said. "Please." She rubbed her thumb back and forth over the inside of Elena's wrist as she pushed all of her feelings into her voice. "I've read all those stories about soul mates and true love and all that stuff, but I never thought they were real, you know? I never thought any of that could happen to *me*."

"Okay," Elena whispered, the quiet word dying quickly in the roar of the shower rain.

Allison's breathing was shallow and made tiny bursts of white fog as each breath hit the heated water raining down around them and soaking through her hair and clothes. "I never thought I'd feel that way about someone. I never thought anyone could ever feel that way about me, but every time I'm with you and every time I think about you, I find myself hoping that you do." Her voice cracked terribly as her throat tightened and tears began to blend with the shower water on her cheeks. Still, she pushed through it. Putting herself out there, laying her feelings bare, scared the hell out of her, but she had to say this. She *wanted* to say this.

"I find myself hoping that you feel that way about me," she confessed, "or that you *could* feel that way about me someday, because all those books say that you only get one, you know? You only get one great love to last a lifetime, and I think it's you. I think you're mine. I want you to be mine."

Elena's eyes widened and her lips parted around a sharp breath.

"You and Lucas," Allison continued, her voice now shaking so hard that she could hardly get the words out, "are always on my mind. You're always in my heart, both of you. I love Lucas like a son, Elena. I want to be in his life. I want to watch him grow up. I want to be there beside you watching him play Little League or singing in his first school play. I want to be there. I want you to *want me* there. I've never wanted anything more in my whole life."

"Allison," Elena croaked, her hand now clasped over her mouth as her body trembled and she blinked through her tears.

Allison took a step forward, the shower spray now beating down on top of her head as she pulled Elena closer. "Remember when I told you that I learned to say something in Spanish that I wanted to say to you?"

Elena nodded, eyes locked on Allison's.

"Bear with me, okay?" Allison sniffled and pushed wet hair back from Elena's cheeks. "I know my Spanish sucks, but it's important that you know that mi corazón es tuyo." She said the words slowly, doing her best to pronounce them as perfectly as possible while conveying how much she meant them, and she did. Her heart was entirely Elena's.

A small sob escaped between Elena's fingers, still cupped over her mouth.

"It's yours," Allison promised, "because I love you. I'm in love with you, and I know that I don't have anything to offer you. I don't have any money. Hell, I don't even have a job right now, and I'm just a goofy kid who will probably never fit into your fancy lifestyle, but I don't really care. I don't care, because if you love me, then I'll do whatever it takes to make you happy. If you love me, I—"

Her next words died against Elena's lips as Elena surged forward and kissed Allison hard on the lips. She pressed her soaked bare body against Allison, arms wrapping tightly around her neck, and sobbed into Allison's mouth as she said, "I do," over and over. "I do love you."

They stood beneath the shower rain, wrapped around one another and soaked to the bone, and the world drowned away in the hum of the spray, until the heated presses of desperate kisses and of fingertips to flesh became all they knew.

"You do?" Allison asked, needing to hear the words again.

Elena nodded against Allison's forehead, their soaked skin sliding together. "I do," she whispered in a puff of fog. "Te amo, Allison."

Allison smiled at the words, letting them fill her up. They pressed together again in a perfect kiss, long and deep, and, as the spray beat down around them, they gave themselves over to the feeling of loving and being loved in return.

Chapter Thirty-Four

NEARLY TWO FULL WEEKS PASSED without Allison and Elena seeing one another. Elena was swamped with work, as she had several spring shoots back-to-back to organize, and Allison was neck-deep in final classes and exams. The separation wore on them both, but they bore it the best they could. They filled in the spaces with texts and phone calls, talking as often as they could. Their conversations ranged from the silly to the serious, but each one drew them closer and closer together.

This class is so boring.

Which class?

It's one of my lit courses, and it's not the subject that blows. It's the prof's book choices. I seriously can't get down with stuff that's SO classic that it's barely understandable.

Some classic literature is wonderful, but I know what you mean.

Yeah, and my prof's voice is sooo monotone, so it's even worse. Seriously, if I had a chisel or, hell, a friggin' SPOON right now, I'd be digging a hole in this wall straight prison style and escaping.

You only have a few days of classes left.

Good point, but then I'll be starting all over again with new classes for my master's.

Well, that was your choice, Allison.

You know, complaining with me is way more of a turn-on than playing devil's advocate.

I see. In that case, what I meant to write was that that class sounds awful, and I would certainly assist you in your grand prison escape were I there.

Much better.

Elena sent Allison pictures of Lucas or the both of them with little stories of the games they played on their evenings together and how much they wished Allison could join them. Allison laughed out loud when she received one of Lucas with his hair wild and sticking up and his face covered in black smudges.

Why are you harboring a child Batman in your house, Elena?

I allowed Lucas to indulge in finger painting. This is the result. He is calling himself Wild Boy and is pretending to be a caveman.

Ha! I love it.

He is now asking me to make him 'leaf clothes'.

DO IT, and make sure you send me some pics.

Allison laughed even harder when she later received a follow-up photo of Lucas, still sporting his paint-smudged face and wild hair. He looked like he was covered in mud. The paint smudges covered his limbs and belly, which were visible since the boy wore nothing but his pull-ups now covered in giant green leaves cut out of paper and taped to the material. The smile on his face was radiant.

Oh my God. I wish I could see him in person right now.

Do you want to come over?

I can't. I'm in the middle of studying with Macy for our one and only shared final. It's a huge one. I wish I could, though. I miss you guys.

We miss you too. Wild Boy and I are going to go build a (paper and blocks) campfire. Study hard, darling.

Sometimes, they would simply tell one another how they felt, and, sometimes, those confessions spiraled into ridiculous, teasing discussions that could go on for hours.

I love you, Allison.

I love you more.

Not possible.

Totally possible.

I disagree.

Well, I agree…with myself, I mean.

Of course you do.

I'm just saying: I love you more.

Well, then, I propose that I love you MOST.

**narrows eyes* Touché sir.*

I am not a sir.

Yeah, I know. It just sounds cooler when you add the "sir".

You are ridiculous.

Me? Ridiculous? Not a chance. YOU'RE the one who just went all thirteen-year-old girl on me with the "I love you most" text.

Excuse me? You started it with YOUR "I love you more" text.

I don't know what you're talking about, therefore it never happened.

You are impossible.

Can I just butt in a moment to say you're BOTH impossible? Because you are, and Alli's message alert going off every three seconds so you two can argue about who loves the other more or most or whatever the bloody hell is ten seconds away from making me go completely apeshit. Also, I'm looking forward to seeing you at Lucas's party, love. Thanks for the invite.

Erm, sorry. That was Macy.

Yes, I gathered as much. I am mortified.

Don't be. She's just sour because she's been studying non-stop and getting hardly any sleep.

Regardless, I think perhaps that is enough texting for the night.

I can switch my phone to vibrate.

Goodnight darling.

Ugh. Goodnight.

When you were a kid, did you ever lie outside and look up at the stars?

Often. Did you?

Yeah. All the time. I'd have to sneak out to do it most of the time, but it was always worth it. I'd just lie there and think about things.

What sort of things?

My parents, mostly. I wondered about them, you know, like where they were, why they abandoned me, if they were happy, if they ever thought about me, if they missed me, if they were even still alive and all that. I used to think about that movie The Lion King and that scene where Mufasa tells Simba about all the kings of the past living up in the stars, and I'd imagine that that was the case for me, too. That maybe my parents only gave me up because they couldn't help it, because of some tragedy or something, but that they never left me. They were up there in the stars, shining down on me when I felt lonely.

Did you ever find them?

I never went looking. Honestly, I don't know that I would even want to know who they are now. They could be monsters.

Or they could be wonderful people.

Yeah, but if they weren't, then I would never be able to go back to my Lion King thing. I'd never be able to just lie out under the stars and imagine they were looking down on me. That would be tainted. I think sometimes it's just better not to know. Sometimes it's just better not to have all the answers.

Perhaps you are right, dear. Sometimes mystery is better than clarity.

And besides, maybe I was always just meant to be a lone little lion.

I hope not, Allison.

Why not?

Because I seem to have this intense desire to keep you.

Oh, do you now?

I do. I don't want you to be alone. I want you to be taken care of.

I've done a pretty good job taking care of myself.

You have, but if it is okay with you, I would like to lend a hand.

You want to take care of me?

I want us to take care of each other.

Deal.

Macy rubbed tiredly at her eyes as she reached for the key dangling from her lanyard. She used it to let herself into her dorm room, already talking to the lump of blankets inside that was her sleeping roommate.

"Alli, wake up," she said through a yawn as she dropped her bag on the floor by the door and made her way over to her small bed. She stopped before she could collapse onto the mattress, though, when she realized that Allison hadn't answered her. She sighed and shuffled over to Allison's bed instead.

"Allison," she said a little louder, reaching down to nudge the part of the blanket pile that she was fairly certain was Allison's shoulder, "wake up."

"*Unh.*"

"Wake up!" Macy pushed Allison's shoulder a little harder.

The blanket pile that was Allison wiggled around a bit, but then the material of the blanket grew tighter as the person beneath it pulled it closer and snuggled further inside. "Seriously?" Macy sighed. "I will pull that blanket off of you."

"No," came the muffled reply.

Macy understood Allison's desire to stay in bed. They both were exhausted from cramming for finals and bingeing on snack foods in order to avoid leaving their room or the library. She kept herself motivated by reminding herself that these were the last finals she would ever have to take, but that didn't really work with Allison, considering she was pursuing a higher education after graduation. Still, she at least had the motivating truth that she could sleep all she wanted once this week was over.

"*Yes*," Macy snapped. "You have to get up, Alli."

"*Why*?" Allison groaned, squirming angrily beneath her blanket.

"Because you've got your final seminar in forty minutes." Macy put both hands on the blanket mound and vigorously rocked Allison's body. "Get up. Get up. Get up!"

Suddenly, the top of the blanket jerked down to reveal Allison's wild blonde hair and angry green eyes. She glared at Macy as she hissed at her like a cat. She held up her hands, laying her index fingers over one another to resemble a cross, and shouted, "Go away, Satan! The power of Christ compels you! The power of Christ *compels* you!"

Macy suddenly shrieked and pretended to gag and choke. "My devil horns!" She gasped. "They're melting!" She dropped onto Allison's bed and writhed around while Allison chuckled, but then she rose to her feet again, propped her hands on her hips, and pinned Allison with a deadpan stare. "Sorry," she said, "still here."

Allison groaned and sat up. She rubbed at her eyes and yawned. "I hate finals week."

"Me too, mate," Macy agreed around a yawn spawned by Allison's, "but I hate having to wake you up even more."

"I know," Allison grumbled. "I'm an ass when I'm tired. You've told me like fifty times this week. I know, and I'm sorry. I can't help it."

"You know what you need?

"Seven energy drinks and a box of chicken nuggets?"

"That too, but I was going to say that you need to get laid."

"Oh God, I'd kill to be able to crawl into bed with Elena right now."

"I'm sure you would." Macy dropped onto her own bed. "But then you would be missing your finals and failing right before graduation."

"Totally worth it," Allison said, pushing her tangled hair away from her face. "I just keep reminding myself that it's only two more days until these finals are over. Two more days until Lucas's party. Two more days until I can see them."

"God, you've got it bad," Macy teased. She then snapped her fingers. "Hey, don't forget to go down to the bar after seminar."

"Okay," Allison said. "Wait. Why am I doing that again?"

"How many times do I have to repeat myself? I got you that interview with the manager, remember? He's looking for a bartender and part-time performer."

"Oh right," Allison said, nodding. "You think he'll hire me? I've only bartended once before, remember? I wasn't great at it."

Macy shrugged. "Seems likely. You know everyone there loves you from open-mic nights, and you can get better at the drinks, yeah?" She winked.

"Hope so," Allison said as she rolled out of her bed and began dressing. "I could seriously use the money, and I can't keep working for my girlfriend."

"I know." Macy sighed. "Besides, you're going to need to start saving so you can come visit me in Oz."

Allison stiffened in front of her small dresser but said nothing.

"You know," Macy said, "you're going to have to talk to me about this at some point, and soon."

"I don't want to talk about it," Allison croaked, her back still to Macy. "It doesn't feel right."

"Talking about it? Or just in general?"

"Just in general. You leaving. It doesn't feel right."

"I know."

Allison turned to face her and her voice cracked. "I don't know what I'm going to do without you."

Macy's eyes watered, but she smiled at her friend regardless. "You'll be fine, Alli. I know you will, and you won't be without me. Not really. You can call me every day if you want, and we can Skype and e-mail and text."

"It's not the same," Allison said, swiping at her cheeks before pulling a fresh shirt over her head.

"I know it's not, but it's better than nothing."

Allison said nothing as she finished dressing and went to brush her teeth and hair. Once she was finished, she grabbed her bag and headed for the door. "I've got to go," she said, gripping the handle.

"Well try not to climb into anyone's shower and confess your undying love while you're out," Macy teased, trying to clear the air of the weight thickening it.

Allison didn't laugh but just swallowed and nodded. "See you later," she said, and then she was out the door.

Chapter Thirty-Five

"You're going to fly out of this car like a torpedo as soon as it stops, aren't you?"

"Yup."

"Thought so," Macy said. "So whipped."

"Yup."

"And apparently proud of it."

Allison grinned at her. "*Yup*."

As soon as the cab stopped, Allison threw a crinkled wad of cash at Macy and then bolted out of the back door. She reached Elena in record time. The woman was bent over a long table of snacks and finger foods when Allison barreled into her, denim-clad arms wrapping firmly around her waist.

"Yeeeeesssss." Allison sighed as she latched onto Elena's side like a koala.

Elena laughed and turned in the embrace so that she could wrap her arms fully around her girlfriend. "Well, hello to you, too," she whispered, pressing a light kiss to Allison's cheek.

Allison buried her face in the crook of Elena's neck and breathed in deeply, taking in the familiar scent of the woman she loved. She sighed, warm breath puffing against Elena's flesh, and whispered, "Hi."

Elena rubbed her back before trying to pull back. It was a futile attempt, though, because Allison held onto her, squeezing tightly around her and grumbling her obvious disapproval of separating.

Elena settled back into the embrace. "I take it you missed me, dear?"

"If that's not obvious, love, then I don't know what it is," Macy said, walking up and setting the small present she had gotten for Lucas on the table near the snacks.

Elena managed to peel away from Allison just enough so that she could offer Macy a one-armed half pat, half hug and a smile. "Macy," she said, "I'm so glad you could make it."

"Yeah, of course. Glad to be here. Thanks for the invite." She rolled her eyes then as she watched her best friend grip onto Elena a little tighter. "You're probably going to regret inviting that one by the end of the day, though. She'll be stuck to you like a leech the entire party."

"Jealous," Allison sang from beneath Elena's hair.

"Psh."

"Reactions like that, dear, make me quick to agree with Allison."

"Jealous of your leech?" Macy asked. "Don't make me laugh."

A shrill squeal suddenly split the air and caught them all off guard.

"ALSON!"

Lucas sprinted across the grass and barreled into Allison the same way Allison had barreled into Elena.

Allison immediately detached from Elena and swooped down to scoop up the little guy. "Lucas!" She swung him around and hugged him close. "Hey, little man! Happy early birthday!"

Lucas grinned and said, "Come on!"

"Come on where?"

"I'm gonna meet you to my friends!"

"Introduce," Elena said. "You are going to *introduce* Allison to your friends."

"That's what I said!" Lucas tugged on Allison's hair. "Come on!"

"Okay, kid, but first, I want *you* to meet one of *my* friends."

His eyes widened. "You got a friend here?"

Allison nodded and pointed toward Macy. "That's her right there. Her name is Macy, and she's my best friend."

Lucas narrowed his eyes at Allison.

"Other than you, of course," Allison added, grinning.

Lucas smiled shyly when he looked back at Macy. He tucked a little closer into Allison, but she just patted him on the back to encourage him. She knew he had a bit of a shy streak when first meeting new people, but once he opened up, it was instant best-friends-forever, and Allison *really* wanted him to like Macy.

"Hi Lucas," Macy said. "It's nice to finally meet you."

Lucas frowned as he stared at her. He then leaned into Allison's hair, cupped his hand around his mouth, and whispered in her ear. "She talks funny."

Allison nodded along to Lucas's words and then answered him out loud. "Macy sounds like that because she is from a different country."

Eyes widening again, Lucas gaped at Macy.

"That's right," Macy said. "I sound funny, don't I?"

Lucas giggled and nodded. "I like it."

"Well, good, because I like *you*."

Lucas smiled at her and then tugged on Allison's hair again. "Can we go now?"

Allison laughed. "All right, kid. Let's go." She leaned over and pecked Elena on the cheek. "I'm off to make some friends."

"So much for my leech," Elena said, and Allison kissed her once more.

She winked. "I'll be back."

Lucas climbed around onto Allison's back and cheered when she took off galloping toward the other kids.

Allison and Lucas barely made it back to the snack table before Macy, who was leaning on Elena like they had been best friends for years, called out to tease her best friend. "Oi! If I send Elena off to get a saddle, will you wear it?"

Allison stuck her tongue out at Macy as she walked over and carefully let Lucas down from her back. As soon as the kid was down, Allison playfully punched Macy's shoulder and pulled her off of Elena. "Geez," she said. "I leave for a few minutes and you start trying to make a move on my girl? Not cool."

"If she finds me more charming, then so be it," Macy said, pushing Allison back.

"Children, please," Elena said, laughing, before picking up her son. "Come on, birthday boy. Let's get you some food."

Macy smacked Allison's arm. "Alli, who's that?"

"Who's *who*?"

"Leggy blonde headed this way. Ten o'clock."

Allison looked where indicated and let out a laugh. "Oh boy," she said. "That's trouble."

"Meaning?"

"That's Vivian."

Macy smirked. "No shit?" She didn't wait for a reply before she took off to meet Vivian halfway.

When she reached Vivian, she dipped into a dramatic bow.

"Um, do I know you?" Vivian asked.

"No, but *I* know *you*," Macy said, straightening again. "Teach me your genius ways."

Vivian smiled and said, "That would take years. Sorry, stranger."

Returning the smile, Macy held out her hand. "I'm Macy. Allison's roommate."

"Oh!" Vivian said, eyes widening. "Oh right! Macy!" She reached out to shake Macy's hand. "I've actually heard a lot about you. It's nice to meet you."

"And you," Macy replied. "I'm a big fan of your work."

"My work?"

"Your matchmaking, of course. I heard all about your little scheme from a secondhand recounting of Allison and Elena's pillow talk. It was a bore beyond the bits about you, all love and rainbows and other sappy shit."

Chuckling, Vivian slipped her hand into the crook of Macy's elbow and they made their way toward the others. "Don't tell me you aren't a fan of epic romantic moments," she said. "Allison seems to be a master of them. I find myself swooning over her on a daily basis. It's disgusting."

"Eh." Macy shrugged. She grinned at Allison when they reached the table, now close enough to be heard. "She stumbles into most of those moments. She's just good at improvising."

"Is that so?"

"No, I'm totally romantic and, um, dashing and stuff," Allison said.

Elena leaned over and kissed Allison's cheek. "Quite dashing, dear."

"See!" Allison smiled triumphantly, showing all her teeth.

"Sure you are, mate."

While the kids were crowded around Allison and Lucas Sr., listening to the two playing guitar, Elena spent time sorting Lucas's presents and making sure that Vivian had marked each one on the list so that she could send out thank-you cards the following week. She was pulled from her task, though, when Macy approached her.

"Macy," Elena said. "Are you having—"

"Fun?" Macy asked. "Are you kidding? Watching Allison get trapped in the Bounce House as it deflated was one of the highlights of my life. I'm having a blast."

Elena chuckled. "It *was* rather amusing."

"Right? I'm kind of pissed that I didn't get it on vid."

Elena grinned wickedly, glancing at the other woman. "*I* did."

"Score!" Macy's smile was brilliant as she stepped in closer until they stood side-by-side. They turned to lean against the table and look out on the bustle of Lucas's party. Silence settled between them, stretching on for several moments before Macy sighed and, without looking at Elena, said, "Sorry to get serious, but we need to talk."

Elena's stomach knotted instantly, but she kept her composure. "About?"

Crossing her arms tightly over her chest, Macy rocked on her heels a bit as she muttered, "I need to know that you're not going anywhere."

Elena turned to look at her. "I'm sorry?" she asked, confused.

"Allison," Macy said. She smiled almost sadly. "I need to know that you're not going to leave her. I need to know that you're not going to abandon her, you know?"

Elena frowned. "What do you mean?" she asked. "I…Macy, I *love* her. More than I ever thought possible."

"I know you do," Macy said, "but sometimes that isn't enough. I mean, even if you two don't work out as a couple, I need to know that you won't just kick her to the curb, Elena. She's had enough of that in her life, and, with me going back home, she's going to need someone to lean on. I want to trust you to be that person, but I need you to tell me that no matter what, you won't just abandon her."

They held each other's gazes a long moment before Macy whispered, "Is that a promise that you can make?"

"I can," Elena said, voice firm. "I can make that promise."

Macy held out a hand. "Shake on it?"

Elena slipped her hand into Macy's and shook it firmly.

"Right," Macy said. "Now that that's taken care of, I just need one more thing from you."

"Oh? And what is that?"

"Make sure she doesn't shut me out," Macy said, glancing up and looking more vulnerable than Elena had ever seen her. It was almost startling, the need in Macy's eyes. "That's what she does, you know? When she thinks things won't work out or when she's scared, she isolates. She'll try to do that when I leave. She'll assume that we'll lose touch, so she'll try to force it to happen quickly. Don't let her do that, Elena. Don't let her shut me out. Make sure she calls me and accepts my calls. Make sure she sits her ass down to Skype with me at least once a week. I mean it. She's my best mate. She's the most important person in my life, and I don't want to lose her."

Elena placed a hand on Macy's shoulder and squeezed. "I will make sure of it, Macy," she said. "I promise."

Macy let out a soft breath. "Thanks."

"I was actually hoping that you wouldn't mind a visit," Elena said after a moment, and Macy whipped around to face her, brows shooting up.

"Both of you?" she asked, her voice squeaky with obvious excitement.

Elena nodded. "I was thinking sometime this summer. Would that be acceptable?"

She startled when Macy suddenly yanked her into her arms, but quickly sank into the embrace. "Thank you," Macy whispered. "I would love that. Thank you."

Elena patted her back and nodded atop her shoulder. When they separated, Macy subtly wiped at her eyes and then turned to put her back to the table so that they were standing side by side again. Elena let her gaze fall on Allison across the park, playing for the kids, and she smiled.

"You *will* protect her, won't you?" Macy whispered, and Elena's smile widened.

"I will do better than that, dear. I will love her."

Despite the few snags, Lucas's party was a great success. Lucas had certainly exhausted himself with an overload of fun. He conked out on Allison's shoulder halfway to Elena's car.

"Are you sure you want to come home with us?" Elena asked Allison as she buckled Lucas into his car seat. "Would you not rather spend a bit of extra time with Macy?"

"I'm sure," Allison said. "I've been missing you guys like crazy and, besides, I'm pretty sure Macy has plans to go to the bar tonight to have a little goodbye party with a few of her friends."

Elena smiled at her. "Excellent. I was hoping I could get you all to myself today."

"I'm all yours, babe."

Elena took Lucas to bed once they made it home, and Allison wandered off toward Elena's bedroom, knowing Elena would want to change clothes before settling in for the night. She stepped into Elena's room, collapsed onto the massive fluffy bed, and reveled in its softness and the overwhelming smell of Elena wafting up from the sheets. Her gaze scanned over the room, absorbing the details of the little sanctuary she felt she hadn't seen in decades, even though it had only been a couple of weeks.

It was exactly the same, except...

Allison jumped to her feet and crossed the room to get a better look at an obviously new addition to Elena's bedroom décor. She stared up at the large photo for several long moments. She found it so beautiful that she could hardly believe it was *her* in the frame.

But it was.

It was one of the photos Elena had taken that day in the studio. Allison stood front and center in the photo, skinny jeans and tank, hands tucked into her pockets, shoulders drawn tight, but it was her face that drew her in. Caught in a moment of…Allison didn't know exactly, but she could tell it was genuine. She had never seen herself look so open before, so tender.

Her eyes in the photo were wide and light as she stared directly forward, her cheeks painted a soft pink and her lips slightly parted.

"That one was my favorite."

Allison jumped as hands slipped around her waist from behind and Elena's voice whispered against her neck. "Your eyes."

"Yeah," Allison breathed. "I look so…"

"Beautiful," Elena said, and Allison melted into her. "I know that word often seems so terribly generic, but I've never seen anyone embody it quite as perfectly as you do in this photo, Allison. It still takes my breath away."

Allison turned in Elena's arms and pulled her into an embrace. "I've never *really* felt that way before."

Elena stroked a hand through Allison's long hair. "Beautiful?"

"Yeah," Allison said. She pressed a kiss to Elena's neck. "But I do with you."

"But it even *looks* pretty," Allison said, shaking the bowl in Elena's direction as they lay on opposite ends of the couch, their legs entangled. "How could you not want to eat something so pretty?"

As soon as the words were out of her mouth, Allison grinned mischievously and bit her lip.

Elena smirked and gently shook her head. "Your mind just went somewhere else entirely, I take it?"

"Yup."

Elena clucked her tongue and arched a brow. "Dirty girl."

"Whatever. It's *your* fault."

"I can live with that."

"Of course you can." Allison threw a piece of popcorn at her head, but Elena ducked to the side just in time and it missed her.

"Throwing it at me is hardly the way to make me want to try it, dear," Elena told her, and Allison shrugged.

"I'm just gonna keep throwing them, and then maybe the next time you open your mouth to say something, BAM! One will land in your mouth, and then you'll be all, 'Wow, this is delicious. I want more, except *this* time, I want to add a piece of candy to it.'"

"My," Elena drawled, "that is an elaborate plan, and of course, that sounds *exactly* like something I would say."

Allison laughed out loud and threw another piece of popcorn at Elena. "Try it, woman!"

"No."

"Try it because I'm so cute when I ask."

"No."

"Try it because you love me."

"I do love you," Elena told her, leaning forward to kiss the side of Allison's calf.

Allison threw a piece of popcorn at her head. "I love you too."

"I'm still not trying it."

Allison threw a whole handful at her. "Try it!"

"You're going to wake my son," Elena said, grinning, so Allison whispered as loud as she could so that she sounded like she was hissing the words.

"*Try it*!"

Elena let out an exaggerated sigh. "Why is it so important that I try this ridiculous concoction of yours?"

"Because it is delicious." She then put on a straight face, as solemn as could manage, and clasped a hand around Elena's ankle. "It's because I love you, Elena." She stressed the words dramatically. "I don't want you to miss out on the delicious things in life."

"Well, it looks disgusting to me." Elena shook her head and poked Allison's side with her toes. "Even the description of it sounds disgusting."

Allison smiled. "That's the thing, though, you know? It's part of why I love it, even more so now that you and I are together."

"What do you mean?"

Allison popped another handful of her popcorn and Reese's into her mouth before crunching it down to nothing and swallowing. She then pulled Elena's foot up toward her face and pressed a kiss to the inside of the brunette's exposed ankle. "It's us," she said.

Elena stared at her curiously, and Allison pointed to the popcorn. "This stuff," she said. "It's *us*, you and me."

"You and I are popcorn and candy?" Elena asked.

"Totally."

"Dear, you are going to have to elaborate."

"Two things that maybe were never meant to go together," Allison said, one hand rubbing up and down Elena's shin. "Two things that people look at or even just hear about and automatically sneer at or assume it won't work. It's two things that are completely different and that shouldn't go so well together, but they *do*." Allison squeezed Elena's leg. "It's us. You get it?"

Elena stared at her for a moment, and then a soft sigh escaped her. She shifted on the couch and climbed over Allison's legs to get to the bowl in her lap. Reaching in, she pulled out a small handful and funneled it into her mouth. She chomped it down, somehow managing to make it look graceful, and then shrugged a shoulder. "It isn't terrible," she said, "but it isn't heavenly either."

Allison laughed and pulled her down into a long kiss. "I can't believe you tried it."

Elena grabbed the bowl of popcorn and moved it to the small table nearby before settling more comfortably in her lap. She rested a hand over Allison's heart and pressed a kiss to her lips. "You've always had a way of winning me over."

Allison ran her hands down Elena's back. "Same."

They kissed each other, long and languid. Their fingers tangled together, squeezing and holding tight, as those slow, soft kisses grew deeper and hotter. Their bodies moved together, slowly beginning to grind to the rhythm of Allison's quickening pulse.

"Momma?"

Elena instantly jerked up at the sleepy sound of her son's voice, slipping off of Allison's lap, and Allison followed. They turned to find the sweaty, pajama-clad toddler standing a few feet away and watching them as he rubbed at his eyes.

Clearing her throat, Elena patted at her hair and pulled her shirt down where it had ridden up. “What’s wrong, baby?”

“I’m thirsty.”

Elena let out a soft breath, and Allison began to shake with muted laughter. A few moments later and Lucas probably would have walked in on something a little more heated than a quiet kissing session. “Okay, munchkin,” Elena said. “Let’s get you some water.”

She smacked Allison’s shoulder as she rose from the couch and scooped up her son.

Allison just continued to laugh as she pushed off the couch. “Maybe we should hire a babysitter,” she said as she followed Elena.

Elena glanced over her shoulder and smiled, arching a brow.

Allison narrowed her eyes at the look. “*No*, not a hot one. I’m the only hot babysitter allowed.”

Elena let out a soft laugh and disappeared into the kitchen.

Allison shook her head, smiled, and followed.

She knew she had a lot of trying times ahead. Graduation was looming, and that meant the end of the last four years of her life. That meant saying goodbye to Macy, her closest friend and the only family she had ever had in her life before taking the babysitting gig that turned her world upside down and gave her more than she could have ever dreamed possible for her.

She knew she and Elena would face challenges, and that things wouldn’t always be like this, so easy, so perfect, but those thoughts faded from Allison’s mind as Elena’s laughter spilled into her ears. Her heart was so full in that moment that she could feel it in every part of her, beating out the rhythm of this new life and this new hope. This was only the beginning. Whatever the future held, she wasn’t concerned. She wouldn’t face it alone, and neither would Elena.

Whatever it was that had always been missing, she knew they had found it in one another.

They found home.

About KL Hughes

KL Hughes is an American poet and fiction author writing in multiple genres. Growing up in a small town of just over 1500 people, she spent much of her time inventing various ways to entertain herself as well as others. Whether it was through vocal performances of original children's songs or theatrical re-enactments of books, movies, and actual events, Hughes showcased her extensive imagination and creativity at a very early age.

She began writing poetry at the age of nine, a passion that rapidly grew and expanded to include short stories, novellas, and eventually novels. Throughout elementary school and high school, Hughes won several contests and competitions focused in original poetry and short-story composition.

After graduating valedictorian of her high-school class, Hughes went on to pursue and earn a Bachelor of Liberal Arts degree in Theatre Arts and English Literature. Her collegiate studies allowed her to develop and hone her skills in poetry, playwriting, screenwriting, and fiction prose.

Working as a writer full-time, Hughes lives in the United States with her wife and their Dalmatian. When not writing, she enjoys theatre and film, travel, visits to old cemeteries and haunted houses, putting on one-woman musicals for her wife, long walks and hikes, and family time.

CONNECT WITH KL Hughes:

Tumblr: http://chrmdpoet.tumblr.com

Other Books from Ylva Publishing

www.ylva-publishing.com

All the Little Moments

G Benson

ISBN: 978-3-95533-341-6
Length: 350 pages (approx. 132,000 words)

Anna is focused on her career as an anaesthetist. When a tragic accident leaves her responsible for her young niece and nephew, her life changes abruptly. Completely overwhelmed, Anna barely has time to brush her teeth in the morning let alone date a woman. But then she collides with a long-legged stranger...

A Story of Now

Emily O'Beirne

ISBN: 978-3-95533-345-4
Length: 367 pages (approx. 128,000 words)

Nineteen-year-old Claire knows she needs a life. And new friends. Too sassy for her own good, she doesn't make friends easily anymore. And she has no clue where to start on the whole life front. At first, Robbie and Mia seem the least likely people to help her find it. But in a turbulent time, Claire finds new friends, a new self, and, with the warm, brilliant Mia, a whole new set of feelings.

Once

L.T. Smith

ISBN: 978-3-95533-399-7
Length: 295 pages (approx. 77,000 words)

Beth Chambers' life is no fairytale. After four years in a destructive relationship, Beth decides enough is enough and leaves her girlfriend, taking Dudley, her dog, with her. At her lowest point, she meets Amy Fletcher, a woman who appears to have it all–and whom she believes would never want more than friendship. Beth needs to believe in magic once more for her dreams to come true. But can she?

Under a Falling Star

Jae

ISBN: 978-3-95533-238-9
Length: 369 pages (approx. 91,000 words)

Falling stars are supposed to be a lucky sign, but not for Austen. The first assignment in her new job—decorating the Christmas tree in the lobby—results in a trip to the ER after Dee, the company's COO, gets hit by the star-shaped tree topper.

There's an instant attraction between them, but Dee is determined not to act on it, especially since Austen has no idea that Dee is her boss.

Coming from Ylva Publishing

www.ylva-publishing.com

Getting Back

Cindy Rizzo

At her 30th college reunion, Elizabeth must face Ruth, her first love who bowed to family pressure long ago. As they try to reconcile the past, Elizabeth must decide whether she is more distrustful of Ruth or of herself. Is she headed for another fall or does she want to be the one who walks away this time? It's not easy to know the difference between getting back together and getting back.

Cast Me Gently

Caren J. Werlinger

Teresa and Ellie couldn't be more different. Teresa still lives at home with her Italian family, while Ellie has been on her own for years. When they meet and fall in love, their worlds clash. Ellie would love to be part of Teresa's family, but they both know that will never happen. Sooner or later, Teresa will have to choose between the two halves of her heart—Ellie or her family.

Popcorn Love

ISBN: 978-3-95533-265-5

Also available as e-book.

Published by Ylva Publishing, legal entity of Ylva Verlag, e.Kfr.

Ylva Verlag, e.Kfr.
Owner: Astrid Ohletz
Am Kirschgarten 2
65830 Kriftel
Germany

www.ylva-publishing.com

First edition: September 2015

Credits
Edited by Michelle Aguilar
Proofread by Blu
Cover Design & Printlayout by Streetlight Graphics

Made in the USA
Middletown, DE
01 October 2015